Prais

MW00640550

AWAKE
THE LEGACY OF AKARA

"A visionary page-turner! We must tell new stories if we're going to wake up and heal, and *Awake: The Legacy of Akara* is one of those stories."

—IYANLA VANZANT,
#1 *New York Times* bestselling author of *One Day My Soul Just Opened Up*
and Host of *Iyanla, Fix My Life* on the Oprah Winfrey Network

"*Awake: The Legacy of Akara* is a fabulous, pulse-quickening adventure as well as a spiritual road map toward an evolved humanity. In the midst of a grand quest that spans the cosmos, it offers a vision that raises us out of this time of uncertainty, divisiveness and upheaval toward a time of miracles, happiness, and oneness. Get this book and raise your vibration!"

—MARCI SHIMOFF,
#1 *New York Times* bestselling author of *Happy for No Reason*
and *Chicken Soup for the Woman's Soul*

"In a time of apocalyptic crisis, it is a healing experience to read this luminous book. We are clearly in a state of need for an evolutionary vision of who and what we yet may be. This is a book of healing, of insightful story into the possibilities that remain for us and our world. We are looking at another world that works. What appears here as science fiction is actually spiritual guidance and a way to create and re-generate our own time and planet."

—DR. JEAN HOUSTON,
Pioneer of the Human Potential Movement, former United Nations advisor
and author of over thirty-five books,
including *The Wizard of Us: Transformational Lessons from Oz*

"I dare you to put this book down before you absolutely collapse into sleep at night! It's a riveting adventure with a profound and important message especially designed for the challenging times we are living through now. The Akarans, a fascinating and evolved race of beings, bring blessings of wisdom and love to Earth— divine assistance that we could certainly use right now. If we use this book as an allegory for our own path toward an evolved humanity, it could help us transcend the current consciousness on the planet and experience the kind of enlightened civilization that we are capable of. If you enjoy a blockbuster story and are at all concerned with the future, I urge you to read *Awake: The Legacy of Akara*. I bet you'll be awakened by it!"

—DR. RON HULNICK,
President of the University of Santa Monica and Co-Author
of *Loyalty to Your Soul* and *Remembering the Light Within*

"Truly brilliant! Like classic science fiction films such as *Star Wars* and *The Matrix*, *Awake: The Legacy of Akara* has a spiritual theme and beloved archetypes that go to the heart of the hero's journey. It affirms our sense that technology without spirituality leads to dystopia and extinction, very real possibilities in today's world. *Awake* portrays spiritual development not as adopting a set of beliefs, but as realizing our deeper potential, including extraordinary abilities, by more fully embodying the "Wisdom"— the fundamental field of infinite energy, intelligence, and creativity from which the universe and our individual lives emerge. With a generous dose of fast-paced action, the story stimulates not just our adrenals, but also our minds, hearts and souls. I loved the book and believe it is destined for the big screen."

—RICK ARCHER,
Host of *Buddha at the Gas Pump,* Co-Founder of the Association
for Spiritual Integrity, and frequent presenter
at the Science and Non-duality Conference

"Few stories have the power to permeate the collective unconscious with a truly new paradigm, and to set the imagination free from the consensus reality we have become habituated to. This is one such story. *Awake: The Legacy of Akara* is a full-on heart-pounding sci-fi thriller with a profound spiritual message for humanity. In order to save the world, the characters learn to trust and connect to something beyond themselves, "the Wisdom" that pervades the universe. Many crises on Earth today stem from our own inability to connect to this wisdom, and it has resulted in apocalyptic suffering; the inevitable result of the egoic mind running amok. Akara, an alien world that has gone through the same historical trials as Earth, offers both a mirror for humanity in this moment of history and a possible path of redemption and evolution of human consciousness."

—DANIEL SCHMIDT,
Spiritual Teacher and Creator of the films *Samadhi*
and *Inner Worlds Outer Worlds,* viewed more than 30 million times worldwide

"*Awake: The Legacy of Akara* is a dazzling spiritual science fiction that offers the reader a rich and engaging storyline as well as a deeper message about the collective awakening of humanity. It aims to show us a glimpse of what our destiny may hold, and what it will take us to get there, while delivering a message of hope and inspiration. Truly a must read in every regard."

—AARON ABKE,
Spiritual Teacher

"*Awake: The Legacy of Akara* is absolutely brilliant and possibly one of the most important epic tales to be told since *Star Wars* or the *Matrix*. It is equally deserving of the big screen. Containing a message that is both timely and essential, this story brings much needed insight, wisdom and hope for humanity at this critical time on Earth. We know the power stories hold—they shape our culture. Now more than ever we need a story that has the capacity to reshape our future. This story has that power. What an extraordinary adventure!"

—ISIRA SANANDA,
Spiritual Teacher and Author of *Buddha on the Dance Floor* and *Awakening You*

"*Awake: The Legacy of Akara* is beautifully written and a delightful and creative expression of how we can live on the Earth from wholeness and love; how we can wake up from the illusion of separation, our own Ravaging Era. This message is of vital importance to us all at this time."

—SHARON LANDRITH,
Spiritual Teacher in the lineage of Adyashanti

"A remarkable story empowering our innate ability to wake up to a prophecy of light versus a prophecy of darkness. Awake: The Legacy of Akara is a fast-paced science fiction adventure and quest to discover our authentic self beyond our egoic identity so we can evolve and dream a new beautiful dream for Earth. This book is just the inspiration we need right now. Awake is engaging and a must read!"

—SANDRA INGERMAN, MA,
Award-winning Author of twelve books, including *Walking in Light*
and *The Book of Ceremony: Shamanic Wisdom
for Invoking the Sacred in Everyday Life*

"Brilliantly written. This is the very best that sci-fi has to offer, expertly woven with suspenseful adventure, humor, heart and deep wisdom. Through masterful storytelling the vivid, unforgettable characters sweep you up into an un-putdownable, entertaining journey that cleverly invites the reader to reflect on themes that are as old as time, but more relevant today than ever. Eagerly awaiting the next book in what is certain to be a wildly successful series!"

—TANYA MAHAR,
Co-Creator of the films *Samadhi: The Illusion of the Self (Part 1)*
and *It's Not What You Think (Part 2)*

AWAKE

THE LEGACY OF AKARA

A NOVEL

DAYNA DUNBAR
JULIA NADINE PADAWER

awakethenovel.com

Cover design by Ruslan Us
Torus art by Anamaria Stefan
Map art by Carlos G. Rios

ISBN: 978-1-7359248-2-3 (trade paperback)
ISBN: 978-1-7359248-1-6 (ebook)

Library of Congress Control Number: 2020923109

awakethenovel.com

For

Jesse Robertson

and

Lucien Padawer

In the universe there is a core from which we obtain knowledge, strength, and inspiration. I have not penetrated into the secrets of this core, but I know that it exists.

—Nikola Tesla

I have learned to use the word "impossible" with the greatest caution.

—Wernher von Braun
Father of rocket science

AWAKE

THE LEGACY OF AKARA

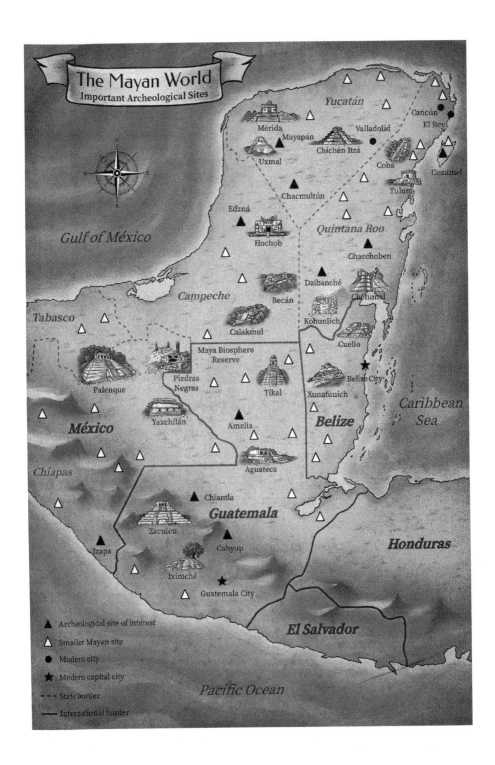

The Mayan World
Important Archeological Sites

Yucatán

Cancún
El Rey

Mérida
Mayapán
Valladolid
Chichén Itzá

Uxmal
Coba
Cozumel

Chacmultún
Tulum

Edzná
Quintana Roo

Hochob

Chacchoben

Gulf of México

Campeche
Dzibanché
Chetumal
Becán

Kohunlich

Tabasco
Calakmul
Cuello

Maya Biosphere
Reserve

Piedras
Negras
Belize City

Palenque
Tikal

Yaxchilán
Xunatunich
Caribbean
Sea

Amelia
Belize

México

Aguateca

Chiapas

Chiantla

Guatemala

Zaculeu
Honduras

Izapa
Cahyup

Iximché

Guatemala City

▲ Archeological site of interest
△ Smaller Mayan site
● Modern city
★ Modern capital city
- - - State border
——— International border

El Salvador

Pacific Ocean

PROLOGUE

On December 21, 2012, the world was supposed to end. According to Mayan prophecy, the Earth would somehow just cease to exist. The ancient Mayan civilization (2000 BC – AD 950), once located in what are now Guatemala, Mexico, and Belize, is widely recognized for its great accomplishments in hieroglyphics, architecture, mathematics, and astronomy. But it is most renowned for its highly advanced and precise measurement of time. Mayans were obsessed with time, counting it and tracking its passage over great epochs. The accuracy of their calendars is unparalleled by any other ancient civilization on Earth—so much so, in fact, that a number of respected historians believe it is possible that they had assistance from extraterrestrial beings. But all the Mayans' various calendars— and archaeologists have found many—came to an abrupt end on the same date—December 21, 2012. When the apocalyptic day came and went, the world concluded the prophecy was a myth.

But it was not. It was averted by an extraordinary course of events that began simultaneously on two different planets—Earth, and Akara, home to an awakened civilization far more evolved than our own. In order to protect the individuals involved, this story has been a well-kept secret. Until now.

Pleiades star cluster

CHAPTER ONE

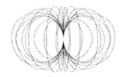

ANOMALY

Location: *Planet Akara—Pleiades star cluster, Milky Way*
               Galaxy, 445.7 light-years from Earth

Earth Date: *December 19, 2012*

Mobius clenched and unclenched his long, four-fingered hands. He had to make a choice, and he had to make it fast. If he decided to go to Earth, it would change everything for him, but if he didn't go, it could change everything for them. For a moment, he wished he had just put the relic back in the ground and covered it over with dirt.

•

Six days earlier, before he even knew Earth existed, Mobius stood on the jump platform of a hovercraft as it moved high in the lavender skies of Akara over the final testing site. As the arm display of his energy suit's control panel counted down, he grew more and more agitated. *I'll never make it,* he thought. In an attempt to calm down, he looked out the transparent ribbon that encircled the craft's hull. His two enormous blue and orange eyes squinted at the Twin Flames, Akara's binary light source. The sun and dwarf star were caught in a gravitational embrace that made for some radical astronomical phenomena, but today, they seemed only to shine a further light on his deficiency. He was eighteen, but suddenly felt like a child again. Mobius shifted his gaze to Akara's moons; seven of the eleven hung visible in the day sky, and they brought him a bit of comfort, like sentries watching over him.

Suddenly, the aperture beneath his feet flashed open, and he heard his mentor say, "Candidates, make the leap," as he dropped into the upper atmosphere, free falling toward the ground. The cold geostrophic winds battered him around until he flipped over and dove headfirst, slicing through the air to stabilize his fall. As he hurtled toward the dense, green gas cloud below—a toxic remnant from the Ravaging Era a thousand years before—he tried to quiet his mind. He didn't want to obsess about his chances of getting admitted into the Discovery Corps, Akara's renowned space exploration program. From the age of nine, he believed his entelechy, his innate creative potential and purpose, was to become a flier with the DC. It was the only thing he ever really wanted to do and the one thing he was certain could never happen. But now he was on the verge of the impossible. If only he could pass the final test today.

As he plummeted downward, he felt a slight surge in his head followed by a mild cool sensation throughout his body, alerting him that a thologram with the mission details had just uploaded to his neurolink. He reviewed the instructions on the three-dimensional thought hologram, but the instant he entered the radioactive cloud, the neurolink glitched out. *No way*, he thought. *It's not enough.* He knew he'd have limited intel about the mission, but he'd expected more.

For a few moments, the gas cloud obscured his view of the

ground, but then the noxious mist thinned, and he glimpsed the ghostlike outlines of ancient ruins of what was once a thriving community. Just as he cleared the cloud, he activated the anti-gravity landing sequence on his suit, slowing his acceleration until he could reorient himself feetfirst. Upon touching down, Mobius struggled to find his footing on the arid ground, kicking up a plume of lapis blue dust. Residue of radioactive waste hung thick in the air, and heat from the effects of the greenhouse gasses pressed down on him like defeat. An ominous, phosphorescent glow rose from the ground, reflecting the paltry light that forced its way through the cloud above. Mobius looked around, his eyes adjusting to take in more light by decreasing the proportion of blue and increasing the proportion of orange.

One by one, each of his Supernova Crew members, Nava, Tru, and Barj, landed nearby. Their translucent suits accentuated each of their various skin colors—Tru purple-black, Barj pale yellow, and Nava burnished gold, her tone close in color to Mobius's own warm bronze.

The crew quickly gathered around Nava, the leader for their last mission together as candidates and the most important one to date.

"Set your timers for forty minutes," she instructed. "On my mark—three, two, one."

In unison, they initiated the countdown on their control panels; over the last year at Entelechy Academy, they had become a tightly knit team.

"Remember," Nava said, "head back to the rendezvous point immediately when the alarm sounds. We have only twenty minutes to get back to the ship before our shields are breached. After sixty-five minutes our exposure will be critical, and at seventy-five, fatal."

Protocol required her to remind them, but it wasn't necessary. They all knew the gravity of the mission, which simulated an off-planet scenario with extreme field conditions—a toxic environment, comms down, no scanning tech, and a limited energy supply. It was only a test, but the circumstances were real.

Mobius, Nava, Tru, and Barj began making their way toward the vestiges of the ancient community—gray hulking masses of crumbling structures that emerged from the ground like exhumed corpses. The ruins sat on the rim of a canyon that was one of the planet's last sources of retainite, Akara's most precious resource and the only material capable of containing torus energy. Without it, Akara would plunge back into the dark age that reigned before the Rebirthing.

Mobius was fascinated by the rare substance, a liquid-crystal that existed in a liquid state underground and crystallized into a solid above ground as soon as it was exposed to the argon in Akara's atmosphere. Even though he'd never paid much attention in planetary sciences, he'd learned everything he could about retainite and was heartbroken to find out it had been mined to near depletion during the Ravaging Era for use in technology and weaponry, leaving enormous pockmarks all over the planet. The small amount that remained was buried in the canyon Mobius trudged toward, and he was excited that his current mission was to locate an extraction site. The only problem was that he'd have to do so using nothing more than his intuition.

Supernova's rapid pace slowed. They were a physically impressive group—their hairless bodies tall, muscular, and fit—but the menacing ruins still presented a steep challenge.

"This place is unnerving," Nava said. "The energy here is so dark."

The candidates blinked twice, indicating their agreement.

They continued on in silence, walking through the desolate community that was one of thousands around the planet left over from the Ravaging Era. Mobius could almost feel the souls of the billions who had died during the hundred-year reign of self-inflicted destruction. Environmental disasters, including severe droughts and mini ice ages due to extreme climate fluctuations; worldwide pandemics; contamination of the food and water supply; and out-of-control warfare as a result of overpopulation, dwindling energy supplies, and a radical imbalance in wealth distribution had all brought the Akaran race to the edge of extinction. By the end of the Final War, only a few million individuals had survived. The shock of it hit Mobius harder than ever before, since he could see and feel the effects all around him. He shuddered at what it must have been like when neighbor fought neighbor over the last remaining resources.

Even though the poisoned graveyard Mobius was walking through gave no indication, a series of synchronistic events had pulled the race back from total annihilation. Most of those who endured were the more evolved, conscious members of the species, who became known as the "Wise Ones." They had joined together in collaboration and cooperation rather than participating in the savagery and competition that had taken hold during the Ravaging. Retreating into the last unadulterated areas called "vital zones," they created conscious communities across the planet.

It became survival of the wisest.

Mobius climbed a half wall of an ancient building and dropped to the other side, landing in a morass of sludge that came up to his knees. As he slogged along, he couldn't help but think about what had somehow miraculously emerged from all this ruin; how the concentrated communities of wise beings had sparked a planetary awakening to the true nature of reality and the oneness of all life. That awakening had brought an end to the conflict and the dawn of a new era—the Rebirthing. With it came access to previously unused parts of the brain, a harmonization of brain wave patterns, as well as a profound opening to intuitive, telepathic, and healing faculties. Connection to levels of compassion and awareness far beyond the five senses became known simply as the Wisdom. Within a few generations of the Rebirthing everyone was born with this more highly evolved matrix of consciousness and ability. Everyone but a rare few.

Mobius's breath came heavily, and the eeriness of this place made him even more anxious. He continued to struggle against the obstacles in his way, but mainly he fought against his handicap. Mobius was one of the rare few. He had been born an Anomaly.

•

After trekking for a while longer, Supernova had made their way past most of the ruins yet still couldn't see the edge of the canyon. "This is taking too long," Barj said. "I wonder if the sites the other crews were dropped at are as challenging as this one."

"I hope so. I don't need anything more going against me," Mobius said, then checked the display on the inside of his forearm—30:13 to go. He looked at Nava. "This is impossible. What if I don't get in?"

In the last few years at Entelechy Academy, he had explored many other life paths, including archaeology, holo-design, environmental rehabilitation, and quantum travel. After trying it all, he was more desperate than ever to get into the DC.

Nava put a hand on his arm for the briefest of moments. He

became distracted by her touch and her beauty, as he had been many times since they'd met a year ago. And once again, he struggled to keep his feelings for her at bay.

"Mobius, take a breath and get centered."

He squeezed his eyes shut for a moment, trying to focus on his breathing.

"You've made it this far, and Kaia believes in you," Tru said, referring to their beloved mentor.

"And remember what she told you," Nava added. "Open your mind and focus positive. You don't know what's possible."

Barj tapped Nava on the arm. "Easy for you to say."

"No kidding," Mobius said. Everyone knew that out of all twenty-four candidates, she had the strongest intuitive ability.

The group moved along in silence for a few more minutes until Nava yelled out, "There it is!"

The four of them broke into a run and soon stood on the edge of the canyon, looking down on an expanse of burnt orange and yellow spires that rose like enormous pointed hats out of the flat, dry canyon floor. Some of the formations were smaller with little round balls at the top, but they were all in the same conical shape—larger at the bottom, then tapering up to a point.

"It's fantastic," Mobius said, taking in the extreme vertical drop and rugged landscape below.

Tru looked at him like he was crazy. "Fantastic? More like intimidating."

Mobius felt a thrill of energy run through him at the enormity of the moment. He had the chance to become the first Anomaly—one of only .0002% of the current 500 million population—to make it into the Discovery Corps and become a flier with the space program. Even though, like all Anomalies, he had limited access to the Wisdom, he also had advanced physical abilities. Luckily, Mobius had one of the highest aptitudes in survival and adventuring the DC had ever seen, and only because of it did he have a chance of getting in.

Nava glanced at her control panel. "Okay, let's move. Twenty-three minutes to go. See you back here at the rendezvous. Make the leap, everyone."

"Make the leap," they said back, repeating the phrase taken from the Discovery Corps motto—"From data to information to knowledge to Wisdom—Make the Leap."

Mobius reached into his pack, pulled out a silver tube, and threw it down like a dagger. Five claws unfurled and burrowed into the ground, then a ring popped out the top. He clamped his rope onto the ring, then onto his suit's harness, and hurled the rest off the side of the canyon. After backing to the edge of the cliff, he hung suspended for a moment, took a deep breath, then pushed off backwards, sliding down the rope much faster and longer than safety protocols advised. Swinging to the wall, his feet hit the rock face, then he pushed off again; he loved the rush of rappelling. On his backward arc, he looked up and saw his crewmates still far above. His speed and greater athletic ability were his only hope of finding the retainite in time.

As soon as he touched the ground, he unclipped from the harness, left the rope dangling, and pulled out a handheld probe that would confirm the presence of retainite once he located a possible extraction site. The access points to the underground reservoirs of liquid retainite were no bigger than his hand, and he knew his detection would have to be precise. Pushing the thought out of his mind, he bolted in the direction he had been assigned by his thologram.

Moving through a gap in the enormous conical formations that now towered above him, he encountered a slot canyon so narrow that he wasn't sure he'd be able to squeeze through. The sliver of a canyon receded into the distance with huge, striated rock walls rising at a sharp angle on either side of him. Racing forward, he followed the natural trail of the canyon. At times, the path was so constricted he had to turn sideways, inch through the gap, and scuttle over rocks blocking the way. He moved as fast as he could for a while, then stopped inside a cavernous rock enclosure to check his display. With only a narrow slit of murky sky visible at the top, his eyes adjusted to read the time remaining—15:36.

Anxiety rose in his throat, and he was about to rush out of the cave when something stopped him—a subtle feeling that he should remain still for a moment. *Where is the extraction point?* he asked inwardly, then waited. But all he heard was his own heaving breath, quickly followed by his doubting mind. He looked around, trying to find any clue that might lead him to the retainite. *It can't be in here,* he thought, *it's too narrow. And it's too near the start. It can't be this easy. Keep moving.*

He sprinted on, bursting out of the slot canyon. The sky opened up above, but he was still in a tight space, surrounded by three huge spires closing in on him. The cone-shaped structures blocked his view completely, and he couldn't tell which way to go. Without thinking, he shoved the probe into his pack and began working his way up the tallest formation, climbing freestyle without securing a rope. The rock was unstable, and it slipped away in pebbles as he climbed, and he knew he was taking a risk the mentors would question. Finally, he reached the top—8:49 remaining. With his feet stable underneath him, he held on to the pointed apex of the enormous cone with one hand as the other swung free while he looked in every direction. To the south, just beyond the cluster of formations, he could see an open field, and hope spread through him like warm liquid. *That has to be where it is.* He studied the best way to navigate through the spires to get to the field, then anchored a hook and slid down a rope in a matter of seconds.

Moving easily through the undulating pathway he'd seen from above, he ran ahead and finally reached the open space dotted with dead scrub-brush. As he crossed the broken terrain, he looked at the countdown—only 2:54 to go. *It's not enough time!* His heart punished him, not so much from exertion as from fear. He began looking around frantically.

Slow down, Mobius. For a moment he thought he heard Kaia speaking to him telepathically, but it couldn't be her since she wasn't allowed to guide him in any way. Besides, he wouldn't have been able to hear her even if she tried. While she was the only person he was able to pick up any telepathic thoughts from, that was only when he was physically near her and highly focused. He figured that she'd told him to slow down so many times over the past year, her words must just be ringing in his head. Forcing himself to stop, he tried to tune in to his intuition by quieting his mind, closing his eyes, and slowing his breathing like he'd been taught in mindfulness training. He struggled to listen for an answer, to access the Wisdom, but all he could think about was the display relentlessly counting down.

He opened his eyes—1:38 left before the test was over. He could hardly breathe. Desperate, he pulled the retainite probe out of his pack, ran into the field and began plunging it into the canyon floor time and time again—covering as much ground as he could in the seconds remaining—trying to locate the retainite by sheer force of will.

Suddenly, the control panel's alarm pierced the silence. Time was up.

He had failed.

•

Several minutes later Mobius heard Nava call out from behind him, "Mobius! What are you doing?"

He glanced over to see her standing nearby, deep concern on her face.

"It's got to be here," he yelled, as he continued to obsessively stab his probe into the ground. "I have to find it!"

Nava rushed to him. "Mobius, we have to go. Even if you find it at this point, it won't count."

"No!" he cried.

His control panel sounded, imploring his departure as well. *"Suit degradation begins in fifteen minutes. Evacuate the area."*

"I don't care. It doesn't matter anymore," he screamed back at it, then futilely slammed the impenetrable display with his probe before stabbing it into the ground again. This time the probe clanked on something hard.

He dropped to his knees and began digging furiously. "What is that?"

"I don't know, but it's not an extraction site. Let's go," Nava begged.

"It may be retainite that made it all the way to the surface and crystallized."

"That's incredibly rare!"

He continued to dig and uncovered not crystal, but metal—a silver cylinder encrusted with centuries of dirt and grime.

"Mobius, we have to get back to the drop-off. You're putting us both in serious danger!"

"It's okay. We'll just take off from here. But where are Tru and Barj?" he asked, suddenly aware of his crew.

"I sent them back to the hovercraft when you weren't at the rendezvous. They're fine, but we're not. We don't have enough power to clear the gas cloud from down here."

At these words, he snapped out of his rage and stared wide-eyed at Nava for a split second, then yanked the relic out of the ground, and they began to run.

CHAPTER TWO

ENDANGERED

Location:	*Planet Earth—Guatemala, Maya Biosphere Reserve, 75 miles south of the Mexican border*
Date:	*December 9, 2012*

The drug gang cowboys no longer wore bandanas over their faces when they confronted Diego Villela. The jungle ranger tightened his hands into fists as he stared at the four barefaced men who had suddenly erupted out of the jungle and stopped his Jeep.

"What do you have for us, college boy?" Pedro, an oily-skinned *narco* who usually did all the talking, asked in Spanish as he slung his AK over his shoulder.

Diego had to tell them something. If he didn't, they would take him down, but if he did, it would endanger everything he'd sworn to uphold. Once again, he wished he had handed the drug lord back his blood money and kept his eyes to the ground.

The *criminales* had first ambushed Diego eight months ago on the side of a remote, rutted-out road just after he'd started working for the paramilitary ranger patrol in the lawless jungle of Guatemala. His job was to help protect the Maya Biosphere

Reserve—8,000 square miles of rainforest and one of the most threatened and important habitats in the world. After running off a group of illegal pet traders trying to capture scarlet macaws, he had emerged from the jungle to find the *narcos* waiting for him, lined up in front of his vehicle with their faces covered and armed like terrorists. Now that Diego was on the take, they no longer bothered to conceal their identities, but he wished they still wore the damn rags, because Pedro, a rawboned *pendejo,* had a mug like a ghoulish Mexican mask out of *Día de los Muertos.*

"You'd better start talking, Diego," Pedro barked while the jungle ranger stood silent, trying to figure out what to say.

"I've been working on it," Diego finally replied, his words laced with bile. *The* diablos *own me now.* The insidious thought came to him before he could push it down, and he gritted his teeth against it. He'd believed that allying with their money, power, and the *narco* culture that was worshipped by the poor, powerless young guys he grew up with in the *barrio*—the ones who kicked his ass on a regular basis—would prove that he was not the asthmatic, scared little kid he used to be. At twenty-four, he had grown to be 5'10" (taller than any of the outlaws in front of him), made his body fit and strong, and gotten a fierce jaguar tattoo that took up the length of his right forearm. Despite all this—even standing there in his fatigues, armed with an assault rifle and empowered with paramilitary authority—he still couldn't shake the feeling of self-doubt and weakness.

"The boss is counting on you, *cabrón,*" Pedro said. "You've got to give me more than that."

Diego's stomach turned to molten lava at the mention of the boss. All he'd seen of the notorious drug lord, Manuel Menendez, was his feral black eyes above the mask he'd worn when he'd offered Diego more money than his parents had ever imagined and a chance to prove he was turning out to be impressive after all, unlike his father. "Uh, I'm telling you, there's no real news ... They're talking about some kind of crackdown from the *Policía Nacional Civil*, but nothing is certain yet. Their biggest concern right now is stopping the slash and burn deforestation and illegal logging."

Pedro raised his eyebrows and whistled under his breath, and the other men exchanged glances, all of them wearing the typical *narco* uniform of cowboy boots and jeans. The news was a big deal—the slash and burn areas, where outlaws like these had cut out huge swaths of rain forest, were important for drug running. The *narcos* used them to land their planes to drop off and pick up cocaine and heroin on their way to Mexico and the United States. They also used the clear-cut areas to create cattle ranches as fronts for laundering their money, as well as money for Salvadoran and Chinese gangs who illegally logged the timber to sell in China.

"Who is the leader of the police for the crackdown?" Pedro asked. Diego knew this meant, "*Who do we need to threaten or pay off this time?*"

As the ravenous December sunshine beat down on him, he wiped the sweat off his face with his sleeve. "I don't know. They haven't mentioned any names."

"When is it happening?" Pedro pressed, raising his voice above the howler monkeys that bellowed in the trees.

"I don't know that either. They keep changing the date because of all the tourists coming for the end of the Mayan calendar."

Suddenly, a short, stocky guy with a missing ear was in Diego's face, his AK rifle pressed up under Diego's chin. "It's your job to know."

Diego tried to stand his ground, but he stepped back, his heart thundering. "If I pry, my uncle will suspect me," he stammered, suddenly picturing the distinguished Domingo Hernandez, who was head of the jungle patrol, scowling at him from under imposing eyebrows. "He isn't like me. He's on a mission."

"Don't worry, Rafael," Pedro said. "Diego will do his job. His job *now* is to get his uncle to tell him who is in charge of this police crackdown and when it is happening. If he does what he's told, he keeps getting paid more money than he thought he'd see in his whole, stupid little life. And if he doesn't ... he will suffer very badly. So you see? It's easy for him."

Diego gripped his rifle tighter, for a moment fantasizing about how he could get himself out of this mess. "Give me a week. I'll have more for you."

Rafael backed off but glared at Diego with disgust. Moments later, the men melted back into the jungle and were gone. Diego drove away as fast as possible on the rugged road, fear pulsing through him like thick blood. He had given them some information but had concealed the fact that the police offensive was set to begin sometime in the next two weeks. Stalling allowed him the temporary illusion that he was thwarting the *criminales*. But he knew if he didn't warn them before the strike happened, they would kill him for sure.

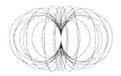

CHAPTER THREE

RELIC

More than twenty pairs of eyes stared at Mobius and Nava as they emerged into the cabin of the hovercraft from the airlock where they had removed their energy suits and gone through decontamination. At first, Mobius wished he could crawl back into the airlock, but when all the candidates started cheering and shaking their fists, a sheepish smile crossed his face.

Kaia stepped into the cabin from the cockpit where she'd taken over the pilot's chair to conduct the harrowing last-minute rescue. All the candidate crews exploded out of their seats, the craft's light glinting off their bald heads and their cheers growing even louder. She had performed an impossible vertical flight maneuver in order to pluck Mobius and Nava from the canyon wall just before they reached toxic exposure.

What a badass, Mobius thought, even though he dreaded having to face her after what he'd done. More than just a deep space pilot, Kaia was a planetary hero, and he was still amazed that he'd landed her as his mentor. Just the year before, she'd been part of a mission to rescue a crew on a scouting expedition that had been stranded on an uninhabited planet where noxious vegetation had degraded their vessel and poisoned the crew. She had defied mission parameters and helped save all eight fliers and recover the ship. But she was poisoned to the point that she had to stop flying for a while to let her body recover, even after undergoing quantum-healing treatment. Since being grounded, she'd decided to help select the next generation of fliers for the Discovery Corps.

"Settle down, everyone," Kaia said, gesturing for the candidates to lower their fists, but it was the stern look on her face—something many of them had never seen before—that quieted them.

She then turned to the other mentors aboard and began discussing the situation, without even glancing at Nava and Mobius. As the two of them took their seats, Barj, Tru, and the others started peppering them with questions, but Mobius ignored them and instead studied Kaia, trying to determine if she already knew why he hadn't returned to the rendezvous when the alarm sounded. As always, her golden eyes sparkled with a mischievous fire, a stark contrast to her rare opalescent white skin, which originated only in the snow-covered region of Sintaura.

After talking to her colleagues, Kaia announced to the still-buzzing candidates, "You all may not be so excited in a few hours, when we're still onboard because the hovercraft now has to undergo extensive decontamination, thanks to our little unplanned excursion into the gas cloud."

The candidates groaned, and Mobius shifted uncomfortably in his seat, feeling more claustrophobic than if he actually were riding back in the airlock.

"Supernova Crew," Kaia said, "With me."

The four of them followed Kaia into an open alcove, where they sat around the stone conference table as Kaia touched a panel, bringing a convex wall down to give them privacy. She looked at Mobius. "Barj and Tru told me you weren't at the rendezvous point," she said, crossing her arms in an X, with one hand resting on each shoulder. "What happened?"

He put a hand on top of his head, knowing he couldn't get away with lying to her. "I don't know. I just ... I lost my mind. I couldn't locate the extraction point. It had to be there. I had to find it."

"That was my sense of it, but I had to hear it from you." She drew in a deep breath. "Wait here. I need to consult with Melekai."

"Seriously? Do you really need to tell per?" Mobius asked, using the gender-neutral pronoun "per," because Melekai, like many Akarans, was a person who identified as neither male nor female.

"Yes, seriously. You could have died out there," she said, then turned and left the room to contact one of the highest-ranking members of the Discovery Corps.

Mobius's crewmates sat around the long table staring at him, but he looked away, focusing on the ship's energy source just outside the alcove. As he watched the torus, a spectacular ball of multi-colored light revolving inside a transparent retainite sphere, he felt a wave of shame at not being able to locate an extraction site. Torus energy was critical for their survival; the revolutionary technology was able to harness the infinite power of the universe to provide Akara with unlimited free, clean energy. But it needed retainite to make it work. If he had gotten into the DC, he would have been exploring space to find the thaumaturgic liquid-crystal—one of the most important areas of lifework on the planet. But now what was he going to do? He looked back at his crew, knowing the answer to the question he was about to ask before he spoke. "Did all of you find an extraction site?"

They blinked twice, and Mobius squeezed his eyes shut.

Nava turned to Tru and Barj. "I'm going to tell Kaia you two shouldn't be here."

"Seems to me, you shouldn't either," Tru said.

Mobius slumped in his chair. "I'm really sorry," he said, then mumbled to himself, "Nice move, Anomaly. You really screwed up this time." They sat in uncomfortable silence for a few moments until Mobius suddenly grabbed his pack. "Hey, wait, I found something down there."

"What do you mean?" Barj asked, leaning forward.

"Yeah," Nava said. "He insisted on digging it out of the ground ... that's what almost got us killed."

"I think it's a relic," he said.

"Really?" Tru asked. "Wait a minute. It could be contaminated."

"No, it went through the decon chamber in the airlock. It's fine." Mobius pulled the metal cylinder out of his pack, and they all took turns examining it. When it made its way back to Mobius, he worked off some of the encrusted grime and noticed what appeared to be a cap on one end. He tried to turn it, but it didn't budge. "Here, hold it," he said to Nava.

As she gripped the cylinder tightly, Mobius used both hands, trying to work the top open. Finally, it loosened, letting out a pneumatic whooshing sound as it released its vacuum-seal. He looked inside and saw nothing but a dark, padded chamber, but when he overturned it, a small object fell out. Mobius picked it up, and everyone stared at the shiny gold cube he held in the palm of his hand.

"What is it?" Nava asked breathlessly.

"That area's been uninhabitable since the Ravaging Era. Whatever it is, it has to be at least a thousand years old," Barj said, gaping at it.

"Come on, what are we waiting for?" Nava said, her eyes flashing with curiosity. "Someone capture it and do a search."

Tru, the tech geek of the crew, reached into a pocket on the upper sleeve of her arm and pulled out her cognizer, a small transparent disc. She pinched the cog, opening it into a three-dimensional orb that floated out in front of her, then dropped the cube into the device, using her neurolink to command the cog to define the object.

As the glowing sphere started to spin and they waited for the results, everyone watched intently. "It looks like a game piece or something, maybe a toy," Barj said.

After a few moments, the cog began vocalizing. "The object is an ancient form of information storage known as a data cube. It was used in the late Ravaging Era."

"Cool!" Mobius said as Tru snatched the cube out of the orb, then flattened her cog, using it as a magnifier to examine the relic more closely.

"I wonder how you access it," she said. "Look, there's a tiny hole in the corner."

"Really? Where?" Nava asked.

Before anyone could stop her, Tru pulled out a needle-thin tool from the utility belt she was still wearing and plunged it into the hole.

"No!" Mobius yelled, but it was too late. The needle was already inside the cube.

"I felt something click," Tru said.

"Are you crazy? You probably broke it. Now we'll never—" Mobius stopped griping because the top of the cube flipped open, and a faint beam of light shone out.

They froze, watching it there in Tru's long hand, unable to make anything out of the flickering light. "You can't see that old imagery in light like this; it's too bright."

"Lights off," Mobius commanded, and the room darkened.

Just then, Kaia entered the room, and Mobius grabbed the cube, tossed it back into the cylinder, and shoved it into his pack.

"Why are the lights off?" Kaia asked. The candidates just looked at each other and shrugged.

"Lights on," Kaia commanded as she walked to the front of the alcove and touched a clearscreen panel floating near the wall. A holographic image of Melekai, the stoic senior commander, projected into the room. At the sight of per, the candidates rose from their chairs and nodded their heads in respect.

Nava jumped in before either Kaia or Melekai could speak. "I just want to say that Tru and Barj followed my orders and shouldn't be—"

"There's going to be a full inquiry," Melekai said, then looked at Barj and Tru, "but for now you two can go."

Barj squeezed Mobius's shoulder, and they left the room.

"Mobius, I was shocked when Kaia relayed what happened. How can you justify this behavior?" Melekai asked.

Mobius shot per a look. "All I can say is I've never worked this hard or cared about anything as much as getting into the DC." He grew visibly more upset as he spoke. "I was told anything is possible, even for an Anomaly." He looked directly at Kaia for the first time. "*You* told me that!"

"Never mind that you failed the test," Kaia said. "If this is how you respond under high stress situations and then refuse to take responsibility for your actions, you didn't belong in the Corps in the first place."

"The test is unnecessary anyway," Mobius continued his protest. "We have advanced scanning instruments that can find retainite. I don't need to find it using my intuition—"

"Mobius, at the very least, show your mentor some respect," Melekai cut in. Per had been Kaia's mentor when she first entered the space program, and they were close. "The test is by no means unnecessary. The ability to function without tech is critical. You know perfectly well that during Kaia's mission all comm systems and tracking devices, even neurolinks, were rendered inoperable."

Mobius looked at the floor, hoping Melekai would stop the rebuke, but per continued. "That is why you *must* be able to open your heart and mind to access the Wisdom. Valuing technology over Wisdom was one of the great mistakes made during the Ravaging Era."

"I know," Mobius sighed, having heard this lecture countless times in his training.

Kaia drew in a deep breath, and Mobius could feel her disapproval. She had gone out on a limb for him, convincing the Discovery Corps Council to lessen his intuition admission requirements, and now he was displaying the kind of thinking and behavior typical of an Anomaly.

"But I thought the Wisdom was telling me the retainite was in that field."

"Clearly, it wasn't," Kaia said. "And it wouldn't have mattered anyway. The test was over."

"I know. I made a mistake," he said, his anger giving way to guilt. Kaia's disappointment in him was almost as unbearable as not getting into the DC.

She looked at him, her fiery eyes momentarily turning warm and kind.

"What's going to happen now?" he asked.

"The Council will determine that. I'll let Kaia take it from here. An important mission is underway that I need to get back to,"

Melekai said, and the hologram vanished.

The possible consequences raced through Mobius's mind, but he shifted his focus to Nava. "She came back for me," he pleaded. "She shouldn't be disciplined for my mistake."

"And as the team leader," Nava said, "I'm requesting leniency for Mobius. His record has been excellent up until today."

Mobius felt a burden lift from his heart; he'd always been certain she'd never be attracted to him, but he couldn't bear the thought of losing her as a friend.

"The DC made an exception for him once," Kaia said. "I doubt that they'll do so a second time. We're done for now." She walked out of the alcove.

Nava turned to Mobius, who sat frozen in his chair. "We all know how much you wanted this. Try to forgive yourself. I do."

He blinked twice, and though he was relieved to hear it, he couldn't bring himself to look at her, so he stood and walked to the viewing ribbon and stared at the landscape below— a sea of tall, colorful grasses spreading out in all directions. He imagined what it had looked like during the Ravaging Era and felt an odd connection to the past, to a time when he wouldn't have been an Anomaly. "Sometimes I wish I had lived back then."

"Back when?" Nava asked, joining him.

"The Ravaging."

"Are you kidding? It was *horrible.* I think the gas cloud messed with your head. They almost killed themselves off, and they wiped out animal species by the thousands. What part of that would you have wanted to live in?"

"At least I wouldn't have felt so alone."

Nava glanced out the window. "Oh. I hadn't thought of it that way."

"Plus, it would have been incredible to be part of the Rebirthing. But I doubt I would have been evolved enough to be one of the Wise Ones." Many times, Mobius had imagined what it would have been like to have joined the brave leaders at the end of the Ravaging Era who had left behind their ancestors' toxic ways of life.

Nava smiled gently at Mobius. "I know you would have been one of them."

He glanced at her, unsure. Though he lacked full access to the Wisdom like all Anomalies, he was on the more evolved end of the spectrum. Because of it, he'd thought he was going to be a trailblazer like the Wise Ones had been, a hero to his kind everywhere. But now he served as just more proof that they couldn't be trusted. Once again, he was lost in a world where he didn't belong. Though he wasn't treated like one, he felt like an outcast, like the object he had pulled out of the ground—a relic from the past.

INTANGIBLE ZONE

Diego scanned Domingo's face for a sign that his uncle might be onto him. Domingo had called him into his office at the Laguna del Tigre ranger station, and as usual, ever since Diego had made a pact with the drug gang, he worried that the great man, whom everyone called *El Jefe*—The Chief—had somehow discovered what he'd done.

"I have something important to discuss with you," *El Jefe* said in Spanish.

Diego's body tightened as his uncle casually sipped his *café con leche* and set the cup back down on his desk.

"I'm giving you a special assignment," Domingo said finally, and Diego exhaled, relaxing into his chair. He even allowed himself to get excited—until his uncle described what it was.

"I received a phone call from the Natural Resources Defense Council. Apparently one of their volunteers is arriving from New York tomorrow for an eco-tour. They've asked if we could please show her around a little bit before her tour begins in a few days."

Diego sighed. "Can't Alejandro do it? I'd rather be hunting down animal poachers."

"I would rather you not give me grief when I give you an

assignment," *El Jefe* said. "You know you are the best person for this. Miguel didn't spend two years at university in the United States. He doesn't know their American culture like you, and he doesn't speak fluent English."

Diego burned at the mention of his two years at San Diego State. It would have been *four* years and an environmental science degree had Domingo not convinced him he had to drop out of school to come home and help support his mother and younger sisters after his father died and his mother fell ill. Before that, Diego had been given such an incredible opportunity. The wealthy coffee plantation owners his mother had spent twenty years housekeeping for—cleaning everything from their floors to their children—had been paying for him to go to college in America. He hated being reminded of what his life might have been. But he knew not to argue any further; his uncle would not be swayed. "Fine. I'll drive her around."

El Jefe leaned in. "Diego, more than just driving her around, your job is to show her the splendor of the jungle and how tragically it's been desecrated. The NRDC has made a number of donations to us over the years. I want to stay in good standing with them."

Diego walked out of the ranger station with mixed feelings roiling inside him. He revered Domingo, knowing that he had dedicated his life to saving the Reserve, but Diego also resented his uncle for making him leave college. Although he felt guilty about being in bed with Menendez, he'd justified taking the blood money because he was supposed to be helping his family. Isn't that what Domingo had wanted?

•

Jillian Savoy gaped at the pipeline running alongside the dirt jungle road. "My God, how long does it go on?" she asked Diego, who was driving the Jeep.

She looked to be around Diego's age—in her early twenties—and unfortunately for him, she was pretty in a very distracting way, with mahogany brown hair, pale, smooth skin, smoky green eyes, and high, patrician cheekbones. Diego kept telling himself to be professional and cool because he tended to get a little stupid around attractive women.

"The pipeline goes on another ten miles or so," he said. "There are illegal petroleum extraction sites all along here, deep into the forest."

"But this is in the intangible zone, isn't it? It's supposed to be off-limits. How can they get away with this?"

He shrugged, defeated. "The problem is that there are only six members of the ranger patrol for the entire Laguna del Tigre National Forest, which is one of four national parks in the Maya Biosphere Reserve. We have a budget of about one hundred fifty U.S. dollars per square mile for equipment, staff, and everything else. We are not able to hold back all the drillers, poachers, loggers, and drug cartels. There's no one to shut them down, and even when we do, another one pops up the next day." This is how he rationalized working with the *criminales*; the forest was being decimated, and there was nothing he could do to stop it.

"Wow." She shook her head in dismay. "It's one thing to read about all this ... Six rangers for an area that's over a thousand square miles? That's a joke. Why don't they assign more?"

Diego smiled at her naïveté. He had encountered this kind of thinking often with gringos. "Ms. Savoy, this is not—"

"Please, call me Jillian."

"Okay, Jillian, this is not the United States. Guatemala is a third world country. And an oligarchy. All our wealth and political power are in the hands of a few ruling families. These billionaires have no interest in the environment. It's not good for business."

"Believe me, I know." She sighed heavily. "At this point, the U.S. is pretty much an oligarchy too, though no one wants to admit it. The top ten percent own seventy percent of the wealth. It's a serious consciousness of greed."

Diego looked at her with admiration; she was anything but naïve. "That's true." He forced himself not to think about the corrupt choices he'd made based on his own consciousness of greed, as she'd put it. Every once in a while, he glanced over at her, trying to size her up. She had a vitality about her, and yet a look of tenderness and vulnerability in her eyes. Her body was fit, and he hoped it meant that she could handle the rigors of the jungle.

As the Jeep bounced over some rocks in the road, Jillian grabbed the roof handle. "It's just heartbreaking that there are only six people to protect this area. It should be a worldwide responsibility. The rainforests are the lungs of the planet—they're a global resource, not just a national one." When Diego didn't respond, she looked over at him. "I'm sorry. I'll get off my soapbox."

"Don't apologize," he said, though he wasn't sure what a box of soap had to do with it. "I agree with you. But until the world realizes how important the jungles are, we need help from organizations like yours."

"Is that a fundraising pitch?" she asked. "Because they told you I'm just a volunteer, right?"

"No. It wasn't a fundraising pitch." *I'm wasting my time out here,* Diego thought. "So, what would you like to see today? There are some beautiful waterfalls at the end of a great animal trail ... there's a bridge that crosses a river that has a lot of alligators, or ... I do need to check one of the cat cameras to replace—

31

"Cat camera?" she said breathlessly. "As in *big* cat?"

"Yes, in the jungle. It helps us get an accurate population count."

She bounced up and down excitedly in her seat like a five-year-old. "Yes, yes, yes," she said. "Let's go check the cat camera!"

Diego chuckled and they rode for a few more minutes in silence until he pulled off the road into the jungle, stopping behind a stand of trees where he was sure his car could not be seen from the road. "Here we are."

"Great," she exclaimed, starting to jump out of the Jeep.

"Hang on!" Diego pulled her back into the vehicle.

"What's wrong?"

"Nothing ... I just want to make sure there are no ... dangerous animals." He checked that his pistol was in the holster on his hip and that the safety was off, then he got out and scanned the area for *criminales*. This was nowhere near their usual territory. That's why the camera had been placed here, and the reason he'd felt comfortable bringing her to this area, but he still breathed a sigh of relief when he noticed no signs of human presence in the last several days. He could deal with animals, even the most dangerous. It was poachers and *narcos* he was worried about. "Okay. *Está bien*," he said, then grabbed his backpack. "Let's head in. Did you put on bug spray?"

"Yes, sir," she said, tying her hair into a ponytail.

"Good. You'll need it. Okay, before we go in, the main thing to remember is to stay quiet. Keep your eyes open above and below for snakes and insects, but also for big cats. We might get lucky and see something."

CHAPTER FIVE

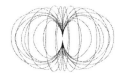

THE CUBE

When the hovercraft finally docked at Discovery Corps headquarters just outside Metanom City, Akara's global capital, Mobius told the rest of Supernova Crew to go on without him. He ran to catch up with Kaia as she headed to the mentor lounge. "Kaia, wait. I need to know ... where was the extraction site?"

"Where you sensed it was."

Mobius squeezed his eyes shut and mentally retraced the steps of his quest. "In the opening in the slot canyon?" he asked tentatively.

"That's right."

He dropped his head as Kaia's words hung in the air. "But it didn't make any sense. It was so narrow and close to the rendezvous point—I thought it had to be harder."

Kaia put her arm around Mobius and started walking again. "Remember, Mobius, the Wisdom doesn't always make sense to the linear, logical mind. The logical mind is valuable, but it isn't the highest authority. And you let it override your intuition today."

"I know," he sighed. "I'm sorry I let you down."

"Actually, other than today, you have made me very proud.

Remember that and learn from this experience. That's all you can do."

•

Mobius walked along the path from DC headquarters to his eco-dorm on Entelechy Academy's sprawling campus, in shock at the events of the day. The Twin Flames were beginning their descent in the early evening sky, and crisscrossing streamers of light pierced the gold and pink clouds that hung low in the distance, creating a warm glow on the smooth sandstone and glass fractal architecture.

When he got to his room, he found the door open and his crew waiting for him. He dropped onto his suspension bunk with a sigh. He'd loved being a part of their team for the last year, but now it was over. He was the only one who hadn't made it into the DC, and he felt more like an Anomaly than ever. *I just want to be by myself,* he thought. "What are you all doing here?"

"You have to bring the cube to Kaia," Barj said.

"No way," Mobius replied emphatically.

"Barj is right," Nava said. "We're required to turn in any artifacts."

"I'm not going to let them take this away from me too," he protested. "Besides, it's probably just somebody's household data anyway."

"What if you're wrong?" Barj asked.

"Maybe whatever's on there could be interesting enough to get you into the Archaeology Corps," Tru suggested. "I know that's not your first choice, but it's still fascinating."

After space exploration, archaeology was the only other thing that actually interested Mobius. And Tru was right, it was one of the most exciting and important areas of lifework on Akara. The planet had only recently recovered enough to be explored again and allow Akarans the time and energy to dig under the layers of history and rediscover their past. A breakthrough in the last year enabled archaeologists to detect brain wave residue left behind by their ancestors, helping to locate ancient ruins previously undetectable. This led to the discovery of new wonders across the planet—historic landmarks, buried metropolises, and treasured artifacts. But what Tru didn't know was that even though he loved archaeology, he wasn't very good at it. At least not compared to his older brother, who was already in the Archaeology Corps. His brother had advanced access to the Wisdom, and while Mobius loved him dearly, he chafed at their differences. Even though everyone around him, especially his parents, were careful not to compare them, Mobius himself couldn't help but do so, and the contrast was rough. The last thing he wanted to do was to put himself back in the long shadow cast by his brother's light.

Nava put her hands on Mobius's shoulders and leaned toward him, pulling him out of his reverie. "You have to turn it in," she said. He stared into her striking multicolored eyes, mesmerized. The four separate colors—pale blue, fuchsia, yellow, and green—were a rare genetic inheritance that occurred only when both parents had two eye colors and passed on their recessive genes. Her face was so close to his, he could just tilt forward and kiss her. For a breathless moment, he thought she might be feeling the same way he was.

They stayed like that for what seemed to him like a very long time, until Barj said, "Mobius, what are you going to do?"

Nava smiled and squeezed his shoulders. "Yeah, what are you going to do?"

"Anything you want me to," he felt like saying. Instead he nodded, "All right. Let's go." He knew they were right. Besides, maybe finding the relic would redeem him with Kaia, at least a little bit.

•

Once inside the arched entryway of the Community Hall, Supernova Crew hesitated outside the mosaic tile doors to the mentor lounge, because no one wanted to disturb the mentors in their lair. Mobius finally pushed the doors open and stepped quietly inside, trying to draw as little attention as possible.

He scanned the lounge—a microcosm of Akaran civilization, with mentors of all colors from across the globe gathered together. Most of them wore some type of traditional adornment from their home regions, along with their uniforms or civilian attire. Because Akarans had lost so much from their past, they celebrated their cultural diversity and did everything they could to keep it alive. Mobius always felt as if he were at a world heritage festival when he walked around Entelechy Academy.

As he scanned the room for Kaia, more and more mentors noticed him. He greeted them by putting a hand to his heart or by using the more formal gesture of putting both hands on his heart and extending them open in front of him. They all responded in kind. Finally, one of them—a woman wearing the traditional arm rings of the Lerenza region—pointed to the back of the spacious room. Mobius brought his chin to his chest in thanks and made his way through the gauntlet of leaders to where Kaia sat with Melekai. "Kaia, your renegade is here," the commander said and smiled. Mobius wanted to bolt, but another of the mentors said in a strong Qalarian accent, "Stay at peace, candidate, we're just having fun."

Kaia looked at him with amused consternation. "Have I not seen enough of you today?"

"I have something important I need to talk to you about," he said, looking around at Melekai and the others nearby. "Privately, please."

Kaia rose to her feet and put a hand on his shoulder as they began walking back through the lounge. "Don't ever let anyone tell you that you're predictable, Mobius," she said, and he smiled even though the other mentors started teasing Kaia about her rogue candidate.

"Everyone is so clever," she said. "I'm glad you're all having a good time."

When she walked out the door and saw the expectant faces of the other crewmembers, she said, "Now I'm getting curious. What is it?"

"I forgot to tell you something before. I excavated a relic down there, in the canyon."

"You *forgot* to tell me?" She looked at him, incredulous. "Mobius, what were you doing *excavating* down there?"

He opened his mouth to speak.

"Don't answer that," she said. "I'm going to overlook the fact that you didn't show me right away. I know you were dealing with a lot. Let me see it."

Mobius took the gold cube from his pocket and showed her.

"What is it?" Kaia asked.

"It's some type of data storage from the Ravaging Era, but we don't know what's on it," Mobius said. "We need to go somewhere dark to see it."

"This just gets better and better. Come on, follow me."

After everyone gathered in a meeting room next door, Mobius placed the cube on a pedestal in the center of the room, and they stood around it in a circle. Tru inserted the tool into the cube like she had before, and instantly, the top flipped open and a beam of light shot out. Instead of forming a three-dimensional holographic projection that they could all see from wherever they stood, it beamed images on the ceiling above them.

Kaia came closer, studying the object. "I'm amazed this old thing still works." Suddenly, she was as excited as they were—all fun and fire as usual. "It's only two-dimensional," she explained and pulled Tru and Barj out of the way, turning the cube onto its side. Suddenly, they could see what they hadn't been able to before, as the flattened moving images displayed on the wall, like in times past.

As he watched the unfolding footage, Mobius's enormous eyes grew even bigger. "This isn't possible," he whispered.

CHAPTER SIX

OBSESSION

"What cats live in this area?" Jillian asked excitedly as Diego led them into the jungle.

He held a tree branch out of her way. "Jaguar, jaguarundi, ocelot, puma, tigrillo."

"So all of them," she said, her eyes gleaming. "Awesome."

"Any one in particular you're hoping to see?"

"I'd be thrilled with any of them, but it looks like you've got a personal favorite," she said, pointing to his forearm. "That's a jaguar, right?"

"Yes," he said, running his hand over the image of a leaping spotted cat that was inked from his wrist to his elbow.

"It's so cool. I really like the way the tail wraps around your wrist," she said, touching it.

His face flushed at her touch. "Thanks."

"Maybe it will bring us good luck."

"I've only seen two in the last six months, so it hasn't worked that way so far, but we can hope." He led them off the road onto the animal trail that meandered through the forest dominated by bayleaf palm and logwood casha trees. Mosquitoes and sand flies buzzed around them. Only a few steps in, the canopy overhead rustled.

"*Un mono* ... monkey," Diego said, catching his Spanish and pointing to a funny-faced, black howler looking down on them.

Delighted, Jillian pointed her iPhone at the big girl and clicked away, but the howler screeched at them, not as enthused to make their acquaintance. "Whoa," Jillian said. "It's so loud."

"They're the alarm clock of the jungle. No sleeping late around here."

"I noticed. I was up at six this morning." She followed him as he moved farther into the thick vegetation. "Not that long ago, I was usually just getting into bed at that hour."

"Did you work at night?"

She laughed. "Uh, no, I partied at night."

"So what's a big partier doing down here?"

"Oh gosh, that's a long story," she said, crinkling up her nose.

"I'm sure I'd love to hear it. How about you tell me on the ride back?"

"We'll see ... It's magical here," Jillian said, clearly changing the subject.

"It is," Diego said with pride, as if the jungle belonged to him. "You want to see something magical?" He walked over to a tree with a long, narrow trunk. "Do you know what this is?"

She looked at him sideways. "I'm pretty sure it's a tree," she said, her voice playful, pitching up into a question mark.

He smiled, shook his head, and took out a pocketknife. He made two parallel downward diagonal slashes a few inches apart around the trunk, then stripped away the bark between them. A white, milky sap began to ooze from the tree, then drip down the spiral carving.

"What is that?" Jillian asked, her voice filled with delight.

"Latex," Diego said. "This is a rubber tree. They're indigenous to this area."

"You're kidding. I didn't know rubber came from trees. I thought it was synthetic."

"Most of it is now, but about a third is still natural. The ancient Mayans used this sap to make the first rubber balls in the world."

She nodded appreciatively. "You're a fascinating guide, *Señor. Muchas gracias* for the demonstration."

"Your Spanish is very impressive," Diego said, teasing her.

She chuckled. "I hope you enjoyed it, because that was pretty much the extent of it other than ordering from a menu. By the way, your English is so good, I'd barely know it wasn't your first language if it weren't for your cute little accent."

They continued deeper into the jungle, and it became impenetrable in places. Diego pulled his machete off his pack and hacked at the curling vines and undergrowth that blocked the way until the path opened up again. Within a few minutes, his shirt was soaked with sweat in the dense humidity. At one point, Jillian insisted that he let her give it a try, and she took over while he drank some water and watched the ripples of her back and shoulders move the fabric of her tank top.

"How am I doing?" she asked and turned around.

"Impressive. You're really strong."

She smiled. "I do a lot of yoga."

"You can get muscles like that from yoga?"

"The kind I do," she said, using the machete to swat at a mosquito buzzing around her face.

"Hey, watch that thing!"

"Why? Don't you think I can handle it?" Jillian asked, crossing her arms.

"Well, if I didn't, I certainly wouldn't tell you while you're holding a machete in the middle of the jungle."

She laughed loudly, and in response a monkey howled and a macaw squawked, which made her laugh even more, and Diego laughed with her. While they were cracking up, she pulled back the machete as if to hack off his head, and he flinched. Then she gently brought it down and handed it to him. They laughed harder, and because it had been months since Diego had even smiled, it felt like tasting fine Champagne after subsisting on brackish water.

"It's a good thing we're not close to the animal viewing platform, or we would see nothing with all the noise," he said as he led the way farther into the jungle, trying to regroup. Any attempt at acting like a professional guide had been completely undone by her.

"I'm just getting a kick out of watching a jungle Zorro in action."

He stopped and looked at her. "Is that how you see me? Like Zorro?"

"Well, it works, doesn't it? A macho Latino dude who wields a sword and protects the helpless creatures of the wild."

If you only knew, he thought. He turned quickly and walked on so she wouldn't see the shame that burned on his face.

●

Deep in the jungle, Diego and Jillian approached a waterproof, motion-sensitive camera mounted on a tripod and concealed with leaves and underbrush. It sat at the edge of a small clearing, where shafts of sunlight sliced through the forest canopy and created exotic patterns on the jungle floor. Diego made sure there were no snakes around, then removed the camera's memory card and replaced it with a new one. He put the camera back on its mount, then fished his secret weapon out of his pack.

Jillian's eyes widened. "Perfume?"

"Cologne," he said. "Specifically, Calvin Klein Obsession for

Men. They go *loco* for this stuff."

"Seriously? I won't even ask how you figured that out."

He went to the fallen log that the camera pointed at and sprayed Obsession all over it.

"Okay, *vámonos*," he said, pointing to a lookout platform twenty feet above the ground in an enormous ceiba tree.

"Oh my God, this tree is majestic," Jillian said, gazing into its far-reaching branches. "I've never seen anything like it."

"The ceiba is the national tree of Guatemala. It's sacred to the Mayans. Even the illegal loggers always leave at least one standing."

They climbed the crude ladder to the platform and perched themselves on the small plywood square amidst the canopy of branches. Diego loaded the memory card into his own camera, and they looked at the pictures it had captured over the last few weeks. It had caught almost every kind of cat around these parts except for the little tigrillo and the elusive prize, the jaguar. Most of the shots were too dark, but a few of a large male puma and one of a young ocelot were excellent.

"The pictures are awesome," Jillian said. "I feel like I'm in the middle of a National Geographic documentary."

They ate some trail mix, then sat back to wait. After forty-five minutes, they had only seen some birds and a few spider monkeys. Jillian shifted impatiently then whispered, "Do you think there's really any chance we'll see a big cat?"

"Like I said, it is rare. They're like ghosts."

"I have an idea," she said. "You might think it's silly, but it works with my cat at home, and she's pretty aloof."

He looked at her with a raised eyebrow, then whispered, "I'm not sure what you're about to say, but I'm guessing she's a *house* cat."

She laughed quietly. "I know, but it's worth a try."

"Okay, what is your trick?"

"Meditation."

"Meditation?" Diego's face screwed up into an expression of disbelief. "I'm not sure what that's going to do, unless that word means something different than I thought."

"No. That's what I mean. Every time I meditate, Cheerio winds up in my lap. I think she's drawn to the peaceful energy."

"Uh ... okay," he said, holding in his laughter. "*Adelante*, go ahead. It's not going to do anything, but why not."

"Wanna bet?" Jillian said, crossing her arms.

"Sure," Diego replied, crossing his own.

"Great. If I win, you take me to the Mayan ruins at Tikal," she said, referring to what had been one of the greatest cities in the ancient world.

"Sure. You've got a deal."

"But wait, what about if you win?"

"I'm good. It's not a fair bet. You're not going to win."

"Aren't we cocky?" Jillian quipped.

"Well, I'm a jungle Zorro, no? What do you expect?"

She squeezed her eyes shut for a moment, annoyed. "I expect a real bet."

"Fine. On the drive back, you have to tell me the story about all the partying and how you ended up here in Guatemala."

Jillian stuck out her hand to shake on it. "Deal," she said.

"We should stop talking. Even whispering. The cats can hear very well."

"Okay," Jillian said, then crossed her legs and closed her eyes to meditate.

Diego watched her curiously and saw an expression of serenity come over her face in spite of the bugs flying around her. As Jillian sat perfectly still, Diego's heart swirled in confusion. He was intensely drawn to her and envied her freedom to laugh so easily. But she also scared him—her beauty and lightheartedness threatened to unravel him, and he could not afford to let down his guard. Not only would *El Jefe* not be happy, but it would seriously mess with his head while dealing with Menendez's men. He had to stay sharp.

She opened her eyes. "What?" she whispered.

"I didn't say anything."

"I know. I can feel you staring at me."

He lowered his gaze. "You look so *tranquilo,* so peaceful."

"You should have seen me six months ago; I was a mess." She rolled her eyes then put her hand over her mouth, realizing she had spoken too loudly and looked around to see if she'd scared anything off. "Oops, sorry."

For some reason, the idea of her being a mess intrigued Diego. "What happened six months ago?"

"Later ... but only if you win, of course," she whispered.

"Oh, come on—"

"Shh." Jillian put her finger to her lips. "I'm meditating, remember?"

She closed her eyes again, and her peacefulness, the sounds of the jungle, and the fact that Diego hadn't slept well in weeks lulled him to sleep within minutes. He awoke a few times but then dozed off again into a deep slumber. Finally, after what could have been thirty minutes or two hours, he opened his eyes and heard movement below. His breath caught as a large, female jaguar languidly moved toward the Obsession-covered log, and he touched Jillian's knee. When she opened her eyes and saw the big cat, she gasped, then stared at him, astonished. He put a finger to his lips to keep her from saying anything. Her eyes seemed double their normal size as she stared at the magnificent creature with black rosette-shaped rings and spots decorating her golden coat. The jaguar sniffed at the log, then started rubbing her face on it and licking it over and over, climbing on it and pawing at it. She was obsessed with the Obsession and looked like a big kitten playing with a toy.

They both took pictures of the jaguar, and when a shaft of light hit her feline face and she looked up at them, her smoldering golden eyes sparkled, and her radiant beauty took their breath away. Finally, she'd had enough of the cologne catnip and slinked back into the jungle as quietly as she had come.

Jillian looked at Diego and, like little kids, they celebrated by shouting and cheering, jumping to their feet and high fiving.

"That's the coolest thing I've ever seen! I told you the meditation would work!" she yelled, then hugged him so fast and hard that he stumbled backward and nearly fell off the platform. But she pulled him back toward her and steadied him.

As they stood there with their arms around each other, his stomach trembled, and his legs felt watery. He wanted to kiss her. *Ni lo pienses,* he said to himself. *Don't even think about it. You have to get serious. This cannot happen.* He gently pushed her away from him, then scrambled down the ladder and headed back toward the Jeep.

"Why are you going so fast?" Jillian asked as she rushed to keep up.

"I just need to get back. I've spent enough time playing around."

Finally catching up to him, she grabbed his arm. "Hey, you owe me—Tikal tomorrow!"

"Not possible. My boss won't allow it."

"You made a bet!"

"Well, I didn't think you'd win."

They rode back to headquarters in silence, as he stewed in resentment at her presence. He didn't want to be around her anymore. He didn't want to think about the fact that they saw a jaguar on her first time out, or how the local Mayans believed that jaguar sightings, which were extremely rare, were a gift from God. And he certainly didn't want to think about God. She had penetrated his veil of denial and made him furious at himself for what he'd done and angry at her for making him feel this way. He gripped the steering wheel as if he wanted to choke it and vowed to stay away from her. When he dropped her off, he tried not to notice the hurt in her eyes.

CHAPTER SEVEN

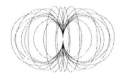

ANCIENT ALIENS

Mobius stared in shock at the moving images that the data cube projected onto the wall. "Is that ... are those ...?"

"Aliens?" Nava said, finishing his sentence.

The old-fashioned footage, stamped "International Space Agency Mission Log," showed a view from an ancient Akaran spacecraft hovering over a gathering of alien beings on a lush planet rich with life. The aliens stood amidst large, pyramid-shaped structures, some of which were under construction in the middle of a clearing in a dense, green jungle. As the craft moved down and landed on the ground, the beings came into better view. They were like Akarans in many ways—anthropoids with two legs and two arms, but they had tiny eyes and dark fur on their heads.

Mobius couldn't tell if there were pers among them, but he did see two genders for sure. Most of the men wore primitive loincloths, but some were more elaborately adorned with tunics, jewelry, and headdresses. The women wore colorful pieces of cloth draped around their bodies. Their skin was a deep brown, a shade darker than Mobius, but not as dark as Tru. As the craft landed, the aliens lost control, raising their hands and falling on their knees. Even though there was no sound, they were obviously crying out.

The five Supernova crewmembers stood there, awestruck at what they were seeing.

"This is unbelievable!" Tru exclaimed.

"Unreal," Barj said.

"Look at them, they're beautiful," Nava said.

"They have to be from L'Azman," Kaia whispered. "Wow."

"That's mind-blowing! I thought L'Azman was a myth," Mobius said, an electrical current of energy running through him. For as long as he could remember, he'd known the legend of L'Azman, which meant "Precious Jewel." It was said to be a planet inhabited by intelligent beings and located in the Serpent, a tiny constellation visible from Akara. No one but conspiracy theorists took the legend seriously; the chances of finding another planet like Akara were one out of the billions and billions of worlds, solar systems, and galaxies in the universe. Everyone agreed that there had to be other sentient beings out there, but sadly, they had never found any. Given this lack of contact and Akarans' obsession with space, even though there was no evidence of its existence, L'Azman had achieved a cult-like status.

All of a sudden, the imagery cut to a new scene, showing what seemed to be the commander of the mission to L'Azman. He was wearing an old space suit, with a helmet that had a large coiled tube coming out the top of it. He stood at the exit portal of the ancient craft and said something to the camera.

"What is he saying?" Barj asked, frustrated that there was no sound.

Through the helmet's clear visor, the commander's features were visible—a long nose and pearl white skin and golden eyes.

Like Kaia, he was clearly Sintauran. When the portal opened, the commander clomped in his heavy space boots down the steps to the ground and stood before the crowd of aliens. He towered over them, two heads above even the tallest males. They all prostrated themselves before him, except for one man who walked toward him, then spoke and knelt down. The ornately dressed man, who wore an enormous feathered headdress, placed something at the commander's feet.

The commander posed with a triumphant look on his face, then with a flourish removed his helmet, revealing his hairless head and big Akaran eyes. The aliens completely lost their minds, wailing and crying.

"Who is that?" Mobius asked.

Suddenly, the image glitched out and disappeared.

The room vibrated with wonder and excitement as they stared at each other in the low light. "What did you stumble onto here?" Kaia asked, nearly breathless.

"Proof that the myth is true! That has to be L'Azman. It really exists and is inhabited by aliens!" Mobius said, turning up the lights.

"It's also proof that there actually *was* footage of the planet that was lost or destroyed during the Final War, like the conspiracy theorists have always claimed," Tru said.

Nava picked up the cube. "This may be the only footage that survived."

"It's the biggest find since the Xaxen Cathedral," Barj said, referring to a recent important archaeological find. "Maybe the biggest find since the advent of torus technology!"

Kaia turned to Mobius. "I have to hand it to you. You're the most anomalous Anomaly on the planet. Assuming the footage is real, this is groundbreaking."

Pride lifted Mobius's chest and relief relaxed his shoulders. *Maybe my life isn't ruined after all,* he thought. But his attention quickly returned to the mission log. "How did data this important end up in that canyon? It makes no sense."

"It seems like someone intentionally buried it there," Nava said. "They went to great lengths to hide it."

"But why keep it a secret in the first place?" Barj asked.

Nava looked at Kaia, studying her face for a moment. "What is it?"

"What do you mean?" Kaia asked.

"Something's wrong. I can tell."

"Nothing's wrong," she insisted.

"I know you're not telling us something."

"Stop that, Intuit," Kaia said. "There are a lot of questions to be answered. At this point we need to turn the cube in to the Archaeology and Discovery Corps."

They all erupted in protest.

"Let's try to find out what else is on it," Mobius urged.

"This isn't a game. It's a serious discovery," Kaia said.

"Come on, Kaia. I brought it to you, and I could have kept it," Mobius said, a tinge of anger in his voice.

"You're not helping your case, candidate."

"Kaia," Nava said, gently putting a hand on her shoulder. "Mobius risked his life, and mine, to retrieve this. He found it for a reason."

Mobius felt his heart thumping its triple beat in his chest. *Was that possible?* He felt energy running up and down his body again. The room became almost eerily quiet.

Nava leaned in and whispered into Kaia's ear, "What's the harm in us looking at it first? Mobius is devastated. Just give him this."

"Well ...," Kaia said. "I'm not even sure what we've got here. I suppose we could try to find out what else is on it before turning it in."

"Yes!" exclaimed Mobius.

"How would we even access the rest of the data, assuming there is any?" Barj asked.

Kaia remained silent, deep in thought. "I might know a guy," she said finally.

"A guy?" Mobius asked, filling with excitement.

"A guy who's an expert in ancient technology. His name is Piphus—he was on my team in the Discovery Corps for a while, but he turned out to be too much of a recluse to work in a group."

"Sounds perfect," Barj said jokingly.

"Do you think he'll help?" Nava asked.

"I don't know," she said. "He's very unconventional, so it's hard to tell what he'll do, even though this seems like the kind of thing he'd jump at. But I'm not even sure where he is. He's pretty off the grid. Last time I heard, he was in Dalusia, in the mountains doing his own thing."

"So, does this mean we can keep it?" Mobius asked.

Kaia stood contemplating—placing one of her fingers at the center of her forehead, just above her eyes, where she and all Akarans had an azure blue circular mark. "I should say no. But the Wisdom is telling me to go ahead." She smiled. "But then we're turning it in right away."

The group looked at each other in disbelief and started to vibrate with anticipation. They loved that she wasn't afraid to bend protocol.

"Don't get too excited. I have no idea when or if I'll be able to find Piphus. If I don't reach him in the next couple of days, we'll have to turn it in."

"You'll find him," Mobius said, unable to hold back his excitement. He took the cube from Nava, shut the top, and handed the tiny artifact to Kaia. Nava flashed him a smile, and it seemed ten times brighter than the sun and dwarf star combined.

•

As soon as the candidates stepped outside the Community Hall, Nava stopped and looked up at the dark sky, now filled with stars. "Look at the Serpent," she said. The five tiny stars visible to the naked eye formed a squiggly line in the shape of a snake, with the biggest star at the top as its head.

"Come on you guys, follow me," Mobius said. He cut diagonally across the quad and headed toward the Tenzin Observatory, named for the legendary brother-and-sister science team who developed the first torus at the end of the Final War. They'd helped bring civilization back from the abyss of the Ravaging Era and usher in the Rebirthing. A regal structure, the observatory towered over the campus. During the day, its dome—covered in mirrored fractal geometric patterns—reflected the spectrum of light from the Twin Flames, shooting laser-like beams back into the sky. At night it refracted the softer light of Akara's moons.

Inside the foyer, the group walked past a display that housed the first torus, then they wound their way up a suspended glass spiral staircase. At the top, one by one, they looked through the imposing telescope that shot into the glimmering night sky. Even here on the outskirts of the city, there was enough darkness to see well; since the Rebirthing, Akarans had put an emphasis on minimizing all pollution, including light and sound. The telescope was nowhere near the strength or capability of the ones used by the

DC in remote locations, but it was good enough to turn the faint, faraway constellation into a dazzling pattern of colorful stars and planets of various sizes. Somewhere among them—possibly even one that they could see—was L'Azman.

Nava backed away and let Mobius look again. "I hope the footage turns out to be real."

"If it does, do you realize what it means?" Mobius whispered as he gazed across the galaxy. "We're not alone."

CHAPTER EIGHT

HOT SEAT

D iego pulled into the Laguna del Tigre Ranger Station in a near panic. His Uncle Domingo had summoned him when he'd radioed in his patrol report an hour ago, and he was convinced that this time *El Jefe* had definitely discovered his secret. The man knew pretty much everything that happened in the jungle. Diego sat in his Jeep and tried unsuccessfully to pull himself together. Not only was he stressed out about getting busted, he was exhausted.

As usual, he'd tossed and turned all night, but this time it wasn't because of the drug gang; it was because he couldn't quit thinking about what had happened with Jillian the day before. But as he prepared to face his uncle, she was the last thing on his mind. If he were found out, not only would he lose his job and devastate his family, he'd be locked up for sure.

Finally, he made his way to his uncle's office through sheer force of will, even though his stomach threatened to come up. *El Jefe* was on the phone, trying as always to get more funding, more support, more rangers, more help to fight against the human greed and desperation that threatened to destroy the rainforest. He motioned for Diego to sit down, then finished his call, hanging up the phone with a sigh. He said in Spanish, "You look like hell. What's going on?" Domingo stared at him with deep brown eyes under his heavy, jet-black eyebrows.

He knows, Diego thought, but smiled as convincingly as he could. "Nothing, nothing. *Estoy bien*, I'm fine."

"How is your mother doing?"

"She's still having a lot of trouble with pain from the arthritis and is unable to work much." Diego had already given her some of Menendez's money. When she asked how he got it, he claimed he had made it online with a friend from the U.S. She knew nothing about the Internet; there wasn't even a computer at home, so he kept it vague and said he'd lucked into working with the guy on his time off. His mother's gratitude had helped lessen his guilt.

"Is there enough money for her and your sisters to live on?"

Diego wondered how long his uncle was going to drag this out, but then again, Domingo's tone seemed warm and caring. Maybe he didn't know after all.

Diego forced himself not to look away when the subject of money came up. "Oh yes, we're managing."

El Jefe looked at him curiously; he knew that Diego's dad, Domingo's brother, a small-time handyman, hadn't left them anything but debt when he died. He also knew that Diego's job didn't pay enough to cover the expenses of his mother's care or his sisters' education. But since his mother rarely ever spoke to her brother-in-law, Diego wasn't about to tell Domingo the story that he was moonlighting after work, afraid his uncle would see through the lie.

"Tell me what happened this morning on your patrol," Domingo said, dropping the subject of money.

His uncle's casual tone convinced Diego that Domingo didn't

know anything, and he felt like he could breathe for the first time in an hour. Running his hands through his hair, Diego let out a little nervous laugh, and relaxed back in his chair. "I was patrolling the southern border near the river and right off the road, I saw six wood poachers cutting down mahogany trees and loading a truck. I came up on them with my bullhorn and told them to freeze, that I was taking them in. Two of them drove off in the truck and the other four bolted into the rainforest. I chased them on foot, but it seemed like they knew the trails, because I couldn't catch up. After about ten minutes, I realized I was in danger of being ambushed, so I bailed out and called in the plate number of the truck."

"You are too brave sometimes." Domingo shook his head, but there was a slight grin under his thick mustache.

Diego steered the conversation away from his supposed bravery. "I can't believe how bold these *pendejos* are getting. They were right next to the main road."

"Well, at least some of them are going to be hurting soon," Domingo said. "I just got word that INTERPOL is joining the police strike against the loggers and *narcos*, giving us manpower, weapons, and vehicles."

Diego's face twitched at this news. He wished he didn't know about it. *If a strike happens, and I don't warn Menendez* ... "That's good news!" Diego finally said, forcing excitement into his voice. "When does it happen?"

"Soon, within the next two weeks. The date isn't set yet, but I think they will want to coordinate it with the festivities at the end of the Mayan calendar to get as much international media attention as possible." He put his hands on the back of his head and leaned back. "Can you believe how big this thing has become? I am very glad because of the attention the Reserve is getting, but it is surprising—the reaction people are having. And the entire world is focused on us right now."

"No, I can't believe it or understand it. But as you said, hopefully it will be helpful for our cause. So, when is the raid?"

"My guess is sometime between December eighteenth and twentieth. I'll be giving all the rangers orders as soon as I know more."

"*Bueno.* I can't wait." He was going to ask who the local police leader was so he could just give Menendez a name and be done with it, but he simply couldn't bring himself to say the words. He hoped that giving up the timing and the fact that the International Criminal Police Organization was involved would be enough to keep himself alive through this crisis. He just wanted to make enough money from the drug cartel to give his mother enough to live on for the rest of her life and to get himself the hell out of the third-world jungle and back to his first-world college in the States. Even though he loved his country, all the time he'd spent over the summers in the U.S. with his mother's employers in their seaside mansion had made him intolerant of the poverty and struggle in Guatemala.

As Diego got up to head back out on patrol, Domingo leaned forward and crossed his arms on his desk. "Sit back down. I'm not done with you."

Diego's stomach tightened up again as he lowered himself back into his chair. "Oh. I thought that's why you called me in—to tell me about the raid."

"No, I called you in to talk to you about Jillian Savoy."

"What? What about her?"

"Apparently, you were a bit of a *pendejo* yourself."

"I didn't act like an asshole. What are you talking about?"

"Is it true that you went back on a promise to take her to Tikal?"

"How did you even hear about that? What the hell is her problem?"

Domingo leaned forward, a serious look on his face. "Listen to me, *mijo*. The president of the Natural Resources Defense Council called me this morning and told me we need to fix whatever happened between you and *Señorita* Savoy. Apparently, her family is extremely wealthy—billionaires in fact—and the young lady has persuaded them to give the NRDC a significant endowment, a large percentage of which was earmarked for the Reserve."

Diego was barely able to stay seated at that point. "Oh, so I pissed off some spoiled, rich girl from the U.S., is that it?"

"Diego, forget about your *machismo*. Your behavior may have put her contribution at risk!" Domingo glowered at him. "Let me be clear. You need to get yourself together and act like the Queen of England has come for a visit, and you are her personal guide to Tikal. I don't know what your problem is, but if I hear you're anything but a perfect gentleman, your ass will be back in that chair and you'll be in very hot water."

"Just have Alejandro take her," he said. "He speaks English well enough. Clearly, she doesn't like me."

El Jefe leaned forward and raised a finger. "We're not going to give her a single reason to tell her family to take their money somewhere else. Right now, you are a reason," he said, pointing his finger at Diego. "And you're going to fix it. This is your job, Diego. Now stop acting like a child. Go find her and tell her you'll be escorting her to Tikal whenever she wants. And afterward, she'd better be convinced that her family's contribution is going to the right place."

Diego stood up. "Is that all?" he asked through gritted teeth.

"That's it. Oh, and not a word about her money. She doesn't want anyone to know who she is."

Diego clenched his fists and walked out of the office to his Jeep, leaving skid marks as he pulled away from the station.

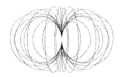

CHAPTER NINE

OBSOLETE

Mobius stood with Kaia and the rest of Supernova Crew on a raised platform, waiting for the skyway to take them to the mountains where Piphus lived. It had taken Kaia a few days to locate the eccentric recluse, but now that she had, they were abuzz with anticipation. They also couldn't stop talking about the news that had captivated everyone for the last two days—for the first time, a DC scouting crew had discovered retainite on another planet. Scans revealed a large quantity under the planet's surface, but interstellar geologists were still trying to figure out how to extract it given the planet's frigid temperatures and intense winds.

As he waited, Mobius scanned the scene below. The skyway station overlooked an open-air market. The streets were filled with citizens dressed in a kaleidoscope of colors and styles from regions around the world, and he watched as they moved among the stalls of art, jewelry, and clothing. The air was filled with the aroma of flowers and food, and it made him realize he was hungry. His appetite had become a bonfire of late, especially with all the training. He downed some nuts he had in his pocket, but there was no time to get anything else.

Moments later, the skyway descended noiselessly from above

and floated to a stop. As the doors of the long, transparent tube opened, they stepped on board, sat down, and activated their energy harnesses. Immediately, the transport shot directly upward from the ground. The skyways traveled at a high elevation so they wouldn't clutter up the lower airways.

When the tube finally reached the required altitude, it stopped, and for a moment Mobius felt as if he were suspended weightless before the transport moved forward, this time horizontally, toward the mountains. Immediately, Mobius got up and started pacing. The days since the test had dragged as he waited to hear the consequences for his actions in the canyon. Word was supposed to have come down from the DC yesterday, but it had been delayed amidst the news of the retainite discovery.

"Can you check again?" he asked Kaia.

"All right, Mobius. You're relentless." She got up and stepped away.

His worst fear was that he'd have to enter the Anomaly Rehabilitation program, something typically reserved for the least evolved Anomalies. While it wasn't punitive, he'd always prided himself on being on the higher end of the spectrum and going into rehabilitation would be humiliating.

A few moments later, Kaia walked back toward him. "Well, you definitely have some luck on your side. They've determined that not making the Corps is consequence enough."

"Yes!" Mobius exclaimed. "Thank you!" He walked by each of his crewmembers and bumped forearms. Though he was grateful and relieved, he knew he would continue to obsess about his failure if he didn't have the relic to distract him.

An hour later, the skyway arrived in Dalusia, and most of the passengers headed off on foot or pedicycle, but Piphus lived many miles up the mountain, so the crew checked out uni-hovers. As Mobius straddled his machine and pulled out of the station, he was glad that the day was warm, with clear lavender skies so they could ride without using enclosures. They moved into the light traffic skimming the roadway and fell into a staggered formation with Kaia in front. As soon as they hit the outskirts of town and started up the mountain—a huge monolith rising out of undulating prairie—Kaia bent into an aerodynamic position over the handlebars and gunned her uni-hover to maximum speed. They all looked at each other and smiled, speeding up to keep on her tail, banking back and forth into turn after turn. Even though it was impossible to crash—the autopilot would kick in and prevent the uni-hover from flipping or hitting anything—the speed was still a thrill for Mobius.

Finally, Kaia slowed the pace and came to a stop in front of a small freemarket so they could get something to eat. "Thank the Wisdom!" Mobius said. "I'm famished."

"*Always*. Why do you think I stopped?" Kaia said and smiled knowingly at him. "Make this quick everyone, I'm going to wait here."

Mobius envied her; she was an Absorber—someone who didn't need to eat food. She was able to live off the life force provided by the biosphere, as well as the background energy of the universe. After mastering the technique, Absorbers could still eat, but it was purely for pleasure. Even though he wished he could absorb, he couldn't imagine voluntarily not eating; he enjoyed it too much.

Supernova Crew walked into the market and picked out what they wanted. Unlike in the city, where attendants worked in the food markets to keep them stocked around the clock and to assist individuals in finding what they were looking for, the smaller country markets were empty except when food arrived. Otherwise, there was no need for an attendant since the food was free, and no one took more than they needed.

After Supernova Crew ate, they continued on, turning off the road just past the freemarket into woods dominated by trees with white bark and pale blue-and-silver leaves. Piphus's house was so remote there wasn't even a side road leading to it, so they had to dodge around the trees on their uni-hovers. Mobius barely slowed his speed, testing his reflexes and his nerve. Finally, they came to a clearing and saw a dome house that seemed to grow out of the ground, the curve of the roofline matching the distant horizon it overlooked.

They parked the uni-hovers and walked to the house, where the arched front doors were already open. Kaia called out to Piphus, and two fuzzy, orange winglings—a cross between an insect and a reptile—flew out the door just over their heads, and they all ducked. "What else is in there?" Mobius asked.

A few moments later, an unusually short, heavyset Dualie man appeared at the door. Adding to his already peculiar appearance, he wore a hat made of spiked, pale yellow faux fur. Akarans were completely hairless, so they tended to be fascinated by fur and hair. Almost every culture on the planet included clothing and head-wear that imitated it, and Piphus's hat was a modern version of headgear that dated as far back as Akara's earliest history. Like all Dualies, he had two-toned skin—light pink and a kind of bronze that traded off in big swaths all over his arms, neck, and face, the only parts not covered by his baggy clothes. The pink areas on his arms were decorated with tattoos that looked like intricate lace patterns, which Mobius couldn't stop staring at.

Piphus stood blinking at the group and squinting as if just

coming up from below ground.

"It's good to see you, Piphus," Kaia said. They greeted each other as friends by placing one hand on their hearts and reaching out and touching palms with the other.

"These are the Discovery Corps candidates I told you about," she said, introducing each of them. When she got to Mobius, she put a hand on his shoulder, "This is the one who found the relic."

Piphus eyed him for a moment before darting his eyes from one to the next. "There are so many. And they're bigger than I expected."

Mobius glanced at Nava, wondering what size Piphus expected them to be.

"Show me the relic," Piphus said, getting right to business.

Mobius held out the data cube, instantly focusing Piphus's scattered attention. The cyber-engineer leaned forward, studying the small golden object with fascination, then took it from Mobius and walked quickly inside without saying a word. They followed him into a large central room filled with gadgets, computers, and technology they had never seen before—a junkyard of old electronics. The piles of what seemed like random, useless stuff made Mobius even more skeptical than when he first laid eyes on Piphus. Looking more closely, however, in the far-left corner of the room, he noticed a set-up of the most current technology on Akara, with four holo-docks running at once.

Once inside his bizarre lair, Piphus seemed to relax a little. He picked up a twig that he'd obviously harvested from one of the trees outside and began chewing on it as he examined the cube, his pale blue eyes only inches away. "This is Late Ravaging Era for sure. You said it opened and you saw some 2D imagery?"

"Yes," Kaia said. "But it cut out, and there was no sound. We're hoping you can recover it."

Piphus set the cube on his workstation and began a search through stacks of spare parts and drawers full of junk. "Did you force it open with the insert hole?"

"Yes," Tru said.

"I hope you didn't ruin it," he mumbled.

"We wouldn't have known what it was if I hadn't opened it," she protested.

After rummaging around, Piphus finally held up a part that looked like a wire with a square end dangling from it. "I don't have a computer old enough to plug the cube straight into, but I have an adapter."

He powered up what looked to Mobius like a centuries-old machine with a clunky oval screen. It actually had a wire that had to plug into a torus because it didn't have its own energy source. He put the cube into the adapter and the adapter into the side of the computer, then punched a few buttons on a flat pad that lay on the table in front of the computer screen.

Barj looked on nervously, then whispered to Kaia, "Um, how long is this going to take? I really do have to make it home tomorrow night for Concordance. It's our first holiday since my sister died. That's not going to be a problem, is it?"

She put a hand on his shoulder. "That is the tenth time you've told me, Barj. I know how important it is that you're there, and I assure you that we all have places to be. We'll be back in plenty of time."

Concordance was the biggest holiday of the year, commemorating the official beginning of the Rebirthing Era. The day was named after Akara's planetary governing document drafted by the first World Wisdom Congress. The Concordance had unified and brought peace to the planet and ended the Final War. Mobius was expected to be home with his family too.

An indicator light on Piphus's screen blinked. "So far so good," he said. Then he strung a long cable from the back of the old computer to the corner near his modern computing station and plugged it into a clear narrow tower that was as tall as he was.

"What is that thing?" Tru asked.

"It's a transformer that I invented," Piphus said. "It has about eight hundred and fifty different inputs from computers that date back over thirteen hundred years, and it deciphers almost a thousand different languages and operating systems. If I can get the data from the cube to download onto it from that old machine, the transformer will put it directly onto my system, which will decode it, repair it, and recode it automatically."

"Wow," they all said almost simultaneously.

Piphus laughed, and suddenly he seemed like an excited child. And so did the rest of them. What he was describing was essentially impossible to anyone outside the Archaeology Corps or a few technology museums. Ninety-nine percent of technology from the past had been lost to time—no one really cared about old, outdated electronics when there was newer, faster, smaller, cooler tech available, not to mention that the older technology wouldn't even work anymore. The hardware had been treated as junk, and all electronic waste—as well as huge landfills of trash—had been incinerated by blasting it into the furnace of a distant sun. No one had any of this old stuff lying around, let alone the capability to use it.

When the transformer indicated that the transfer was complete, Piphus looked over the converted data with a scowl of frustration.

"What's wrong?" Kaia asked. "You weren't able to make it

work?"

"Some of it won't repair, but I think we have most of it. Let me just convert it to holographic projection."

"Oh, for the way of peace," Kaia exclaimed, "Don't worry about that. We can handle 2D. Come on, let's see."

"Speed over excellence," he quipped. "You're reminding me why I'm glad not to be taking orders at the DC anymore."

Kaia rubbed his furry head. "You know you've missed me."

Piphus picked up a miniature clearscreen, pinched it to open it to its full size, and fed the holo-dock with commands via his neurolink to open the data. Suddenly, drumbeats pounded through his sound system, and Mobius jumped off the floor, his heart pounding to a new, faster rhythm.

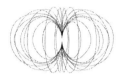

CHAPTER TEN

ITZAMNA

Transfixed, Mobius watched Piphus's screen as alien men with chiseled faces, feathered headdresses, and bare chests stared out at him. With eyes glossed over, they beat on large animal-skin drums, as if in a trance.

"Look at all that hair on them!" Piphus said over the noise of the alien drumming. "I cannot believe what I'm looking at."

They gathered around the clearscreen, pulling up rickety chairs that looked as old as the obsolete technology surrounding them. Piphus started the data-imagery from the beginning, and they looked at the scene they had already watched at Entelechy Academy, but this time it was much clearer and with sound.

The spaceship's commander stood wearing the helmet with the big air tube, and he spoke to the camera, his voice gravelly and low. "We have just landed on L'Azman for the first time since we discovered the planet and its primitive inhabitants three years ago. We have been exploring this solar system but have not found life on any other planet, so we have returned. These beings are easily dominated and subdued because of our superior intellect and technology, and that makes them quite useful. And they should present no obstacle to fulfilling my vision of establishing an Akaran colony here. We are eager to see the progress they have made since we were last here and showed them how to cut rock and lay stones more easily for their buildings, how to improve their canals for irrigation, and how to create more accurate calendars using the stars. Their understanding of time was admirable, but we have added to their knowledge significantly."

As the commander walked down the ramp and removed his helmet, the aliens' cries were now audible. Their wildly exotic-sounding language was not understandable except for one word, which they chanted over and over —"Itzamna!"

"Am I hearing correctly?" Mobius asked. "Are they saying—"

"Itzamna," Nava whispered. "They're saying Itzamna."

Piphus paused the recording and they all looked at each other. Tru jumped out of her chair. "Is this guy *actually* Itzamna? Is he real too?"

She and all Akaran children had heard tales about a tall evil being from ancient times named Itzamna. But no one, not even the conspiracy theorists, believed the Itzamna myth was actually true.

"If he's real," Mobius said quietly, "our childhood nightmares have just come to life."

"Piphus, can you authenticate this footage?" Kaia asked. "We need to make sure it's not just some form of entertainment or possibly even a hoax."

"That would take some time, and I'd need access to both the Archaeology and Discovery Corps databases. But from what I'm seeing, it looks authentic to me."

"Incredible," Kaia said, shaking her head.

When Piphus started the mission log again, they watched as Itzamna inspected an enormous, though partially completed, stepped-pyramid structure. The male alien who had approached Itzamna when they first landed, and who appeared to be the aliens' leader, joined the Akaran commander. Of all the aliens, the leader wore the most ornate tunic, cape, and ornamental jewelry made of a beautiful green stone, and the biggest headdress with the most impressive feathers. Itzamna and the leader spoke in the alien language, but the log was subtitled at the bottom of the screen.

Itzamna climbed the steps of the unfinished pyramid. "I am extremely displeased with you, King K'awiil," Itzamna said, his nostrils flaring.

The king bowed a little. "My Lord, we are ashamed that we have not finished your temple before your return."

"Why is this?" Itzamna demanded. "It was halfway complete when I left."

K'awiil bowed his head for a moment. "The problem is that we don't have enough workers to get the stones to the higher levels. On this building where we stand, many workers died finishing it, so the pace of construction is slow."

"That is no excuse!" Itzamna bellowed, his eyes narrowing and his jaw jutting forward. He turned toward the throng of people staring at him with worshipful attention. Half a dozen members of his crew stood together behind the aliens. They also looked up at him, but the expressions on their faces showed not admiration, but fear.

Itzamna raised a hand over his head dramatically. "Hear this! It shall be known from this day on that the power of this place will be increased with each drop of blood that touches its holy ground! The temple will be the first structure we will complete now that I have returned. It will be the most important structure not only here, but in all the universe. It will be a testament to me, your

Creator Sky God, for the rest of time!"

The crowd cheered wildly in response to Itzamna, and King K'awiil turned and frantically motioned to two men who stood behind him. "I hope this at least will please you."

The men moved to a low bench and picked up a large round stone carving from it. It was almost as tall as they were, and its great weight showed in the strain on their faces. They brought the carving to King K'awiil and Itzamna.

"This will grace the top of your temple, my Lord. We have named it Temple of the Sky God."

An uncanny likeness of the commander—with his big, upward slanting eyes, large nose, and full lips—was incised in the stone. A serpent with its mouth open and fangs showing sat on top of his head.

Kaia pointed at the screen. "Clearly they thought the air tube on his helmet was some kind of snake." Snakes were still common on Akara, having survived the Ravaging Era much better than most species.

Itzamna smiled, then laughed—his mood changing abruptly— and put his hand on King K'awiil's back. "You have made me very happy with this."

"And, my Lord, please accept this as well," The king removed a large, ornately carved green pendant that hung around his neck. As he placed it over Itzamna's head, he said, "It is made of jade, our most precious stone, and it is my most prized possession. This necklace is worn only by the king. By giving it to you, I am proclaiming to all that there is no power higher than you."

Itzamna took K'awiil's hand and raised it with his own, and both L'Azmanians and Akarans roared their approval. All but one, who did not cheer as wildly as the rest—a female crewmember from Akara.

Piphus paused the mission log. "What in the name of all that is unholy did you bring me here?"

Mobius was numb. He didn't know how to process it all.

"This guy is completely insane!" Kaia said.

"Surely the translation is wrong," Barj said.

"Did you see the look in his eyes?" Nava responded. "I don't think it's wrong."

Piphus started the log again, and the scene changed to Itzamna sitting on a magnificent carved throne at the top of stairs that were flanked by some kind of carved animals. The throne was recessed into a stone frame, so that Itzamna was protected from the rain that poured down. He wore a headdress with feathers, fur, and the head of a large serpent on it. A fascinating, fur-covered animal with an anthropoid face and a long tail sat on the top of the throne above his head.

"What is he looking at?" Barj asked.

Just then, the footage changed to reveal hundreds of alien slaves using ropes and logs to drag a huge stone along the wet ground during a rainstorm. When any of them faltered, they were beaten by a guard, their blood blending with the water and running in rivulets down their bodies.

"I can't believe an Akaran did this ... that this is our legacy," Kaia said. "It's horrible."

Piphus blinked twice. "I'm struck by the fact that he taught them how to cut and move the stone manually, but he didn't give them the wheel. It would have been so much easier."

"I'm sure it's because he enjoyed watching them suffer for him," Nava said, her voice quivering. "I need a break."

She got up and walked out the front door, and Mobius went

after her. Immediately, he felt uplifted by the warmth of the Twin Flames and the solidity of the woods. Being in nature offered the comfort of something beautiful and true and good.

"This is our legacy on L'Azman?" Nava said. "The aliens there were primitive. They were still in the tribal stage of evolution, and Itzamna took advantage of that. But what about his crew? Why didn't they do something?"

"They all seemed to be either under his spell or terrified of him," Mobius said. "Except that one female member."

By now the entire group was standing around breathing in the fresh air. Mobius looked at them, and every last one of them looked ill.

Kaia had her hands on top of her head, and she breathed deeply and slowly. "Our history is filled with wars and violence and cruelty, but to know that we exported it to another planet is tragic. How could they have let this guy near another civilization?"

"He had to have been obsessed with power to start," Piphus said, "but encountering the aliens must have changed him. Their worshiping him as a god clearly made him insane."

"And look how many leaders in our history were crazy as hell, but for some reason people followed them," Barj said.

They all blinked their eyes in agreement.

"You all don't have to watch any more of it," Kaia said. "You can just stay out here. But it's important that I see the rest."

TIKAL

At *El Jefe's* orders, Diego left the ranger station and headed directly to speak to Jillian. She was staying at an eco-tourist sanctuary in the middle of a vast freshwater wetland area that was only accessible by boat. He had to leave right away to find her, or he'd miss the last boat back and get stuck there for the night.

He drove to the docking area on the river and boarded a little, dilapidated motorboat, greeting the wrinkled old driver, Pepe—a native with a great, chiseled Mayan face imprinted with antiquity. Five eco-tourists and birdwatchers holding various sizes of cameras and backpacks boarded with Diego. The twenty-minute boat ride was serene. Even the alligators sunning themselves onshore seemed tranquil, and it helped him to calm down a bit. By the time Pepe brought the boat to ground at the station, Diego was still furious with Jillian Savoy, but at least he felt he could pull off seeing her without betraying how he really felt.

He asked around and was told she'd gone zip-lining. He found her on a wide trail that led into the jungle, on her way back. When she saw him, she came to an abrupt stop.

"How was it?" he asked, trying to sound casual.

"Pretty cool, but not fast enough for me. What are you doing here? You're the last person I expected to see today."

"I came to make out on our bet."

Jillian snickered. "I think you mean make *good* on our bet. Maybe your English isn't that great after all."

He rolled his eyes. "English phrases make no sense half the time. Anyway, I am here to tell you that you are getting your way, *señorita*. I'm taking you to Tikal."

"No. You're not."

"What? Why not?"

"Because I don't want to go with you anymore."

"Are you kidding me? *¡Ay! ¡Chica loca!*" Diego exclaimed, muttering in Spanish under his breath, but then stopped himself. He had to pull this off; she couldn't know he'd been ordered to take her, so he dropped his annoyance. "I didn't like how things ended with us. I would like to make it up to you and make *good* on our bet."

Jillian just glared with her arms crossed.

"Please, Jillian," he said, unnerved, and forced himself to flash her his most winning smile. "I know you want to go. And I want to take you. I promise."

She looked him up and down for a moment as if she were trying to decide if he was telling the truth. Finally, she let out a big sigh. "I bet that Latin charm helps you talk your way into an awful lot. Fine, I'll go."

She began walking again, and he fell in beside her, moving beneath a canopy of twisted vines and flowering trees on the well-manicured path back toward the bamboo dwellings of the eco-resort. After a couple of minutes she exclaimed, "I can't believe I'm finally getting to go to Tikal! Part of why I decided to come on this trip is because of the end of the Mayan calendar celebrations. It should be amazing."

"It will be crowded with a lot of weirdos, that is for sure," Diego said.

"You aren't a believer, it seems."

"In the end of the world in a few days?" Diego asked. "No."

"I hope you're right," she said, "but I guess I'm one of the weirdos. I've kind of gotten into the Mayan prophecy. So have a lot of people I know. I have an aunt in Oklahoma who stocked up on bottled water and cans of beanie weenies."

Diego laughed. "What are beanie weenies? And how will they help her if it's the end of the world?"

Jillian shook her head, smiling. "I don't know, but my point is a lot of people are taking it really seriously. I do think there's something significant about it."

"Why?"

"Because the Mayans had unbelievable knowledge for an ancient civilization, and I don't think it's just random that their calendar ends on December 21st, 2012. Many people think if it's not the end of time, it must be some kind of turning point on the planet."

"I guess we'll find out soon enough," he said. "So, when do you want to go?"

"How's tomorrow?"

Whatever the rich girl wants, Diego thought. "Fine. I'll pick you up at the dock first thing in the morning." He went to shake her hand, trying to create a little distance and professionalism between them.

"Don't be ridiculous," she said, hugging him, and he pulled away a little, surprised.

Gringos can be so forward sometimes. On the boat ride back, he vowed that tomorrow he would maintain a strict, formal air with her at all times.

•

As they drove into the heart of the Mayan ruins of Tikal the following morning, Diego wasn't doing a very good job controlling his anger. It had been two hours since he'd picked Jillian up from the boat, and he was getting more irritated by the minute. He was not happy that she had badmouthed him to his boss, or rather to the head of a global non-profit who had then badmouthed him to his boss. It made him think that because of her family's money, she felt she could treat people any way she wanted and get away with it. He'd been around enough rich people to know they often felt entitled. At least he knew that there would be no visitation from the *criminales* this close to Tikal, especially with the number of tourists already swarming around five days before the end of the calendar. But as always, he was nervous, and even more so with her at his side.

He stopped at the main parking area of the ruins. "I think it's best if you take a tour with one of the guides here. They'll know more about the ruins than I do."

She looked disappointed. "No, I want you to come with me. Come on, it'll be fun."

If he refused, he assumed she would report it as *pendejo* behavior to the NRDC, and then his uncle would hear all about it again. "Fine," he relented, feeling pushed around. "But I hope you'll be satisfied. Don't say I didn't warn you."

Over the next two hours, Diego guided her around the magnificent Mayan city of Tikal with its great plaza, enormous stepped pyramids, and carved stelae—large upright stone slabs depicting the greatness of gods and legendary Mayan leaders. Tikal always had a grand, noble air about it, but that atmosphere had increased noticeably because of the preparations that were being made for the three-day festival leading up to the fateful day—12-21-12.

Jillian stopped and looked at one of the stelae with small, carved symbols all over it. "Wow, I wonder what all those etchings mean."

"I know what a couple of the glyphs are," Diego said.

"Glyphs?" Jillian said. "Is that what they're called?"

"Yeah. You know, like hieroglyphics."

"Oh, right. You know what some of them mean?"

"Well, only a couple of the simple ones. There are about a thousand different Mayan glyphs." He studied the carving, then finally pointed to one that looked like several squiggly lines. "I think that one means fire."

Jillian got up closer to the stone. "Yeah. I can see that. It looks a little like a flame."

He pointed at another, more intricate symbol. "That one represents the city of Tikal."

She smiled at him. "Impressive, *señor*."

At her compliment, Diego relaxed a bit, and they kept walking until they came to a ball court with walls and stone rings. "This is where the first games with rubber balls were played," he said. "The games were great ritual events and seen as a battle of good against evil."

Diego told Jillian everything he had learned about Mayan culture over his years growing up in Guatemala and working as a ranger here. He recounted theories about how the Mayans had built the pyramids without use of the wheel, work animals, or any sophisticated technology, and shared about their worship of deities, practice of human sacrifice, and, of course, their obsession with time.

"The ancient Mayans were incredible astronomers," Diego

explained as he stood in front of a large stone Mayan calendar, intricately etched. "The reason they could track time so far into the past and into the future is that they somehow knew exactly where the planets and stars were at any given time. They knew that ten thousand years before the Mayan culture ever existed, the galaxy was in a specific configuration, and they also knew exactly how long it would take for the skies to return to that same configuration again. It is impossible for scientists to explain how they figured out all that they did."

Surrounded by a horde of people, Jillian examined the detailed carvings on the stone. "That's why people are paying so much attention to the end of the calendar and believe it could be the end of the world," she said. "The Mayans knew what they were doing."

A young man with glasses and an unkempt beard had heard them talking. "They got help from aliens," he said with a French accent. "That's how they knew what they did."

Diego glanced at him, shaking his head, then pulled Jillian away. "See what I mean about weirdos?"

"A lot of people believe that, you know," Jillian said.

He smiled as if he were dealing with a naïve child. "A lot of people are *muy loco,* Jillian."

"So, you don't believe there's a chance the world will end even though the Mayans seemed to know impossible things? Things that were possibly taught to them by aliens?" She laughed a little.

"See, you laughed. You know it sounds ridiculous. It's like Y2K. It was supposed to be this big disaster, but nothing happened. It will be the same as that."

As they began making their way back toward the entrance, Jillian pointed to a large round stone carving. The etching at the center was a male head in profile, with a huge nose, large eyes, and full lips. He wore a headdress topped by a serpent with its mouth open and fangs showing. Three concentric circles of elaborate glyphs surrounded the image. "Who is that guy? I've seen him depicted a lot."

"That is Itzamna," Diego replied. "The Mayans considered him to be their creator sky god."

"He's got a big nose," she said.

"You know what they say about men with big noses, don't you?"

She looked at him sideways. "I don't think I want to know."

"They have big egos." He laughed. "What did you think I meant?" He realized he had let down his guard again and was having a good time with her.

They walked to the Jeep, and he reminded himself that he must remain distant and formal. On the way home, a light rain began to fall as Diego talked about the dismal state of the Maya Biosphere Reserve, hoping to erase any doubt Jillian may have developed about the money she and her family were planning to give to the NRDC.

"A few months ago," Diego said, "I drove into a local village and saw several men standing around a dead jaguar that was poached for its coat. The men had chased the poacher away, but the jaguar was already dead. The species has been endangered since the '70's, and the poachers are more ruthless than ever."

He went on and on with horror stories about severely threatened wildlife; out-of-control fires set by people who were colonizing the rainforest; illegal logging by Chinese-backed criminal groups who cut down prime tropical hardwoods; money laundering by drug cartels who ranched cattle on razed forest land; and more. By the time they got back into Laguna del Tigre, Jillian was crying. Even though what he told her was harsh, it was all true, and he was proud because tomorrow he would be able to tell *El Jefe* that he was confident the Reserve would be getting her family's donation.

The rain stopped, and the setting sun was turning the remaining clouds into a canvas for a warm-hued, painted sunset. Diego turned onto the narrow dirt road that led to the river dock and let out a grateful sigh. He had made it through the day without pissing Jillian off and, just as importantly, without telling her off. In his mind, not only had he carried out Domingo's orders, but he'd also secured a huge investment of money for wildlife conservation. He knew that only that kind of money and the resources it could pay for would really help the jungle; his own paltry actions one way or the other made no difference. He felt good about himself for the first time since he had met Manuel Menendez.

Glancing in the rearview mirror, he noticed a truck that had turned off the main road behind him was speeding up. The vehicle didn't slow down until it was on his tail. Then he heard shouting, "*¡Alto! ¡Alto!* Stop, stop!"

Diego's mouth filled with bile, and his heart began thrashing like a dry fish in his chest.

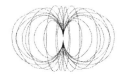

CHAPTER TWELVE

THE CAPSULE

A ll of Supernova Crew had decided to join Kaia back inside to watch the rest of the mission log, however horrible. When Piphus started the ancient data-imagery again, they watched the progress the aliens had made on the temples. Mobius was grateful that nothing disturbing took place for several minutes. But then an Akaran crewmember suddenly piqued their attention again. A woman with purple-black skin who was obviously from Enshala, like Tru, walked into frame. She stopped before Itzamna, who wore a huge brown and black snake draped over his shoulders—a live version of the headdress etched into the stone carving of him.

Mobius leaned forward in his chair. "That's the woman I pointed out in the beginning who didn't seem too happy about being there."

"You asked for me?" she said to Itzamna.

Itzamna looked down at her. He was very tall—not just compared to the aliens, but even for an Akaran man from those days—about the average height of most Sintaurans now. "Your crewmates informed me that you have continued to work on restoring communication with Akara, even after I ordered you to stop."

She looked up at him defiantly. "I was only trying to let them know we are alive."

"I don't care what you were trying to do!" he roared. To her credit, she barely flinched. But then he became eerily calm and spoke to her as if she were a child. "You do not disobey my orders. I want this city completed before we make contact with them. When they see what I have accomplished and how I am able to rule these aliens, I will be able to command full control of colonizing this world."

"You are exploiting these people and using their primitive beliefs against them," the woman protested.

"We are superior to this species," Itzamna said. He waved a hand, and two alien men came into the frame and took her forcefully by the arms.

She resisted them while shouting at the commander, "You've gone beyond wanting to just colonize and rule this race. You want to be a god. You've gone insane!" She spun around—using a combat technique that originated in the Enshala region—and escaped the guards' hold. She punched one of them in the nose with the base of her hand, then wheeled around and kicked the other one in the chest.

Itzamna called out, "Subdue her!" and six other alien men attacked. The woman was bigger and faster than they were and trained in more sophisticated fighting techniques. She fought them off with remarkable speed and skill, and everyone yelled at the screen hoping she would win. The aliens started to back off, looking like they were beginning to believe she was supernatural, like Itzamna, and therefore invincible. She began moving toward Itzamna, still in her fighting stance, but an Akaran crewmember ran at her out of nowhere, and plunged a long, black blade into her shoulder.

Mobius and everyone else groaned as she crumpled to the ground.

"It's not possible for this to get any worse, is it?" Nava put her hands on her head.

Onscreen, Itzamna congratulated the attacker as the woman was dragged away. "You have proven your loyalty, Lieutenant."

The man nodded gravely. "Thank you, Commander."

"Do you think she was able to communicate with Akara?" Itzamna asked.

"Not that I could tell. It is possible but very unlikely that she could cover her tracks that completely."

"Do the other crewmembers remain loyal to me?"

The lieutenant blinked twice. "So far, yes, I believe they do."

"Good, keep watching them. How is progress coming on the time capsule?" Itzamna sat on his throne again, as if nothing had happened.

"Very well, Commander. We are nearly finished preparing it."

"Excellent. It must be ready for Dedication Day."

"It will be, sir," he replied. "Do you want me to delete the footage of today from the drone cameras?"

Itzamna thought for a few moments. "No, for now I want to have a record of everything."

The image jumped to a different scene altogether, showing bare-chested drummers on the screen, their pounding rhythm beating again inside Mobius's chest as a wild event unfolded before him. A dozen ornately feathered, painted, and adorned men and women danced in a plaza situated at the base of the Temple of the Sky God.

"What a sight," Piphus said. "This has to be the dedication day he was talking about."

The image jumped again to Itzamna, who now sat next to King K'awiil in a stone stadium amid a crowd of people from every class—warriors, aristocrats, peasants, and even slaves bound in ropes—yelling and cheering. They watched two teams playing a game using a rubber ball on a court with two walls on either side of it, each one bearing stone rings through which the players tried to pass the ball.

"What an impressive race of beings," Nava said. "Even though they're violent, they are unbelievably creative and talented. Look at those carvings and how beautiful the murals on the stadium are."

"I know, and they may be more primitive than we are," Kaia added, "but they're so much like us."

Piphus blinked his eyes twice. "I'd sure like to get my hands on their genetic material and compare it to ours."

"This game is impossible," Barj said. "How do you get that heavy ball through one of those little rings?"

"It seems like you don't," Mobius said. "Can we move this along?"

On Akara, sports seemed to go at lightning speed compared to this. Piphus fast-forwarded, and the game was decidedly more exciting sped up. Finally, K'awiil's team scored for the second time and won the game.

A huge celebration rocked the stadium for several minutes, so Piphus sped up the footage again until the imagery cut to another location. On top of the Temple of the Sky God, Itzamna and King K'awiil stood surrounded by ghoulish-looking men with wild headdresses and skulls painted on their faces. The best player from the losing team—painted blue and wearing a peaked headdress—was forced to kneel in front of King K'awiil. Several of the men with painted skulls brought forward a low, convex-shaped platform. Mobius and the others watched in horror, hands partially covering their eyes, as K'awiil's warriors laid out the athlete on the platform—its arc pushing his chest upward. The ceremonial leader who wore the most intricate face makeup and headdress stepped forward. He pulled out a knife with a black blade and, with all his strength, sliced into the man's chest just under his left ribcage. He then reached inside the wound with his other hand and yanked the man's heart out with one hideous pull. Holding the still beating heart over his head, he looked at Itzamna and cried, "For your eternal nourishment, my Lord!"

"Stop!" Nava cried. "Stop it, Piphus. Enough."

"That's disgusting!" Tru shouted.

"It's the grossest thing I've ever seen," Barj whispered, his hand over his mouth.

Nava trembled visibly, and Mobius bent over, gripping his stomach, "I just don't understand how they could ..." his voice trailed off.

"Remember," Kaia said, so quietly Mobius could barely hear her, "there were sacrificial practices long ago in Akara's history too."

"Yes, but we didn't have to watch it," Tru said.

"How much more of this is there?" Nava asked.

"It's almost done," Piphus said, resuming the mission log once again, wincing in anticipation of what might be next.

Onscreen, Itzamna was still standing on the enormous pyramid, facing the crowd below as the single sun set behind him. "You have honored me on this sacred day. I am filled with power and nourishment from the blood that has consecrated my temple," he shouted. "This is a glorious day that will be remembered forever. Our city and this temple are what I have envisioned. It will last for the rest of time, and I will never be forgotten."

He then turned away from the people and beckoned to two slaves. "I want to show you something," he said to K'awiil. The slaves carried over a large, round stone carving etched with an image of Itzamna in the center, surrounded by concentric circles of intricate symbols. Itzamna pointed at the calendar and said, "This sacred calendar ceases at the end of the 13th baktun—the final baktun in this Great Cycle of time. If on this day, 1,292 years from now, I am not still honored and worshipped as I am today, this calendar will be your last. I will open a great mouth of darkness in the sky that will swallow your world."

King K'awiil took a step backward, horror flashing across his face. "But, my Lord ...you would never do that to us ..."

"I would and I shall!" Itzamna shouted.

K'awiil put his hands to the sky. "There will be no need! You will always be honored and worshipped."

"If you are wrong, L'Azman will pay dearly." Itzamna paused and gazed out across the city built for him, a frightening fire burning in his eyes. "I will know from the other side if I have been forgotten, and when this planet meets its end, Akara will know it was at my hands, and they will be awed by my power. I will be remembered forever."

Itzamna turned to K'awiil, and the king quickly changed the expression on his face from horror to reverence. The commander placed a firm hand on K'awiil's shoulder and said, "Let me show you what I have done to ensure my plan. The place where this instrument of destiny resides will also be your royal tomb, so you can guard its contents even from the underworld."

Itzamna led King K'awiil through an opening in the top of the pyramid, which Mobius and the others hadn't realized was there until the commander walked through it.

The screen went dark.

Everyone stared in shock for a moment until Kaia burst out, "Is that it? Is that all we have?"

"That's all we have," Piphus said, leaning back in his chair.

Everyone started talking at once.

"What did he say?"

"A mouth of darkness?"

"He's going to destroy L'Azman in the future?"

"Is it still there?"

"How would we even know?"

Finally, Piphus turned to Kaia. "Can you quiet them please?"

"Hey!" Kaia shouted. "Let's calm down. I need to hear that again. Maybe we misunderstood him."

Piphus played back the last part of the log and confirmed what Itzamna had said. "Unfortunately, we didn't misunderstand," Kaia said after hearing it a second time. "He said he's going to destroy the planet."

"What if he's just saying that to scare the aliens, to gain more control of them?" Barj asked.

Piphus pushed back from the computers. "No, remember, he spoke of a time capsule with his lieutenant earlier. They were talking about engineering something for the dedication day. This must be it."

Nava blinked twice then said, "He said whatever it was ... the instrument of destiny as he called it ... would open in the future—"

"And create a mouth of darkness," Mobius said. "What does that mean?"

"I hope I'm wrong, but I think—" Piphus stopped.

"*What?*" Kaia asked.

"I think he meant he was going to create a black hole."

CHAPTER THIRTEEN

HUNTED

Diego drove frantically down the muddy jungle road, trying to evade the truck that chased after them.

Jillian turned around to see a pickup with armed men standing in the bed holding onto a roll bar, and two others in the cab. "My God, Diego! What's going on? Who are they?"

"I don't know," he said, barely able to speak. "It looks bad though."

"You're damn right it looks bad—they have guns!"

"You need to get down!"

When his uncle had insisted he take Jillian to Tikal, Diego wondered if he might be putting her in harm's way, but he'd convinced himself that the *criminales* would never stop him in the tourist zone. Besides, what excuse would he have given *El Jefe* that he couldn't take her?

The truck sped up and overtook them on Diego's side of the vehicle, barely able to squeeze next to him on the narrow road. Looking over, he saw several guns pointed at his head and slammed the accelerator to the floor. Shots fired, and a bullet pierced the driver's side window, shattering the front windshield.

Jillian screamed and raised her head to look.

"Stay down!" he yelled as he fishtailed all over the dirt road, slicked with new rain. Gunshots continued to ring out as the truck moved from side to side behind them, trying to catch up again. It began to overtake them on Jillian's side, and when a bullet entered the passenger window and blasted a hole in the dash just above her lowered head, Diego slowed down and brought the Jeep to a stop. Jillian started to sit up again.

"No, no." He put a hand on top of her head. "Stay down no matter what. Hopefully they won't see you."

"What's happening?" Her voice was panicky.

"This is what I was talking about," he said, his body trembling with fear. "A drug gang probably. Stay in here, and don't make a sound."

He opened his door, and she grabbed his leg. "Don't leave me."

"I won't. I promise. I'm going to try to get rid of them."

He got out of the Jeep with his hands raised and faced the truck. Four men jumped out, two of them with AKs pointed at his chest. When he saw Pedro's gaunt face, he wanted to scream.

"Why do you run from me?" Pedro said in Spanish. "I thought we were good friends."

Diego was grateful Jillian didn't speak Spanish. "I didn't know who you were!" he replied though gritted teeth, trying not to lunge at Pedro's throat. "All I knew was someone was shooting at me. Why the hell were you shooting at me?"

"I have heard nothing more from you about this police action. And now you run away when you see me then you lie about it. I know you saw me."

Rafael, the earless one, walked toward the Jeep, probably looking for something to steal—guns, money, equipment.

"I couldn't tell it was you. I swear," Diego stammered. "I have important information for you. I was going to contact you tomorrow." He prayed he could keep Rafael from continuing toward the vehicle.

Rafael stopped and looked at him expectantly.

"You'd better have something good after making me hunt you down like this," Pedro said.

"It's only been three days! I told you to give me a week!" Diego yelled but then forced himself to calm down. "The police operation is going to begin in the next week or so. I don't know the exact date yet. No one does. And INTERPOL is involved too."

"INTERPOL? This is important," Pedro nodded his head, impressed. "And the head of this operation? What is his name? How many men will they be sending?"

"I don't know," he said. "I wasn't told that yet. I will get the information tomorrow."

Pedro's eyes narrowed as he stared at him scornfully. Rafael moved toward the Jeep again.

"Francisco Medina! That's his name!" Diego shouted, lying to try to stop Rafael. But it was too late; he'd already seen Jillian. He opened the door and dragged her out.

"See, I told you I saw someone," Rafael bragged.

When Pedro laid eyes on the pretty American, a creepy smile widened across his face. "*Dios mío, cabrón*, what do we have here?"

CHAPTER FOURTEEN

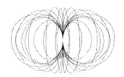

PROTOXAN

A clear sense of urgency pervaded the air; Mobius could feel the clock ticking inside of Itzamna's time capsule. An Akaran had planted something on an alien planet that could destroy it, if it hadn't already. Just from the people he saw on the data cube footage, it was clear that L'Azman hosted an amazing race with incredible intelligence and artistic abilities. No doubt they were primitive and believed that they were separate from one another, but they must have evolved significantly by this time. Mobius felt his mind expanding with wonder at what they must be like now. "There's no way he could possibly create a black hole!" he said, as if his sheer conviction could bend the facts to his will.

"Right?" Tru said, looking back and forth between Piphus and Kaia, hoping the answer could only be no, but the alarm on their faces said otherwise.

"How?" Barj asked.

Kaia leaned forward in her chair as the realization sank in. "Protoxan."

There was a pause as the crew stared at one another in horror. Within seconds, they all jumped on their cognizers. Mobius scoured the data. He knew a little about protoxan, but what he found was more fascinating—and concerning—than he remembered. Protoxan was an extremely powerful energy source with rare attributes that was discovered in the late Ravaging Era, on the planet Protox. The energy was created by an incredible phenomenon—ravenous bacteria fed off a super-dense, radioactive gas resulting in the release of massive amounts of energy—which scientists named protoxan. Until protoxan's discovery, plasma energy created by nuclear fission fueled space travel, but at high costs—radium mined to near depletion and catastrophic nuclear accidents. Protoxan enabled the space program not only to replace nuclear fuel, but also to do something more remarkable—stabilize wormholes, bending the limits of space-time and catapulting Akara to parts of the galaxy so far away they'd never before been within reach.

Protoxan was considered a miracle technology, until its own highly unstable and toxic properties were discovered. It was banned after an astrophysicist was infected with its bacteria, causing a rapid, planet-wide pandemic. Then, to make matters worse, a rogue nation weaponized it. The substance became even more frightening when a scientist named Hiro discovered that if he separated the bacteria from the gas and kept it contained, the gas interacted with dark matter and became denser and denser. He theorized that if the super-dense gas were exposed to oxygen, it would implode and create a black hole.

"So protoxan creating a black hole is just a theory?" Mobius asked, looking up from his cog.

"Unfortunately, no," Kaia said. "They actually tested it. They ejected a capsule containing a microscopic amount of the dense protoxan gas into deep space, then tracked the results from Akara. It worked. They actually created a tiny black hole."

"There were advocates of weaponizing the black hole technology in case an alien race ever attacked Akara," Piphus said. "A whole planet could just be erased."

"But did Itzamna's ship hold enough protoxan to create a black hole that could swallow an entire planet?" Tru asked.

"Based on the amount of protoxan required to power the ship and stabilize wormholes for that kind of deep space mission," Piphus said, "he would have had more than enough, I'm afraid."

"But how could Itzamna possibly program it to implode at an exact time in the future?" Mobius asked.

"He wouldn't have programmed it so much as calculated it— well, him or his protoxan propulsion engineer. They could have isolated the gas and contained it in a small space surrounded by a magnetic field, then used Hiro's Equation to compute the rate at which the protoxan would condense. At the required level of density, the capsule would open, exposing it to oxygen, and then it would implode. And boom, black hole."

"For the way of peace," Nava said, "the Ravaging Era practically destroyed our world, and now it's about to annihilate another one."

"What do we do now?" Barj asked. "We don't even know where L'Azman is or if it's still there."

"Actually," Kaia said. "There's something I need to tell you."

Everyone waited vigilantly for her to speak. She leaned back on the edge of Piphus's desk and took a deep breath. "What I'm about to reveal to you is highly sensitive information, and very, *very* few people know about it," she said, her opalescent skin glowing in the soft light of the room. She looked at each of them in turn. "It's going to come as a shock, and I need to know that I can trust you all with it, as well as everything else you've seen."

They gave her their assurances.

"We've known L'Azman exists, that it isn't a myth."

Everyone sat in stunned silence for a moment. Then they all bombarded her at once. "What? Who is *we*? You're kidding! Why didn't you tell us before?"

"Quiet down and I'll explain. The Discovery Corps discovered the planet, or I should say rediscovered it, ten years ago."

"So much for Concordance principle number eight: Governing bodies and planetary agencies shall maintain complete transparency in all activities," Piphus quipped, quoting Akara's sacred document and voicing what they were all thinking.

Kaia took a deep breath before responding. "There *is* transparency—other than with L'Azman."

"Why would they go against the Concordance?" Tru asked.

"Knowledge of L'Azman's existence was repressed long ago, at the end of the Ravaging Era, by something called the anti-encounter movement," she explained.

"That was like a thousand years ago!" Mobius exclaimed. "Why is it still being kept a secret?"

"The DC council decided that the information could still fall into the wrong hands," she said, avoiding eye contact with Mobius. "Space travel is such a curiosity, really almost an obsession these days. And given the rate at which technology advances, the DC Council realized that the possibility of a group of ..." She hesitated. "Certain citizens ... building a spacecraft using the torus that powers their home or hovercraft may not be that far off. They were concerned that these people could contact an alien civilization if they found it."

"*Certain* citizens?" Mobius felt his entire body contract, but he forced himself to stay seated.

Nava put a hand on his leg. "She's not talking about you."

"No, just all the other Anomalies," he said.

"Only the ones on the far end of the spectrum," Kaia said. There were some Anomalies who were completely cut off from their connection to everyone else, and for those people, special programs were in place because they could be very dangerous. "Nava's right. Keeping L'Azman secret wasn't about someone like you."

"Let's move on," Mobius said. "Does the Corps know about Itzamna and what he did?"

"No," Kaia replied. "Almost all the original records were destroyed. All that we know is that *something* really horrible took place on L'Azman, and whatever it was led to the Planetary Non-Interference Regulation—one of the only principles we still use that was handed down from the Ravaging. There was a huge battle between those pushing for colonization and the non-interference advocates, and we know that whatever happened on L'Azman swung the space agency at the time toward non-interference."

"But if everything was destroyed, how does the DC know that the planet that was discovered is L'Azman?" Barj asked.

"The coordinates of L'Azman were wiped from the records, but its exact distance from Akara was recovered. When the distance to the inhabited planet we discovered matched the distance to L'Azman, statistically we knew it had to be the same planet."

"How do we find out if L'Azman is still there?" Nava asked.

Kaia stood up. "Well, the DC does regular planetary scans, but that data won't be current enough to confirm that it's still there now. I'm going to let Melekai know what's going on and ask per about pointing the ANSA Array at L'Azman to confirm its existence. It's the closest telescope that we have to the planet."

"So, is L'Azman *actually in* the Serpent star cluster?" Piphus asked.

"Yes, it is."

"Is there anything else you can tell us about it?" Mobius asked.

Kaia thought for a moment, then smiled. "I can tell you what they call their planet in their predominant language."

"*What*?" Tru asked, and they all stared at Kaia in anticipation.

"Earth," she said.

Mobius looked wide-eyed at the others. "Earth," he whispered, getting his tongue around the foreign word. "For the way of peace, I hope Earth is still there."

•

The group stood around waiting for Kaia, eager to hear about her conversation with Melekai. When she returned several minutes later, she announced, "It's there!"

They all let out a deep sigh. "Oh, thank the Wisdom!" Nava exclaimed.

"At least it was as of sixty-four minutes ago, which is how long it takes the data to reach us from L'Azman, boosted by the Array."

"That's great, but we have no idea when the time capsule is supposed to implode," Tru said.

"I know," Kaia said. "Piphus, Melekai is going to take the footage to the Discovery and Archaeology Corps Councils. Please send it through. While they're reviewing the mission log, we thought maybe you could calculate when the time capsule is supposed to open so they can have that information as soon as possible."

Piphus sent the data, then stood up from his chair. "Of course I can do the math, but I'll need several pieces of information for the calculations, one of which we don't have—when the countdown began."

"Itzamna said it would detonate 1,292 years from when he buried it," Mobius replied.

"Yeah, but we don't know when that was," Nava said. "Plus, that's in L'Azman years, right?"

"Has to be," Tru said. "He was using their calendar to calculate it."

"Yes, that we know," Kaia said. "And another piece of data we have is that protoxan was only used for deep space travel during about a fourteen-year period in the late Ravaging Era."

"We may be able to narrow it down further," Piphus said. "I have cyber-friends who claim to have detailed information about L'Azman. I've never been that interested before but let me see what dates they claim the planet was discovered."

"You mean the conspiracy theorists?" Barj asked.

"You might want to rethink that label," Piphus said. "We've just established it's not a theory and that there *was* a conspiracy to hide knowledge of L'Azman's existence. They clearly know more of the truth than the rest of us."

Kaia just looked at the ground and held her tongue.

Piphus pinched open his cog. After a number of exchanges with his contacts, he reported to the group. "There is a five-year window that keeps coming up regarding a mission to L'Azman."

Kaia sent the information to Melekai and asked if it was possible to search the database for any ancient missions that might coincide with the dates. As they waited for a response, Kaia stood tall and stretched, arching her back and reaching her arms into the sky in the shape of a V. The jeweled band on her upper arm, which held her cognizer, danced in the midday light that poured in through the windows. "My energy is fading," she said, then drew in two quick, sharp breaths through her nose, followed by two quick breaths through her mouth. She repeated the sequence three times to increase her life force, then said, "Okay, I've got something. Melekai just sent me a thologram."

Her eyes moved back and forth as she scanned the three-dimensional thought hologram that her optic nerve projected in front of her, but that only she could see. "Here's something. Apparently, there were two different missions to a planet classified as A281 during that five-year period. Coordinates of the planet are not known, but it seems the only other missions during that time were much closer to home. These were the only deep space probes," she said. "On the first mission to A281, the ship visited the planet twice, three years apart."

"Itzamna said it was their second time to visit L'Azman in three years, so that fits," Mobius said.

"Right. The second ship that was sent to the planet was on a rescue mission, and this is interesting—it was only three months before the Non-Interference Regulation was enacted. The records indicate four crewmembers were rescued, and the commander died on planet, but his remains were not found. One of the crew was nearly dead at the time of rescue but recovered after a few months in a coma. Not surprisingly, the records don't say anything about interaction with an alien life form. Given that the discovery of L'Azman was repressed, any other information would have been destroyed."

"Did the database include the names of the crewmembers?" Barj asked.

"Yes," Kaia said. "Everyone who ever landed on A281, but no one by the name of Itzamna."

"Maybe that wasn't his real name. Maybe the aliens named him that," Nava said. "It could have been the name of one of their gods already, and they thought he'd shown up in person."

"Oh, I hadn't thought of that," Barj said, and the others blinked twice in agreement.

Tru leaned forward excitedly. "It can't be a coincidence that a rescue mission found four crewmembers, one of them in a coma. That has to be that woman from Enshala who defied Itzamna. Maybe her distress signal got through, and that's what summoned the rescue. Then she must have woken up back on Akara and told the authorities what happened."

"It makes perfect sense," Piphus said, "And I don't think it's random that the Non-Interference Regulation was enacted three months after the rescue mission and right around when the Enshala woman came out of her coma."

"But how did that data cube wind up back on Akara and get buried in that canyon?" Mobius asked.

"Could it have been Itzamna's lieutenant?" Nava wondered. "Maybe he lived in the community on the edge of the canyon."

"If it was him, why would he have kept it when it was so incriminating?" Barj asked. "It could have put him away for life or gotten him executed back then."

"It seemed to me he was almost as much of a self-inflated nut as Itzamna was," Piphus replied. "Maybe he hoped it would be found after he was gone, and people on Akara would know what they did. We'll just never know."

"So, it looks like A281 is L'Azman," Nava said. "All the puzzle pieces fit together."

"But there's still one thing I don't understand," Mobius said. "When the Enshala crewmember woke up, wouldn't she have told them about the time capsule? They would have gone back and retrieved it. Are there any records of any other mission to A281?"

"Not according to the thologram," Kaia said. "Nothing at all. But it's highly likely that she didn't know about the time capsule.

Itzamna surely would have kept it secret from a mutinous crew-member. And it seems she was held captive after she lost consciousness, and that happened before the dedication day."

"So we have to assume that the time capsule is still on the planet," Barj said.

"For the sake of L'Azman, I think we do," Kaia agreed.

They all sat in silence for a few moments as that sank in.

"Now that we've established that A281 is L'Azman," Kaia said, "and we have the approximate date of the mission, we have to figure out when the time capsule is going to implode. And when I say 'we,' I really mean *you*." She smiled at Piphus and put a hand on his shoulder.

Piphus took his furry hat off and rubbed his head. "We know that it's set to open 1,292 L'Azman years from the dedication day we saw in the mission log, and we now know the dates they arrived and were rescued, so the time capsule was buried sometime between there."

He got up and started to walk in large intertwining loops that looked like a figure eight as he thought out loud. "Kaia, I need to know the ratio of A281 years to Akara's years so I can convert 1,292 of their years to ours."

"I'm scanning the thologram. It's not here."

"What? It has to be," he said. "At least there's got to be raw data in there that I can use to do the conversion. Just send it to me."

"I don't need to tell you—this *doesn't* leave your brain."

Piphus didn't respond, already lost in thought as he scoured the data she sent. Suddenly, he started mumbling to himself as he continued moving in loops, performing calculations in his head. After several more passes, when he got to the point at the center of the loop, he stopped. "I hope that's not right; I've got to verify it," he exclaimed and bolted to his desk.

Piphus was as odd as he could be, but Mobius really liked the guy. "Is it just me, or is anyone else hungry?" Mobius asked.

"It's you," Barj said.

Already consumed in the task at hand, Piphus absentmindedly opened a drawer and tossed Mobius a packet of myomeal—a plant-based pasty substance that came in different flavors and made for a perfectly balanced meal. DC fliers lived on it while on missions, but Mobius disliked the stuff and never ate it unless he had to. He walked back outside, sucking down the myomeal reluctantly.

A short while later Piphus called out, "Okay, I think I have it!"

Everyone rushed over, and Piphus launched into an explanation. "Based on my calculation of the mass of L'Azman's sun, and adjusting for our own motion and parallax, and given the orbital distance between L'Azman and its star, and *obviously* using the Laws of Astronomical Motion ..."

As Piphus rambled on without pause, Mobius's head was spinning. He looked at the others and could tell no one else was following either.

"*Piphus!*" Kaia finally interrupted. "What does this all mean?"

"Okay," he said slowing himself down. "If my calculations are correct, it means that 1,292 L'Azman years are 993 of our years. Which means the time capsule is going to open ..." He paused and took a deep breath. "Well, soon. Very soon."

Kaia's back stiffened. "By soon, do you mean it could open in weeks, months?"

He looked at her, his pale blue eyes intense. "No, unfortunately I mean it could open any minute."

CHAPTER FIFTEEN

HOSTAGE

Diego and Jillian bounced around in the back of the drug gang's truck, bound like dangerous animals—blindfolded, with their hands, feet, and mouths taped. Diego felt like they'd been getting beaten up by the jungle roads beneath them for hours. He had no doubt that the *bandidos* were taking them out of the national park and onto private land owned by a front man for the cartel. They had hideouts outside the borders of the parks, where the rangers were prevented from going without a warrant— places so hidden no one but the cartels had ever laid eyes on them.

Diego had gone through moments of rage at himself and his captors, straining to free himself and getting kicked in the ribs for his efforts. At one point, he even cried like a child, pleading with them to let Jillian go, but since then he had gone numb. He had no ideas and very little hope. All he knew was that he had to protect Jillian.

The truck made a turn and went through extremely rough terrain, crossing numerous streams and climbing the entire time. Finally, after another half hour, they came to a stop. The *pendejos* cut the tape off their ankles so they could walk, and hauled them out of the truck, pushing them along forcefully over the uneven ground. Diego smelled the rainforest all around, and he heard the familiar calls of toucans and howler monkeys and the buzz of insects. The *criminales* pushed his head down for a moment as he walked, then brought him to an abrupt stop.

"No funny business, Diego," Rafael said in Spanish. "We will kill you both, her first, if you make a move."

They removed the tape from his eyes and hands, and when he saw where they were, he almost dropped to his knees. They stood inside a ten-foot by ten-foot steel cage that seemed like it was made to hold a puma or jaguar. Jillian looked shocked for a moment, then glared at Diego, her hair wild around her head. "What the fuck is going on?"

"Later," he said quietly. He didn't want the *criminales* to tape their mouths shut again. He turned to the gunmen. "Can we please use the toilet and have some water?"

Rafael, and the other armed man Diego had heard them call Miguel, escorted them to the jungle separately, then shoved them violently back into the cage and locked it shut. When they were securely inside, Pedro walked up with Jillian's backpack.

"Why are you holding us?" Diego asked in Spanish. "I can only help you if I'm free. The police strike is happening soon, and I can find out everything about it."

"We have other informants," Pedro said, holding up Jillian's passport. "I have been ordered to find out who this pretty young thing is, and then we will decide what we are going to do with you." He reached through the bars and stroked Jillian's cheek, and she recoiled.

"Don't touch her!" Diego yelled, lunging for Pedro through the cage, but the *narco* had backed away, laughing.

"Let us go, Pedro, and I will get you the exact information you are looking for," Diego said. "I will get you names, times and dates. Everything."

"I have heard these promises before." Pedro turned and walked away.

"I'm the one who told you about the police crackdown," Diego shouted after him, but Pedro kept walking. "Wait, we need water!"

Pedro ignored him, stopping about thirty yards from the cage at a table set up outside a large tent, and sat down. One of his guys was talking on a radio, and Pedro took the handset from him while he looked at the passport.

Rafael and Miguel retreated to chairs near the tent, but they kept an eye on the prisoners as they talked and smoked.

"Diego, who are these people?" Jillian stammered. "He said my name. He has my passport." She was trembling, but he could tell she was trying to maintain some composure, and for that he was grateful. He didn't know what he'd do if she had a meltdown. He was afraid it might break him too.

"They're criminals, part of a gang. I told you the jungle is full of men like these. They are looking into your identity," he said, unable to look at her for long.

A dark shadow deepened in her eyes. "They're holding us for ransom?"

"A ranger is worth nothing. They are holding *you* for ransom," he said. "Especially when they find out who you are."

CHAPTER SIXTEEN

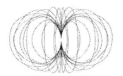

WORLD WISDOM

A Discovery Corps hovercraft descended from the sky and landed in front of Piphus's dwelling. After reviewing the data cube, the DC Council had contacted the Archaeology Corps, and together they had called an emergency session of the World Wisdom Congress. If the mission log was authentic, saving L'Azman would require breaking the Non-Interference Regulation to make contact with the alien beings there, and only the highest decision-making body on the planet could authorize such an action.

Kaia, Piphus, and Supernova Crew boarded the craft and were piloted at top speed to World Wisdom Congress headquarters in Metanom City. When they arrived, Melekai met their ship and escorted them to the meeting chamber where the Congress had convened.

Mobius's legs felt weak beneath him as he entered the grand and intimidating chamber. Because the next day was Concordance, only twelve of the eighty-eight members were present in person—those who lived in the capital or had not yet left to return home for the holiday. The remaining members participated via holo-com, and their holograms appeared as if they were sitting and talking in their respective seats. When Mobius and the others walked in, the members were in the midst of an intense discussion as to the authenticity of the data cube footage, reflecting Kaia's earlier concerns that it might be a hoax or some form of violent entertainment from the Ravaging Era.

"We need to have it verified before breaking the Non-Interference Regulation and sending one of our only remaining ships," a congress member stated, referring to the fact that practically the entire Discovery Corps fleet was off-planet on the retainite mission.

"The footage is being authenticated as we speak," a member of the Archaeology Corps Council informed the body.

The representative from Thal'insus, a diminutive, plum-colored woman, noticed that Melekai had brought in the candidates and their mentor. "Here are the finders," she said. "I have questions for them. Captain Kaia Satya, will you please come forward?"

Kaia stepped to the center of the chamber and nodded her head in respect.

"Captain, can you please explain why you did not immediately turn the relic over to the DC Council after your candidate found it?"

"I didn't think there was any harm in repairing the data cube to determine what we had found before turning it in."

"Let's hope that is the case."

"As soon as I knew the seriousness of its contents, I contacted the Corps," Kaia explained, adding, "Distinguished members, I know you want to verify the footage; however, given Piphus's calculations, I don't believe we can risk any delay. A crew must be sent to the planet immediately."

"Piphus," the Sintauran representative said, "are you certain that the timing is imminent?"

The cyber-engineer stepped forward. "Based on the information we have, there is no way to determine precisely when the time capsule will implode. But within the parameters of the available variables, yes, I posit that it is putatively possible ... I mean probable."

The members paused, trying to decipher Piphus's linguistic acrobatics.

Kaia cleared her throat. "He's trying to say it could open at any time."

"Assuming that Piphus's results are confirmed and the footage is validated," the Enshala representative said, "we must take a vote on Kaia's recommendation, with which I agree. I move that we immediately send a crew to the planet to find and disarm the weapon by any means necessary."

"Pardon me if this sounds impertinent," Piphus interjected a little too loudly, "but I must bring up the fact that this is all being done under cover of secrecy, which is inconsistent with the principles of the Concordance that we are celebrating tomorrow."

Mobius and the rest of Supernova stared at Piphus, surprised. He had been a socially awkward introvert a few minutes ago, and now he sounded like a self-assured statesman.

"I agree with you, my friend," another congress member replied. "We must revisit our policy on L'Azman and will do so as soon as the current crisis is over."

Her fellow representatives concurred, but they asked that Piphus and the others stay quiet about the matter until they could come up with a considered and wise approach to sharing the information planet-wide. Then they returned to the possibility of a mission to L'Azman.

"If we do send a crew, we must keep it to the fewest fliers needed to find and disarm the time capsule, so as to cause the least impact on L'Azman and its population," the Sintauran said. "Four to six should be enough, in my opinion."

"Agreed," another said. "In addition, that would leave us one remaining ship and a small crew of fliers in case a rescue is needed on the retainite mission."

As they continued to discuss the matter, two assistants entered the chamber and reported that Piphus's calculations had been verified, although the mission log footage was still being authenticated. Because of the possible impending danger to L'Azman, however, the Congress came to an accord to send a single spacecraft to the planet right away.

"Melekai," the representative from Thal'insus said, "you are cleared to assemble a crew to travel immediately to L'Azman to locate and disarm the weapon. Given the Non-Interference Regulation, we of course ask for no or minimal engagement with the alien race, but we are aware that some will probably prove necessary."

Kaia made an impassioned plea to join the crew, saying that she was healthy enough to fly even though she was still officially grounded to recover from her rescue mission.

Mobius hoped that her choice to let them hold on to the data cube and take it to Piphus before turning it in wouldn't jeopardize her chances of going on the mission. After Melekai affirmed that Kaia was in good enough health to fly, the members unanimously voted for her inclusion. Since she had been involved in its discovery, they agreed that she should be part of the mission. For a moment, Mobius wished that he could go since he had discovered it, but he hadn't even made it into the DC, and even if he had, they would only send experienced fliers.

The representative from Sintaura stood in his holographic representation with his hands on his heart. "L'Azman—the precious jewel—is in danger," he said. "I move that we take a moment to hold the planet and all its life-forms in the Wisdom and in love, and to keep them and this mission on the highest watch in our consciousness."

They all stood, hands on hearts, and everyone held in the silence for a moment. Mobius felt a powerful presence fill the room until a chime sounded, and the assembly began to adjourn.

●

Sitting on the outer walkway of the Tenzin Observatory at Entelechy Academy, Mobius stared in the direction of the Discovery Corps. He and the rest of Supernova were waiting to watch the spaceship take off for L'Azman and to track it through the telescope until it made the leap across the galaxy. The normally bustling, noisy academy grounds were empty because of the holiday, and the silence seemed to hold impending peril.

"I wonder what's going on," Tru said. They had been waiting for over an hour. "They should have left by now."

"I know," Barj agreed. "I really do have to get home for Concordance."

The Twin Flames sat low in the evening sky behind murky cloud cover, adding a heavy, dispiriting quality to the air, and Mobius couldn't shake a feeling of uneasiness.

"Are you okay?" Nava asked him.

"I just hope they make it in time."

Just then a message came through on everyone's cogs. "Kaia has just summoned us all to the DC," Barj said.

Nava stared wide-eyed at Mobius for a moment, then they all scrambled to their feet.

CHAPTER SEVENTEEN

A QUEEN'S RANSOM

Jillian sat slumped on the muddy ground, sobbing. Rather than making Diego more unstable, however, her emotion seemed to steady him, calling him into his strength. He knew that one of them had to remain in control. He sat down next to her and put his hand on her back. "They won't hurt you. You're too valuable." He was hoping like hell this was true.

"What do you mean by that?"

"After you complained about me, my Uncle Domingo got a call from the head of your environmental organization and found out that you're a billionaire."

"I didn't *complain* about you," she said through her tears. "I mentioned that you acted strangely and that I wasn't going to be getting a tour of Tikal. The president overreacted because of who I am. She didn't need to make that phone call. And I certainly didn't ask her to."

"Really?" Diego asked, sitting down next to her.

"Yes, really," she said. "Is that why you've been so weird? You thought I complained about you?"

"It doesn't matter now," he replied.

"That's for sure," she said, her tears flowing again. "God, my family is going to freak out. I've already put them through so much. They'll think I did something stupid and brought this on myself."

"My uncle will be speaking with your family. He knows you were with me. He'll tell them you were just on a tour of Tikal."

She looked up at him, and it was impossible, but he thought she looked more beautiful than ever. "That man said your name more than once. How does he know you?"

"I have run into these *pendejos* before. They know all the jungle rangers' names." How easily he lied. His father had been a chronic liar, exaggerating everything, especially if it made him look better. Diego had learned well.

"How long do you think it will take them to find out who I am?" She wiped her tears dry with the bottom of her shirt.

"I am afraid your Facebook page alone will be enough to let them know you are worth keeping."

She shook her head. "I can't believe you knew about my family. I didn't want anyone to know."

"I was told to treat you like the Queen of England."

"I'm afraid you've gone a bit off track from the looks of things." She smiled a little, and the fact that she could smile at all, there in that cage, made him think for the first time that he might be falling in love with her. He dropped his eyes, ashamed at how far off track he had actually gone.

"I'm sorry," she said. "This isn't your fault. I didn't mean it like that."

But he knew it was his fault, and a part of him wanted to tell her. To confess that if it weren't for him, she'd be back at the eco-resort eating dinner and looking at her pictures from today. But he didn't tell her—honesty was a luxury he couldn't afford.

He didn't have a rich family to rescue him from his mistakes.

That night, after they were finally brought a few stale tortillas and some water, they tried to sleep but found it impossible. The ground was wet and hard, Jillian was chilled, and the relentless mosquitoes and sand flies drove her crazy. She slapped at them wildly and scratched her bites. "How are you so calm during this onslaught?" she asked.

"I don't scratch," Diego said. "None of the locals do. It's only when you scratch that the bites swell up, and you end up with red spots all over you. They also itch a lot worse."

"So you just let them feed off of you?"

"Yes. Don't resist. It's the only way not to be in misery. Well, to be in less misery, anyway."

She stopped slapping and scratching and wrapped her arms around herself. "I didn't think I'd be shivering in the rainforest."

"It can get a little bit cool at night," Diego said. "People don't realize. And you are wet from the rain before. But there is one way to warm you up."

"What's that?" she asked.

He grinned. "The spoon."

She laughed, and his heart lifted out of his guts for a moment. "You mean spooning?"

"Yes. That's what I said. Isn't that the correct word for holding you like this?" He cupped his two hands together, back-to-back.

"Yes, *spooning*, not 'the' spoon." She smiled.

"Well, you are welcome to sample some authentic Guatemalan spooning if you want to get warm."

She waited for a few moments, thinking and shivering. "Fine," she said.

He moved his body behind hers and held her tightly. Even on

the rough ground, he felt like they fit together perfectly.

"Is this okay?" he asked, but he knew the answer because he could feel her body relaxing.

"Yes," she said quietly. "Thank you."

After a few minutes, she said, "I thought you didn't like me."

He propped himself up on one elbow and looked down at her. "You were wrong."

She turned on her back so that he was just above her. "Really? Because it seemed after we saw the jaguar, you were angry at me for some reason."

Her mouth was so close, and she was so lovely in the moonlight, he was unable to think, let alone speak, for what felt like about half an hour. It was more like twenty seconds. "I, um, was just trying to remain professional."

"Mmmm. It seemed like there was something else. You also seemed irritated when you came to the station and when we went to Tikal, especially at first."

She's using her female superpowers of intuition to read my mind, he thought, and hoped she couldn't do so about everything. "Okay, I was trying to distance myself from you, yes. I didn't want to cross a line that would not be good for my job. But when Domingo found out who you were, he requested that I take you to Tikal."

"Requested?"

"Okay, demanded."

"And he demanded that you treat me like the Queen of England because my family has money?"

Diego lay back down. "Maybe I'll stop talking now."

She turned on her side away from him again. "So if I weren't wealthy, you'd have been free of me."

He wasn't sure what to say, so he didn't say anything, figuring if he opened his mouth, he'd probably just make it worse. After a few moments, she reached back and pulled at his arm. "Give the queen the spoon, please."

Gratefully, he wrapped his arm around her. "So you aren't mad at me?" he asked.

"No. Do you still think I'm a snob?"

"I never thought that," he said.

"*Puhlease,*" she said. "Don't start lying to me now just when you're finally being honest."

"Okay, I *no longer* think you are a snob ..." His voice trailed off but was pregnant with unspoken thoughts.

"What?" she asked.

"Nothing."

"Come on, I can tell."

"I no longer think you're a snob, but maybe a bit of a ..." He hesitated.

"*Yes?*" she said impatiently. "Spit it out."

"I can't remember the word in English—*hipócrita,*" he finally said.

"It's the same word—hypocrite. How am I a hypocrite?"

"You're a billionaire, but on our way to the cat camera you were saying how a bunch of corporations and billionaires run the U.S. and it's pretty much an oligarchy too."

"Just because I come from money doesn't mean I think how the money in our country is distributed is right or fair, or, for that matter, the ridiculous lifestyle my parents and brother live. When they're gone, I plan to put pretty much all the wealth I inherit into an environmental trust." She paused to let that sink in for a minute, then said, "So do you still think I'm a *hipócrita?*"

"No. I think you are unpredictable and interesting."

"Smart boy."

"And I must admit, I also think you're beautiful."

She smiled and snuggled closer to him.

•

The next morning, the howler and spider monkeys were so loud they seemed to be inside the cage. Diego and Jillian watched them jump from limb to limb in the trees, chasing each other. At first they were a welcome distraction but then Diego started to almost resent them; the animals, free and playful, made him feel even more trapped and miserable.

Rafael and Miguel came and let the hostages relieve themselves in the jungle. Their captors gave them bananas, tortillas, and water but refused to answer any of Diego's questions or demands. Finally, Pedro came over with an awful grin on his face. "Your pretty American girlfriend is very lucky. Menendez said to keep our hands off her. *For now.*"

"She's not my girlfriend."

"Whoever she is, it seems we have hit it big with her, Diego. Did you know she is from a very rich family?"

Diego just glared at him.

"Oh, yes, I can tell you did know. And this is why she was getting a private tour, isn't it?"

"What are you going to do?" Diego demanded.

"We are going to contact her father, and he is going to give us ten million U.S. dollars, and then we are going to be very nice and let her go."

"You won't get away with this! You know there will be a manhunt for us!" Diego shouted, grasping for control and power he didn't have.

"No, there won't." Pedro handed Diego a script in Spanish for

Jillian to read on camera, demanding the ransom and threatening that if anyone was sent to try and find her, she would be killed. He ordered Diego to translate.

A few hours later, the *criminales* returned to video Jillian delivering their message to her family. Pedro told Diego she better not try any *teje y maneje*—funny business—because Menendez understood English and was going to review it. As they made the recording, Diego watched, helpless. His entire focus was on keeping Jillian alive and unharmed. If they killed him, and he had no doubt they would if he stepped out of line, then he wouldn't be there to protect her.

When they were finished, Pedro boasted with a smug laugh. "A man like her father can make entire nations do what he commands. And now he will do what *we* command!"

Diego wanted to reach out and strangle him. Instead, he clenched the bars of the cage, wishing the force of his fury could pull them apart.

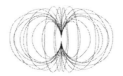

CHAPTER EIGHTEEN

CHOICE

When Supernova Crew arrived at the Discovery Corps head-quarters, the sprawling base was as empty as Entelechy Academy had been, due to the holiday. Kaia waited for them in the gardens outside the main entrance, along with Piphus, whom Kaia had also summoned.

"Something's wrong with the ship's torus," she explained. "We couldn't bring it to full power."

"It sounds like the formulation injector," Piphus said. "It will power up, but not all the way to quantum capacity. If the injection system—"

Mobius scowled and cut him off. "How long will it take to fix?"

"The engineers are saying at least a day or two because so many of our engineers are off-planet. It's too long as far as I'm concerned," Kaia said.

Mobius put a hand to his head.

"I have requested permission to take the only other ship we have left on the planet," she continued, "but that is going to require another meeting of the Congress. Without knowing the precise time that Itzamna's device is going to detonate, or authentication of the mission log, Melekai doubts they will release our only remaining craft in case it's needed for a rescue on the retainite mission. And we don't know how long authentication will take," she sighed.

"I understand your frustration," Piphus said, "but the footage could very well be fake, given the consciousness on the planet during the Ravaging Era."

"It's not fake," Mobius said.

"I agree," Kaia said. "My intuition tells me it's real."

Nava studied her face. "I know that look. What are you thinking?"

"I think we should go. Tonight."

They all stared at her stupefied.

"We?" Tru repeated.

Kaia blinked twice. "I can get us onto the other ship, and I can pilot us to L'Azman. It's Concordance Day tomorrow, so the building is already practically empty."

Tru burst into anxiety-ridden laughter. "You are not serious!"

"Yes, I am."

"Why not ask the other members of your crew to go with you?" Nava asked.

"Because I feel pretty certain they would balk at going without permission and would inform the DC."

"Nothing like this has ever been done," Piphus objected. "I mean, there's no theft anymore, let alone theft of a spacecraft! Are you sure you aren't wanting to do this to be a hero, Kaia?"

Suddenly, a look of world-weariness came over her face. "An Akaran commander found L'Azman in one of our ships, and one of our weapons is about to erase it from existence. They're the only other anthropoid race we've ever found. It's called the 'Precious Jewel' for a reason." She paused and looked up at the stars for a moment before continuing, "I've seen a lot of planets, and ninety-nine percent of them are barren rocks. We've detected what we think are ships from other worlds out in space and in the skies above Akara, but even with our latest technology, we can't be certain; they're ephemeral, like ghosts. The only planets we've discovered with any basic life forms had plant-life that was toxic to us, or unintelligent insect-like creatures crawling all over it. Space is immense beyond the mind's ability to comprehend. Its emptiness is shocking when you get out there. We know the probable number of planets with sentient life has to be high, but so far, we've found only one—L'Azman. And it has to be saved." She touched her fingers to the mark between her eyebrows and closed her eyes, pausing for a moment before continuing, "There's something about being out there in all that space and how alone it feels. I mean, why do we really explore? Why do we keep sending out discovery missions? It's not just to find retainite. It's to find others who love and think and create. When L'Azman was rediscovered, it was the most amazing celebration you can imagine among those who were told in the Discovery Corps. We were all crying. You all told me you were moved when you looked at the Serpent constellation through the telescope. L'Azman is more than just another point of light in the cosmos. It's our sister, our brother ... It's us."

Everyone stood in silence as she looked at them. Mobius could hear the sound of the wind moving through the outdoor mobile sculptures, but he felt utter stillness inside.

Finally, Piphus spoke up. "I'm sorry I questioned you. I suppose I shouldn't be surprised. I did hear that you disobeyed orders on your last mission so you could save that crew of fliers."

"It's all right." Kaia walked away for a few moments to gather herself, then returned to him and asked evenly, "Do you think we have time to let the Congress reconvene for further deliberation?"

"The truth is, I can't say for sure," he said. "But I suppose if I were on L'Azman, I'd want someone to get in a ship, *right now.*"

"So you agree with me?"

"I do … I mean theoretically … but if you are really considering this …" Piphus cleared his throat. "Kaia, I don't mean any disrespect to Mobius, but are you sure it would be the wisest choice to bring someone with limited access to the Wisdom on a mission like this?"

The anger Mobius felt at Piphus's words raced his heart into a sprint, but he stood frozen in place. He wasn't going to prove Piphus right about Anomalies by losing control. He'd done that enough recently.

Kaia looked at Piphus without blinking. "Yes. I'm absolutely sure it's the wisest choice."

Piphus turned to Mobius. "Don't get me wrong; I like you. It's just that this is important to consider." He turned back to Kaia. "He can't merge with the ship—will we even be able to get there with him on board?"

"We don't need him to join the merge, Piphus," she said. "Mobius is an asset. He has unparalleled survival and adventuring skills, and we have no idea what we're going to encounter on L'Azman. And, the fact is that Mobius was the one who found the data cube. It was an incredible synchronicity that he found it."

"I agree," Nava said.

"Piphus, you don't have to come if you are uncomfortable with him being part of the crew," Kaia said.

Mobius was stunned. He couldn't believe that Kaia would choose him over Piphus. He remembered the confusing guidance he'd received at the end of the test—to look in the field, when the retainite had been in the cave. He tried to take in the possibility that it truly had been the Wisdom guiding him after all.

Piphus put his hands up. "Okay, I just wanted to check. This is serious business we're getting ourselves into, and I know there has never been an Anomaly on a Discovery Corps mission before. But if you vouch for him ..."

"I do," Kaia said.

Nava blinked twice. "Me too."

Barj and Tru blinked as well.

"Besides," Tru said, "didn't you get kicked out of the Corps because you couldn't work in a team?"

Piphus's round face twisted into an expression of dramatic offense. "I have a very sensitive system," he said. "I couldn't be around that many people all the time."

Mobius looked at each of his friends and Kaia gratefully.

"I'm sorry, Mobius," Piphus said. "I've just met very few Anomalies."

Mobius sighed. "I hope you can learn to change your mind."

Kaia looked at each of them in turn. "I feel a responsibility to L'Azman and feel called to go. I can't do it alone, but you each need to decide for yourselves if you're coming or not."

Barj shifted on his feet. "I'm so sorry, but I can't go. I just can't do that to my parents. If something happened to me after just losing my sister ..."

"I understand, Barj. You need to be with your family," Kaia said.

"I can't go either," Tru said, looking at the ground, disappointed. "You all know I lost consciousness in the simulator every time I tried to go past minimal g-force settings. I'll end up working in engineering, I'm sure. I don't think I'll ever be a flier."

"It's not everyone's entelechy. You'll make an incredible

engineer." Kaia put a hand on her arm warmly. "Please remember, you and Barj need to keep this completely quiet."

"We will," Tru assured her, and Barj blinked twice.

"I just don't know if I can go either. I live in the mountains for a reason," Piphus said. "As I mentioned, my nervous system doesn't do well with a lot of stimulation."

Kaia's head dropped in dismay.

Nava looked at Mobius. "It's down to us."

Mobius clenched and unclenched his long, four-fingered hands. He had to make a choice, and he had to make it fast. If he decided to go to Earth, it would change everything for him, but if he didn't go, it could change everything for them. For a moment, he wished he had put the relic back in the ground and covered it over with dirt.

"Excuse me," he said, and walked to a bench across the court-yard to sit down. Just a short time ago, he'd fantasized about being able to join the mission. But now, his only thought was, *I shouldn't go. Piphus is right. I am a liability. What could I possibly add or offer?* But then he glanced back at the crew, and Nava was staring at him with an intensity that moved him deeply. He didn't have to be telepathic to know what she was thinking—*We need you.*

He felt her belief in him filling him up, and he took a full breath for the first time since Piphus began questioning Kaia about him. *I can only prove him wrong and inspire other Anomalies if I go. And this is my one chance to go into space. But the most important thing is L'Azman.* Mobius reflected on Kaia's words about it being so important, and he knew she was right. *If she thinks I can help ... But what if Piphus is right about me?* Mobius's thoughts ricocheted out of control, like heated atoms bouncing off one another, before clarity finally came over him. He had found the relic and felt compelled to be a part of whatever was going to happen because of his discovery. He walked back to the group. "I'm going."

Nava beamed at him. "Me too."

Kaia turned to Piphus. "Are you coming or not? I need an answer, now."

"I know," he said, plunging his hands into his pants pockets.

"Despite what I said before, you do know I can't do this without you, right?"

He kicked at the ground. "Of course. Someone has to initiate the leap while you pilot."

Kaia's head snapped up. "So you're coming?"

"Yes. Like you said, you can't do this without me. Besides, if I missed the chance to see a populated alien planet, my inner nine-year-old would kill me."

They all chuckled.

"Let's go," Kaia said, and they all started walking toward the round, domed main building.

Mobius knew that getting into the main building of the Discovery Corps would be easy—many areas were open to the public—but getting into the spaceport and stealing a ship would be another story. As they approached the entrance, the massive convex doors spread open. Tru and Barj embraced each of them and told them to follow the Wisdom, but their eyes were filled with worry.

As Kaia, Piphus, Nava, and Mobius stepped across the threshold, Tru called out to them. "You'll come back heroes!"

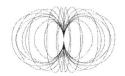

CHAPTER NINETEEN

CONCORDANCE

Mobius and the others walked across the soaring atrium of the DC's main building, a tribute to both galactic wonder and their own planetary beauty. The ground level was filled with a menagerie of rich plant life—towering trees, flowering vines, and whimsical shrubbery. The ceiling was a great dome of crystal, with an enormous holographic sphere floating beneath that depicted imagery from deep space missions. No matter how many times Mobius had been inside the atrium, it always made him slow his pace and look around in awe. He glanced up and was pulled into the virtual reality—a copper-colored planet came into view, which he circumnavigated, then he moved through an asteroid belt, shifting in space, and maneuvering through the debris.

He was so lost in the hologram that he bumped into Piphus and tripped over his feet. "Sorry," he said.

"Gird yourself," Piphus said. "You are about to experience the real thing."

At the far end of the atrium, Melekai stood waiting.

"Thank you for meeting me," Kaia said.

"What are they doing here?" Melekai asked, glancing at Piphus and the candidates.

"We need to talk," she said, and pulled per aside. While Kaia tried to persuade Melekai to support her plan, Mobius was captivated by a large display of early space program technology. Inside the case hung a cumbersome, weighty space suit, reminiscent of the one worn by Itzamna. Next to it sat a very simple pilot's control board. The most interesting exhibit included various-sized golden metal handprints. They had been used as a highest-level security measure to protect the many Ravaging Era major weapons systems. Each imprint was programmed to the unique biometrics, including DNA and hand geometry, of a national leader or top-ranking military officer who had launch capability. Mobius had always loved checking out the old technology, but he could never really imagine living in a world where planetary destruction was a constant threat.

After a few minutes, he looked over and saw Melekai walk away from Kaia, striding across the atrium, hand to mouth. Per paused for what seemed like a very long time before walking back and talking with Kaia again for several minutes. Finally, they both headed over to Mobius, Nava, and Piphus.

"Melekai has agreed to help," Kaia said.

Mobius's breath sped up, and he and Nava looked at each other. He couldn't believe this was really happening.

Melekai remained stoic. "Even though taking this kind of action without consent of the World Wisdom Congress is not something I would typically sanction, I trust Kaia's intuition here. I don't think we can risk waiting for Congress to be summoned from all over the planet on Concordance, then to further deliberate. And you will certainly need ground support to pull it off." Per turned to look at Mobius. "My one remaining reservation is whether or not you are up to the challenge of this mission. Kaia has explained why she wants you to go, and I acknowledge that you took responsibility for your actions, but that doesn't change the fact that this is extremely high stress and high stakes; we've never dealt with anything of this magnitude before. Under normal circumstances, we'd be sending our most experienced and reliable fliers, but they are all out on the retainite mission. And Kaia is sure the remaining crew will not go without approval, and I have to agree. So we are left with you."

Mobius shrunk momentarily under Melekai's gaze, but then something bigger than himself rose up inside him. "Commander, I understand your concern. During the test, I put myself and my agenda before the mission and safety of my crew. I learned a hard lesson that day, but I promise you that I *have* learned it."

"Honestly, I'm not getting clear guidance on this, but I trust your mentor enough to follow hers," Melekai said.

Mobius was grateful that the senior commander was permitting him to participate in the mission, though he wished it was for reasons other than "we're left with you."

Melekai turned to Kaia. "We'll rendezvous at 3:00 a.m. For now, however, you must excuse me. I have some holiday plans to change."

•

After Melekai walked away, they entered the inner sanctum of the base, only accessible to Mobius, Nava, and Piphus because they were with Kaia, a senior flier. Mobius knew that she was seen as a star around here, and no one thought to question her. Nevertheless, Mobius felt like he was trespassing on sacred ground.

As they walked by one of the control rooms, Kaia waved to the engineers. "Peaceful Concordance," she called out. "Sorry you won't be spending it with your families."

"Peaceful Concordance, Kaia," they replied.

"Where are we going?" Mobius asked.

"The most important place in the DC, as far as you're concerned," Kaia said.

He grew wide-eyed for a moment, before realizing where she was taking them—to the expansive dining hall located on the top floor of the building.

"Very funny," Mobius said, and Kaia chuckled.

The dining hall ceiling—undulating waves of glass speckled with sculpted, swimming sea organisms—rose high above them. The hall's design was inspired by the nearby inland sea on which Metanom had been built. Most of the sea life there had been destroyed, so what was left, along with all the wildlife on Akara, was valued more than any technology or possession on the planet; they were even beginning to see some of the sea organisms showing up as the plant life regrew. Suspended in the center of this room that honored the sea was a rotating spiral ribbon of glass, inscribed with the Discovery Corps credo—"From data to information to knowledge to Wisdom—Make the Leap."

Mobius looked around, taking in the oceanic beauty. He'd been in the dining hall during a few of their trainings, but this felt different. "Not much to choose from at this late hour," he grumbled when he saw how little there was on the buffet. "That reminds me, what about food on the ship?"

"Even less to choose from," Kaia said.

Mobius knew what that meant—myomeal. He almost let out a groan but realized it would not be appropriate for a flier, which by some miracle he was about to become. Presuming they could steal a ship, of course.

They all sat down to eat, including Kaia, since she wouldn't be able to absorb life force from the living biosphere while they were in space.

"So what next?" Piphus asked.

"I'll take you all back to my quarters. You need to lie low until Melekai and I can get access to the ship. In the meantime, Mobius and Nava, you need to reach your families and let them know you're not going to be back for the holiday. Tell them ..." she paused, knowing anything she was about to say would be a lie. "Tell them you're participating in ground support for the retainite mission."

Mobius thought about how excited his parents would be that he was working with the DC on an actual mission; he hadn't been able to bring himself to tell them he hadn't made it into the space program. He regretted, however, that he had to lie to them. One of the ways they had realized he was an Anomaly was that they had caught him lying to them to defend himself or to get his way. But he had never come close to a lie of this magnitude. He wondered if his great-great-grandfather had also been caught lying when he was a kid. Mobius's mother had always said that he too may have been an Anomaly and that maybe it was carried in the DNA, but scientists had never found a genetic link. For some reason they didn't understand, a few people were still just born feeling separate from the whole.

Mobius looked at Nava, who was sitting quietly, looking out the massive windows at the fading daylight. "Are you okay?" he asked.

"I will be." She shrugged. "I'm grieving at the thought of saying goodbye to my family. I'd be home right now with them. Concordance has always been my favorite holiday. I want to do everything I can to help save L'Azman, but I wish we could have left after tomorrow."

"I know it's hard but leaving on Concordance definitely makes stealing a ship easier." He smiled.

She seemed to force a smile back, and they both stepped away from the table to contact their families. When they returned, Kaia and Piphus were talking technical logistics of the mission that Mobius didn't understand. He looked at Nava to see if she was picking any of it up, but she wasn't even trying; she was staring out the window again.

He put an arm around her. "You can celebrate with your family when we come back."

"*If* we come back," she whispered. Nava pulled her gaze away from the sky outside and turned her rainbow eyes back toward Mobius. "To be honest, I have a feeling we may never see our families again."

•

Mobius, Nava, and Piphus holed up in Kaia's quarters while she prepared for their mission. Mobius nodded off to sleep but woke with a start every once in a while as Nava's words ran through his head—*if we come back.* The problem was that he'd never known her intuition to be wrong, so it seemed he was headed off to die. At some point in the night, however, the knowing that nothing really ever dies fully sank in, and conviction filled him from the inside. The slight tremor that had been vibrating through him since Nava pronounced their fate slowly receded into the background, and a still, peaceful calm emerged in the foreground. *If it's time for my death,* he thought, *may I die saving L'Azman, not die with it.*

Unable to fall back to sleep, in the wee hours of the night Mobius got up to go see what Kaia was doing. Having successfully avoided running into any DC personnel, he finally found her in the Bioenergetics Chamber, a large freestanding octagonal room, in which the floor and ceiling were lined with intricate latticework in various geometric structures specifically designed to focus the body's subtle energy field. He looked through the viewing window to see his mentor in the darkened chamber, practicing the quantum science of energy projection. Kaia stood with her arms at her sides, hands facing forward. Subtly, almost imperceptibly at first, her body began to emit a warm glow, a beautiful golden luminosity that grew brighter by degrees. When it reached a brilliant intensity, the energy gathered in front of her chest, then shot forward. A transparent image of her physical body made of vibrating light appeared on the other side of the chamber; she had consciously projected her energy body across the room.

Every time Mobius witnessed energetic projection, he felt deep wonder. Far from just a parlor trick, the DC used it for pre-inspection of a planet before sending ships and crews to the surface. But Mobius couldn't learn the skill no matter how many times he'd tried. Unlike accessing the Wisdom, energy projection wasn't a requirement to be a flier in the DC. Even among the mentors, it was a fairly rare gift. In fact, Nava was the only candidate who could do it with any predictability. Kaia, of course, was masterful at it.

Mobius watched as Kaia's energy body turned and moved toward him, then looked directly at him through the viewing window. *Of course she knew I was here,* he thought. Suddenly, Kaia's light-body disappeared, and a moment later she opened the door to the chamber and joined him. "What are you doing here?"

"I'm sorry. I couldn't sleep."

"It was risky of you to leave my quarters."

"No one saw me."

"Thank the Wisdom," she said, shutting the door. "Come on. It's time to meet up with Melekai. Remain silent." They returned to her quarters and roused Nava and Piphus, then Kaia led them through darkened corridors to an engineering room deep in the headquarters' interior, where Melekai waited, looking weary but stolid.

"I need to scan your energy signatures," Melekai said to Mobius and Nava, "so you can enter and interact with the ship. Piphus and Kaia are already in the database." Per directed Mobius to the center of the room, onto a round platform with silver concentric circles beneath his feet. "Stand still," Melekai instructed.

Instantly, the circles rose out of the platform and began to revolve around him, reading the unique makeup of his energy body. He felt like he'd been dropped into a cog to be analyzed. He looked at Nava and their eyes locked, sharing this rite of passage. In that moment, he wasn't sure if he was going on this mission more to impress Nava or to save L'Azman.

When the scan was finished, Melekai said, "Congratulations, Mobius. This is a big moment. You walked onto the platform a candidate and walked off a flier."

Kaia proudly put a hand on Mobius's shoulder, and Piphus rubbed his head affectionately. Nava pulled him into a heartfelt embrace. It surprised him, especially when he felt a subtle current move through his body as their energy fields started blending together. *I wonder if she feels it too*, he thought. When they pulled away from each other, the way Nava was looking at him, and the fact that she continued to hold onto his hand for another moment, made him think she just might.

After she was scanned, Melekai told them, "Once you get in the ship, take off as fast as you can. I'll do what I can to mask your launch signature, but it will only be a matter of time before they find you. Hopefully, it will be long enough for you to get the torus fully powered to make the leap."

"Thank you," Kaia said. "For the sake of peace, it will be."

"Fly well," Melekai said before departing.

Kaia and her crew made their way to the spaceport, an enormous enclosure normally filled with spacecraft of every size. Mobius followed Kaia as she headed to the only remaining ship—an ultra-sleek, hexagonal craft made out of an iridescent, cobalt-blue and silver material. He almost tripped over his own feet, mesmerized by the uber-modern machine.

"Wow," Nava said, as she stood in front of it. "We're definitely being led by the Wisdom."

Mobius looked at what she was pointing to—the ship's name, *Concordance.*

"I don't believe it," he said.

"Only fitting, don't you think?" Kaia said. She reached up and touched the side of the ship, and it scanned her. Mysteriously—since the craft looked totally seamless—the side of it opened, and a walkway lowered to the ground. They entered the airlock, a narrow space that could accommodate up to eight crewmembers.

"Close outer hatch door," Kaia commanded, then touched a control panel. "Override code A281TC. Bypass airlock delay." The inner hatch door retracted, and they climbed into the interior of the *Concordance. "Airlock sealed,"* the ship's artificial intelligence matrix announced moments later.

The *Concordance* was more spacious inside than it appeared from the outside. Mobius and Nava turned in circles looking at everything, while Kaia and Piphus prepared the ship for launch. They had trained in simulators and been inside spacecraft before, but they were still impressed with the *Concordance* and over-whelmed by being on a real mission. In the center of the craft was the ship's torus, housed in a clear atmospheric chamber that maintained proper argon levels so the retainite remained in a solid state.

"This torus is incredible," Mobius said, as he watched it glow dimly with changing, multi-colored light. "It's the biggest I've seen in a spacecraft."

"All right everyone, lock in," Kaia instructed. "We've got to move."

She sat down in the pilot's chair—one of the eight seats in the small scouting craft. Even though the outside of the craft and its instrumentation were high tech, the interior incorporated as much nature-based design as possible—natural fabrics and colors, and even plants. Piphus took the flight engineer's seat, which was surrounded by the most intricate instrumentation. Kaia pointed to two of the empty seats, indicating where Mobius and Nava should sit.

"Welcome, Captain," the vessel's comm system vocalized.

Kaia started to call out a series of commands, the first of which powered up the ship, and suddenly, the torus started to spin and glow brighter.

"Safety protocols," she called out next.

The chairs automatically swiveled, facing inward. Then full-body, energy safety shields surrounded each of them.

"Raise landing gear and drift to clear bay doors." The *Concordance* noiselessly lifted off the ground a few feet, then glided forward across the hangar and emerged into the night.

"Bring the torus to quantum capacity," Kaia instructed Piphus. "I want to make the leap as soon as possible."

Piphus studied the instrument panel. "Affirmative, Captain."

Mobius and Nava looked at each other, smiling at Piphus's sudden change to official protocol.

"Okay, get ready, everyone. I'm going to take us out of here fast before they can stop us," Kaia warned.

Even though there was almost no on-the-ground security, the Corps had highly advanced shielding technology in place in the event a violent or desperate alien race ever found them. But she had no idea what they would do to an unauthorized craft leaving the planet. "Just hang on. I promise you won't die."

"At least not yet," Mobius quipped to Nava.

"Not funny," she replied, but smiled nervously at him as they both gripped their armrests.

Kaia nodded at Piphus, and he held up three of his four fingers. The torus began spinning faster and brighter as he ticked his fingers down one at a time, then pointed to Kaia, "Now."

Instantly, the spacecraft shot straight up. Mobius felt like the Tenzin Observatory had fallen on him as the g-forces smashed him against the seat and nearly peeled his face away from his skull.

CHAPTER TWENTY

POWERLESS

For days on end, Diego and Jillian sat in the cage and waited. Diego finally convinced their captors to give them some blankets, so at least they didn't have to sit on wet ground. With hours of nothing to do, they talked. They told each other their life stories, and the only thing Diego left out was his deal with Manuel Menendez. Otherwise, he told Jillian things he had never told anyone, including how he'd been bullied as a child because he was often sick and weak.

"I bet it feels good to have some power now," she said.

He looked away from her gaze. "I'm still planning to finish my degree." He didn't want her seeing him as some uneducated jungle cowboy, like the gang members who were holding them. "I only came back because my father died. I don't care about power." While the first part was the truth, the second part was a lie, and he hated that he was lying to her again. It seemed like once he'd started, he would need to lie forever. "Besides, what kind of power is this?" He waved his hands at the cage. "The law has no power in the jungle."

"It's powerful to try to protect this place," she said. "It's dangerous, but you do it anyway. That's important, Diego."

"Come on," he said, coughing, trying to clear the humiliation knotted in his throat. "I'm sure your story is much more interesting than mine. Let's talk about you."

"I don't know if it's more interesting. But it is different, that's for sure," she said. "You grew up in the kind of poverty that can destroy you. In the last year, I realized that I grew up in the kind of wealth that can do the same thing."

He looked at her quizzically. "What do you mean?"

"Having the amount of money my family does creates a false sense of reality," she said. "It's like being in a bubble. I went to elite private schools in New York City and was overly protected but indulged at the same time." She looked away, lost in thought for a moment. "It turned out not to be a great combination for me."

"What happened?"

With a slight, sad smile Jillian said, "When I started going out with my friends, many who also came from famous families, we had paparazzi following us around. I was in gossip columns and tabloids just because I was a Savoy. It started when I was only sixteen."

Diego shook his head. "I can't imagine. That must have been really strange."

She rolled her eyes and nodded. "Yeah. It made us feel like we were really important. It was like a drug, and then we discovered real drugs and alcohol, and the party never stopped." She paused for a moment and snapped a twig in two that she had been twisting in her fingers. "I got in way over my head."

"How did you stop?"

"Sometimes it comes down to stop or die, you know? It came to a head last summer. All I was doing was chasing highs. My boyfriend and I were partying all week in LA with a bunch of people at a hotel. It was a crazy scene. One night, I was driving with him, and we were totally fucked up and fighting," she said. "I stopped the car in the middle of a really busy street and got out and ran across traffic. He left the car in the middle of the road and chased me on foot, and about ten people must have called the cops, because we were surrounded within minutes. I managed to spin a story they bought, and by some miracle I wasn't arrested."

"The miracle was that you were white and wealthy. If it had been me, I'd have been thrown in jail for sure."

Jillian shook her head. "I know. Believe me, I've thought of that."

"But, *Dios mío*. You're really lucky. You could have been killed."

"Easily, or I could have killed someone else. It was a huge wake-up call. I mean, I'd had a bunch of them, but that one finally got through to me. I knew if I didn't stop, the next time I wouldn't be walking away."

Diego was grateful she'd told him. He didn't feel quite as bad about his own mistakes.

"I went to rehab for a month to get my head on straight," she continued. "It was an incredible experience; I had a huge change in how I saw myself and how I related to life. That's when I started meditating and doing yoga."

Diego nodded. "What happened when you left rehab?"

"I went to our house in the Hamptons to try to figure out what I wanted to do with my life. In rehab they told me I needed to find something that's not all about me to put my energy into, but I knew I couldn't follow my mom's path. She's always been this 'big philanthropist,'" Jillian said, making quotation marks in the air with her fingers, "doing fancy fundraisers for different causes with famous people, but I knew that wasn't for me. It always struck me as a bit for show—a fundraiser is a great excuse to throw a black-tie party. I don't think anyone who gives away only a small percent of their billions every year and finds creative ways to pay next to nothing in taxes should be called a philanthropist."

Diego listened to her attentively, captivated by her fire and conviction.

Jillian suddenly looked down. "Don't get me wrong. I love my family, and they love me. I just see things differently from them, particularly after being in rehab."

He nodded, and she remained silent for a few moments.

"Anyway," she continued, "I was in the Hamptons, and one morning in meditation, my cat came and sat in my lap like she always did, and I just felt so much love for her. I had this incredible moment where it felt like we weren't separate; there was just this profound connection and oneness. I can't even come close to explaining how it felt. And that's when it came to me—I knew what I wanted to do."

"Save endangered animals and habitats."

She nodded. "I've always loved animals, and I just felt this overwhelming desire to help save the ones that are being threatened. I knew I had to get out of the States and go somewhere wild and see for myself what was happening, so I came here. But now I don't know that I'll be able to save myself, let alone any wildlife."

He could see tears welling up in her eyes. "I am very sorry about this," he said, then stood up and yelled at Miguel to please bring them water before she could tell him again that it wasn't his fault.

●

Besides talking, they also passed the time doing yoga. Jillian had convinced Diego to twist himself into what he thought were ridiculous positions that looked anything but macho. But there was nothing he wouldn't have done at that point to get her to like and respect him, and he had to admit it made him feel a lot calmer. After the first session she put him through, he only agreed to do it again after she convinced their captors, who had been watching and laughing at them, to let them wash with a basin of water. He refused to smell any worse than he already did around her.

One morning, when Jillian opened her eyes after meditating, he asked, "Did it help?"

"Yes, it always does."

He crossed his legs like hers and faced her. "What does it do for you?"

"It relaxes and centers me. I'll never forget the first time I experienced not having any thoughts. I realized my mind had become quiet for the first time ... well, ever."

Diego imagined what it would be like not to be assaulted—for even the briefest of moments—by the relentless thoughts about what he had done and what was going to happen to them.

"But it's more than that," Jillian continued. "In the silence, I feel like I connect to my true self. I know who I am beyond ... beyond my little ego. I feel something deeper, bigger. Greater than myself."

"God?" he asked.

She tilted her head in the way he loved. "If you want to call it that, sure."

"What else would you call it?"

"The Mystery of Life ... Spirit ... Source ... Presence ... the Universe—"

"'The Force'?" he said, raising his eyebrows and smiling. "Like in *Star Wars*."

"Exactly," she said, and they both laughed.

"I'm not normally religious," Diego said, "but I've definitely been praying that we get out of this safely."

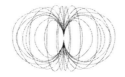

CHAPTER TWENTY-ONE

THE LEAP

As soon as the *Concordance* reached escape velocity, the ship's engines throttled back, and the g-forces let up enough so that Mobius could finally turn his head. Kaia had taken them up to ninety percent of light speed, and when Mobius looked down through the view window in the floor, he saw the breathtaking, iconic image of Akara from space—an orb of swirling opalescent violet, blue, and green—receding in the distance. Kaia turned off the energy shields, swiveling her chair to face them. "Everyone okay?"

"I don't know," Mobius said. "Do I still look the same? It feels like my face was rearranged."

"Sorry about that." She chuckled. "Since I didn't know if Melekai was going to be able to keep the defense system from pulling us out of the sky, I kept the inertial compensation and centripetal acceleration force fields to the minimum settings I felt you could handle. It's a good thing you've been in the simulator, or it would have been a lot worse. In about half an hour, when the torus is at quantum capacity, we'll make the leap to L'Azman."

"In the meantime," Piphus said, "we all need to upload the appropriate languages and tutorials to our neurolinks and cogs.

I have to figure out which ones, so give me a minute. L'Azman doesn't have a universal language yet."

I wonder how that works, Mobius thought. On Akara, though each region continued to speak their local historical language, after the Rebirthing, the World Wisdom Congress had established a universal language to help unite the planet.

"Although L'Azman doesn't have a universal language," Kaia said, "there is one that is spoken most widely across the planet. Make sure to download it, as well as whatever the local language is in the region we're going to."

Piphus blinked twice.

"This craft has L'Azman languages in its database?" Nava asked.

"Yes," Kaia said. "From our scans of L'Azman. All the ships do."

"But why store their languages when we never planned to encounter the aliens there?" Nava asked.

"Never is a very long time," Kaia said. "If they develop deep space travel as quickly as our ancestors did, we want to be ready. They are an unstable civilization, and we need to know how to handle them."

Kaia turned around and went back to piloting the ship, and Mobius found himself lost in the torus again—in its beautiful display of swirling movement and color. He stood and moved closer to it, wishing he could go inside the atmospheric chamber where the torus was housed and touch the retainite shell that held the spinning energy together. Placing his hand on the outer chamber, he stared at the technology and thought about the miracles that led to its invention. When the Tenzin siblings who invented it were born, the planet was in a catastrophic state, but the new consciousness was flowering throughout the vital zones where the Wise Ones lived. The Tenzins, who were gifted with the Wisdom, devoted their lives to developing a new, clean, and renewable source of energy—the only hope for the dying planet.

Akaran scientists had long known that the universe was birthed into existence from a dot tinier than a pinprick. The Tenzins theorized that this dot is not just the origin of the universe, but its center point. They believed that the primordial energy contained in this singularity is constantly creating an evolving universe in the form of a torus—a spherical, donut-like shape of revolving energy. In essence, they hypothesized that the universe is a self-generating field of infinite energy that bursts forth from the center and expands outward until it curves around, returning back to its point of unity, even as it is expanding. It then disappears into the quantum field and explodes back into manifestation again, repeating the cycle over and over.

Through their research, the Tenzins had found that this primordial energy, the mystery that somehow created something out of nothing, persisted through all of space-time and permeated everything in existence, filling the vast emptiness that was not really empty at all, but simply formless.

Since this source energy existed everywhere, they theorized that it could be tapped. If they were to build a structure in the shape of a torus and contain it in a sphere, then accelerate the quantum energy inside and around the structure fast enough, it was possible that the unbelievably rapid movement would actually begin to pull in this immeasurable, ubiquitous energy, in effect creating a tiny universe. Retainite had been the lynchpin, proving to be the only material strong enough to contain the immense energy the torus would create.

Kaia got up from her pilot's seat and stood next to Mobius, then called Nava and Piphus over. "While we wait to make the leap, I want to wish you all a Peaceful Concordance. I'm sorry that we can't be home for the holiday, but let's just take a moment and give thanks to the first World Wisdom Congress for ratifying the Concordance."

As they stood in the silence, Mobius reflected on the Concordance—the landmark agreement signed on this day 998 years ago, in which awakened leaders not only ended the Final War but also decided to pool the planet's remaining energy resources for the torus experiment. Testing the Tenzins' theory had required enormous amounts of electrical power, which was in very limited supply and was being used for only the most critical needs. The decision to use the last remnants of non-renewable resources had been a huge leap of faith.

Kaia reached into her pocket and pulled out a small, clear bag. "I have something for you." She handed them each a bracelet.

"When did you—?" Mobius asked.

"When you were sleeping," Kaia said. "You're a flier now."

His throat closed off, choking back his emotion, as he put the bracelet on his wrist and watched it glow gold, then red, then blue. The iconic amulets were a tradition at the Discovery Corps—all the fliers wore them as a display of unity. Made of a beautiful metal that intermittently changed colors in homage to the torus, each bangle was inscribed with the insignia and motto of the Discovery Corps and the names of the flier and their crew.

"Thank you," he said to Kaia, as the charm lit up his name and the name she had given to their four-person crew for this mission—L'Azman.

•

Mobius and Nava stood looking out the window at the millions of stars and planets that rushed by the spacecraft. "Since my junior space exploratory, I have imagined going back into space," he said, "but I never thought this is how it would happen."

At the age of nine, all Akaran children are taken into the cosmos, when their imaginations are at their peak. The trip is made so that they can have the life-altering experience of seeing Akara from space. Without thinking, he reached out and took Nava's hand.

"I know what you mean," she said, and pulled his hand closer to her.

Mobius didn't want to breathe or move; he wanted everything to stop, with them standing there, holding hands, for a very long time.

Just seconds later, however, Piphus interrupted his perfect moment. "I'm sending everyone language tholograms. I used the footage from the mission log when the ship descended onto the planet and compared the shape of the land mass with our planetary scans. Based on what I found, we'll be learning two languages—the current language from the region where Itzamna was located, and the predominant language on the planet."

Mobius felt the familiar surge in his brain and cold sensation flowing through his body as his neurolink received the Spanish and English tholograms.

"The thologram will give you language dictionaries and tutorials," Kaia said, "as well as help with pronunciation. But we're also going to need to administer proboscis nano-technology. It will stimulate the area of your brain in charge of language, so you'll be able to learn very, very quickly. One of the amazing things about L'Azman, or Earth, is that we can actually learn to speak their languages."

"The fact that we have the necessary oral and vocal structures is incredible," Piphus said. "It has always been suspected that if we ever found other sentient life, they would be so alien as to be incomprehensible. I cannot get over how similar we are to them in so many ways."

"Do you really think we'll have to interact with them?" Mobius said, feeling both squeamish and excited at the thought.

"Maybe we can just go grab it and get out before anyone sees us," Nava said.

"There are seven billion aliens on L'Azman, or ... I mean Earth," Piphus said as he put his hand on top of his head. "That's going to take some getting used to. Anyway, it seems fairly likely we may have to communicate with one or two of them."

"I've never had anything implanted other than my neurolink when we started training, and that was weird enough," Mobius said.

Nava swallowed hard. "Me neither."

"Most fliers never will," Kaia said. "It's only under very special circumstances that we use proboscis technology. And this is certainly one of those. Are you guys up for this? You knew what we were doing here."

"Just give me a minute," Nava said.

Kaia grinned a little. "Fair enough. I'll go first." She held the tube to her nose and inhaled.

The rest of them followed.

Mobius waited for a moment but felt nothing. "I don't think it worked."

"Just give it a minute," Kaia said.

Suddenly, he definitely started to experience something—a buzzing in his head and a high-pitched ringing in his ears. He put his hands over his ears, and so did Nava.

"Will this go away?" Nava asked.

"It will," Kaia said.

Within minutes, they were able to begin talking to each other in their newly acquired L'Azman languages.

"Go through the tutorials, and from here on out, let's speak their languages as much as possible," Kaia said.

"We sound hilarious!" Nava said.

Suddenly, an alert sounded on the main console, and a voice boomed into the ship. "This is Discovery Corps command. Return to headquarters immediately."

"This is Captain Kaia Satya," Kaia responded. "I take full responsibility for taking the *Concordance* without consent. Given how high the stakes are, I felt it was my duty to L'Azman to follow my inner guidance. I hope that my actions will prove worthy of such a breach of protocol."

"Kaia, this is outrageous. Return now and—"

"End communications and turn off sound," she commanded, and the sound ended abruptly.

Nava's mocha skin turned pale. "They must think we've lost our connection to the Wisdom."

"Somehow, this will all end up being my fault," Mobius said.

"I just told them it was my responsibility," Kaia said. "You need to leave the Anomaly story behind, Mobius. It doesn't define who you are." She turned to Piphus. "We have to make the leap and get out of visual range as soon as possible. I've disabled tracking so they won't be able to find us once we do."

"Almost there," Piphus said.

Mobius wished they could leap right then so he didn't have time to think about it.

"Ready to not exist?" Nava asked him.

"Sure," he said. "Why not?"

"Nava, come here," Kaia said. "You need to help with the merge. The approximate celestial coordinates from Akara are 3 hours 47 minutes right ascension and +24 degrees declination. That should get us pointed in the neighborhood of L'Azman."

Mobius felt a familiar defensiveness at not being able to join the merge for the leap necessary to get them to Earth. After initially thinking the torus was just an energy source, quantum scientists later discovered that it could be used to enable a spaceship to leap to any location in the universe. Because the torus was constantly moving in and out of the quantum field, they found that it was possible to "ride it" into the formless and then back out into form. When the crew's conscious intention was merged with the torus through the ship's artificial intelligence, the ship and everyone in it would move into the quantum field, then reformulate at whatever location the crewmembers were holding in their consciousness when the leap occurred.

Mobius clenched and unclenched his hands. The truth was, he had answered Nava with false confidence. *I don't know if I'm ready to not exist,* he thought. They were playing with the laws of the universe, and something could go terribly wrong.

"Are we ready, Piphus?" Kaia asked.

"I don't think we're ready for any of this," he said. "But yes, the ship is energized."

Mobius winced and closed his eyes.

Kaia looked at Piphus. "Make the leap."

CHAPTER TWENTY-TWO

KING OF THE JUNGLE

It had been four days since Diego and Jillian were kidnapped, and it felt like an eternity. They were hungry, thirsty, bug-bitten, and damp because of the frequent rain. The *criminales* had refused to tell them anything about the ransom negotiations.

Jillian sat across the cage from Diego, leaning against the bars, trying to meditate as the jungle animals squawked and screeched all around them. Suddenly, Jillian opened her eyes, put her hands to her face, and screamed, "I have to get out of here! I'm going to go completely insane if I don't get out of here right now!" She jumped up and started yelling at the guards to let them out.

"Hey, *tranquilo*. Calm down!" Diego said, panicked. He feared that Rafael and Miguel were going to hurt her if she kept screaming—they were heartless and seemed to enjoy watching him and Jillian suffer. "Jillian, they just want an excuse to hurt the rich American girl so they can feel powerful." He put his arms around her, but she fought him, her strength fueled by adrenaline, and he was barely able to keep her contained.

"Let me go!" she screamed. "I'm done! I don't care anymore!"

He didn't know what to do, so as he held her, he started singing to her in Spanish.

"Stop it," she said, but he could feel the struggle leaving her body, so he kept singing softly into her ear as he pulled her close to him.

Finally, she let go completely and leaned her head against his chest.

"What do the words mean?" she whispered.

"A heartbroken man is asking the moon to make his love return to him."

She leaned the rest of her body into him, and he wished he could pick her up and carry her away. "It's beautiful," she said. "You have a pretty voice."

He looked down at her. "Pretty?"

She pulled away from him and lay down on the blanket, curled up on her side. "Don't worry. You're manly enough."

But he didn't feel manly; he felt weak and pathetic. Rage crept into him like poison from a tropical sting. He turned toward Rafael and Miguel and a new guy named Carlos. They sat smoking and playing cards at the table under the shade tarp, as usual. "Miguel!" he called out. "Hey, come here. I have to tell you something."

Jillian lifted her head from the ground. "What are you doing?"

Rafael looked at him for a while, chatted with Miguel and Carlos a moment, then sauntered over, his AK slung over his shoulder. "¿Qué quieres?" he asked. "What do you want?"

"I need to tell you something about the lady," he said in Spanish, as Jillian looked on, trying to understand what they were saying. "Come here."

Rafael refused to get closer than a foot away, but it was close enough. Diego reached out, lightning fast, and grabbed the rifle strap, yanking him against the bars. But Rafael clamped his arm down on the strap, and they screamed a string of Spanish curse words at each other as they struggled for the gun. Just as he was about to wrench it free, Diego's head exploded with pain, and he stumbled backward, holding the place just over his eye where Miguel had run up and hit him with the butt of his rifle, then he fell to the ground.

Enraged, Rafael opened the cage door, and Jillian threw herself in front of Diego to keep Rafael away from him. "No!" she screamed. "Leave him alone!"

He pushed her out of the way, and Diego got up and lunged at him, but the other two men grabbed him and dragged him out of the cage. Diego had heard of the beatings people had taken from *narcos* like these, and he knew that he was about to be killed or crippled for life.

Rafael left Jillian yelling in the cage and locked the door, then stood over Diego as Carlos and Miguel watched, rifles at the ready. Just as Rafael landed his first blow, Diego found himself praying that Jillian be safe. Suddenly, Rafael stopped. The men turned to look at something, and Diego heard the sound of a vehicle approaching. When it cleared the trees, he saw a black Range Rover. Pedro was driving, and another man sat in the passenger seat wearing an army fatigue mask over his head and face. Diego knew that could be only one man—Manuel Menendez.

Pedro and Menendez got out of the car and began shouting at the guards. "What have you done? I can't leave you alone for one day!"

Miguel and Rafael tried to defend themselves, describing how Diego had attacked Rafael, but Menendez ordered them to lock Diego back up. As they argued, Carlos pulled Diego to his feet and led him, staggering, back to the cage, where he was grateful to be back in confinement.

"My God, Diego," Jillian said as he faltered on his feet. She pulled him down to the ground, putting his head in her lap and stroking his hair. "What were you trying to do?"

Tears fell from his eyes. He had no strength to hold them in anymore. "I was trying to get you out of here."

"They were going to kill you," she said. "You scared me to death."

"How lucky for you," Manuel Menendez said in Spanish, walking toward them with a swagger, the mask still on his face. "Pedro tells me you keep her calm, and now I see she keeps you calm too." He laughed. "Obviously you have not told her the truth. That would not keep her calm, I think. Maybe not so many caresses, eh?"

Diego pulled away from Jillian, trying to reclaim what he could of his *machismo*. "Let us go," he demanded, his voice croaking.

Menendez laughed harder, his white teeth set off by the dark green color of his mask. "You are filled with yourself. I understand. Beautiful women do the same for me."

Jillian stood up, so Diego did too. "Are you the leader? What's happening? Why are we still here?" she asked.

Diego tried to memorize the drug lord's visible features—his teeth and lips and eyes. He noticed the shiny, snakeskin cowboy boots he wore. He was so powerful and secretive. No one knew his real name or identity, even though it was believed that he was Salvadoran. If Diego ever had the chance, he wanted to be able to identify him and bring him down.

"I feel the Americans are playing games with me," Menendez said in heavily accented English.

"What about my father?" Jillian asked.

"I have spoken to your father. He seems like a reasonable man who is trying to do the right thing, but he is pressured from your government, I am sure. We are getting closer to handing you to him, but first we have to move you."

"When?" she asked.

"Tomorrow," he said, and pointed at Diego. "Your boyfriend is only alive because of you. If you want him to stay that way, make sure he is sweet like a kitten. If he breathes in a way I don't like, I will put a bullet in his skull."

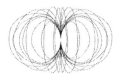

CHAPTER TWENTY-THREE

L'AZMAN

When Mobius opened his eyes, he was on the other side of the galaxy. The leap had been like dying—no sense of self, no anything—and then coming back to life. He slowly became aware of being in form again, of inhabiting a body. Then he watched his mind slowly come back online, and with it the thoughts that made up his individual sense of self and his interpretation of everything around him.

He looked out and saw Earth and felt like he couldn't breathe for a full minute. It looked so much like Akara. His crewmates were all spellbound too. After taking in the precious jewel, they gazed back toward Akara from the perspective of Earth. Invisible to the naked eye, it sat amidst a tiny cluster of seven visible stars, dwarfed by the immensity of the cosmos. To Mobius, it seemed for a moment like Akara simply was not there. A pang of loneliness gripped his heart. In all the years he had longed to be in space and explore, he had never imagined that once he traveled to another planet, his deepest desire would be to return to his own.

His face must have revealed his thoughts, because Kaia smiled at him and said, "We'll get back home. I'll make sure of it. But for now, we have a job to do."

"Yes, we do," Piphus said, clapping his hands together. "Now that we've learned the languages, we need to get more conversational. We also should familiarize ourselves with the aliens' world as much as possible, and specifically the region Itzamna landed in."

Within minutes, Piphus had tapped into Earth's Internet, and Kaia piloted the ship behind the moon so they could review a broad range of information and entertainment. Mobius was disturbed by what he saw. The news was dreadful—ninety percent of it was about people doing horrible things to one another. And the entertainment was just as dark, if that were even possible. He was shocked that over a thousand Earth years after Itzamna's mission, these aliens were still so violent and disconnected from each other. "Is this what an entire planet of Anomalies would look like?" he wondered aloud.

"Come on. Let's focus positive. There is also a lot of good in this species," Kaia said. "Remember, their evolutionary stage is similar to the one Akara was in when Itzamna came to Earth. Although we were a little further along technologically. Remember, our race was nearly extinct before we stopped killing each other."

"It's just hard to watch," Nava said.

"Well, at least this is encouraging ..." Piphus said. He had researched the latest quantum scientific theories to determine how advanced the aliens were at understanding the universe. "The ability to access the Wisdom isn't widespread, and they are far from tapping its full potential, but it looks like some of their scientists and philosophers have made significant advances. Listen to this—someone named Albert Einstein, whom they consider to be their greatest scientist, said: 'Reality is merely an illusion; albeit a very persistent one.' He also said: 'The intuitive mind is a sacred gift, and the rational mind is a faithful servant.'"

Mobius started to feel more hopeful after hearing that and watching some more inspiring stories of the aliens helping each other and the incredible wildlife on their planet. He particularly loved watching sports, which were also popular on Akara, and this similarity between their two worlds helped him to feel more connected to the beings on L'Azman. He watched soccer, the primary sport in the region, but he was most excited by basketball, which was similar to *corasala,* one of the biggest sports on Akara and one that he was really good at. He couldn't help but notice how upset the players often seemed to get, and he had to admit he related. People were constantly telling him that it was just a game.

Piphus reviewed Earth's space program and found that they were still in the earliest stages of interstellar travel. "Although there are numerous accounts of extraterrestrial visitations—how fascinating, very similar to Akara in that they seem to not show themselves fully or communicate directly. Individuals claim to have direct experiences at times, and some countries recognize what they call Unidentified Flying Objects, but there is no consensus about extraterrestrial existence. I wonder if it's the same beings visiting both planets. However, unlike Akara, none of these visitations are officially recognized planet-wide."

They watched samples from all the movies he could find about space and contact with other beings. Visitors from other planets came in a variety of creative forms, but the stories almost always had one thing in common—the aliens were all portrayed as psychotic and evil.

"I'm not sure how great a reception we're going to get," Nava said. "It seems like they're obsessed with the idea of a hostile race from outer space destroying their planet."

Mobius blinked twice. "We have to assume that people are going to think we are like this."

"Maybe part of the reason they feel this way," Kaia said, "is because of contact from someone like Itzamna in ancient times. Even if they don't overtly remember, it might still be in their collective consciousness."

"It must be," Nava added, "because look at how many of their depictions of anthropoid aliens have no hair and eyes much bigger than their own."

Piphus began a sweep of the geographical area where Itzamna had been. "This isn't going to be easy," he said.

None of the records about A281 included the location of the city Itzamna had built. Although Piphus had been referencing the mission log, which showed the ship descending to Earth, the footage was not seamless. The imagery showed a long shot from far above the planet, in which the general area of a particular land mass was visible, but then it cut to a view hovering directly over a jungle and the aliens reacting to Itzamna's ship.

Fortunately, the correct hemisphere was rotating toward the *Concordance* when Piphus began looking, so it didn't take him long to find the distinctive strip of land connecting the two large continents, which he recognized from the mission log. When he started scanning the area, he found many ruins with pyramid-shaped buildings. By comparing the scans to imagery on the Internet, he found all kinds of information about the ancient civilization that lived in the area at the time of Itzamna, including pictures of the round stone calendar from the mission logs. "Mayans," Piphus said in English. "The aliens Itzamna ruled are called Mayans."

"We might want to start calling them 'humans' or 'people' rather than 'aliens,'" Kaia said. "To them, *we're* the aliens."

"True," he said. "Okay, here is a map with the location of important Mayan sites. There are dozens."

"Can you search for King K'awiil?" Kaia asked. "Where did he rule?"

"Already on it." After a few moments Piphus sighed. "Turns out there were many kings named K'awiil, and at least five who ruled in four different Mayan cities during the time period of Itzamna's mission."

They reviewed pictures of each location on the Internet, and each one showed the familiar stepped-pyramid buildings from the mission log, only now they were ruins.

"It could be any of these," Nava said. "They all look so similar."

"Let me grab aerial images of each of the four cities and compare them to the footage of the landing. Maybe we'll recognize something."

Despite their efforts, they couldn't find a match. The mission log footage cut away before the layout of the city below was recognizable.

"I wonder if Itzamna did that intentionally so the exact location couldn't easily be found," Nava speculated, as Piphus continued to toggle through the pictures of the cities from above.

"Stop!" Kaia said suddenly, as Piphus scrolled past one of the aerial shots. "Go back. There's something interesting about the placement of the buildings. It looks so familiar." She stood with her arms crossed, one hand on each shoulder, intently looking at the picture. "What is it?"

They all stared at it for a while, then Piphus shouted, "Wait! Let me check something. That looks like ..." He brought up an image of a constellation of stars.

"I see it!" Mobius said. It was the very constellation they had just gazed at to find their planet.

"They call it the 'Pleiades' or 'Seven Sisters,'" Piphus said, laying the image of the star cluster on top of the layout of the buildings. It matched perfectly.

"Wow. That has to be it!" Kaia said. "Itzamna built his city in the form of the Pleiades constellation because it is where Akara is located."

"What is it called?" Mobius asked Piphus.

"Tikal."

They had found their ancient city.

CHAPTER TWENTY-FOUR

STARGAZING

Diego lay awake as Jillian slept with her head on his shoulder. He grappled with whether or not to tell her the truth about how they had landed in this hell. Suddenly, there was a rustling near the cage, and Jillian woke with a start. "What is that?" She bolted upright, alarm in her voice.

"Shhh," he whispered, sitting up and stroking her hair. "Just an animal. Go back to sleep."

They had heard animals all around them every night, but after the day's violence, they were both more on edge than ever.

"I don't think I can." She looked at him, the moonlight glowing on her face.

Without thinking, he kissed her. When she kissed him back hungrily, he felt like he was being filled up from within. A loud noise pulled them out of their kiss, and they turned their heads to see a massive tapir staring right at them. "Wow," Jillian said breathlessly, fascinated by the enormous six-hundred-pound mammal that snuffed around looking for vegetation to eat. "It looks like a huge black pig with an anteater snout."

As frustrated as Diego was that they'd been interrupted, he loved that she was like an awestruck child seeing this rare, endangered giant. When it lumbered away, Jillian lay down, her head on Diego's chest. "You're a very good kisser."

"You too," he said, but suddenly, he was preoccupied with his thoughts of telling her the truth about his alliance with Menendez. He was filled with love for her and the feeling of her lips on his, and at least for that moment, he wanted to do the right thing. It seemed to be the right time—maybe the only time—because he didn't know what would happen the next day, if they would even be kept together, or if he would live.

She sat up and started swatting away the battalion of mosquitoes that had just moved en masse into the cage, and the moment of their beautiful connection was lost in the circumstances of their suffering. "God, this is such a nightmare," she said, quite loudly. "I'm starving!"

"Please whisper, Jillian. Don't give them a reason to come over. I'm sure your parents are putting all their money and power into looking for us. Well, for *you* anyway. They'll find you. I'm sure of it." But his confidence was an act; these *bandidos* were pros and were hiding them deep in the impenetrable cover of the jungle.

"They can't hear me. They're all passed out from drinking rum," Jillian said.

"Look at *Escorpión*," he said pointing at the sky, trying to distract her. "It's beautiful tonight."

Jillian gazed at the night sky, seeing the curves of the constellation Scorpio, its stinger and claws poised and spread across the firmament. But the full, incandescent moon and the wafting smoke of the guards' campfire dimmed the glow of the stars. Oddly, one was much larger than the rest and shone brightly. "What is that?" she asked, pointing at the large, orange-hued point of light above the tree line, just beyond the clearing where the kidnappers had their camp. "It's huge."

"A planet?" Diego said, looking upward. "Or maybe the international space station."

"No way ... it's too big. Oh my God, it just moved!" She exclaimed in a loud whisper.

"It's probably an airplane. Actually, it's hovering, so it must be a helicopter. But there's no air traffic here. It's got to be a rescue mission!" Diego jumped to his feet. "Jillian, they found us!" He put a finger to his lips then whispered, "They found us."

She grabbed the bars of the cage, pushing her face between them. Just as she did, the light began to move away from them. "Oh God, they're leaving!"

"¡*Mierda!*" Diego exclaimed, watching the aircraft recede into the night sky in an S-shaped pattern. "It's moving so strangely. Maybe it's a drone they sent out to search for us."

"Come back," she cried as it withdrew farther away, becoming a distant pinprick. "Please come back." She fell to the ground and put her hands to her head, trying to hold back tears. She had already cried so many.

"Jillian ...," Diego whispered.

"What?" she said, looking up at him.

"It's coming back."

She scrambled to her feet and locked eyes on the point of light, watching it moving toward them again.

"Diego, what *is* that?" Jillian grabbed his arm. "I've never seen anything like it."

"It has to be some high-tech, military plane," Diego said, his voice trembling.

Moments later, they knew it was neither. A honeycomb-shaped object arrayed with lights hovered just above the tree line a few hundred yards away.

"Diego, that's not a military craft," Jillian said, breathless, gaping up at the object. "That's a UFO!"

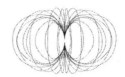

CHAPTER TWENTY-FIVE

CANDIDATES

The *Concordance* hovered at an altitude visible from the ground and in the line of sight of two particular humans Kaia hoped might be able to help them. "They see us," Kaia said. "Let's find out what they do next."

"I still think this is a really bad idea," Mobius said, crossing his arms in an X.

After they had located Tikal, the city Itzamna built, Kaia had insisted that they couldn't find the time capsule on their own. Though the structures in the city were uninhabited, information on the Internet revealed that it was a popular tourism site, and Kaia wasn't willing to risk navigating through all those people to find the right temple without help. She had instructed Piphus to scan the area to look for people who could potentially assist them on their mission.

But Mobius wasn't convinced. "I realize we might encounter aliens down there, but to seek them out? That completely goes against the Non-Interference Regulation. Besides, we don't need a guide. We can find it ourselves. This race is too unstable. Many of their *leaders* behave as badly as Itzamna. What does that say about everybody else?"

"Mobius, we have no idea how to navigate this planet. We're unfamiliar with Earth's culture and customs, and it's too easy for us to misstep and be discovered. We need someone who can guide us, not to mention hide us. I agree that most of them believe they're separate and are run by primitive, survival instincts, but that's why we performed the scans—to find humans who have a high enough vibration. And these two have the highest we've found."

In order to find potential candidates to be their guides, they had focused in remote areas where they would be seen by the fewest number of people when they landed. It was easy to prevent tracking on radar, but the *Concordance* didn't have camouflage technology to keep from being seen—it had never been necessary, since the Non-Interference Regulation prevented getting close enough to an inhabited planet to be detected. But now Mobius wished they did. Piphus had surveyed the area extensively, but it was not easy to find humans who would be open to them and not panic. To help them decide if people on the ground were a good fit, Piphus measured their overall vibrational blueprint based on their brainwave activity, the stability of their nervous systems, and the frequency of their energy bodies.

He located a couple in a remote area of the jungle whose blueprints were stable enough, but they had children with them, which created a complication. He had also found a man on his own, camping at the base of some cliffs, and they thought they might have their guide, but his blueprint was a mess, suggesting some type of intoxication.

Finally, he came across two people he thought were a possibility.

"Excellent," Kaia said. "I may be able to communicate with them telepathically."

"I can only hear you telepathically when I'm really focused and close to your energy field," Mobius said. "You think they'll be able to?"

"There is a tremendous amount of love between them, and it's raised their vibration to a very high level, so I'm hopeful," Kaia said. "Also, the female is generally quite open, and the male appears to be weakened physically and emotionally, so he is less guarded than he might otherwise be."

Nava blinked twice, adding, "They seem like good candidates to me too. And, when I tune into the male, he seems very knowledgeable about the area."

"I agree," Piphus said.

"Even if they respond well, what are we going to do about the five men nearby who have negative blueprints?" Mobius asked.

"We'll have to work around them," Kaia said. "My intuition is telling me that these two are the right people, and I need to trust that."

Mobius relented, realizing he couldn't argue with her wisdom. "What now?" he asked.

"We find out how much more they can handle," Kaia said, then sat down and closed her eyes.

CHAPTER TWENTY-SIX

EXTRATERRESTRE

D iego felt like he could barely breathe. "It ... it can't be a UFO. It must be something manmade."

"I don't think so," Jillian said, fixated on the ship suspended over the center of the clearing, directly in their line of sight. "And whatever it is, it seems like it's watching us."

"*Mierda,*" Diego said. "Now you're really scaring me."

Jillian put her hand up to quiet him. "Wait, oh my God. I may be totally crazy at this point, but I hear something ... It's a voice—I think they might be trying to communicate with us."

"*They?* They who?" He raked his hands through his hair. "We're talking about *extraterrestres*—aliens, for God's sake?"

"Yes, I can really feel them. But don't worry. They're peaceful ... I think."

"*Jesucristo,* you *think?* I hope you know. This is totally *loco!* You're communicating with aliens?"

Jillian sat down in her familiar cross-legged position and closed her eyes.

Diego's mouth dropped open. "You're going to meditate *now?*"

"Shhh! I'm trying to listen."

As she became quiet, an expression of bliss came over her face, and she looked almost angelic. His eyes kept moving from her to the mysterious object in the sky. Sweating and scared, he felt his throat tightening, but after a minute or so, a feeling of profound peace began to wash over him. Instead of feeling freaked out, now he just felt calm. And perplexed. Somehow everything that had been so upsetting just moments before, suddenly seemed just fine, and he found himself sitting down next to Jillian and closing his eyes as well. Almost immediately, he heard a female voice that seemed to be talking to him from a few feet away.

"Don't be afraid. We're here to help you," she said.

"Did you hear that?" he asked Jillian in a breathless whisper.

"Yes," she said. "It's okay. She's communicating with us telepathically."

"Are you still there?" Diego asked silently to whomever was talking.

"Yes," the voice said. "I am."

"Who are you? Why are you here?"

"My name is Kaia," she said. "I am from a planet called Akara. We have come to L'Azman ... to Earth ... on a very important mission to assist your planet, and we need your help."

"You need *our* help?" Diego couldn't believe this was happening, but oddly, something about it seemed natural, because the unexplainable sense of peace was so strong.

"Yes. We are looking for something." Her voice was beautiful and soothing. "We need a guide. May I come down in my energy body?"

Diego hesitated. "Your what?"

"Yes," Jillian said out loud.

A moment later, Diego felt the presence of someone sitting in front of them, but he could barely see her body, just a glowing thread of light forming an outline of her shape. "This is your energy body?"

"Yes," she said. "It is a more subtle level of form. You have one too. It is what connects us to the quantum field."

Suddenly, a breeze blew smoke toward them from the fire the guards had left burning. And her body showed up clearly, like a flashlight beam when pointed at the smoke of a campfire. He and Jillian both inhaled sharply as they saw the left side of her beautiful face and her long, flowing body. *She's really here!* he thought.

Kaia reached out a hand and put it on Diego's shoulder, but it penetrated his body, her hand actually going through him, and suddenly, his body started shaking, completely thrown out of balance. "You can't touch me," he said. "I can't handle it." His heavy human energy was not vibrating at the same rate as hers.

Kaia pulled her hand back, and Diego got the sense that he was like a precious child to her. An exotic, magical being—kind of how he would see a newborn jaguar cub in the jungle—and she wanted very much to touch him, even hold him in her arms. The love and affection he felt radiating from her was so intense, he completely lost himself in the joy of it.

Kaia touched Jillian's arm, and she seemed to tolerate it much better, allowing Kaia to stroke her affectionately. "You are incredible beings," she said.

Jillian and Diego both laughed at the unusual compliment. "So are you," Jillian whispered.

The *extraterrestre* finally pulled her hand away and focused on why she was there. "If we land our craft here and come to you in our physical bodies, are you going to be able to handle that?"

Diego's stomach pinched with fear, but the smoke flowed over her again, and he saw the smile on her face and once again felt the radiant love and peace she exuded. "I can't believe this is actually happening," he said, "so I can't say for sure. I mean in real life, are you sure you're not scary looking? Are you as peaceful as you are now?"

She giggled, and the sound was sparkly like the ringing of small bells. "I'm just like I am now. Just more solid."

"But we're being held captive by some very violent men," he said. "We're locked in this cage."

"This is a cage?" she asked, shocked. "You mean like for confining and displaying animals?"

It sounded to Diego as if she were reading from a dictionary. "Well ... yes, normally that's what they're for."

"Why are you being held captive?"

"Some very bad men have kidnapped us," he said.

"Taken us against our will. For money," Jillian said. "But if you get us out of here, we will help you."

Diego looked at Jillian. "We will?"

"Yes, of course we will," she said, raising her eyebrows at him.

Diego turned to Kaia. "Yes, of course we will."

"We are coming down then," Kaia said.

"Be careful—!" Jillian said, but the alien was gone.

"That was extravagante! Absolutely incredible," he whispered, his hands on the sides of his head.

Jillian turned to him, her eyes filled with tears of joy. They stood up and embraced each other, watching as the spaceship descended from the sky.

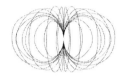

CHAPTER TWENTY-SEVEN

TOUCHDOWN

Kaia emerged out of telepathic communication with the humans and faced her fellow crewmates. "They agreed to help us."

"Excellent," Piphus said.

Kaia cocked her head to the side. "Well ... except for the fact that they told me they are locked up in some type of cage. Piphus, how did we miss that?"

"I ... I thought it was some kind of dwelling," he stammered. "There was no reason to suspect captivity."

"We have to keep looking for other people who can help us, then," Nava said.

"No." Kaia squeezed her eyes shut for a moment. "They're our guides. I can feel it. And they need our help. I'm landing the ship."

"What?" Mobius said. "This is crazy!"

As Kaia brought the *Concordance* down to land, Mobius felt as though they were descending into a war zone. He realized that maybe he was more afraid of humans than his friends were because humans were like Anomalies, and he didn't trust himself. He took Nava's hand again and was grateful when she held his tightly as he looked out the window, barely able to see the clearing below. Kaia had extinguished the outer lights, and only the waning moon illuminated the area. The jungle around the clearing moved like a giant breathing beast as the energy from the craft disturbed the trees. As they got closer, Mobius saw people moving below. Even though he knew they couldn't see inside the ship because the window was transparent in only one direction, he still felt exposed.

"They're running!" Piphus said, looking at the ship's surveillance imagery on the clearscreen. "There are two vehicles. One of them is leaving."

"Our guides?" Kaia asked.

"No. They're still locked up," Piphus said. "It's their captors."

"Look!" Nava said. "One of the five men is opening the cage door. He has some kind of mask on his face."

Kaia descended quickly, and their landing jolted Mobius nearly off his feet. She turned on the full array of outer lights, and the whole area was lit up in an orange glow. The man turned and looked at the ship, caught like an animal in the lights for a moment, then started running toward the remaining vehicle. Even though he wore a mask, his fear was obvious.

The male in the cage started screaming, pointing furiously and jumping up and down.

"Piphus, quick. Turn on the sound sensors," Kaia said.

"Don't let him take the car!" the man in the cage yelled over and over.

"Stay here," Kaia commanded as she jumped out of her seat and ran to the airlock, closing the inner hatch behind her. As soon as the outer hatch opened, she ran down the ramp after the man, bounding with huge strides across the clearing. The man screamed, "*¡El demonio!* It's a demon!" then bolted into the jungle.

Mobius realized that Kaia must have been a powerful sight to the alien, whose idea of manned space travel was landing on their own moon decades ago.

Kaia ran back to the ship, and Mobius watched her, amazed. He knew the gravitational force would be less here since Akara's mass was greater than Earth's, but he hadn't imagined what it would look or feel like.

"Is the area clear?" Kaia asked Piphus over comms.

He looked at the scanners. "Yes, all clear."

Kaia turned her attention to their two guides, who had stepped out of the cage and were staring at her. She looked back up at the ship and said, "Piphus, I need you to stay with the *Concordance*, but Mobius and Nava, if you want to, join me out here."

She hadn't finished her sentence before the two of them were in the airlock. When the outer hatch door opened and they stepped onto the outside ramp, Mobius inhaled deeply, taking in the warm, humid Earth air. "It's weird."

"Harder," Nava said, blinking twice.

"We'll get used to it," Kaia said, looking up at them from the ground.

Earth's air had higher oxygen and lower argon levels than Akara's atmosphere. Lower argon levels or not, any fresh air felt good to Mobius after the stale air of the ship. He walked down the ramp and onto the ground and was overcome by the terrestrial smell of L'Azman—rich and sweet and fruitful. He also immediately felt the weaker gravitational field, which filled him with a sense of lightness. He jumped straight up just to check it out and was thrilled at his ability to go twice as high as he normally could. *And the landing is so soft!* he thought, feeling giddy.

They walked across the clearing to the humans, and the five of them stood there for a moment, just looking at each other in wonder and disbelief. It wasn't difficult to tell that the humans were deeply affected. The woman had water streaming out of her eyes (a very strange-looking phenomenon) and the man couldn't stop laughing and saying, *"Ala gran, ala gran.* Wow, wow." Mobius was as stunned by what was happening as they were.

Mobius put his hands over his heart and extended them outward in the traditional Akaran greeting. The humans repeated the gesture back to him. Then he shook hands with the woman, knowing it was a customary human greeting. "My name is Mobius," he said in English, looking into her eyes, which were sparkling. She was different than he, but not much. She had hair on her head and around and above her eyes, which were small compared to his, and she had no mark between them like Akarans did. Her other features were similar to Akaran features, but she was shorter. He felt an immediate and intense love for her.

"I'm Jillian," she said.

"May I touch your hair?" he asked.

She nodded and laughed.

He reached out and stroked it. "There's so much. Does it stay this length?"

"No, it grows," she said. "I have to cut it, or it would go all the way down my back."

"Fascinating," Mobius said.

He moved to the man and repeated the Akaran gesture. "My name is Mobius."

"I'm Diego," the man said, his eyes almost as big as an Akaran's from the state of shock he was in. *"Whoa,* you only have four fingers."

"Whoa, you have five," Mobius replied, and they both laughed,

Diego with his head back and mouth open, and Mobius with a rapid breath in and out of his nose.

"This is completely mind-blowing," Diego said. He opened his hands next to his head and made a noise like an explosion, and Mobius mimicked him, and they laughed again.

Mobius pointed to the injury on Diego's head. "Does it hurt?"

Diego shook his head slowly. "It did before you all arrived, but I don't feel anything right now."

The hair on his head was black and wavy, but Mobius was most intrigued by the hair that grew right out of his face. *What a remarkable creature,* he thought. Diego seemed to think the same about Mobius, and as they stared at each other in awe, Mobius felt the same love for him that he did for Jillian and was filled with overwhelming ecstasy.

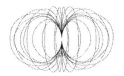

CHAPTER TWENTY-EIGHT

UNCONTAINED

Suddenly, the terrifying sound of three gunshot blasts tore apart the night.

"Get down! Gunfire!" Diego yelled, and they all dropped to the ground.

"It's Menendez!" Jillian said, covering her head with her hands. "He's the one who kidnapped us."

More shots blasted through the clearing as the man with the mask ran out of the jungle toward the vehicle, shooting his handgun as he went. Without thinking, Mobius jumped up and made a break for the car. Luckily, Menendez was preoccupied with the others and didn't see Mobius. With his gravity-assisted speed, Mobius got to the car first and hid on the driver's side. When Menendez came around the front of the vehicle, Mobius jumped on top of him, and they wrestled for the gun. As he pinned the criminal's arms to the ground, he realized he was much stronger than his opponent. Menendez cursed at him in Spanish; many of the words Mobius didn't know, but he did know "demon" and "freak," which the man repeated several times. Mobius finally was able to force the weapon out of Menendez's hand, but the crazed gunman kept fighting, and Mobius didn't know what to do to stop him.

"Mobius!" Nava yelled out. "Kaia is wounded! She's been shot."

Hearing this, Mobius suddenly felt an overwhelming rage rise inside him, and without thinking, he hit the man in the head with the end of the gun, and the man went limp. As a deep red blood oozed from the criminal's head, Mobius became horrified—he had never committed an act of violence in his life—and he was afraid he'd killed the man. He stood there, frozen, until Nava's cries jolted him out of his shock. He ran back to find everyone kneeling over Kaia, her own purple blood staining her clothes and spreading out beneath her.

Kaia's eyes opened slightly. "It's bad. I can't self-heal this."

"We have to get her back to the ship!" Nava shouted.

Mobius handed the gun to Diego, then scooped Kaia up in his arms. "She'll be okay!" he said, but panic filled his voice. He bounded across the field toward the *Concordance* as Nava, Diego, and Jillian followed. Inside the airlock, he yelled, "Override code A281TC. Bypass airlock delay."

"*No,*" Kaia groaned, barely conscious, and whispered something he couldn't understand. The inner hatch door opened, and Mobius ran to the medical station inside, where he laid Kaia out on a platform.

Suddenly, an alarm went off in the ship. "*Warning: Inner Atmosphere Destabilization.*"

Jillian jumped and grabbed Diego when they heard the blaring alarm. "What's happening? What's it saying?"

"Cancel warning," Piphus commanded in Akaran. "Don't worry," he said to Jillian in English, pointing to the open hatch door, "Earth's atmosphere has gotten into the ship, but we can breathe your air, so it's okay." He turned back to Nava and Mobius.

"How many times was she shot?" He had witnessed everything from the ship but hadn't been able to stop Menendez.

"At least twice. In the chest and stomach," Mobius said. "I can't tell. There's so much blood!"

Nava ran to Kaia, whose injuries far surpassed Nava's quantum healing abilities, so she activated the medical AI. "Do you think it can extract whatever is inside her?"

"I don't know. I think so ... it should be able to," Piphus said.

Jillian and Diego stood transfixed near the hatch; they alternated between taking in the exotic alien craft with its unfathomable technology and watching Kaia on the medical bay platform. Suddenly, rapid machine gun fire blasted into the ship, bouncing off the interior. Everyone dropped to the floor except Diego, who ducked, then bolted for the hatch, pulling the pistol from his waist and shooting back at Menendez, who had obviously regained consciousness and found a more lethal weapon.

"I should have shot the *pendejo* when I had the chance," Diego yelled, as he fired from the ship.

"*Warning: Torus Integrity Compromised,*" another alarm sounded.

Jillian looked over at Piphus, but instead of him telling her not to worry like he did last time, he yelled "Oh no! No, no, no," as he ran to the engineering control panel. "The retainite. It's liquefying!" He turned around to look at the torus and stared in disbelief—the atmospheric chamber protecting it was filled with puncture holes.

"Why is it liquefying?" Mobius yelled.

"Argon," Kaia whispered.

A look of terrified recognition came over Mobius's face as he realized what he'd done. Earth did not have enough argon in the atmosphere to maintain retainite's solid state. After he overrode the airlock, the ship had filled with alien air. When the gunshots punctured the torus's atmospheric chamber, the retainite holding together the torus started to liquefy. "Close the hatch!" he yelled and bolted for it just as Diego screamed like a wild animal and ran down the ramp shooting at Menendez.

"Diego!" Jillian called out as Mobius closed the hatch behind him.

"Piphus, can you restore the argon levels?" Mobius asked frantically after the ship was sealed.

"Yes. It will stop the liquefaction process, but it's already lost some of its shape."

"What do we do?" Nava asked.

"We have to leave immediately. The torus could collapse before we make the leap. If we don't go now, we may never get back."

"Can you pilot this thing?" Mobius asked.

Piphus put his hands on his head. "I think I can tell you and Nava how to initiate the leap while I pilot. I just hope the merge with just Nava and me will be enough."

"It will. It has to be," Nava said.

Jillian stepped toward Mobius. "Can someone please tell me what's going on?"

"You have to disembark. We need to leave right now. There's a problem with the ship."

Water started coming out of her eyes again, but this time from sadness rather than joy. "I understand. I'm so sorry. Find us if you come back," she said. "We'll help you. I promise."

Kaia reached out and grabbed Nava's arm. "You all have to stay," she whispered in Akaran. "You have to find the time capsule."

"No way!" Mobius said, walking back to her. "We have to get

you home. You're dying."

"No, no. It doesn't matter. This is more important," Kaia said.

Piphus, Nava, and Mobius looked at each other, struck silent for a moment. Nava finally spoke. "She's right. We have to complete the mission."

"I think we should return to Akara," Piphus said. "It's not just Kaia. We need to get a functioning ship to help locate and disarm the time capsule."

"I'll stay," Mobius said.

"We're not leaving you alone here," Nava argued.

Mobius felt like he was going to drop to his knees, they were so weak. "Before we left Akara, you also said it doesn't matter what happens to us. We have to do everything we can to save L'Azman. I can't help with the leap, Nava. You two don't need me. But they do. I'll do whatever I can until you return." *If you are even able to,* he thought, knowing something could go horribly wrong when they tried to make the leap, since the torus had been damaged.

She squeezed her eyes shut, and Mobius took her silence to mean that she agreed that he needed to stay, even though she couldn't bring herself to say it.

"Mobius, you have to go if you're going," Piphus said as he looked out the viewing ribbon.

"Is it clear?" he asked.

"Yes. The gunman is unconscious, and Diego is dragging him toward the cage."

Mobius squeezed Kaia's hand and turned to go, but she held on.

"You are a Discovery Corps flier now," she said when he looked back at her. "Remember—make the leap."

He forced a smile, then Kaia let go of his hand, and he ran toward the hatch.

Piphus shoved several bags of myomeal into his hands as the hatch opened once again to the humid air outside. "Follow the Wisdom," he said soberly.

Nava rushed to Mobius and pulled him to her before he could go. "We'll come back for you, I promise," she said, then kissed him.

He stood frozen in disbelief for a moment, until they heard Diego over the comm, "We have to go now! I hear vehicles approaching, and they'll be heavily armed."

Mobius turned to Jillian. "Let's go. Stay behind me in case of more gunfire." The two of them raced down the ramp and across the clearing to Diego as headlights slashed across the area from a vehicle that was headed their way.

"Come on, come on, come on!" Diego shouted as he jumped behind the wheel of the remaining car.

Jillian dove into the backseat, but Mobius couldn't figure out how to get the passenger door open—there was no scanner or anything he recognized.

"Get in the car!" Diego shouted as he looked in his rearview mirror and saw Menendez stand up inside the cage, holding his now unmasked head.

"How?" Mobius yelled.

Diego reached across the seat and pushed the door open just as gunshots erupted from the SUV that was now headed straight for them. Mobius jumped in, and Diego punched the accelerator, veering wildly around the oncoming car.

As they sped away, Mobius looked back to see the *Concordance* lifting off the planet and leaving him behind.

CHAPTER TWENTY-NINE

THE PROPHECY

The road was a narrow, rutted slash through the jungle, and it was taking everything Diego had to keep the Range Rover from barreling into a tree or getting stuck in one of the many stream crossings.

"Are those men going to follow us?" Mobius asked.

Diego checked his rearview mirror. "I'm sure they'll try, but I have a pretty good lead. They have to get Menendez out of the cage first. Hopefully, this is the only key." He picked up a ring with a padlock key from the console. "You clocked him in the head, and I beat the hell out of him too, so that will slow them down." He glanced at his knuckles, which were raw and hurting.

Mobius put a hand on top of his head.

"Are you okay?" Diego asked.

The alien dropped his head. "I've never experienced violence like that before … and I hurt that man. I could have killed him."

"We had no choice," Diego said. "We probably *should* have killed him, to be honest. He's a bad man." He tried to sound matter-of-fact, but he hadn't been able to stomach executing the *narco* when he'd had the chance.

They rode along without talking for a while, and Diego couldn't help but glance over at the alien as often as the road would allow. He found Mobius fascinating—hairless with golden bronze skin and huge two-toned eyes with a blue mark between them. All four of the aliens had this same mark, so Diego assumed it was a feature everyone on their planet shared. Mobius's teeth were white, and his lips were thin and kind of a light purple, which Diego guessed came from the fact that Akaran blood was the color of an eggplant. His nose was narrow and well-proportioned, and his ears were small and lobeless. Diego thought Mobius looked nearly human until the alien turned toward him with those eyes, and Diego shuddered a little, trying to get used to them. Mobius's eyes seemed twice the size of human eyes and slanted upward, but most unusual was the color of his irises—nearly all pale orange and a little blue. But he'd noticed that in the light of the spaceship, they were about half and half.

"Can you see a lot with those?" he asked Mobius, who had turned slightly away from him to look out the passenger window into the dark night.

"Well, I can see you staring at me," he said. "We have up to two hundred and ten degrees of peripheral vision. Yours is much less." His speech had started out halting and slow, but with everything he said, it became smoother, like the language was getting easier for him.

"Whoa ...," Diego said, imagining the ability to see something halfway around his head.

Mobius reached up and grabbed the handle above the door, and Diego was impressed by how lean and muscular he was. Diego had seen him take down Menendez and get his gun easily, and he wondered what kind of combat training a guy from a race advanced enough to travel through deep space would go through. Then he remembered that Mobius said he'd never experienced violence before. Diego was about to ask him about it when he lost focus on the road and hit a bump that almost made him run into a tree.

"Diego, you have to concentrate," Mobius said, his voice strangely musical, like it was in surround sound. He put his hand on Diego's shoulder. Diego swallowed hard, chills running up and down his arms, as he tried not to be creeped out by the alien's four-fingered hand. It seemed that the profound sense of ease and peace he had felt around Kaia was waning.

Jillian, who hadn't said a word since they sped away, sniffled in the back seat.

"Are you crying?" Diego asked.

"I don't know why people have to kill the most beautiful things," she said. "Kaia is like an angel, and he just shot her."

Diego felt a knot forming in his throat, and tears started to burn his eyes. Kaia truly was like an angel. The love she exuded was like nothing he'd ever felt. He could feel it coming from Mobius too, just not as much as he had with Kaia.

Mobius put his hands over his face. "I can't think about that right now."

"I'm sorry," Jillian said.

Diego cleared his throat and squeezed his eyes shut for a moment to push back the tears. The alien was right. This was not the time. "Mobius, where do you need us to take you?"

"The ruins of Tikal. Do you know where it is?"

"Of course," he said. "But I have no idea where we are right now, and the GPS isn't working this deep in the jungle, so I'll have to get to a main road and figure out where we are from there."

Jillian leaned forward. "Mobius, why Tikal? Why are you here?"

Mobius looked back and forth between Diego and Jillian,

clenching and unclenching his hands. "I ... I don't know how to tell you this," he stammered.

Jillian and Diego exchanged glances, even more concerned than they already were.

Mobius closed his eyes for a moment, took in a deep breath, and started again. "About a thousand Earth years ago, someone from my planet ... a rogue space commander named Itzamna came here and—"

"Did you say *Itzamna?*" Diego interrupted. "He's a Mayan god!"

"Well, no actually, he is from my planet, but the Mayans thought he was their creator sky god. They worshipped him, and he became insane with power and ...," Mobius paused.

"And?" Diego demanded.

Mobius had a pained look on his face. "And, he planted a time capsule that would ... explode, or really *implode*, in the future."

"What do you mean *implode?*" Jillian asked, her voice tremulous.

"I mean ... it will create a black hole that will devour the Earth."

Diego and Jillian sat in silence, trying to process what they'd just heard.

"I'm so sorry," Mobius said, pressing on the mark between his eyes.

"When exactly in the future?" Diego asked.

"We don't have a precise date but, according to our calculations, very soon."

Jillian put a hand over her mouth. "Oh my God ... the Mayan prophecy is *real.*"

CHAPTER THIRTY

COMANDO CÓSMICO

D iego had already thought he was going to float out of his
body, but he really felt lightheaded after Mobius told them
about the time capsule. *The entire Earth getting sucked into a black
hole because of ancient alien contact with the Mayans? The Mayan
deity Itzamna an out of control alien?* It was like trying to wrap his
arms around the sun. He couldn't possibly hold it all.

"What prophecy are you talking about?" Mobius asked Jillian.

"The Mayan calendar ends on December 21st, 2012. They have
a prophecy that it will be the end of the world."

"In the mission log, Itzamna pointed to some kind of stone calendar when he was talking about the time capsule. December 21st
must be the date it's going to implode!" Mobius exclaimed. "But
we still don't know exactly what time."

"People say it will be at 11:11 a.m.," Jillian said.

"Okay, at least we've determined when the device will detonate.
What is the date today?"

Jillian turned to Diego. "I have no idea, do you? I've lost track
of the days."

Diego stared straight ahead, his eyes fixed on the road as if in
a trance.

Jillian shook him. "Diego, are you listening?"

"Oh ... sorry. I'm not sure what day it is," he finally responded in a monotone.

"We need to find out as soon as possible," she said, alarmed. "I do know that the 21st is really soon. Mobius, please tell me you know where the time capsule is and how to stop it."

"No. Unfortunately, I don't."

"Then why are we going to Tikal?"

"We are not certain, but we believe the time capsule is located there because Tikal's layout mirrors the Pleiades star constellation."

"That's fascinating, but what does that mean?"

"That's where Akara is located."

"Really? That's amazing!" Jillian turned to Diego. "Did you know that Tikal was laid out like the Pleiades?"

"Yeah, but I never thought much of it," Diego said, still in a fog of denial about what was happening, even though the evidence was mounting.

"We think Itzamna designed the city as a monument to his home star system," Mobius said.

They plunged down the dark road in silence for a little while, all of them trying to process the situation. Suddenly, Diego came out of his brain fog and had a million questions, but he realized Mobius was still trying to deal with the fact that his crew was gone, along with his ride home. Not to mention the fact that Kaia was dying, and the planet that he was stuck on was about to implode. At least that's what Mobius believed. Even though he could think again, Diego still couldn't bring himself to believe that it was true. He felt like he was in a strange dream.

Finally, they came to a crossroads, still dirt, but at least wider and smoother than the one they'd been driving on. Diego still had no idea where he was. He sat for a moment looking left and right, then glanced in his rearview mirror and was relieved to see they were not being followed. "If Menendez and his men haven't caught up to us yet, they're not likely to. We may be okay for now." He looked both ways again and finally turned left.

"Why did those men shoot at us?" Mobius asked.

Diego and Jillian laid it out for him—with Diego, of course, leaving out the part about being an informant for Menendez.

"I was right," Mobius said, after hearing about the drug gang. "We did descend into a war zone. What did I get myself into?" He held his head and started breathing strangely, his mouth opening and closing, with a low moaning sound coming from deep in his throat.

"What's going on?" Diego asked Jillian in the rearview mirror.

"I think he's crying," she said.

"Okay, great. Looks like everybody's gonna cry. Come on now," Diego said. "It's going to be okay."

"Really?" Mobius said. "I don't have any idea what I'm doing. I didn't know anything about Earth or the time capsule until two days ago. I didn't even make it into the space program."

"*What?*" Diego looked at him in disbelief. "And you're supposed to save us? Who the hell sent you to do this?"

Jillian put a hand firmly on Diego's shoulder and scowled at him in the mirror, but that didn't stop him.

"I thought you were some kind of highly trained, special forces *comando cósmico* or something!"

Mobius looked away but was still crying—opening and closing his mouth like a giant catfish. "Hardly. I'm an Anomaly; I'm the last person on Akara who should be here."

"What do you mean?" Jillian asked gently.

Mobius stopped crying and paused. "Just a moment. I'm scanning my language database."

"What language database?" Diego asked.

"It's on my neurolink ... Basically, I have a computer chip in my brain."

"Whoa," Jillian said. "I keep feeling like I woke up in the middle of a sci-fi movie."

"No kidding," Diego said.

"According to my language program," Mobius continued, "Anomaly is the best translation for what I am called on my planet—someone or something that falls outside the norm."

"But how do you fall outside the norm?" Jillian asked.

Mobius explained how the Akaran race had almost gone extinct during the Ravaging Era, and how after the Rebirthing, everyone but a small percentage of beings was born with a highly evolved consciousness. Anomalies, he said, were those less evolved beings.

"You might be an Anomaly on Akara," Jillian said, "but compared to most humans, from what I've seen, you're pretty damn evolved."

Mobius looked at her with his enormous eyes, warm and grateful. "Thank you, Jillian."

"Thank you for getting us out of there, Mobius. I'm so sorry about your friend Kaia. You love her very much, don't you?"

He blinked twice. "It's strange. Your language has only one word for love. On Akara, we have many—there are so many different kinds of love. But yes, I do love her very much. I love her as a mentor and with a kind of love that I only feel with some people—I love her as myself."

"That's beautiful," Jillian said.

When the road straightened out a little more, Diego glanced over at Mobius. "That's quite a shirt," he said, studying the mesh-looking material that resembled dragonfly wings and almost glowed.

Mobius looked down at the iridescent blue and white webbed fabric. "It allows for optimal ventilation, and it repels dirt and odor. The design is based on the wings of one of our insects. Many of our designs are inspired by nature."

If I can get it reverse engineered, I could make a fortune, Diego thought.

The Range Rover hit another hole in the road, and they all bounced off their seats. As the car slammed back down, Diego winced and put a hand to his head where Rafael had hit him.

"If you liked my shirt," Mobius said, "you'll really like this." He took a small disc out of the pocket on the arm of his shirt and held it over the gash on Diego's head.

Diego flinched. "What is that? What are you doing?"

"It's a cognizer. It can do many things, including helping you heal. It repairs the tissue at the molecular level. Many people where I'm from can heal themselves of a lot of injuries and illnesses with just their conscious intention. But for those who can't, the technology works almost as well."

"Brilliant!" Jillian exclaimed.

Diego looked at Mobius skeptically. "You're not giving me alien DNA, are you?"

Mobius smiled. "No. Don't worry. And I promise, no probes."

"What are probes?" Diego asked.

Jillian laughed. "He was making a joke."

"We viewed some parts of your movies about space visitors," Mobius said. "I couldn't help myself."

"I still don't understand," Diego said, looking at Jillian bewildered.

"Just relax and drive the vehicle," Mobius said, continuing to hold the cog over Diego's wound.

Diego felt heat and tingling in and around the gash above his eye and inside his head.

"So people where you're from can heal themselves?" Jillian asked, watching closely.

"Yes. It's something almost everyone on my planet can do now," Mobius said. "Many evolutionary scientists believe it was a gene that turned on to help us survive after the Ravaging. But it doesn't occur in everyone." He pulled his hand away and asked Diego how he felt.

"Better, I think," Diego said. The headache and the pain of the cut had gone away as soon as he'd started talking with Kaia, so he wasn't really sure. He looked in the mirror, and the gash did look significantly better.

As the dawn was just starting to pink the sky, they finally came to a dusty little village lined with a few rundown adobe dwellings. "Mobius, get down. We have to find out where we are and get some food and gas." Diego pulled into the one tiny gas station in town.

"We don't have any money," Jillian said.

Diego smiled and held up Manuel Menendez's wallet. "Yes, we do, and it's full of Guatemalan quetzales and American dollars."

"Thank God," she said. "In that case, let's also see if we can pick up a disposable cell phone."

Diego burst out laughing. "Are you serious? We're in the middle of the jungle, Princess, not Times Square. We'll be lucky if they even have gas."

"Oh. Right," she said sheepishly.

"Let's make this quick," Diego said, looking behind them. "Menendez and his men might still be coming."

Jillian and Diego got out of the car, but Diego looked back at Mobius. "Stay down and stay in the damn car," he said, but Jillian shoved Diego and scowled at him, so he put his hands together and bowed at Mobius, "*Please* stay in the damn car."

They walked to the door of the crumbling house next to the closed gas station as Jillian grumbled. "He's innocent and sweet. Don't treat him like he's some tough guy."

"He needs to get tough if he's going to be with us down here in the *war zone*," Diego said, then yelled out, "*¡Gas, por favor!*"

A young girl looking no more than twelve came out in bare feet, and without a word, opened the shop and turned on the gas. As it was pumping, Diego and Jillian went inside.

"*Señórita*, where are we?" Diego asked in Spanish. "Can you please give us directions to Tikal?"

"You're in *El Conacaste*," she replied without looking at him and pulled out an old, tattered map. "I don't know how to get to Tikal. You can look."

Jillian walked around to buy whatever food she could find as Diego studied the map. She grabbed three gallons of water, a few dusty bags of plantains, a bag of *chicharrones*—the pork rinds she'd seen Diego eating at Tikal—and two loaves of *Pan Bimbo* white bread.

"Can we use your telephone?" Diego asked the girl, holding out money.

Jillian heard the word *teléfono*. "No phone calls," she whispered.

"What? You just wanted to buy a cell phone a minute ago!"

"Yes, but not to call anyone."

He gave her a frustrated look. "*No comprende, princesa.*"

"I want to have one in case we need it."

"We *do* need it. We have to let your family know you're okay and make sure they're not paying off Menendez."

"No, it will cause a huge mess," she said. "They'll insist we come in, and then what do we do about Mobius? I believe that this time capsule is about to blow, and we have to help him. Can you imagine what would happen if the government were to find out about him? Do you think they'll just believe him, or do you think they'll treat him like an alien invader and lock him up first, especially with his story about the end of the world? Those muggles would completely rip him apart."

"Muggles?" he asked.

"You know, from Harry Potter. The people without magic. I use it to mean people who are ..."

Diego raised his eyebrows and nodded. "I get it. They are definitely muggles. Then we should just let our families know we're okay and tell them not to tell anyone."

"I guarantee you the cops have all the phones tapped. Look, Diego, if Mobius is right and there is about to be an apocalypse, that will be a lot worse than waiting a few days to call them, don't you think?"

"How can we trust that he's telling the truth?" Diego asked, looking back at the car. "What if they came here for another reason?"

Jillian just stared at him, her arms crossed. "You think it's just a coincidence with the whole Mayan prophecy thing? Plus, I know you felt their energy, Diego. I saw your reaction to Kaia."

"I feel it less with him."

"I know. Me too, but it's still there. Come on, from what you've seen, you really think he's hiding some evil intention?"

"Well, if it were a movie, he'd for sure be hiding some evil intention."

197

She rolled her eyes. "They're not like that. It's not a movie. That's why Mobius joked about the probes, which by the way, means shoving things inside every hole in your body to do experiments."

"Oh, *sondeo*! *Sondeo* is the word for probe." He laughed, finally understanding what Mobius had been saying. "Alien joke."

"I know, right?" Jillian said. "They knew that's how people would see them, and they came anyway. To save us. And by the way, your wound is totally healed."

He touched it and was shocked that the cut was gone. "*Dios mío*, this just keeps getting weirder by the minute."

They walked toward the car, and he looked down the road to make sure the *criminales* weren't coming, then stopped Jillian and turned her to face him. "If we have to be going through this, I'm glad we're in it together."

"Me too," she said, smiling, and when he kissed her, she held the sides of his face.

"Um, excuse me, Earth people," Mobius called out from the car. "That's really nice but get in the *damn car please.*"

Diego and Jillian turned and looked at him—all they could see were his huge, two-toned eyes over the bottom of the window frame. Jillian laughed. "His accent sounds kind of Russian, don't you think?"

"Mmmm, I thought Scottish at first, but sometimes he sounds kind of Jamaican."

Jillian smiled. "I know. It seems to change."

As Diego got behind the wheel, Mobius whispered to him, "It is exalted that she will put her mouth on yours with all that hair on your face."

Diego laughed. "That's one way to put it, I guess. With her, even if I didn't have hair on my face, I'd be lucky to get kissed."

"Yes, you are lucky," Jillian said as she climbed into the back seat. "Since, we're on the topic ... Mobius, I've been wondering. I know that Akarans kiss because I saw you and Nava on the ship, but do you ... I mean ... you know ...?"

Diego raised his eyebrows and looked sideways at Mobius. This he had to hear.

Mobius just looked at Jillian blankly.

Diego cleared his throat. "I think what she's trying to ask is, do you have ... sexual relations ... like with ... members of the opposite sex?"

"Actually yes, but it's not necessarily with the opposite sex."

"On Earth, it's not necessarily with members of the opposite sex either, Diego," Jillian said, slapping him on the arm.

"Of course. Sorry," Diego said. "I was struggling to explain it. I didn't mean to assume you're straight."

Mobius paused then laughed. "Oh, you mean heterosexual. We don't define everything the way humans do. If I had to use a word, I guess you could say we are ... I don't know. Maybe transsexual?"

Jillian and Diego chuckled. "Um, I'm pretty sure that's not the word you're looking for," she said.

Mobius paused for a moment. "Oh, no. No it's not. Maybe omnisexual? But again, we don't use these labels. You love who you love—it could be anyone."

"Cool," Diego replied, starting the car.

"I love that," Jillian said.

As Diego began to pull away, Mobius asked, "When do we arrive at Tikal?"

"I'm guessing in about two hours, based on the map. But it's filled with tourists ... there's no way you can walk through there looking like that," Diego said, eyeing the strange alien up and down then he suddenly hit the brakes. *"Mierda*, I forgot." He rolled down the window and called out to the girl, who was walking back to her house. "*¿Señorita, qué día es?*"

"Diecinueve de diciembre," the girl yelled back.

"December nineteenth," Diego translated then looked back at Jillian, whose eyes were filled with fear.

"Holy shit," she said. "We only have two days."

CHAPTER THIRTY-ONE

ACCIDENTAL TOURISTS

A few hours later, Mobius sat in the front seat incognito, wearing a huge pair of dark, wraparound sunglasses (which covered not only his eyes, but also the azure mark between them), a baseball cap, white T-shirt, and too-short nylon athletic pants, all with *Parque Nacional Tikal* and Mayan symbols on them. The gear was from a roadside fruit stand and tourist shop they had passed on the way to the ruins. Jillian and Diego had gone into the bathroom and brushed their teeth and washed up with paper towels as best they could. Jillian even washed her hair. Then they changed into tourist wear too. Paranoid about being tracked by Menendez's men, Diego had carefully wrapped his filthy fatigues in Jillian's old clothes before throwing them in the roadside trashcan.

As they drove, Mobius squeezed myomeal into his mouth from a thin, clear pouch. After he was finished, he put the empty pouch in his hand and made a fist. When he opened it, the baggie was gone, and just a little moisture wetted his palm.

"That's incredible!" Jillian said. "Where did it go?"

"The material breaks down into water vapor and carbon dioxide when it's under pressure and heat, but only if there's nothing inside. The food keeps its molecular structure from breaking down."

"So no trash?" she said. "Isn't that amazing, Diego?"

"*Yes*, it is," Diego said. He stared intently at Mobius's hand. *Forget about the shirt*, he thought. *I can make billions on those bags.* He couldn't even imagine what would happen if he could get ahold of the cog. Presuming they survived this supposed Armageddon, the bag's technology alone would make him the richest man on Earth. Besides, he rationalized, it would help save the environment. His mind raced with possibilities—maybe he could even be with Jillian if he became rich, especially if he launched a revolutionary eco-product. He had no doubt that she, not to mention her family and friends, would never have anything to do with a poor Guatemalan jungle ranger under normal circumstances. *But*, he thought, *if I were the next Steve Jobs ...*

"You seem to be doing better," Jillian said to Mobius as she ate some plantains.

"I am," he said. "But I keep wondering if Kaia and the others got home. The ship was damaged."

"Kaia was your leader?" Jillian said.

"Yes. She is a pilot from the Discovery Corps, our space program."

"What would she be doing right now if she were here?"

He breathed deeply. "She'd be figuring out how to get to the top of the temple in Tikal where the time capsule is hidden and get inside without being seen."

"There are at least a dozen temples at Tikal, and all of them except for Temple IV are off limits to climbing," Diego said. "I've been to the top of IV. There's nothing up there, no opening or doorway; I know that much."

Mobius fingered his bracelet nervously. "Hopefully, I will recognize Itzamna's temple when I see it. From the pictures Piphus found, we all thought that Temple I looked like the closest match, but it's hard to tell because it's so much older now."

Jillian looked at the bracelet as it changed colors. "That's so beautiful," she said, pointing to the inscription. "What does it say?"

He paused for a moment. "'Make the Leap.' It's part of the Discovery Corps motto, 'From data to information to knowledge to Wisdom—Make the Leap.'"

"What does it mean?" she asked.

"It has two meanings. The first one is making the leap from using only the logical mind, to a deeper intuitive knowing that accesses the Wisdom. We say, 'make the leap' to each other as a reminder to stay connected to the Wisdom."

"What do you mean by 'the Wisdom'?" Diego asked.

Mobius thought for a moment. "Well ... that's the best word we could find in your language. There's no direct translation. It's really more like heart-wisdom. It's the infinite love and intelligence of the universe."

"You can connect to that?" Diego asked.

"Well, not as much as everyone else on Akara since I'm an Anomaly. But I can, yes. Actually, all self-aware, sentient beings have the potential to connect to it because it's the essence of who we are. It's just that people are able to connect to it to different degrees based on their level of evolution."

"Gorgeous. I love it!" Jillian said.

"That's deep," Diego said, but then thought, *Too damn deep for me*, as Mobius kept talking.

"The other meaning is about our interstellar travel. We jump in and out of space-time. When we do, it's called 'making the leap.'"

"Really?" Diego said, suddenly a lot more interested. "Does that mean you can travel faster than the speed of light?"

"Of course," Mobius chuckled. "Otherwise it would have taken us hundreds of years to get here."

They sat in silence for a moment before Diego said, "Then Einstein was wrong."

"Oh, Einstein. We learned about him on your Internet. I like that guy. He was pretty evolved. What was he wrong about?"

Diego looked at Mobius. "His theory of relativity said that nothing can travel faster than the speed of light."

"Well, that's true. *If* you add *'through* space-time' to that. You can't go faster than light-speed in dimensional travel. But we leap in and out of it, so we're operating at the quantum level where the laws of macrophysics don't apply."

"*No me digas,*" Diego exclaimed. "You're kidding me. How do you do that?"

"Diego, pay attention!" Jillian said, as they blew past the entrance to Tikal.

He spun around and drove through the arched gateway to Tikal, joining the tour buses and rental cars in the parking lot. When they got out of the car, Diego and Jillian looked Mobius over. At first glance, with the sunglasses on, he looked like any other tourist, except for his high-tech, bright green neoprene-like shoes and color-changing bracelet—two more materials Diego needed to get his hands on. He hoped people would assume the shoes were just the latest thing from Nike, and not examine them too closely. The best thing they all had going for them was that Mobius had goldish brown skin, which looked closer to Polynesian or Indian, but could pass for Latino. Piphus and Kaia would have never been able to walk through a dark bar at midnight, let alone Tikal in the middle of the day.

"You're going to have to keep your hands in your pockets and keep the hat and sunglasses on at all times," Jillian said.

"But you'd better take off that bracelet."

Mobius grasped the talisman. "No, I'm not taking it off. No one will see it." He thrust his hands in his pockets, and the bracelet was no longer visible. "See, it's fine."

As they walked toward the ruins, Mobius towered over Diego and Jillian.

"*Madre mía*, try to look shorter somehow," Diego reprimanded Mobius.

"You're at least six foot five," Jillian added, "and you stand out."

Mobius threw his hands in the air in frustration.

"No!" Jillian said, and a few Guatemalan men holding signs offering guided tours stared at him as he stuffed his hands back in his pants pockets.

One of the men walked straight up to Mobius and held out a flier, "Hey, big man," he said with a heavy accent. "We give you the best tour, very cheap." Mobius froze in response to being addressed and just stared down at him, without saying a word.

Diego snatched the flier out of the man's hand. "*No, gracias,*" he said, pulling Mobius along by his elbow.

"The little human just talked to me like I'm from L'Azman," Mobius said. "How amazing!"

Diego sighed. "You can't stop for these people. Like I said, you're going to get a lot of attention because Guatemalans aren't used to seeing anyone as tall as you. They look at you like you're an alien."

Jillian and Mobius both groaned, and Diego was struck once

again by how human Mobius seemed—his mannerisms and humor and emotions.

Mobius bent his knees and kept walking, trying to be shorter. "Okay, no. That's worse," Jillian said. "You look like a chicken."

The ruins were hemmed in by jungle, which Mobius kept gazing at in wonder. But when they emerged into the central plaza with its carpet of bright green grass, ancient cathedral-like pyramids, and people milling about everywhere, he halted abruptly and made a sound that seemed like a cross between a gasp and a sob. "It is so exalted! And humans are so exotic looking," he said, capturing several images surreptitiously on his cog. "How can they see with those tiny eyes? So many different body sizes and shapes, and so small. This is ... this is," Mobius stuttered, his eyes darting left and right as he searched for the right word, "breathtaking."

Jillian took his arm and smiled proudly. "It really is, isn't it?"

"I can't believe I'm actually here. L'Azman really is a *'precious jewel,'*" he said, then started fish blowing again.

"*Ay,* stop crying!" Diego said. "You look ridiculous."

Mobius looked down at him. "I wonder how you'd react if I dropped you on my planet in the middle of exotic ruins with aliens everywhere?"

Diego thought about it for a moment. "Good point. I might actually cry."

Mobius shifted his focus to the business at hand and studied a towering stepped pyramid hulking on the edge of the central plaza. "That temple looks very familiar. Is that Temple I?"

"Yes," Diego said. "That's it."

At the bottom of the temple steps, a man stood holding a sign written in English on one side and Spanish on the other: "DECEMBER 21ST IS THE END OF THE WORLD. MAKE YOUR

PEACE WITH GOD TODAY."

When Diego read it, he felt something begin to quake inside of him, like the blood was draining out of his body. Until that moment, he hadn't fully believed what Mobius had told them about the time capsule, and he had never believed the Mayan prophecy business for a moment, but looking at the dark message, it crashed in on him, and somewhere deep inside he knew it was true.

He looked up at Temple I, and suddenly, he had a vision. A great chasm opened up from within the pyramid, like a giant gaping mouth that screamed out the piercing, incomprehensible sound of the fabric of space time ripping apart. The mouth then seemed to inhale, sucking into itself all the people and buildings and land he could see. All of life, all the Earth imploded, ingested by the void as it rushed into the apocalyptic sink hole and vanished forever.

The vision was so real that he felt like his guts were coming up.

"Are you okay?" Jillian asked, her hand on his back.

Diego bent over, his mouth watering with the taste of bile on his tongue as images of carnage and decimation barraged him. Under his arm he saw a little Latino boy wearing a superhero cape racing around the stelae and laughing. Normally, Diego wouldn't even have noticed him, but looking at the child in that moment, he was overcome with love for this little boy he didn't even know. And somehow, impossibly, he had a chance to protect him, to protect everyone.

"Yeah, I'm okay," he said, standing upright and wiping his mouth with the back of his arm. "I will be."

"I want you both to know that I am so sorry for this," Mobius said.

"Thank you," Jillian said. "It's not your fault. But thank you anyway."

"Okay," Diego said. "*Vámonos*. We've got a disaster about to happen."

.

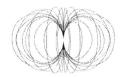

CHAPTER THIRTY-TWO

TEMPLE I

M obius stood at the foot of Temple I, looking up. "How can I get to the top?"

"We have to wait until dark," Diego said. "There are security guards everywhere, and even more than usual right now."

"Oh yes, I didn't consider that. We don't have security or law enforcement on Akara."

"Wow, I can't even imagine," Jillian said, then looked at Diego. "Wouldn't that be amazing?"

"I'd be out of a job, that's for sure," Diego said.

As Mobius walked around the grounds and inspected the temple, he noticed the ease of his breathing and realized he'd adjusted to Earth's atmosphere. People stared at him despite all Diego and Jillian had done to camouflage his appearance. Fear wormed its way through him as images of a terrified and violent mob attacking him kept pushing their way into his consciousness. He reminded himself what he'd been taught—that for survival, the mind was designed to fear the unknown. He realized that the fear itself was more of a threat than the possibility of a crazed mob; if he let it run wild, it could paralyze him or cause him to do something stupid. He knew he had to focus on connecting to the

Wisdom, or he'd lose the only thing that he had going for him on this alien planet.

When Mobius stopped and looked up at the top of the temple again, studying it intently, Jillian asked, "What are you doing?"

"Scanning the top of the pyramid to see if I recognize any of the carvings from the mission logs."

"You can see that far?" she asked. "That thing is over fifteen stories high."

For a moment, Mobius imagined how fun it would be, under different circumstances, to try to free climb up the side of it without using the staircase. "Yes. Actually, I can see even farther than that."

"Can you see *through* things?" Diego asked.

"Of course not," Mobius replied.

"Oh, right. *Of course not*," Diego repeated, throwing up his hands. "How am I supposed to know?"

Just then, the little boy Diego had seen earlier ran by in a black cape and facemask, wielding a red lightsaber and yelling, "It's the end of the world! It's the end of the world!" Mobius watched quizzically, and Diego chuckled, seeing that the boy wasn't dressed as a superhero; he was dressed as Darth Vader.

"I know him!" Mobius said, quickly capturing an image on his cog, then putting his hand back in his pocket.

"What?" Diego said. "*Itzamna* was one thing, but I refuse to believe you know Darth Vader."

"You know that's not actually *him*," Jillian said. "Just a kid dressed like him."

"Yes. Sure," Mobius said, but in truth, he was so far beyond his familiar world, he wasn't sure of anything. "He was in one of my favorite Earth movies."

"The street vendors sell merchandise from *Star Wars*. A scene from the first movie was filmed here," Diego said.

"That's exalted!" Mobius exclaimed.

Jillian smiled at Diego. "That is, um, exalted I guess."

Diego laughed. "He seems to love that word, although he has no idea how to use it."

They turned to another side of the four-sided temple and were confronted with a carved image on a stela. Mobius stopped cold. "For the way of peace, it's Itzamna," he said quietly.

"Yes, creepy looking," Diego said. "Is that what he really looked like?"

"According to the stories, yes, pretty close." Trying to control his nerves, Mobius studied the carving. While this was not the round carving K'awiil had given Itzamna in the mission log, it was an encouraging sign to see Itzamna's image here, in whatever form. "The Mayans treated Itzamna like a god because of the advanced technology, but he was just a self-obsessed tyrant. The people on Akara weren't evolved enough back then to use that level of technology responsibly. Him least of all."

They walked under a tree to get out of the sun. "So when can we try to get to the top of the temple?" Jillian asked.

"Not until very late tonight," Diego said. "They're having ceremonies every night right now because of the end of the calendar, so it will have to be around three in the morning, when everyone has finally gone to bed."

"Did you see anything else that convinced you this is the right place?" Jillian asked Mobius.

"It looks similar, but I can't tell for sure," he said. "I wish I had uploaded the mission log to my cog or neurolink, but I never thought I'd be here alone."

Diego sighed. "Hey you guys, I've got to get something to eat. I'm starving to death."

Mobius looked at him, alarmed. "What? Oh, no! Here, eat this," he said, handing him a packet of myomeal from his pants pocket.

Diego looked at him, annoyed, and Jillian laughed. "He's not literally dying from lack of food. It's just an expression. He means he's hungry."

Mobius sighed with relief and mumbled, "Oh. I'm hungry too."

"Let's go get something to eat at one of the restaurants up front, then rest until we can get to the top of the temple," Diego said.

In the waning light of evening, they walked back toward the entrance, through an open area with campsites huddled closely together and visitors' tents set up on the grass. Numerous pointy-faced animals with striped tails, which Mobius learned were called "coatimundi," and large birds with iridescent colorful feathers named "turkeys" walked around like they owned the place. A busy group of the animals with brown fur and long tails that he'd seen on the mission log made their way through the trees nearby.

"Itzamna always had one of those with him. What are they called?" Mobius asked in awe at the diversity of wildlife, as he captured several images on his cog. He wished all Akarans could see this—what it must have been like before the great extinctions.

"Spider monkeys," Diego said. "We call them *bandidos* because they're little bandits and love to cause trouble."

At the restaurant, Jillian went in and got some *tamales*, grilled plantains, and bottles of water, and they sat near the tents under a tree. Diego was lying low, like Mobius, because he didn't want to see anyone he knew. Mobius ate some myomeal, but it was not satisfying, as usual, so he convinced Diego, Jillian, and himself that he could eat Earth food—he figured, *why not?* He could breathe

Earth's air, after all. He bit into the *tamale*, and it tasted like nothing he'd ever eaten before. Then he got to the reddish-brown stuff inside and asked, "What is this? It's making my mouth feel strange."

"It's chorizo," Diego said. "Spicy pork."

Mobius checked his thologram and exclaimed, "Oh no ... For the way of peace, it has a face!"

•

The next thing Mobius knew, someone was shaking him and yelling, "Mobius! Wake up!" He felt like he was in a dark void that weighed on him so heavily, he couldn't bring himself out of it, until the shock of ice water hit his face, and he sputtered to the surface. He groaned in frustration, certain that his brother was taunting him.

"Mobius! Wake up," Diego yelled again, even louder.

Mobius took off the sunglasses covering his eyes and looked around.

"Thank God. I was starting to panic."

"Heavens to Betsy, I'm on Earth!" Mobius exclaimed.

Diego put a hand to his forehead and closed his eyes. "Where did you hear that expression?" Before Mobius could answer, Diego said, "Never mind, yes, you're on Earth and you passed out for almost two hours. It must have been something in the *tamales*."

"Oh ... I remember now. You fed me an animal!"

"I guess that means you don't eat animals on Akara?"

"That's disgusting. No. Not since the Ravaging."

"Well then, if I ever get to go to Akara, remind me to pack a cooler."

"What?"

"Nothing. We'll make sure to get you something vegetarian

next time," Diego said, cleaning off Mobius's sunglasses. As he handed them back, he exclaimed, "Whoa! Your eyes are almost entirely orange now."

"Yes, they change to adjust to light, so I can see in the dark," Mobius said, looking up at the stars as the details of all that had happened came back to him.

"Cool, like built in night vision goggles," Diego said to himself.

"What time is it?" Mobius asked, sitting up.

"It's nine o'clock."

"Can we climb the temple yet?"

Diego took the sunglasses out of Mobius's hand and put them back on his face. "No, it's not late enough yet. They're still having those damn ceremonies."

Mobius heard drumming in the distance and the sound of a large crowd. He pushed the glasses down on his nose and peered at Diego. "Something is wrong," he said. "Did you sleep?"

"A little," Diego said, but he was visibly agitated, sighing and running his hands through his hair.

"What's wrong? Where's Jillian?"

"I don't know," he groaned.

"What do you mean?" Mobius asked, starting to feel anxious himself.

"I was sleeping, and when I woke up, she was gone. It's been freaking me out. I didn't know what to do ... I couldn't just leave a giant alien lying around half dead to go find her."

Mobius looked around, trying to shake off the grogginess; the food had been like a tranquilizer, but thankfully a short-lasting one. By the light of campfires and torches and his exceptional vision, he saw Jillian in the distance. "There she is. She's coming this way."

"Where?" Diego asked, scanning the area in the direction Mobius was looking. "I can't see her."

Moments later, Jillian came weaving her way toward them. "Hey! Hezawake," she slurred. "I thought you might be dead!" She laughed like she'd said something hilarious, then fell to her knees next to Diego and pulled him into a kiss. "You are so hot, you know that? Since I met you, I've been kidnapped, been on a spaceship, and hung out with an alien! That's what I'd call a killer first date!"

Diego pulled back from her. "*Dios Mío*, Jillian, keep it down. We're trying not to be noticed."

Mobius looked at Diego, confused. "What's wrong with her?"

"She's drunk out of her ass!"

Jillian cracked up. "*Off*, Diego. *Off* my ass. And I'm not drunk. Jusa li'l tipsy. I did a few rum shots with my new frenz," she said too loudly, gesturing toward the crowd. "They're American, like me!"

After Mobius realized what "drunk" meant, he was surprised at first, but then he thought about it. "I guess that is one possible response to our situation."

Diego fell back on the grass and put his hands to his head. "Jillian, we've got a bomb to deal with and you're off getting wasted. I thought you gave all that up after you went to rehab."

"It was all just too much. I needed to numb out," she said, looking at him soberly for a moment, but then shifted back into party mode and yelled, "Iz the end of the world! May'zwell have a good time." She struggled to her feet again and stumbled off, calling back to Diego and Mobius, "Come on, you guys, you're missing the show. It's exalted!"

"That is *not* how you use that word!" Diego yelled as he and

215

Mobius scrambled to their feet and hurried after her.

As they approached the central plaza, Mobius saw the spectacular light show that was playing on the stepped pyramidal surface of Temple I—patterns of palm leaves moving and morphing into stars and Mayan symbols—as drums beat a rhythm to the dancing lights. Just as they joined the crowd, the drumming stopped and the lights faded out, and a spotlight shined on a wall that stood near the temple. The wall bore an image of the round Mayan calendar that foretold when it all came to an end. Above the image hung a ring like the one used in the ballgame from Itzamna's mission log.

A tiny plump brown woman, round-faced with big dimples and dressed in a ceremonial skirt and blouse, stepped onto a small stage in front of the wall. For some reason, Mobius was drawn to her, and the pull was so strong that he began to move closer.

"Where are you going?" Diego asked, following him.

"Come on," Mobius said, pulling Jillian along with them.

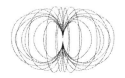

CHAPTER THIRTY-THREE

SHAMAN

Mobius skirted around the edge of the crowd so that they were now looking at the woman from the side.

"I am Ix Chel Inka Mazte, named after the Mayan moon goddess Ix Chel, and I am known as Inka," she announced into the microphone in a lovely, lyrical accent. "I am a shaman from a lineage that dates back to the ancients, and I am proud to welcome you to our homeland!"

The crowd erupted in applause, and her face lit up in a huge smile. She pointed to the round, intricately drawn calendar, with a mask-like face in the middle surrounded by concentric circles of glyphs. "You all have heard the prophecy that in a few days, December 21st, 2012, which is the end of our 13th baktun, will bring the end of the world at 11:11 a.m. on the winter solstice. A baktun is 144,000 days or almost 400 years. Thirteen baktuns—which is over 5,100 years—comprise an Age or Great Cycle of time. The end of the world coming at the close of this Great Cycle is a prophecy of darkness. It is *one* of the prophecies written in the etchings. But it is not the only one. What most of the world does not know is that there is also a prophecy of light. An alternate prediction that says the end of the calendar does not represent the end of humanity, but an end to the dark times, and the beginning of a significant shift or evolution in human consciousness."

The raucous crowd applauded and cheered, and Mobius had a sense that Jillian was not the only one who was drunk.

"I love her," Jillian gushed, standing on her tiptoes and hanging on Diego's arm to see over the people.

"Me too," Mobius said.

"Don't you think we should make a plan, Mobius?" Diego asked.

"This is the plan for now." He kept his eyes glued to the little woman, whose energy he could feel from where he stood. "She is so wise and loving."

Suddenly, the shaman noticed him and smiled, and he wondered if it was because he was so tall, because he wore sunglasses at night, or because she could feel his energy too. Then she turned and moved to a nearby stela. "This is the symbol for the 13th baktun," she announced, mesmerizing the crowd as she pointed to a tower of eight glyphs that looked like strange masks, animals, and other images arranged in two stacks of four. Crowning the columns of glyphs was a larger etching that looked like it bore wings.

Mobius looked down at his T-shirt. It had the same symbol she was pointing at, with "13th baktun" written next to it.

"These symbols," Inka continued, pointing to another set of glyphs, "spell out the prophecy of light. It says, 'Malevolence and secrecy will then be consumed upon fiercely burning altars. And the fire quenched will bear thick smoke. And the smoke will cleanse the old vision. The dawn will pour out a new vision. The dawn will open the Flower of Life.' This is the promise of a new time. A sacred time. If the prophecy of light is true, this will be an important moment in our evolution; a time of transformation on the planet, in which we all must decide if we are going to stay with the old, dying way built on greed and selfishness, or if we are going to live the new way of cooperation and peace."

"She understands the symbols," Mobius whispered. "And she has access to the Wisdom."

"Very few people, even among the shamans, understand the glyphs," Diego said, obviously impressed. "But the prophecy of light is clearly wrong."

"Let's hope not," Mobius said. "I have to talk to her."

"No, you do not," Diego said emphatically as Jillian clapped and cooed, "Yes, yes, yes, yes, yes. Let's talk to her."

Inka Mazte continued, her voice bigger than she was. "But the prophecy of darkness is clear. It says that at the end of baktun 13, a god will descend from the sky and bring with him the end of the world. We don't know if this is pointing to some kind of apocalyptic event, or what it means."

Mobius, Jillian, and Diego looked at each other, astonished. "I'd never heard about a god descending from the sky," Diego said.

"That's you!" Jillian slurred loudly to Mobius, then covered her mouth and whispered, "That's you. You descended from the sky."

"No," Mobius said. "The prophecy is talking about Itzamna returning."

"Are you sure about that?" Diego asked.

Inka went on, "We must stop and say a prayer together that the prophecy of darkness does not come to pass." She bowed her head, and everyone got quiet for a few moments. Then she looked up and said, "Remember that you are here in this place, at this time, for a reason. If, God willing, we survive, you must go back home and take the prophecy of light with you and spread it all over the Earth." She extended her arms wide. "Call out where you are from if you have traveled here to be with us."

Different voices and accents yelled out places from around the world—France, Norway, the United States, South Africa, Canada, Brazil—until it seemed like the whole world was represented. The crowd cheered with each name, but no one louder than Jillian who yelled out, "Outer space!" and everyone laughed and cheered.

"Shh!" Diego scolded her.

"But he did," she said loudly, then fell onto Mobius, looking up at him. "Yur so cool in those glasses ... You look jus like a really tall, bald Bruno Mars."

"Who?" Mobius asked. "Isn't Mars a planet in your solar system?"

"Never mind," Diego said. "We have to get her out of here."

"Not yet," Mobius said, keeping his eyes fixed on Inka Mazte. "Please keep her quiet."

"Thank you again for coming," Inka yelled. "Now let's play ball!"

The drumming, performed by bare-chested men in Mayan clothing, started again as several other men removed the stage. Four warriors with painted faces wearing long loincloths, skirts, and Mayan jewelry came out from behind the wall and began to play a far less violent version of the game that Mobius had seen in the mission log. As he watched the men try to hit the ball through the ring at the top of the wall without using their hands, he simultaneously tracked Inka with his peripheral vision.

She joined the crowd to watch the game, and Mobius maneuvered through people until he was standing next to her, with Diego and Jillian hovering just behind him. "It's a good thing the loser won't have his heart pulled out of his body," he said to Inka.

She looked up at him, and he did his best to shrink down to be closer to her. *She's so cute*, he thought. She seemed to be half his size.

"My ancestors took their sport a little too seriously," she said, smiling politely. "But every culture has a history of brutality."

"I agree with you. My planet most of all," he said, deciding to take a risk. "You should have seen the expression on Itzamna's face when King K'awiil's team won the ball game on the holy day that this temple was dedicated."

She looked up at him again, this time confusion and concern playing on her face. "What are you talking about, *señor?*"

"Mobius, what are you doing?" Diego pushed his face between Mobius and Inka.

"I need to talk to you," Mobius said to Inka, then leaned over and whispered, "Please come with me. It's very important."

From her expression, he could see that she was beginning to think he was dangerous. He was sure the sunglasses didn't help. "No. I am busy here," she said, then began to move away.

"Wait," he said. "Please." When she looked back, he leaned over, took his hand from his pocket, and pulled the sunglasses down to the tip of his nose. When she saw his two-toned blue and orange eyes and four-fingered hand, she gasped and clutched her heart.

"Mobius, what the hell?" Diego said as Mobius pushed the sunglasses back up and hid his hand again.

"He's a space alien," Jillian whispered drunkenly in Inka's ear, and the poor woman looked around frantically like she was about to run or pass out.

"No, don't go, please," Mobius said. "Itzamna was from my planet. You must know your ancestors encountered *extraterrestres.*"

She stared at him, open-mouthed, barely breathing, until a young man moved through the crowd to stand next to her. "*¿Mama, estás bien?* Are you okay?"

Inka looked at him, then back at Mobius. Suddenly, Mobius could feel his heart bashing against his chest and the presence of the crowd on every side of him. *What will they do if she tells them I'm an alien?*

"I promise, I am not here to hurt you," Mobius whispered. "What I have to say is very important—it's about the prophecy. I desperately need your help."

Inka looked at him and then at her son. As she opened her mouth to speak, Mobius held his breath, knowing that whatever came next would not only decide his fate, but possibly also the fate of the Earth.

CHAPTER THIRTY-FOUR

THE KINGDOM OF THE SNAKE

"*Si, mijo*. I'm okay," Inka said, placing a hand on her son's arm. "I'm going to talk to this man for a few minutes. I'll see you back at the campsite."

Relieved at her response, Mobius led Inka away from the crowd, and Diego and Jillian followed. As he told the shaman about the time capsule, she leaned against a tree to keep from crumbling to the ground. "This isn't possible," she said in Spanish, nearly hyperventilating

Mobius walked away from the shaman, and Diego figured it was to give her space to try to compose herself; he could tell Mobius felt bad about pulling her into this mess.

"Here, have a shot of this. It will help you get ahold of yourself," Diego said, handing Inka a flask of rum that Jillian's new friends had given her.

"No," she said. "The liquor creates dull energy."

"What kind of energy does an emotional meltdown create?" he asked and shot back some rum himself.

He thought she was angry with him for a moment, but then she said, "You're right. I need to get control of my emotions. My grandfather would be disappointed in me." She stood up straight and looked at Mobius, who paced nearby, glancing her way every few seconds. "My grandfather was a great shaman and taught me everything I know. He believed our ancestors were contacted by extraterrestrials. It is the only one of his teachings I didn't accept, but now it seems he was right about that too." She wiped her forehead with her sleeve and walked to Mobius, pulling on his arm until he removed his hand from his pocket. She grasped it in both of hers, and Diego could see that she was still trembling. "The prophecy says that a god will descend from the sky and destroy the Earth, but you do not seem like this evil power."

"No, the prophecy is about the return of Itzamna, my ancestor, but he is not coming back, I assure you. His legacy of destruction is about to erupt, however. So, the prophecy is true in its way."

Inka nodded. "So then you are here to save us from this evil? Your spirit is so clear and strong. I feel the energy of great love in you. Are all of your people this way?"

"Yes, they are now. Much more than I am actually," he said. "I'm not as evolved as most people on my planet. I'm an Anomaly."

She looked at Diego quizzically. *"¿Anomalía?"*

Diego nodded.

Inka's eyebrows raised in surprise. "It is difficult for me to believe this."

"It's true," Mobius said.

Despite his claim, she looked at the alien with reverence. "Mobius, you are an Anomaly on our planet too, but because you are *more* evolved than most people, not less."

"Maybe, but I hope humanity will have the chance to wake up like we did on Akara. We weren't always this evolved, as you can see from what Itzamna did."

"How did your people come out of the time of ignorance when

Itzamna lived?" she asked.

He smiled sadly. "Great, great suffering. We almost caused our own extinction."

"Do you think we have to go through this kind of suffering in order to change?"

"I don't know. Maybe it can be different for Earth."

"I pray so," Inka replied, then kissed his hand as if she were kissing a saint. "How can I help stop this time capsule from opening?"

When Mobius told her that the capsule was buried with King K'awiil under Temple I and that he needed to get to the top of the pyramid to find the access to the tomb, she shook her head. "Temple I is a funereal temple, yes, and K'awiil's tomb was found when Tikal was excavated in the 1960s. But there is no way to get to it from the top, only from tunnels dug underneath."

"It's probably a secret passageway that they didn't discover. I need to find it," Mobius said.

"Even so, my grandfather was with the archaeologists from the United States when they entered it. There were remains of the king and much artwork, carvings, and jewelry, but nothing else. It was emptied out at that time, and the tunnels were sealed."

"It must be hidden somewhere. We believe the time capsule may be quite small," Mobius said. "It doesn't need much reactive material to make it work, and it requires a lot of pressure from a condensed space. What if they just didn't find it?"

"Tikal was excavated inch by inch for fifteen years," she said. "It is very unlikely, but I suppose it is possible."

Mobius turned away in thought, paced to a nearby tree, circled it, and returned. "I admit it doesn't sound good, but we have to go up anyway. I have no other ideas."

"Then I will go with you and help in any way I can," Inka said.

"First, I must go to my campsite to get water, food, blankets, and flashlights."

"What will you tell your family?" Diego asked. "No one else can know about this."

"I will tell them I am helping an archaeology professor decipher some glyphs. They will suspect nothing. I consult with academics often."

"At this hour of the night?" Diego asked.

"Very little that I do seems strange to them at this point." She smiled and started to walk away. "Follow me; I will show you a place to wait where you will not be seen."

•

Mobius shook Diego awake. "We must go to the top of the temple soon."

Diego sat up and saw that Jillian was still out. Inka, who had returned while they were asleep, was rubbing her eyes and yawning as she rose from the blanket she'd been lying on.

"What time is it?" Diego asked.

"Almost three o'clock in the morning," Inka said, turning on a small electric lantern. When she saw Mobius lit by the warm glow of light, without his sunglasses on, she gazed at him in wonder.

As Mobius gazed back at her, he reached out and touched the medallion that hung around her neck. "What is this? It's beautiful."

"*Sí, así es.* Yes, it is. It's *Madre Mia*—Mother Mary, the Virgin of Guadalupe." She smiled and told him the story of Jesus and his mother. "This is an image of her that appeared to a peasant named Juan Diego a long time ago in Guadalupe, Mexico."

"She is beloved in this part of the world," Diego said. "You ought to see the celebrations for her."

"May I capture her image?" he asked.

Inka pulled a notebook from her hand-woven bag. The cover depicted a larger image of the Virgin. "This one will be better," she said, and he took his cog out of his pants pocket.

The device was so thin it was almost invisible when Diego looked at it sideways. The entire thing glowed faintly and looked like it was made of a material similar to the disappearing bag. Diego hadn't gotten a good look at it when Mobius had used it to heal the gash on his head, but now his eyes grew wide, as Mobius held it over the image of Mary for a moment. *What else can that thing do?* He wanted to know, but he would make himself wait. The first order of business was to find out if they would live or die.

Mobius pocketed the cog and stood up. "Okay, I can't stay here any longer," he said in Spanish. "*Vámonos.*"

"You speak Spanish?" Diego asked.

"*Sí. Hablo español muy bien,*" Mobius replied, then rattled off a few more sentences in Spanish, his accent even funnier than in English, while Diego stared at him with his mouth hanging open.

Mobius looked down at Diego and smiled mischievously. "Pretty good, eh?" he continued in Spanish. "I bet I can kick your alien ass in *fútbol* too."

Diego laughed and wagged his finger. "Oh no, no, no. That would not happen. Earth owns *fútbol, cabrón.* Even though I have to admit you were like a puma chasing Menendez across that field."

Inka looked at Diego. "Does he sound a little Israeli to you? I know an Israeli archaeologist, and he sounds a little bit like him."

"Jillian and I have had an ongoing debate about what his accent sounds like," Diego said.

"Is it time?" Jillian turned over and asked when she heard her name.

"You can stay here and sleep," Diego said.

"No," she insisted, sitting up, her hair a mess. "I want to go."

"You're drunk," Mobius said.

"No, I slept long enough. I promise I'm sober now." She looked at them with regret. "I'm sorry. It won't happen again. I just lost it for a minute but see ..." She stood up. "I'm good."

"You've already been through a lot, so if you can't handle it, I understand," Mobius said. "You didn't ask to be part of this."

Jillian rubbed her hands over her face, trying to clear the after-effects of the booze. "I want to help. I feel like I'm meant to be doing this."

"Come on then," he said. "But no more drunk, or next time you have to stay behind."

"No more drunk," she said. "I promise."

As they made their way to Temple I, Jillian said to Inka, "I'm so glad you are with us."

Inka put her arm around Jillian's waist and smiled up at her.

When they got to the temple, Inka, Jillian, and Diego agreed that the nearly half-full moon was bright enough to see by, even though the crumbling central staircase would be treacherous. The flashlights would make them too easy to spot, and if they were seen, they would be arrested. Mobius looked up at the ancient structure, lit silver by the moonlight. He ran a finger across his bracelet and whispered, "You can do this. Make the leap," then started up the steep steps, taking them four at a time.

"*Extraordinario,*" Inka remarked, watching him climb.

Diego looked at Inka, momentarily concerned about how she'd make it up the small and crumbling steps, but she held her skirt up and began to climb. Then he remembered that she was a Mayan, and they were some of the toughest people he'd ever known. The stairs led directly to the roof comb, a square structure that sat at the top of the temple. By the time everyone arrived at the summit, they were all winded except for Mobius, who'd been waiting for several minutes.

"My goodness," Inka said to Mobius between breaths, "you are so fast and strong."

"That was amazing. With the reduced gravity, I was able to get up here a lot faster than I could have on Akara."

"Glad you're having fun," Diego said, bent over and gasping for breath.

•

Mobius ran his hand along the stone surface on the sides of a short doorway that opened into the interior of the structure. "In the mission log, there was a round carving with Itzamna's face on one side of the entrance, and the calendar on the other. They're not here."

"No," Inka said. "But they could be in a museum, or taken away by looters, or worn away over time. We have lost much of the artwork."

They ducked through the short doorway and followed Mobius into a dank, dark altar room. He stopped and closed his eyes, connecting to his intuition. *Where is the time capsule?* he asked inwardly, then waited. But he heard nothing. *It has to be here. I just can't sense it.*

As Inka and Diego turned on their flashlights, and Mobius shined light from his cog, the walls came to life with etchings of warriors, sacred symbols, and frightening masks. The small, square room had a low ceiling and a doorway that led into another chamber.

"This is where the priests would make offerings to the gods," Inka said. "The etchings here tell the creation story."

Mobius had to duck down even further to move into the next room, and the others followed. It was smaller, but also covered with glyphs.

Inka shined her light on the walls. "This is where the priests would prepare themselves for the ceremonies. They would do ritual bloodletting, where they pierced themselves so their blood would sanctify this place and the ceremony they were about to perform."

"I'm not surprised," Mobius said. "They were really into blood." He ran his hands over the walls, feeling and looking for any opening, for a way into a hidden passageway down to the tomb.

"There's nothing here," he said finally. "Is there anything in the etchings about the end of the world or Itzamna?"

"No," Inka said. "I'm sorry."

"Are you sure it was this one?" Diego asked him. "Maybe it's in a different temple."

"Itzamna's temple was definitely on the central plaza." Mobius looked around. "The only other temple on the plaza is Temple II, but its shape is not right at all."

"And there is no tomb under Temple II," Inka said.

Mobius slumped against a wall and slid to the floor. He sat there with his head in his hands.

"Maybe Tikal is not the right city," Diego said.

"But the city is laid out like the Pleiades," Mobius said, his voice strained, "and Akara is in the Pleiades."

"*¡Increíble!* Your planet is in the Pleiades?" Inka exclaimed.

"Yes." Mobius looked up at her. "Why?"

"The Mayan people who lived in Tikal believed they came from the Seven Sisters. Now I know why."

Diego sighed. "That's fascinating, but—"

"This has to be the city from the mission log," Mobius said. "Why else would it be laid out like the constellation Itzamna came from?"

"Itzamna was a god to the entire Mayan world," Inka said. "Everyone would have known where he came from."

"If this isn't the right city, I have no idea where else the time capsule would be," Mobius said, squeezing his eyes shut. "It has to be here. Itzamna told King K'awiil he would be buried with the time capsule. You said his tomb was found in this temple."

"Yes, but I am sorry to tell you, there was more than one King K'awiil in ancient times."

"Oh, yes. Piphus told us that. I forgot," Mobius groaned then mumbled under his breath, "I can't fail this time."

"It has been many years since I was up here," Inka said, "but I believe I remember an etching of the Pleiades on the wooden lintel above the doorway outside."

"Show me."

"We'll have to use the flashlight for me to see it," she said, as they gathered outside the ceremonial chamber.

He blinked twice, then nodded. "We have to risk it."

Inka pointed the flashlight above the passageway and lit up a rough-hewn panel of wood. On the left side of the lintel, there were seven starburst markings that made up the familiar constellation of the Pleiades. "You see," she said. "There it is."

"I thought that was called the Tiny Little Dipper," Jillian whispered. "A friend of mine calls it the coke spoon."

Mobius didn't respond, not knowing what she was talking about, but Inka glared at her and Diego shook his head.

"Sorry," she said. "I'll shut up."

"What else is on there?" Mobius asked.

Inka moved the flashlight further to the left, illuminating a jagged edge—the beginning of the lintel had broken off, leaving a partial glyph with just a few faint marks remaining. She then shined her light on the glyph to the right of the Pleiades, revealing an etching that looked like a circle inside a shallow bowl, which sat on top of a triangle-shaped platform. "I am not sure what this symbol means," she said. Next to it sat a glyph with another pattern of starbursts. It was made up of five stars. "This one is something I am not sure about either," Inka said. "I recall now that the meaning of this lintel has never been fully understood."

"I understand it!" Mobius said, pointing to the five-star symbol. "That is the Serpent!"

"What are you talking about, Mobius?" Jillian asked.

Mobius's eyes grew even bigger than their normal size when he looked at her, and they were almost completely orange. "The Serpent constellation is where Earth is located when viewed from Akara. It's called the Serpent because if you connect the stars, it looks like a snake with a head at the top. See?" he asked, tracing it in the air.

"So the lintel shows where Earth is when seen from Akara and where Akara is when seen from Earth," Diego said. "Only someone from Akara would know both of those. Wow."

"He's right," Jillian said. "Maybe it was put here by someone trying to communicate with someone like you, Mobius."

"I agree," Inka said. "This has to be a message to someone from your planet."

Mobius could feel a rush of energy moving through him and among the four of them. The night felt pregnant with it. He suddenly had a feeling, a subtle knowing, that this was indeed a message. *Was it Itzamna who left it, or was it someone else?* He didn't sense that it was from Itzamna, but he didn't have any idea who else might have put it there. He took out his cog, pointed the small transparent disc at the lintel, and captured an image of it.

They all stared up at the etching again.

"Inka, do you have any idea what the missing glyph on the left might be?" Jillian asked.

Inka shook her head. "No, *mija*, it could be anything ..." She shined her flashlight on the final glyph on the far right of the lintel. It portrayed a snake with feathers, about to eat its own tail. "But this one is the symbol for the god Kukulcan. He shows up in many Mayan cities. He is a creator—"

Just then, a female voice broke through the silence, *"Alguien esta ahi arriba.* Someone is up there!"

They looked toward the ground below and saw a flashlight beam shining up at them, the moon illuminating the faint outline of the person carrying it.

"Someone saw the light!" Jillian said.

"We must go now," Inka said urgently, turning off her flashlight.

"Not yet. I need to look more—the entrance is probably near the lintel."

"We will be put in jail!" Inka cried in a loud whisper.

"She's right." Diego grabbed Mobius by the arm, and they began the harrowing trip down the steep steps.

Inka nearly stumbled over her skirt. *"¡Ay, Dios mío!"* she shouted.

Mobius scooped her up and carried her as he ran. As they made it to the bottom steps, flashlights rapidly moved toward them from across the plaza as men yelled, "Stop! You are trespassing!" in both Spanish and English.

Mobius instinctively ran directly into the jungle for cover, and

Diego and Jillian followed, racing to keep up. Once out of sight, Mobius put Inka down, and they all moved through the dark, claustrophobic woods as quietly as possible, trying to make their way back to where they had left their things. But the jungle was impenetrable, and the security guards didn't give up easily, shouting commands for them to come out, so they stopped and waited, trying to remain silent while the insects practically ate them alive.

•

Half an hour later, after the guards finally gave up, they made it back to their little camp.

"So what now?" Diego asked as they sat on the blankets.

"It's not here," Inka said. "We knew it was unlikely."

Jillian nodded. "We have to figure out what the message on the lintel means to see if it helps us know where the time capsule might actually be."

Inka dug through her bag, pulling out a pencil and the notebook with the Virgin of Guadalupe on the front. "*Mijo*, can I see the photo you took of the glyphs?"

Mobius took out his cog and projected a three-dimensional holograph of the lintel in front of them.

It looks so real, Diego thought—like if he touched it, he could feel the roughness of the wood. "Wow. That thing is amazing."

Glancing back and forth between the hologram and her notebook, Inka proceeded to sketch a simplified version of each symbol, in the order in which they appeared. Under the first one—the partial etching—she wrote *missing glyph*. Then she drew the others and labeled them *Pleiades, ball inside a bowl on top of triangle, The Serpent,* and *the god Kukulcan.*

Jillian pointed to the first full drawing in the series. "So, we know what this one means. Your planet is in the Pleiades. That's obvious."

"Yes," Inka said, then pointed to the glyph of a ball inside a bowl on top of a triangle, "but I have no idea what this one means."

"I might," Mobius said. "It looks a lot like the spacecraft Itzamna came here in when its landing gear was down, and it was on the ground."

Diego nodded. "Yeah, that could be a spaceship."

"Great," Jillian said and took the pencil from Inka and wrote the word *spaceship* below the glyph.

"And we know what the Serpent means," Inka said. "It's the constellation Earth is in when viewed from Akara."

"So, you obviously have snakes on your planet," Diego said.

"Oh, yes," Mobius answered. "We have all kinds of snakes. We lost many species, but snakes were one of the least affected by the destruction."

"Do you have cockroaches too?" Diego asked.

"Can we focus, please?" Jillian asked.

"*Sí, por favor,*" Inka said, pointing her pencil at the final symbol—the snake with feathers eating its own tail. "As I was starting to tell you when the guards found us, Kukulcan is a creator god, and the god of resurrection and reincarnation—" Suddenly, she stopped and looked at them, her eyes widening. "And he is supposed to return and save the Earth and bring in a new order of peace and wisdom."

"Okay, I just got goose bumps big time," Jillian said, tracing her fingers along her arm.

"Goose bumps?" Mobius asked, then quickly scanned his thologram and found the phrase. "Fascinating! Let me see them."

Jillian stretched out her arm, and he examined it with the wonder of a child.

"Remember about the focus?" Diego said, nudging her with his elbow.

"Sorry, back to Kukulcan," Jillian said.

"The symbol for Kukulcan is a snake with feathers," Mobius said. "On Akara, there's only one like that, and it's from the Enshala region. It's called the *daoyi*, but it can't fly. Do your snakes with feathers fly?"

"Mobius," Diego said. "We don't have snakes with feathers. And none of our snakes fly."

"*Gracias a Dios*. Thank God for that," Inka exclaimed.

"Let me see if I've got this right," Jillian said. "So the god Kukulcan, who is supposed to return to Earth and bring about a new world, is represented by an animal that *only* exists on Akara. Not only that, but the symbol for Kukulcan is a serpent just like the constellation that Earth is in when you look at it from Akara!"

"Yes, that's right," Mobius said. "It can't be a coincidence. Someone from Akara had to be trying to communicate about the time capsule. I can feel the time passing. We need to start moving toward the capsule, wherever it is, so is there anything in this that might tell us where we should look next?"

"Calakmul," Inka said. "We must go to the Mayan ruins of Calakmul in Mexico. It's about fifty miles north, across the border."

"Why there?" Mobius asked.

"Another King K'awiil ruled there and was entombed there."

"You said there were several K'awiils in the Mayan world. Why there?" Diego asked.

"Because," Inka said, "Calakmul was known as the Kingdom of the Snake."

Mobius jumped up. "That has to be it!"

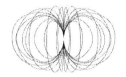

CHAPTER THIRTY-FIVE

OUR LADY

An hour later, they were bumping down a single-lane, dirt-and-mud jungle road heading north to Calakmul. As daylight spread upward through the cover of the jungle, Mobius wished it away. It reminded him that they only had one day left before the apocalyptic legacy from his planet imploded. Since he needed as much time as possible to figure out how to disarm it, he desperately hoped that they would find it at the Kingdom of the Snake.

Until they got there, however, he had to survive road-bound travel once again. He had never experienced it before, and now he saw firsthand why it was part of Akara's technological past. Not only was it far less energy efficient, with all that friction, but also it was brutal on the internal organs. He longed for Akara and the ease and fun of a uni-hover. Unfortunately, this road was their only option.

Diego had told them that no one ever took this route to get to Calakmul from Tikal because it was extremely rough, and also because there was a lot of illegal activity up and down it. Mobius could see large areas of the jungle that had been destroyed and left like a scar on the Earth. In the rainy, summer season, Diego said it was usually impassable, so they were lucky it was mid-winter.

Even though they were going much slower than on a real road, Diego had chosen this route because it was a straight line to Calakmul and so the fastest way to get there—it would only take them an hour and a half—and the ruins were only a few miles on the other side of the Mexican border. The highway, a paved but indirect route, would take about nine hours. More problematic was that the highway would take them to two border crossings— through Belize and then Mexico. Without proper identification and papers showing they weren't driving a stolen car, none of them would ever make it through, and Mobius would be discovered. All this was a strange phenomenon to him, since there were no longer guarded borders between regions on Akara. There was no need for boundaries that kept people either in or out of a place.

As he bounced up and down in his seat, he alternated between looking at a large map of all the Mayan ruins, which they had picked up at Tikal, and flipping his cognizer between his fingers, willing it to come to life with some news—and help—from Kaia, Nava, or Piphus. But it sat dormant, as did his neurolink, giving him no hope. He was bombarded with thoughts—*Where are they? Is Kaia okay? What's taking them so long? Did they even make it back? If not, it's my fault for overriding the airlock. That's what I get for not staying centered.*

He took a deep breath, mentally pivoting to give his thinking mind something else to do, and started scrolling through the thologram dictionaries, learning new words in English since Jillian didn't speak Spanish. Mobius was sure that if Piphus were there he could get the cog connected to Earth's Internet, which might be able to help in their search, but that was way beyond Mobius's abilities. Looking once again at the map, it fully sank in that there were way too many Mayan ruins to get to, and panic rose inside of him. Despite the road conditions, Inka and Jillian were sleeping in the back seat, and he wished he could join them. He was exhausted and needed a break from this horrendous responsibility. On Akara, as an Anomaly, he had an excuse to avoid responsibility. He usually kept up with the little that was required of him at home and with his studies, but now he saw how much he had used his condition to not try that hard—that is, until he got to Entelechy Academy and decided he wanted to get into the Discovery Corps. But by then, he'd missed out on a lot of opportunities to improve his access to the Wisdom, even as an Anomaly. He wished desperately that he'd paid better attention in metaphysics and in mind training.

He kept reminding himself to use his intuition, but since they hadn't found the time capsule at Tikal, he was becoming more and more convinced that finding it was way beyond his capabilities. *Nava would be doing so much better at this than I am*, he thought. Suddenly, her kiss came racing back to him. *Did that actually happen? Does she really have feelings for me, or did she kiss me just to build my confidence?* Mobius could no longer tolerate all the noise in his mind. "Can you talk about something, please?" he asked Diego. "Tell me about your work, this place, something."

"Sure. Actually, I was just thinking about when I first started with the rangers. I patrolled this area for two weeks with a partner so we could give a report to headquarters about any new criminal activity since the year before."

"What did you find?" Mobius asked.

"That it had gotten a lot worse. Slash-and-burn clearing of the jungle like we've seen along the road keeps increasing. Drug smugglers use the cover of the jungle to hide the landing strips for their planes and for laundering money through cattle ranching. Illegal logging and wildlife poaching is on the rise too. It's really bad."

Mobius didn't understand most of what Diego said, but he'd seen the devastation he was talking about with his own eyes. "Why do they do this?" he asked.

"Some of the people are desperate and hungry, but others are just selfish and greedy."

To Mobius, it sounded like a level of suffering and insanity he'd only heard about from the Ravaging Era. He realized that he was struggling so much, not only because he was on an alien planet, but also because the consciousness of the beings was unlike anything he'd ever experienced in his life. Only a few of the most disturbed Anomalies would even consider engaging in the kind of behavior Diego was talking about.

Even though they were part of a less evolved race, his human friends seemed to be holding up much better than he was. After her initial breakdown, Inka had been a mountain of strength, and Diego too. Diego had told him that Jillian was from a privileged family living in a wealthy country, but other than getting drunk, she'd been pretty stable too.

Mobius shared his self-doubt with Diego, but the Guatemalan shook his head. "Mobius, you've kept your cool and made good decisions. I thought you'd gone too far by telling Inka about yourself the way you did, but we needed her, and we didn't have time to play around. Don't start questioning yourself now."

Mobius's heart swelled, filling with even more love for the hairy human. Even though there were obviously many dangerous people on this world, Diego was not one of them.

As morning broke in full above the canopy of trees, Diego groaned that he needed coffee. Mobius groaned that he was sick and tired of myomeal and that he was on his last bag. He wished he were an Absorber, like Kaia, because he had no idea what he was going to do when he ran out of food. But when he focused on it, he got hungry, so he tried to keep his mind on the bigger issues.

"So, have you thought any more about who left the clues for you to find?" Diego asked.

"For *me* to find? I think maybe they were hoping for a little better than me," Mobius said, forcing a smile.

"Listen," Diego said. "You're the only alien on Earth—as far as we know, anyway. So as things are going, the clues were put there for you."

Mobius looked at him for a moment, trying to take that in, but it was too much, so he thought about Diego's question instead. "It could be Itzamna who left the clues, but why would he have done that? And, I keep sensing it's not him."

Diego nodded. "Okay."

"The mission that rescued Itzamna's crew was the last one to Earth. And the records show that the rescue crew were only on-planet for a few hours, so it couldn't have been them. After that mission," Mobius continued, as Diego maneuvered the car over yet another massive tree root in the road, "Akara banned all contact with intelligent alien life-forms. So other than doing periodic planetary scans, we stopped coming here."

Diego looked intrigued. "But your ships still come here?"

"Yes, but only for observational missions."

"I know people who swear they've seen your flybys," Diego said. "Now I believe them. If we ever get a chance to sit down and have a *cerveza* together, you have to tell me everything, *amigo*."

"I hope we get to have both a coffee and a beer together. I want to taste them," Mobius said, "Even if it means passing out for a few hours."

"They're really good. It may be worth it." Diego laughed.

"I'm happy to tell you whatever you want to know, Diego, but whoever is flying by, I doubt it is us—I don't think we'd ever come so close to the planet you could see our ships."

"Wow," Diego said. "So, there's more than one alien race out there visiting Earth?"

"There must be, because we also have had visitations from aliens who have not made contact."

"That's too much for me to think about right now," Diego said, pushing harder on the gas pedal. "Go on about who you think left the clues."

"There was this one rebellious crewmember on Itzamna's mission. At first, I thought that she left the clues. We think she was the one who informed the authorities on Akara about Itzamna's insane behavior. But she must not have told them about the time capsule, or there would have been at least some record of another mission to Earth to retrieve or disarm it. That means she didn't know about it."

"So if it wasn't her, then who was it?"

Inka, who was awake and had been listening, said, "Maybe it was a shaman who found out about the time capsule. Maybe they were praying another sky god would come to stop it from ending the world."

Jillian stretched and yawned. "That sounds like a possibility," she said, leaning forward to look down the road. Suddenly, she cried out, "Diego!" and he slammed on the brakes. Up ahead, uniformed men with rifles were crouching behind three armored vehicles stopped along the side of the road. They fired into a clear-cut area of the jungle at a group of at least twelve armed men who were trying to hide behind a pickup and a flatbed truck filled with downed trees. Both trucks had flat tires from being shot out and were stranded in a still-smoldering ruin of massacred jungle. One of the men hiding in the bed of the pickup rose up and tried to fire back but was shot instantly.

Chaos erupted inside the car, with everyone screaming at Diego to back up. He shoved the SUV into reverse and backtracked as quickly as he could. As they retreated, Mobius saw a man come out from behind the pickup screaming, shooting a rapid-fire weapon like the one Menendez used to damage the ship's torus. One of the uniformed men was blasted with a barrage of bullets, then went down hard.

"What's going on?" Mobius screamed in a high-pitched wail and grabbed his head, overwhelmed by the violence.

Diego fishtailed backward, coming dangerously close to the trees on either side of the narrow road. "*¡Mierda!*" he shouted as he backed into a barely visible side road and stopped the car. The jungle on either side made them invisible to the gunmen on the road and protected them for the moment. "I forgot about the raid against the *criminales!*" Diego said, wiping sweat off his forehead with his T-shirt sleeve.

"Why are they doing this?" Mobius cried. "It's like I'm living in the Final War."

"What if they come after us?" Inka asked, her whole body trembling.

"They're too busy with each other," Diego said. "I think we're okay for a minute."

"What raid are you talking about?" Jillian asked, trying to calm down.

Diego turned off the car to conserve gas. "An international

police force is cracking down on the drug cartels and illegal loggers and poachers this week," he said. "This is an area that has gotten a lot worse lately. And it's an extremely sensitive one for wildlife. I should have known they'd come here, but it was the last thing on my mind." He pounded the steering wheel. "¡Mierda!"

"How long will the fight last?" Mobius asked.

"This kind of standoff could go on for hours."

"It's true," Inka said. "I know these kinds of narcos. They won't give up. They have probably called on the radio for more help, so it will get worse before it gets better."

"Oh my God," Jillian said. "What are we going to do?"

"We can't turn around because the only other road going to Calakmul has a border station," Diego said.

"So, do we just wait as long as it takes for them to finish killing each other?" Mobius asked.

"I don't know," Diego said, rubbing his brow.

The four of them just sat there and waited, flinching when the screams or gunfire intensified. Mobius found himself staring at the medallion of the Virgin of Guadalupe that Inka wore, and an idea came to him.

"You said that people here worship this saint on your necklace?" he said, pointing to it.

Inka looked at him, confused, touching the pendant. "Many do ..."

"Even those men?" Mobius asked Diego.

"Well," Diego said, "even though they might not be Catholic, the criminales were all raised Christian, though you wouldn't know it by how they act. So, yes. She is loved because she is Mary, the mother of Jesus."

"Okay then, I have an idea." Mobius took out his cog, pinched it open into a small sphere and let it hover in front of him.

They all stared, breathless, at the floating orb as the shooting and shouting continued unabated.

"What are you doing?" Diego asked.

"I'm programming the cog with my neurolink. We may all die if this doesn't work, but that's going to happen anyway if we don't keep going."

"*Ay, ay, ay,*" Inka said and started praying quietly in her Mayan dialect.

When Mobius was finished with the cog, he looked at Diego. "Okay, we need to drive toward them. *Slowly.*"

"What? Are you crazy? We'll get gunned down," Diego exclaimed.

Jillian leaned forward between the bucket seats. "Does that thing turn into a laser gun or something?"

"You'll see," Mobius said. He didn't want to give it away; he wanted to see their reaction even if it was the last thing he ever experienced. "If this works, we should be able to drive through." He knew that he was asking for a miracle, but it was the only choice he had.

"And if it doesn't?" Inka asked.

Mobius just looked at her for a moment, then put his hands out toward them. Inka put her hands in his, and Jillian and Diego added theirs.

Inka continued praying.

"Can you say it in English, please?" Jillian asked.

"It is the shaman's prayer," Inka said. "It says, 'We are already given to the power that rules our fate. We cling to nothing, so we have nothing to defend. We fear nothing, so we remember our spirit. Unattached and calm, we will dart past the sun to be free.'"

"Amen," Jillian said.

Diego inhaled deeply then exhaled, "Yes, Amen." He turned to Mobius. "At least tell me this. Are you going to be using force?"

"None at all," Mobius said.

He turned to Jillian and Inka. "In that case, do either of you have a white piece of cloth of any kind? We need a surrender flag."

They searched the car, but the only white thing they had was Mobius's T-shirt, so he took it off and handed it to Diego, who turned it inside out.

Jillian did a double take when she saw Mobius without his shirt on. "Damn, you are one ripped alien."

Diego rolled his eyes and shook his head, then went to the back of the car and returned with a tire iron.

"What's that for?" Jillian asked. "I thought we were going to wave a flag of surrender, not join the violence."

"Really, Jillian?" he snapped. "What the hell could I do to them with a tire iron? I'd rather not hold my arm out the window."

"Diego, are you *actually* jealous of an alien? He's not my type—I prefer men with eyes that *aren't* the size of golf balls."

Inka giggled, and Mobius widened his enormous eyes as far as they could go.

They all cracked up until Diego restarted the car, put the SUV in reverse and said, "I guess if we're about to drive to our death, we may as well die laughing." He backed the car onto the main road, holding the T-shirt, now tied to the tire iron, out his window, and waved it as Inka prayed in Mayan.

"Remember, go slowly," Mobius said.

When they got closer to the gunfight, the law enforcement officers on the right side of the road up ahead saw them, and several trained their guns on them. Once the authorities saw the surrender flag, they shouted and motioned for Diego to turn around. "I think this is close enough," Mobius said.

"It better be, because we're going to get our heads shot off if we go any closer," Diego said.

Mobius held the cog outside the car just above the passenger side mirror and let go, allowing it to hover. Just then, a bullet ricocheted off the hood of the car from the left side of the road where the *criminales* were entrenched, and everyone ducked. Using his neurolink, Mobius initiated the program on his cog, and suddenly, it projected a life-size, three-dimensional hologram of the Virgin of Guadalupe about ten yards in front of the vehicle. The gold and red halo of light that surrounded her glowed and pulsated, and her radiant blue cloak with luminous golden stars moved as if blown gently by the wind.

"What is that?" Diego asked.

Mobius directed the cog, turning the image of the Virgin around to face the car, and had her bow her head.

"*¡Nuestra Señora!*" Inka exclaimed. "Our Lady!"

"Holy shit!" Jillian said.

"How in the world ...?" Diego put his hand to his mouth.

The effect on his friends was as good as Mobius had hoped for.

The beam that emerged from the cog was invisible to the naked eye, so the mother of Jesus really did look like she was walking in front of them.

"Move forward slowly," Mobius said.

Diego wiped the sweat from his face and mumbled, "Okay, okay."

As the Range Rover inched forward, one by one the *criminales* emerged from behind the trucks and from out of the jungle.

"Okay, there they are," Diego said, his voice so high pitched, he sounded like a young girl. *"Jesucristo,* we're going right through them."

For effect, Mobius had the saint look from side to side and open her arms as if in blessing. As they passed, the men on both sides put down their guns, many dropping to their knees and crossing themselves.

"Madre María llena de gracia." Inka whispered the Hail Mary, and tears streamed down her face. Many of the men also wept, their hardened faces changing before Mobius's eyes to the open gaze of awestruck children.

"Look at them," Jillian whispered. "Just look at them."

"Continue slowly all the way through," Mobius said. "Let them experience her as much as they can. Maybe what is happening to them will last a little while."

Finally, they got all the way past the battleground, and when Diego sped up and they were in the clear, the SUV rocked from the celebration that erupted inside.

CHAPTER THIRTY-SIX

CALAKMUL

In all his life, Diego had never seen anything like what they'd just experienced. He didn't know there was anything in this world except brute force that could get men like those not only to put down their weapons, but also to go to their knees in submission. He realized that what he had just witnessed was not of this world, but a miracle from a different realm altogether. He buzzed with energy, not only from seeing it, but also from the thrill of walking through the valley of the shadow of death and coming out the other side. Inka, Jillian, and even Mobius were lit up with energy too, giddy and joyous, and it felt like the road was suddenly much smoother.

They drove by an unreadable, rusted metal sign filled with bullet holes. "I think that means we just entered Mexico," Diego said, and they celebrated as if they'd just disarmed the time capsule.

After following a road sign that pointed them toward Calakmul, fifteen minutes later they pulled into the parking lot of the archaeological site, and Diego was once again unsettled by seeing all the cars and buses already gathered at this hour of the morning. Every Mayan ruin was a hot spot with the end-of-the-calendar phenomenon. *If they only knew they were standing on ground zero,* he thought.

They got out of the car and stopped in the bathrooms at the entrance. The simple act of splashing cool water on his face felt incredible to Diego after staring down death and knowing it was still probably coming tomorrow.

They emerged from the bathrooms a bit refreshed and followed Inka to the central plaza. "Here at Calakmul," she said, "we are lucky because it is legal to climb the pyramids, but we are unlucky because some of the temples were added onto after their original construction. The temple while Itzamna was here might not have looked the same as it does now. Also, the stelae and the structures have been looted and worn away badly. They were made of a soft limestone here that ... how do you say, *erosionada*?" she asked, turning to Diego.

"Eroded."

"*Sí*, eroded very much over time."

She was right about that. The pyramids, while enormous and impressive, were far less intact than at Tikal, and Diego could see very few markings on them or the stelae.

Mobius stopped walking and looked around through his sunglasses.

"What is it?" Jillian asked.

"This doesn't seem familiar. None of these temples look like Itzamna's. It's hard to tell, it's all so worn away. Does it have a ball court?"

"Yes, over there," Inka said, pointing to a flat, open area.

"From the top of Itzamna's temple steps, I think the ball court was to the right."

They passed a park guide, and Inka stopped him and spoke with him in Mayan for a few minutes, pointing and asking questions.

Finally, she turned around. "That one, Structure 11, is the main temple and contains K'awiil's tomb."

"But there's nothing on the top of Structure 11," Mobius said, looking up at the gargantuan decaying pyramid.

"The roof comb probably crumbled at some point," Inka said. "But the temple was built on top of multiple times, so even if there is a secret passageway, there is no way you can get to it."

Mobius groaned and put his hands to his head, at which time the three of them called out, "No!" and grabbed at him to put his hands away.

"Okay, *tranquilo, tranquilo*," he said as he put them back in his pockets, then looked up at the temple again.

"Come on," Diego said. "Let's go up. We don't know what we might find."

The temple, fourteen stories high, was not as steep as the one at Tikal, but they still sweated and panted as they climbed—all except for Mobius. The view was spectacular, overlooking the roof of the jungle for 360 degrees. They could even see the very top of Temple IV at Tikal far in the distance.

Mobius looked around. "This isn't it. It doesn't look familiar at all."

"What if it's because they built on top of the temple?" Jillian asked.

Mobius squeezed his eyes shut then shook his head. "The view doesn't look right."

"Are you sure the time capsule was buried with King K'awiil?" Inka asked.

"Yes, that's what Itzamna commanded. Unless you think they would have disobeyed his orders."

"No, no, not possible," Inka replied. "Not if they believed he was the deity Itzamna."

Diego started sweating even more. They were looking for an object buried in the jungle somewhere with almost no clues and a nearly unlimited area within which it could be hidden. There were dozens of major Mayan ruins throughout Guatemala, Mexico, and Belize, and they'd only been to two of them.

"I have to get out of this sun," Jillian said, her pale face now red and sweating. She looked hungover and scared.

Dejected and tired, they retraced their steps back down the pyramid, then gathered in the shade of a giant ceiba tree. "I think we have to contact the authorities at this point," Diego said. "They can send people to all the ruins to start looking for clues. We don't have time to do this on our own."

Jillian sighed in frustration. "We can't just call some government office and tell them there's a weapon of mass destruction inside a Mayan temple buried a thousand years ago by a sky god, or so says an alien anyway. They'll think we're insane, or terrorists trying to create panic before the end of the calendar."

"You're right," Diego said. "They'll have to see Mobius to believe us."

"You think seeing him will *help*?" Jillian asked. "They'll just think he's some kind of ... I don't know ... Trojan horse."

"What kind of horse?" Mobius asked.

"Ay, ay, ay." Inka shook her head. "They will think he's responsible. God only knows what they would do to him."

"I don't care what happens to me," Mobius said. "All that matters is disarming the capsule."

"So, if no authorities, what now?" Diego asked.

"I don't know," Mobius said. "This is a waste of time. All these ruins have been picked over a million times! I don't even know what I'm looking for." He stopped his rant and closed his eyes. "I need to try to access the Wisdom."

"That's a good idea," Jillian said. "We should meditate."

Inka nodded in agreement. "This is a good place for it," she said, looking up into the branches of the tree. "The ceiba is sacred."

"Are you kidding me?" Diego shouted. "We don't have time to meditate! We need to go!"

"No, we don't want to do something motivated only by fear," Mobius said.

"This is *loco*," Diego said, shaking his head.

Inka put a hand on his arm. *"Es importante, mijo.* There is a natural flow to life. We need to check in and see which direction it is going."

He threw up his hands in defeat as the three of them sat down on the ground and closed their eyes as if they had all the time in the world. *Spirituality is fine if it makes you feel better,* he thought, *but not when you need to get things done, not in a crisis.* "In that case, I'm going to actually accomplish something and get some sleep," Diego said in protest, and lay down and closed his eyes. He was certain that the "flow" was going in the direction of getting some help, and he'd need to be able to stay awake when that finally happened.

A few minutes later, they heard the sound of footsteps on the grass coming closer, and a man clearing his throat. *"Perdóname,"* he said.

Diego opened his eyes reluctantly and saw the young park guide Inka had spoken to earlier looking down at them.

"Yes?" Inka said.

"I am sorry to disturb you, but I found something in the museum that I think you might want to see," he replied in heavily accented but fluent English.

Inka, Jillian, and Mobius were all on their feet within seconds, while Diego laid there looking up at them. "I thought we were meditating."

"We stopped because the flow of life showed up as this young man," Inka said. "So we follow."

The three of them took off with the guide, and Diego scrambled to catch up. "But what about contacting the author—, I mean those people I mentioned before you started meditating."

"Right now, we're going to see what this man ..." Mobius paused. "What is your name?"

"Jorge."

"What Jorge has to show us, then we'll go from there. What did you find?" Mobius asked the guide as they walked.

"After you told me about the lintel at Tikal," Jorge explained, "I recalled that there was a piece of a lintel from one of the Calakmul temples here in the museum."

"Oh yes, we'd be very interested in seeing that," Mobius said, and looked hopefully at the others.

They entered the *Museo de Naturaleza y Arqueologia de Calakmul*, a beautiful building with shiny floors, vaulted ceilings, and low lighting, with spotlights on the artifacts. Jorge led them through several rooms to a table encased in glass, with some broken relics laid out on top. "Here it is."

They looked down at a large piece of ancient wood that was cracked in the middle and had a jagged edge on one end. Obviously, part of it had broken off at some point. The plaque below it said, "Doorway lintel from Structure VII at Calakmul."

"It has the same symbols!" Jillian said, and they all buzzed with excitement.

The lintel clearly showed the glyphs for the Pleiades, the Serpent, the spaceship, and Kukulcan. On the far left, however, in the place where the missing glyph had been at Tikal, was a fully formed image of a man in profile with a large nose and snake on his head. "*Dios mío*, it's Itzamna," Diego said, wonder in his voice.

Mobius whispered something to Inka, then she put her hands on her heart and turned to Jorge. "*Mijo*, thank you so much for showing us this. Do you mind if we study it for a while?"

"*Por supuesto*. Of course," Jorge said. "It is my turn to help in the *museo*, so please inform me if you need anything else."

When he was gone, Jillian said, "With Itzamna being the missing glyph, there's no question someone is trying to communicate about the time capsule to an Akaran."

Mobius lowered his sunglasses so he could see better, and after glancing around to make sure no one was watching, he pulled out his cog and held it close to his chest. Within seconds, a small three-dimensional image of the lintel at Tikal glowed in front of them. "I think the markings on the edge of the broken lintel at Tikal match the Itzamna glyph on this one," Mobius said, gesturing with his head toward the lintel in the case.

"Hey, Dad," a young boy from behind them said in an Australian accent. "What are they looking at?"

Mobius raised his sunglasses and pocketed the cog, along with his hands. They all stood frozen, waiting.

"Don't be rude, Brian," the father said, pulling the boy away.

Diego was grateful that adults could be so oblivious sometimes. In law enforcement training, he'd learned that people see what they want to see. And how much a criminal can get away with because of it. His throat tightened, thinking that he had used that knowledge against Domingo Hernandez to serve his alliance with

Menendez; that *he* was the criminal.

As soon as they were gone, Jillian looked at the lintel case and got back to business. "I don't know if this matches the faint markings from the missing glyph at Tikal. Let me see the image again." Diego felt even worse. She was so smart and beautiful, and he had deceived her too. He moved closer to her so that they were touching.

Mobius glanced around to make sure no one was watching, then took out his cog again. The image of the Tikal lintel glowed in front of them, but this time he pointed at it with a long index finger, and Diego cringed at his creepy alien hand out there for all the world to see. But luckily the kid was gone, and they were in a back room with only a few other people, who were on the other side of the room. Mobius moved his hand over the wood panel in the display, and the floating image moved too, settling on top of it. The lintels lined up perfectly. They were clearly a match.

"Mobius is right," Inka said. "The incomplete glyph at Tikal is Itzamna."

"Definitely," Jillian said, then pointed to the other glyphs on the Calakmul lintel. "I can't get over the fact that Itzamna has a snake on his head, Kukulcan is the image of a feathered snake, and the star constellation you are from is called the Serpent."

"That's why we came to Calakmul," Diego said. "It's the Kingdom of the Snake."

"Yes," Mobius said. "But is there some kind of significance to the snake symbol? What does it mean, Inka?"

"In my culture," she said, "the serpent or snake is significant and can mean many things. Because it can shed its skin, it is a symbol of renewal and rebirth."

"How interesting," Mobius said. "Remember how I told you

that on my planet, the evolution to a new level of consciousness was named the Rebirthing?"

"Oh right," Jillian said. "Wow ... Do you think the snake symbolism on the lintel points to the prophecy of light?"

"Let's hope so," Diego said.

"Also," Inka continued, "among shamans and a number of other spiritual traditions, the serpent often represents what we call the axis mundi, or the world axis. It can be thought of as a column of pure potential energy that runs through the center of the universe. Out of this center of emptiness, all creation arises and appears as duality—good and evil, light and dark, or in this case Kukulcan and Itzamna. The center axis is where we go as shamans to leave the known world and enter the timeless, in order to bring back knowledge and healing."

"That is exalted!" Mobius said, pocketing his cog. "What you're describing as the axis mundi is the same thing as the center of the torus—the emptiness out of which all creation arises."

"Taurus, like the astrological sign?" Jillian asked.

"I think he means torus, like the geometrical shape," Diego said.

"Yes," Mobius said.

Jillian looked at Diego with raised eyebrows.

"Don't be so surprised," he said, puffing up a bit. "I was studying to get a science degree."

"The torus is one of the first things we looked up on the Internet when we got here, to see what is understood about it on Earth and what it is called," Mobius said.

"I've never heard of it. What does it look like?" Jillian asked.

"Kind of like a doughnut," Diego said. "The axis is the emptiness in the center."

"Oh ...," Jillian said. "It also looks like—"

"A snake eating its tail," Inka said, her eyes lighting up. "Just like the image of Kukulcan."

"Okay," Mobius said. "This is definitely significant, but we don't have time to stand here and figure it all out right now. We need to see if the time capsule is here at Calakmul. The presence of this lintel indicates that it might be."

"Yes, let's move," Diego said. "Finally, we're going to *do* something."

They all glared at him, but he ignored it. As they followed Mobius through the museum, Jillian said to him, "You do get that if we had followed what you wanted to do, we would have been driving off to find the police instead of sitting under that tree meditating. Jorge would have never found us, and we wouldn't have known about the lintel."

Diego's pride wouldn't let him "get" anything, at least not out loud, so he just kept walking and wishing she would stop looking at him expecting a reply. But he did decide to shelve the idea of contacting the government for the moment, even though he still thought they probably should, lintel or no.

But Jillian wasn't finished. "And you do realize that even though he's not a trained commando like you thought, Mobius is from a race that is way, *way* advanced compared to ours. Doesn't it make sense to go along with him and an accomplished shaman? And me, your—"

"My what?" he asked, looking at her.

"I don't know ... kidnapping partner." She laughed.

"If you had said 'girlfriend,' I'd go along with whatever you want."

She blushed and pushed his arm.

They finally came to a stop, and Diego realized they'd been walking around in circles through the museum since they left the lintel, and he was getting irritated again. "What in the axis mundi are we looking for?"

Jillian laughed loudly but covered her mouth. He assumed it was because it was inappropriate to laugh that hard when they were supposed to be saving the world from annihilation.

"We're looking for Jorge," Inka said. "He said he was going to be in the museum."

"There he is," Jillian said, pointing to him coming out of the men's room.

"Jorge," Inka said. "May we ask you something?"

"Yes, please," he said, walking over.

"The lintel you showed us said it was from Structure VII," Mobius said. "What is that structure?"

"It is a temple pyramid that originally had a three-room altar chamber on top, but the chamber is gone now," Jorge said.

"When was it built?" he asked.

"It is dated to approximately 731 AD."

Mobius looked excited even with the glasses on. "How tall is it?"

Jorge peered at him curiously. "The temple is only seventy-nine feet tall, one of the smallest at Calakmul."

"That's too small!" Mobius exclaimed. He turned on his heel and stomped across the room in about three strides, then stomped right back. "Okay, that's not it," he said. "It's got to be double that size. We'd be wasting our time even going there."

"Now what?" Jillian asked.

Diego was about to pipe up about going to the police again, but Inka asked Jorge, "Are your computers connected to the Internet?"

"Yes, of course."

"May we please use one? We need to contact a colleague. As I said to you before, we are from Mesoamerican University and are looking for something very important."

"And we have very little time to find it," Mobius added.

Jorge looked up at him. "I hear many accents from all over the world in my job here, but I do not recognize yours. Where are you from?"

"Uh ... well ...," Mobius stammered.

Inka jumped in. "He is an archaeologist from Israel. Please do not tell anyone because he is still doing the research, but he believes there is a connection between our Mayan ruins and some of the ruins in the Holy Land."

Jorge whistled. "Is this possible?" he asked Mobius.

"Anything is possible," Mobius said in stride but clueless as to what particular possibility he was vouching for.

Jorge waved for them to follow him. "Come, I will show you where you can use a computer," he said. "We allow them to be used by scholars sometimes, so it is fine."

He escorted them to a door near the entrance and opened it with a key. "Here you are," he said and let them into a tidy office with a desk, a computer, and a phone. He went to the computer and punched in a code. "I have to get back to the floor, but please let me know when you are finished so I can lock the door."

"*Por supuesto,*" Inka said. "*Muchas gracias.*"

"*Maestro,*" Jorge said, looking at Mobius. "I want to know about your findings when you are ready to publish them. I will give you my email address before you leave."

"Absolutely," Mobius said.

He left, and Diego closed the door.

"*¿Maestro?*" Jillian asked.

"It means 'teacher,'" Inka said.

"Okay, enough standing around," Diego said. "What the hell is the plan?"

"There is a real *maestro* at Mesoamerican University we must contact," Inka said.

"Come on," Diego said, waving his hand in a circular motion. "Let's go then. *¡Ándale, ándale!*"

Mobius looked at Jillian and Inka. "Is he *trying* to be irritating?"

CHAPTER THIRTY-SEVEN

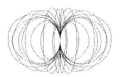

SPEED

Professor Alonzo Acosta peered at the image of the Tikal lintel over his glasses as he spoke to Inka on the computer from his office at the university. The image from the cog floated in front of her, and she had her fingers around it to make it appear as if she were holding a photograph.

"The only ones I have not seen depicted in nearly every Mayan city are those two," Acosta said, pointing to the spaceship and Serpent constellation glyphs. He was a thin, white-haired man with a rich Mexican accent and intelligent, clear eyes (although, to Mobius, weirdly tiny like the rest of the human race). "Those glyphs have always been a mystery."

"We have discovered that they are also on a lintel here at Calakmul, just like the one at Tikal," Diego said from offscreen. "Have you seen them all together in this sequence anywhere else?"

"Who is that?" Acosta asked.

"Ah ...," Inka stammered. "Let me introduce you to ... my colleagues. Diego, Mobius, and Jillian. They're a group of international students doing some very important work for ... Professor Ben-Ezra at the University of Tel Aviv."

The three of them quickly poked their heads in and out of view to say hello.

"Inka, I wasn't aware you were still working with Dr. Ben-Ezra. I thought she'd completed her fieldwork a while ago."

"There have been some new developments," Diego chimed in.

"*Maestro*, I am so sorry," Inka said. "But we are in a big hurry, and it is very important. I hope one day to tell you everything, but I ask you to trust how much we need your help now."

Acosta leaned back in his office chair and crossed his arms. "You have got me very curious, Inka Mazte, and I usually do not let my curiosity go unfulfilled. But since you have come to my aid many times during research projects, I won't ask any more questions. For now." He leaned forward again and started punching on his keyboard. "If we narrow down the search to passageway lintels, perhaps we can find your glyphs elsewhere."

Diego caught Mobius's eye and pointed to the clock on the wall—12:47 p.m.

"I know," Mobius whispered. "Stop freaking me out."

Diego chuckled.

"Why are you laughing?" Mobius asked.

Diego shook his head. "Nothing. You're a funny alien."

"Ssshhh," Jillian admonished him.

A few minutes later, Dr. Acosta was finished with his search. "Okay, I've queried the relics database for lintels with the Pleiades glyph and narrowed it down to nine. But only two contain all the glyphs you are looking for, other than one at Tikal and the broken one at Calakmul."

"Where are they?" Mobius asked.

"Coba and Chichen Itza," Acosta said. "This is fascinating. I never knew that all four of those sites had this in common."

When they heard the additional locations, Inka and Diego

looked at each other in a panic, but they kept it together long enough to get him off the call.

"Thank you, Professor Acosta," Jillian said, glancing at them sideways with concern.

"You're welcome," he said. "If I find anything else, I will contact you. Seeing this connection makes me even more curious about what you are up to. What is a number where I can reach you?"

"We'll get a cell phone on the road," Diego whispered to Inka.

"I don't have the number now, but I will call you with it when I do," Inka said.

"Wait," Mobius interjected. "Professor, do you know if there was a King K'awiil who ruled around the early part of your eighth century buried at either location?"

"In *my* eighth century, no," Acosta said. "But there was one in my ninth century."

Diego shot a look at Mobius.

"*The* eighth century, of course," Mobius said. "Please excuse my English."

The professor continued, "There were no tombs found at the ruins of Coba and no knowledge of a King K'awiil having ruled there. Although admittedly there were many King K'awiil's, so it is possible," the professor lectured on without taking a breath. "But there was a King K'ak'upakal, or possibly K'ak'upakal K'awiil, who ruled in Chichen Itza, and while excavation uncovered skeletal remains, we think those were sacrifices, not burials, because there were no proper tombs. Now, there is a Platform of the Tombs at Chichen Itza—"

"*Okay,* thank you, Professor," Diego interrupted. "I think we have what we need. Bye, bye," and he reached over and ended the video call before Acosta could pontificate any further.

"Diego!" Inka said. "He is an esteemed professor!"

"Well, he won't be an esteemed *anything* by tomorrow if I had let him go on any longer. We need to get moving, and the news isn't good."

"No, it's not," Mobius agreed, taking off his glasses. "There's no King K'awiil buried at either place."

"That we know of," Inka said.

"And we have to follow the clues, anyway, don't we?" Jillian added. "They're all we have."

"That's not the bad news I was referring to," Diego said, putting his hands to his head. "Coba and Chichen Itza are very far away! Several hours' drive for sure. There's no way we're going to make it in time to find this thing, let alone disarm it."

Mobius clenched his hand.

"Where are your friends?" Diego asked.

"I don't know," Mobius said, checking his cog.

"Aren't they supposed to be coming back to help you?"

"They may not have made it back to Akara," he said, pressing his finger to the azure mark between his eyes. "The torus—the ship's power source—was damaged. But even if they did make it, the only remaining ship on Akara was out of service, and the rest of the fleet was away on an important mission."

"So even if they made it, there's no ship for them to return in," Diego said, now exasperated.

"I'm pretty sure they would have recalled one of the others," Mobius said, "but it would explain the delay."

"*Pretty* sure?" Diego asked in a high-pitched voice.

"Okay, let's just all relax and assume they're on their way," Jillian said, stroking Diego's back.

Mobius started to pace, staring at the ground as he clenched and unclenched his hands. "Maybe they came back, but comms aren't working here for some reason. But they should be able to locate me ... I don't know ..." He felt ashamed that they wouldn't be able to communicate with him telepathically if they needed to, but then he stopped himself, catching the downward spiral of negative thoughts and the wake of fear they brought with them. He sensed the fear in Jillian, Diego, and Inka too. "I'm sorry, I'm sorry. We need to focus positive."

"*Is there* anything positive to focus on?" Diego asked.

"At least both cities are in Mexico, and we don't have to cross any borders again," Inka said.

"Good. Good. That's good," Mobius said.

For the next few minutes, they all brainstormed about how to get to the two Mayan cities—one of which they believed had to hold the time capsule—the fastest way possible. Mobius wished they had a hovercraft, but unfortunately, they were stuck with a fossil-fuel-belching monster on wheels. He asked about flying, but they explained it wasn't possible to get him past airport security.

"Why do you need security to use flight transportation?" Mobius asked, baffled.

"People hi-jack them to get ransom money or use them as weapons," Jillian said.

When Diego explained to Mobius what that meant, he tossed his sunglasses on the desk in frustration. "Your species' level of evolution is so inconvenient."

"Can we save the complaints about how primitive we are for later?" Diego asked.

"I have an idea," Jillian said. "Since the only way to get there is to drive, we obviously need to go as fast as we can, but we'll have to worry about cops. So what if we make the car look like an ambulance with that thingy of yours?" She sat down at the computer and pulled up a YouTube video of a Mexican ambulance to show Mobius.

"How important is the noise it makes?" he asked.

"It would make it seem more authentic," she said.

"I don't know how to program my cog to do that."

"*Gracias a Dios,*" Inka said. "I would go crazy with that noise."

Diego shook his head. "Besides, if a police officer saw us go by and radioed in to find out what was going on, they'd find out it wasn't real, and they'd follow us."

Staring at the computer screen, Mobius said, "I have another idea."

•

Forty-five minutes later they were blasting down the highway to Coba, trying to turn a typical six-hour drive into three and a half. Jillian drove as Inka and Diego slept in the back seat. The speed she was going made it seem to Mobius as if the cars they flew past were almost standing still. He loved how fearless Jillian was; she reminded him a little bit of Kaia. For a moment, he allowed himself to enjoy the thrill of the speed, and he couldn't help but wonder if he'd ever get to fly through the Akaran mountains on a uni-hover again.

Mobius was grateful that no one mentioned the obvious—that they had less than twenty-four hours to find the time capsule. At the museum, Inka said that she found it hard to believe it would be at either Coba or Chichen Itza because those two sites were some of the most studied and picked-over of all the Mayan ruins. But the only choice they had was to follow the clues where they led and pray they made it in time. Even if they did, Mobius had no idea what to do with the time capsule if and when he found it.

As Mobius programmed his cog, Jillian said, "It's too bad you can't get the Internet up on that thing, or at least make a phone call."

"We could if Piphus were here," he sighed, touching his bracelet.

She reached out, took his long, four-fingered hand, and squeezed it. "You're doing great." Jillian's compassion reminded Mobius as much of Kaia as her fearlessness did.

"Thanks," he said, even though he didn't feel like he was doing anything at all, let alone a great job. "But we have a problem."

"What now?" Jillian asked.

"I'm extremely hungry."

"Oh God."

A loud, high-pitched whining noise started up from somewhere, and Mobius looked around. "What is that?"

"Our first police car," Jillian said. "I hope this works. I'm going 120 miles an hour."

"I need to get into the back," Mobius said as he spotted the car with flashing lights on top coming after them. He climbed like an ungainly giraffe into the back seat between Inka and Diego, waking them up, then slithered over the seat into the rear of the Range Rover, accidentally kicking Diego in the head.

"¿Qué diablos?" Diego yelled. "What the hell?"

"¡Ay, ay, ay!" Inka exclaimed as she looked around and realized what was happening. She covered her eyes, peeking through her fingers to watch as Jillian swerved through the traffic to evade the police car screaming up on them.

Mobius barely fit in the back, and with all the movement, it took him a few moments to get situated. Jillian was able to stay far enough ahead of the police cars until he was finally able to point the cog through the back window and initiate the hologram.

"Okay, here we go."

Out of nowhere, a large group of spider monkeys appeared on the roadside, ran into the highway, and started jumping up and down just in front of the police car. The policeman swerved wildly into the other lane, sideswiping the car he was just about to pass, and both cars went spinning out of control like they were in a swirling ballroom dance. As the cars behind them slammed on their brakes to avoid the chaos unfolding ahead, the police car spun off the road into a ditch, while the car he had sideswiped flew along the edge of the ditch, kicking up gravel and dirt. The driver veered away from the ditch but went too far and ended up back on the highway, barely missing a big truck, causing the man behind the wheel to blare his horn. Finally, when it was all over and they were speeding on down the highway, Diego raised his arms and shouted, "*¡Adiós policía!*"

"Holy shit!" Jillian said. "It worked! But we could have killed someone!"

"*Ay, ay, ay,*" Inka said again, her eyes rolling to the heavens.

"Now *that* was exalted!" Diego said and reached back to high-five Mobius.

●

Before stopping for gas and food, they tried to get as far away as possible from the mayhem. Using holograms, Mobius was able to change the color of the SUV to green and manipulate the license plate from Guatemalan to Mexican, so they hoped they were not going to find any trouble waiting for them up ahead. But they were nervous as they pulled into a roadside gas station about halfway to Coba. The station was the largest they'd seen and the busiest too. Mobius had to eat, and his human friends thought they should get as big a variety of food as possible to find something that he could tolerate without passing out or who knows what else.

Jillian pulled the Range Rover next to a gas pump and came to a stop. "Let's make this fast," she said. After Diego filled the tank with gas, they all piled out of the car and headed to the bathrooms.

As Diego and Mobius waited for the single men's bathroom to become free, they had a fairly detailed discussion about how they both "go," as Diego put it. It turned out that below the waist they were almost exactly the same.

"Oh, and I have hair down there, and I'm assuming you don't," Diego said.

"You have hair *down there too*?" Mobius asked.

Diego shrugged. "Yes, all adults do."

"No way! Your penis is hairy? Will you show me?"

Just as Mobius said this, an older man came out of the bathroom and stared at them both. He carefully skirted around them, then walked quickly away.

Diego bent over, he was laughing so hard. "No," he said, the strange water coming to his eyes. "But I'll promise you this. If you get us through this, it's the first thing I'll do."

Diego looked so funny that Mobius started chortling, his vocalizations cascading up and down melodically.

"Oh my God," Diego said. "The way you laugh is hilarious."

"The way *you* laugh is hilarious," Mobius replied.

Diego walked into the bathroom, continuing to laugh, as a young guy walked up and stood in line behind Mobius. He was light-skinned with wavy blond hair down to his shoulders and a short beard. Mobius desperately wanted to touch his long hair and his fuzzy face, but he forced himself to keep his hands in his pockets and tried not to imagine all the men he saw with hair on their penises.

Mobius went in after Diego, and when he came out, he found his three companions shopping for food in the market. He still couldn't get over the strangeness of paying for such a basic, universal need. He thought about people who had no money and no way to get food. *How can humans let each other go hungry?*

As the others finished their shopping, Mobius noticed the blonde guy who had been in line for the bathroom join a young woman with shiny black hair and pale skin. She pointed at Jillian and told him something, becoming excited in the process. They walked toward the foursome, staring at Jillian.

"Hey, aren't you Jillian Savoy?" the girl asked.

Jillian stared at them for a moment before stammering, "Uh, I uh ... No. I don't know who that is."

"You know, the billionaire heiress?" the girl said. "It's all over the news—at least in America. We just came in from Texas. She's been kidnapped. I think they said it was in Guatemala though."

"They're offering a reward of like a million dollars for anyone who gives clues to where she is," the guy said, eyeing her greedily.

Mobius noticed Diego looking past him with his eyebrows furrowed, so he turned and saw a rough-looking man in cowboy boots, with tattoos up and down his arms, listening intently as he stood there holding a six-pack of cans that said *Tecate* on the side.

"We don't know anything about it," Diego said to the couple. He herded his companions toward the cashier, but the couple followed, and so did the tough guy.

"I need one of those pre-paid cell phones too, please," Diego told the clerk in Spanish. "And one of these watches." He pointed to a cheap watch in a case a few feet away.

Diego pulled out Menendez's wallet to pay and handed the cashier several bills. The clerk shook his head. "Pesos or American dollars, please," he said in Spanish. "We don't accept Guatemalan quetzales."

"*Mierda*," Diego mumbled under his breath as the Americans and the Mexican man stared at the money in his hands. He shoved the quetzales back in the wallet and replaced them with dollars.

"Where are you from, dude?" the American guy said to Mobius. "Are you from the Middle East or something?"

Diego grabbed their bags of stuff and they all headed toward the door. "No, dude, I'm from another planet," Mobius said, unable to help himself.

Inka's laugh was high-pitched and manic. "He is from Israel!" she said as they finally escaped the store and walked toward the car.

"*Jesucristo*, you're all over the news!" Diego said to Jillian as soon as they were out of earshot.

"Only in the U.S.," Jillian said.

"How do you know this?" Inka asked. "It's a big story any time something bad happens to a rich person."

"Yeah, I guarantee you that guy with the tattoos has heard something about it too," Diego said as they piled into the car. "And they all saw me hand the cashier Guatemalan money. I forgot we were in Mexico."

"Maybe they didn't think anything of it," Jillian said.

As they pulled out of the gas station, they saw the Americans watching them from inside the store; the woman was making a phone call. Then the Mexican man stepped outside and got on his phone too.

"Oh no," Diego said. "That can't be good."

CHAPTER THIRTY-EIGHT

COBA

When they finally got back on the road, Diego drove at the fastest speed the SUV could handle without him losing control of the vehicle.

"*Ay, ay, ay,*" Inka said, clutching the arm of the passenger door in the back seat. "I feel like I'm going to be sick."

Me too, Diego thought. This was the fastest he'd ever driven, and his stomach felt like he'd swallowed a hummingbird, but he tried like hell to seem calm and cool, particularly in front of Jillian. He turned to Mobius, who sat next to him in the passenger seat. "You okay?"

"Definitely. The faster the better," he said.

Jillian looked out the rear window. "No one is behind us. It's going to be okay. Mobius changed the color of the car and the license plate, so if those people were calling about me, the description they give of our car won't match. There's no way anyone is going to look for me at Mayan ruins. Why would a drug gang holding me for ransom take me to Coba or Chichen Itza?"

"We were talking about the ruins while we were shopping," Inka said. "What if they heard?"

"Or took pictures of you without you noticing?" Diego asked.

AWAKE: THE LEGACY OF AKARA

"No way," Jillian said, shaking her head, but the rest of them were silent. She looked at each of them and said, "So ... what? Do you want me to turn myself in?"

Diego kept his eyes glued to the road as he spoke to her. "I'm not saying that. I'm just saying there's a good chance you've been identified and being with me doesn't help. Since I was with you and I fit the description of who you were kidnapped with, that's even more confirmation that you're the billion-dollar girl. And now they've seen Mobius with you. The American asked if he was from the Middle East. Between Mobius's skin color and accent, he probably thinks Mobius is some kind of terrorist."

"Good Lord," Jillian said.

"What do we do?" Inka asked.

"We need to stay focused on the time capsule," Mobius said. "We just have to keep going."

There was really no arguing with that, so while Jillian got the new cell phone up and running, Diego asked Mobius about holograms, trying to calm himself down a little, to distract from the growing pressure. "Isn't there a problem on your planet with people messing with each other all the time?" he asked. "Don't people, especially nerdy guys like you, use it to play pranks on each other and cause all kinds of chaos?"

Mobius smiled a little, took off his baseball cap, and rubbed his bald head. "Kids do that, but it pretty much never works," he said. "We can easily tell a hologram from the real thing. It's kind of like you looking at a movie versus looking at reality. An ancient Mayan would have been fooled, but you know the difference."

"Huh," Diego said. "I guess that makes sense."

"And by the way," he said. "I'm not nerdy, whatever that is."

"Look it up." Diego grinned. "Sorry to tell you, but you kind of are."

Jillian finished setting up the phone, and Inka called Dr. Acosta right away and gave him the number.

"Just a moment, Professor. Let me put you on speakerphone," Inka said as she pulled the phone away from her ear.

"I had to do an interview," Acosta said over the speakerphone, "but I'm looking for more information about that lintel of yours again now. I have a call in to a few colleagues. I'll let you know if I hear back from them with anything that might be helpful."

Inka cleared her throat. "Professor, we're very curious about the significance of the serpent. It is very common among the glyphs we are finding. I believe the symbolism is referring to renewal and rebirth and the axis mundi, but I don't know what else to make of it. Do you have any other thoughts?"

"Let me look into it, and I'll get back to you," he said.

As soon as Inka hung up, Mobius said, "I have to eat. I'm going to lose consciousness."

"You're going to pass out if you do eat," Diego said.

"God, let's hope not," Jillian said. "We can't do this without him."

Jillian, Inka, and Diego debated what food he should try first.

"I think a piece of fruit," Jillian said. "It's simple, natural, one ingredient."

"He needs protein," Diego said. "Vegetarian protein, obviously. But he's got manly hunger, and fruit will only last him five minutes." Jillian rolled her eyes.

"You think you might be projecting 'manliness' onto him? He's an alien from another planet. We don't know *what* he needs."

"Well, he's got real man parts, I know *that*," Diego said.

Jillian raised her eyebrows. "Oh, do you now?"

"Yuh," he grunted. "We talked about it. I promised to show him my hairy penis if we made it through this." He gave Mobius a slap on the back. "Right?"

"Right," Mobius said. "I'm still trying to imagine it."

Inka rolled her eyes. "That's *perfecto*. Men are obsessed with their *penes* throughout the universe."

Jillian laughed and threw her hands in the air. "Fine, you win, Diego. He's got manly hunger and needs protein."

Inka shrugged her shoulders. "The macho man seems to think he knows best."

Diego glanced at her in the rearview mirror, and she stared back at him with an impish grin.

They all finally agreed on a soy protein bar—it seemed most like myomeal and didn't have any of the same ingredients as tamales.

"So, if you pass out again, how do we stop the police?" Jillian asked.

"I'm sure I won't if it doesn't have any animal in it. But just in case, I can teach one of you to start the hologram," Mobius said then looked at Inka.

She held up her hands in protest. "*Ay*, not me. I am bad at these things."

"I'll do it," Jillian said.

Mobius turned around and taught Jillian how to start the hologram in case she needed to. Diego listened intently, even as he raced down the highway, swerving from lane to lane, flying past the traffic. He was starting to get the hang of going fast, and as he'd suspected his whole life, he found that he really liked it. This was the nicest car he'd ever driven by far; it felt like he was going seventy when he was clocking 115 with ease. If he lived, he wanted to buy one for himself. That thought made him focus even harder on what Mobius was saying and on getting his hands on the alien technology, telling himself again that when he did, it would be good for the world, not just for him—a win-win for everyone.

"This is like trying to read Chinese inside a crystal ball," Jillian said as Mobius showed her the cog.

"Here," he said. "I'll just make it so you only have to touch one thing."

Finally, Jillian thought she had it, so Mobius opened the protein bar.

"Okay, let's give this a try," he said, and ate a small piece of it. "Hmmm. It tastes strong. What is the word that is opposite of sweet?"

"Bitter?" Jillian asked. "That's weird."

"Yes, but edible." He quickly ate half of it then said, "Oh, by the way, I changed the hol—" And that was it—he went unconscious as if he'd had a brain aneurism.

"*¡Ay no!*" Inka shouted, shaking him to try to revive him. "The macho man with the hairy penis was wrong!"

"I knew we should have gone with fruit instead of a totally processed food product," Jillian gloated.

"Hey!" Diego said, starting to sweat. "I didn't know."

"Exactly," the women said in unison.

"It's okay," Jillian said. "He's just passed out."

"How do you know? What if he's dead?" Inka cried.

Diego glanced over at the alien's drooping face. "He has a heart," he said, well aware of his own heart thundering inside his chest. "See if it's beating."

Inka put a hand on his chest. "I don't feel anything!"

"Please God no," Jillian said, putting a finger under his nose. "He's breathing." She sighed with relief, then felt his chest. "And I feel a heartbeat. It's weird but it's there. How long was he out last time?"

"Over two hours," Diego said.

"That is not good," she said. "Diego, you better slow down so we don't get stopped. He was saying something, and I don't know—"

"*¡Policía!*" Inka screamed as they blew past a police car sitting on the side of the road. Diego had been so focused on Mobius that he never saw the cop until they were right on top of him.

"Here he comes!" Diego yelled as the police siren wailed at them from behind. "Jillian, you've got to figure it out!"

She grabbed the cog and climbed into the rear of the SUV. She started pressing on the small, translucent disk, but it slipped out of her hand. "Damn, I can't see it! It's almost invisible!" she shouted, scrambling around trying to find it.

"*¡La policía! ¡Más cerca! ¡Más cerca!*" Inka shouted.

"Pull it together, Jillian," Diego yelled. Inka was right. The cop was getting closer. "It's got to be right there."

"Okay, I got it!" She held up the small disc, pinched it into a sphere, then pressed on it, and in the rearview mirror Diego saw a huge Darth Vader, albeit one that looked like a kid in a costume, floating in the air just above the cop car.

"What the hell?" Jillian shouted.

"Lower!" Diego yelled. "Point it lower!"

Jillian brought the image down so the police officer could see it. The cop slammed on the brakes, and the car spun a half turn and started skidding sideways down the highway. Other cars around it dodged and swerved, but Diego heard the sickening sound of tires screeching and metal crunching as several of them crashed into each other. In the rearview mirror, he saw the unfolding wreckage, and the damaged cop car spinning all the way around, then sliding off the side of the road, coming to a stop facing the opposite direction.

"Oh shit!" Jillian shouted. "I hope they're all okay."

Diego glanced back in his rearview mirror. "It doesn't look that bad."

Inka started praying but then put her head in her hands, "*Madre mía*, I am too old for this."

"It couldn't be helped," Diego said, starting to breathe again. "I know one thing for sure—the time capsule going off would be much worse."

They sat in silence for a minute, regaining their composure. The highway was quiet again, at least for the moment.

"—ogram to Darth Vader. I love that guy," Mobius said, suddenly waking up and continuing his sentence as if he'd never gone out.

Inka, Jillian, and Diego laughed. "You better change the license plates and color again," Diego said. "There's going to be an army looking for us after that."

Mobius made the changes so that it looked like they were driving in a pale blue suv. After a brief discussion, Jillian and Inka decided he should try a banana.

"Little bit only," Inka said. "You only slept a few minutes last time, I think, because you ate a little bit."

Mobius took a small bite and swallowed as they watched him.

"Please let this work," Diego said. Even though it would prove him wrong, he wanted it to work for many reasons, not the least of which was that as soon as Mobius could eat, he would allow himself to eat too. *Evolved or not*, he thought, *it's got to be torture to watch someone eat when you're hungry.*

"I think I'm okay," Mobius said and took another bite. "It's good and sweet."

Five minutes later, when he still hadn't passed out, they decided he could eat half the banana. "The other stuff knocked you out within seconds. Seems like you're going to be fine," Jillian said.

Within half an hour, they were all stuffing their faces, and Mobius ate all five bananas. "I'm going to live!" he shouted, his belly full.

Everyone fell silent.

He lowered his voice. "Hopefully."

As they turned onto the road leading to Coba, the cell phone rang. Jillian put Dr. Acosta on speaker.

"I found something interesting in regard to the axis mundi and the sites in question. In addition to the serpent being a symbol for the pillar at the center of the universe that births all creation, as you probably know, the Mayan tree of life is also a symbol for the axis mundi."

"Yes, *maestro*, I know this. How is this relevant?"

"I discovered that the tree of life symbol is prominent on stelae at all four sites in question—Tikal, Calakmul, Coba, and Chichen Itza. It seems to me like more than a mere coincidence."

"Hold on a moment, Professor," Mobius said, then whispered to Inka, "What is the tree of life?"

Jillian pressed the mute button as Inka told Mobius about the tree of life. She explained that it is a sacred symbol across many world mythologies and that it looks like the ceiba tree, with its vast branches arching toward the ground and its root system reaching toward the surface, so that they appear to form a circle. She said that the tree's trunk represents the axis mundi, while the branches and roots represent creation coming into form.

Just as Jillian unmuted the phone, Mobius almost jumped

through the ceiling as he blurted out, "This kind of tree is the primary symbol for the torus on Akara!"

"¿*Perdón?*" Acosta said, and they could hear him typing. "Did you say Taurus—the star constellation? And what is Akara?"

Diego glared at Mobius, but he was still bouncing up and down in his seat. Inka sat, wide-eyed and speechless.

"No, a torus," Diego said, jumping in. "The geometrical shape."

Jillian continued for him. "We have seen it symbolized in different ways in different, you know, places around the world, like in Akara ... the cave Mobius just discovered in Israel ... by the Sea of Galilee near, ah, Nazareth."

Diego gave her a look to show her he was impressed, and she gave him a cocky little nod, until the professor asked, "Where? Did you say Nazareth? That's nowhere near Galilee."

"Exactly," Diego jumped in, clapping a hand to his head. "Anyway, Professor, why don't you look it up? That's T-O-R-U-S."

"Torus. I found it," Acosta said.

"Does it talk about the sacred geometry?" Mobius asked.

"No, let me do a search on that."

Diego rolled his eyes at Mobius and whispered, "We don't have time for this."

"Oh, yes," Acosta said. "I see here, it represents the pattern of the universe from atoms to galaxies ... and, hmmm, even human consciousness. Very interesting. I'll have to read more about that later. But yes, Mobius, I can see how the tree of life resembles this torus shape. Also, similar to the tree of life, this site says the torus is depicted in different ways throughout world cultures and religions."

"Yes, yes, yes," Mobius said, squirming excitedly. He grabbed the phone and put it to his ear. "Can you see it, *maestro*? It's trying to show you that the entire universe is just energy that comes from the same source—it's all one! We are all one. If humans could get this, you could make the leap in your evolution!"

"You cut out. If humans could *what?*" Acosta asked.

Suddenly, Mobius handed the phone back to Jillian and put a hand to his head.

"We're at Coba, Professor," Jillian said. "Gotta go."

"Wait," Acosta protested, "I want to know what Mobius is—"

"Sorry, you're cutting out." Jillian ended the call, then turned to Mobius. "What happened? Are you okay?"

"My neurolink just glitched out," Mobius said. "It's been doing some strange things since I got here, but it went down completely when I put the phone up to my ear."

"I bet it's the damn EMF waves," Jillian said. "I knew it. Those things are toxic. We're all going to die of brain cancer."

"If we make it that long," Diego said, pulling into the parking lot of the Coba ruins. "Okay first, how bad is this? Do you need that neuro thing to function? How much of a cyborg are you?"

"When Kaia and the others return, they won't be able to communicate with me through my neurolink, but I still have my cog, so it should be okay."

"Good. Second, what the hell were you trying to do there with the professor?"

"He's a teacher," Mobius said. "What if he taught his students about the torus and what it means? I was trying to help."

"Well, don't, *hombre.*"

"He's right, Mobius," Jillian said. "You practically told him you're from another planet. You need to keep a lid on it."

•

At Coba, they got out of the car and started what looked to be a very long walk to the ruins from the parking area. At the end of the lot, they found out that it was almost a mile to the actual entrance down a long path. Just then, a small, middle-aged Mestizo man pedaled a bicycle rickshaw up next to them. "Taxi?" he asked, and they climbed onto the two bench seats behind him.

Diego took the opportunity to put his arm around Jillian while they clattered along. He glanced back at Mobius, who seemed to be brooding. "I didn't mean to be a *pendejo* when you got so excited with Acosta," he said. "Are we okay?"

"Yes, we're okay... *Hombre*," Mobius said, smiling.

Jillian giggled and put her head on Diego's shoulder, and he pulled her closer to him.

When the rickshaw came to a stop at the entryway, Diego tipped the man well, grateful that Menendez carried thousands of dollars in cash in his wallet, then headed to the gate to pay the entry fee. As he gave the attendant money, he noticed a uniformed security guard eyeing Jillian. "We have to make this fast," he said when he rejoined the group. "That security guard was looking at Jillian."

Jillian, Inka, and Mobius turned to look at the guard, but he was gone. "You're being paranoid," Jillian said.

"She is a pretty girl," Inka said. "Mexican men are bad about staring."

Diego glared in the direction he'd seen the guard.

"But Guatemalan men are worse," Inka said in Spanish, giving Diego her familiar impish smile.

As they walked quickly down a tree-lined promenade, Diego put his arm around her. "Listen, moon goddess, you and I are going to have to have a talk one day about all this teasing."

She smiled up at him with her little-girl dimples. "You can

handle it."

"Come on," Mobius said, and the others had to speed walk to keep up. His strides covered about three of Diego's and Jillian's, and five of Inka's. He finally stopped when they turned onto the main plaza, looking up at a pyramid hulking before them like a geometric mountain. Even though Diego had just been to two other Mayan ruins, its soaring grandeur took his breath away. At the bottom of the structure was a massive stela with an image of Itzamna on it.

"This has to be a good sign," Diego said.

"We need to go up to the altar room," Mobius said, starting to fill with hope again. "There must be an unknown passageway leading to a tomb in the center of the pyramid."

Inka bent over and put her hands on her knees. "I am too tired, and it is too hot for me to climb. I'm sorry."

"That's fine," Mobius said. "Just stay here."

Jillian nodded. "Let's go."

As Mobius, Jillian, and Diego headed up the crumbling structure, Mobius started to fill with hope that maybe this was the city they'd been looking for.

Halfway up, Jillian said, "Another Mayan Stairmaster. I don't have to worry about working out, that's for sure."

"No," Diego panted. "None of us need to worry about working out."

At the top of the massive temple, they didn't have time to rest or enjoy the dazzling view of the cantaloupe-colored sun descending toward the roof of the jungle. Mobius looked up at a large rectangular indention above the doorway to the altar room. "That must have been where the wood lintel hung."

They ducked through the opening and into a small, enclosed

altar room, and Diego was struck by how different it was from outside. The sounds of the tourists climbing all over the pyramid were muffled to near silence, and the temperature was probably fifteen degrees cooler. The smell was also really old, but in a good way, like earth.

"It feels sacred in here," Jillian said.

"But there is only this one room, and it's so small," Mobius said, running his hands along the walls, trying to find some opening or clue that would lead them to a burial chamber. He closed his eyes. "I'm going to try to access the Wisdom."

An Asian family—mom, dad, and two kids—stood outside, and the dad peeked his head in. "Can you wait just a minute?" Diego said, blocking his view of Mobius. "He had an ancestor who died here."

"Oh sure, sorry," the man said and backed out.

Jillian put her hand over her mouth to muffle her laughter. "So great-grandpa died like a thousand years ago?"

"Whatever," Diego said, grinning. "It worked."

"*¡Mierda!*" Mobius shouted.

"You didn't get anything?" Jillian asked.

"No, I think I did. My access seems to be getting stronger. But I don't believe there is anything here. I don't know what to do." Mobius squeezed his eyes shut.

They walked back out into the warm glow of the setting sun and looked around. "We have to figure out what the glyphs on the lintels are trying to tell us," Jillian said. "There's a message there. We still need to know what it is."

"She's right," Diego replied, glancing at the watch he'd bought at the gas station and seeing that it was just after 5:30 p.m. "But we have less than eighteen hours before the capsule opens."

"I know that, Diego. What I don't know is what to do now," Mobius said, as he spun his bracelet around his wrist, the colors changing with each turn, until Diego made him put his hands back in his pockets.

Jillian pointed down below them. "Hey look, Inka is waving at us."

They started down the steps toward her, and as they descended, it became clear that she wasn't just waving; she was frantically motioning at them to hurry.

CHAPTER THIRTY-NINE

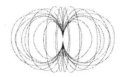

TREE OF LIFE

Mobius, Diego, and Jillian rushed down the steps and ran to Inka.

"Did you find anything?" she asked breathlessly.

"No," Mobius said. "What's going on?"

She looked around the park. "I saw some men who looked like *narcos*. Bad men. I got scared they were looking for Jillian, but I don't see them anymore."

"We need to go anyway," Diego said. "We have to get to Chichen Itza. Maybe it will have a clue."

"First, come look. There is something important you must see," Inka said and led them to the stela of Itzamna at the base of the pyramid. "Look. Look what's on the other side—it's the tree of life that *Maestro* Acosta spoke of." She pointed to an etching in the monument that took up nearly the entire face of the stone slab—a large tree with various glyphs scattered among its mushroom of branches and roots curling upward from below. "Look here," she said, pointing to the center of the tree trunk. "It is upside down so not very easy to see, but that is the spaceship symbol."

"Oh my God, you're right," Jillian said.

Mobius felt a thrill of energy running through him when he

recognized the glyph.

"What do you think all this means?" Diego asked Inka.

"After looking at the etching for some time," she said. "I entered the timeless realm of the shamans and began to see some things. I believe the tree of life has clues to the time capsule just like the lintels. The spaceship glyph is a symbol of Itzamna's godlike power. I think it may be the symbol for the time capsule itself. The tree represents the creation of life—"

"And the time capsule sits at its center about to destroy it all," Jillian said.

"Why is the symbol upside down?" Mobius asked.

"That I do not know," Inka said.

"When you draw a tarot card upside down, it signifies that the meaning is inverted. Is that possible?" Jillian asked.

"Perhaps. Perhaps it represents the defeat of Itzamna and the time capsule by Kukulcan," Inka said. "Look at this." She pointed to another glyph—this one on the upper left side of the root structure. It was the familiar etching of Itzamna with his big nose and serpent on his head. Like the spaceship, it was larger than most of the others on the stela. Unlike the spaceship, however, it was right side up.

"If the time capsule is not here, why do you think that one is bigger than the others?" Diego asked.

"Maybe because Itzamna was a god," Mobius said.

"I don't know. The spaceship glyph is the same size as Itzamna, and so is that one," she said, pointing to a glyph that sat at the top of the stela just above the tree.

"What is it?" Jillian asked.

"The symbol for Coba, where we are now," Inka said. "All of the old cities had their own emblem glyph."

"Right," Diego said. "I am familiar with the one from Tikal."

Mobius took out his cog and captured the tree of life on it. "Dr. Acosta said that there were trees of life at all four cities. We need to see what's on the others as well."

"Yes, I agree," Inka nodded.

"Why is this all so secretive and complicated?" Jillian asked. "If someone wanted the capsule to be found, why not just make it obvious?"

"She's right," Diego said. "Unless Itzamna put them there to mislead anyone who might try to find the time capsule."

Inka shook her head. "If these lintels and stelae are here to reveal the actual location of the time capsule, it would have been much too dangerous to make it obvious. Itzamna had many faithful followers—the entire Mayan world in fact—and they would have wanted his divine commands carried out at any cost. I am sure that whoever was leaving the clues knew they would be killed, and the clues would be destroyed if it were ever discovered that's what they were doing."

"Maybe it was a secret society. More than one person," Jillian said.

"Do you really think a Mayan from back then could create such a complex set of clues in all these different locations?" Mobius asked.

"Yeah, it's like an elaborate scavenger hunt," Jillian said.

Inka cut her eyes at Mobius. "I appreciate that you are very advanced ... at least that's what you say—"

"Listen, tiny human, don't get pugilistic." With an open mouth, Mobius looked around at them. "I have no idea where I got that word."

Inka rolled her eyes and waved a hand at him, then continued trying to make her point. "Let me tell you something about my ancestors, alien *grandote*. They were the greatest astronomers in history, and they had no instruments. They were also the greatest keepers of time in the world. They understood that the Earth went around the sun every 365 days when most of the world thought the sun circled the Earth. I cannot go into all the things my people understood and knew, but let me just tell you, they could have created these clues for certain. It may have taken years to complete, but that did not stop them from building huge cities with only primitive tools. Believe me, they could do it."

"Okay, okay," he said. "I was just asking." Then he mumbled, "I guess I won't mention that they had help from my ancestors."

Inka squinted her eyes at him until they suddenly grew wide, filled with fear. "The *criminales*," she whispered. "They're here."

Mobius glanced over his shoulder and, in the shadows of early evening, saw three intimidating-looking men in cowboy boots and jeans, staring at them.

"She's right," Diego said. "Those guys are *narcos*."

"What are they doing here?" Jillian asked.

"Not learning about the Mayan culture, that's for sure. They're looking for you," he said. "I knew it. That man at the gas station must have heard you talking about Coba. Menendez is connected to a huge criminal network. He could have easily gotten the word out about us escaping. Or maybe they want you for the million-dollar reward."

Mobius looked back again. "They're coming this way."

"Come on, come on," Diego said. "We've got to get out of here." They started walking toward the entrance as fast as possible without breaking into a run.

When they reached the entrance, Jillian said, "We should tell security about those men."

"No," Diego said firmly. "I think the security guard may be the one who told them you're here."

The little man on the bike rickshaw was just about to take off with a foursome of elderly people, but Diego ran in front of the rickshaw and blocked his path. "Come on!" he yelled at his friends, then demanded that the old folks get out. When they hesitated, he began to physically pull them and the driver out of the vehicle. "Now," he said. "It's an emergency! *¡Emergencia!*"

Diego handed the driver a wad of dollars as Mobius hopped on the pedicycle-like transport. He pushed on the pedals with all his might, and the bike surged forward.

"It will be in the parking lot waiting for you!" Diego called back to the taxi driver in Spanish as Mobius propelled them toward the car so fast that people stopped and stared. He hoped he was going too fast for them to notice his hands on the handlebars.

The three *criminales*, now joined by the security guard, ran after the rickshaw, but Mobius was pedaling too fast for them to catch up. When the guard stopped running, he took out his phone, and the other men veered off through the parking lot, presumably toward their car.

Jillian squeezed Mobius's shoulder. "This thing is going to come apart if you keep going this fast!"

But fear pushed him forward, even though he knew she was right. When they approached the suv, he realized he didn't know how to stop.

"Diego!" he yelled, trying to slow down his legs, but the pedals kept spinning around and around. "How do I stop this thing?"

"What?"

"How do I stop?"

They passed the Range Rover as Diego yelled, "Push backward on the pedals! Go the other way around."

Mobius slammed the pedals backward, and the rickshaw went skidding across the pavement. It turned sideways, shuddering as if it would burst apart, then went up on two wheels, tilting crazily toward the ground. "Whoa!!" they all screamed. Just before it toppled over, Mobius put his foot on the ground and pushed, and the rickshaw's wheels slammed back to the ground.

"*¡Ay, ay, ay!*" Inka shouted as they jumped out and ran to the car. Before Mobius had even closed his door, Diego squealed out of the parking lot.

"Are they behind us?" Diego asked.

"No, I don't see them," Jillian said, and they all sat there breathing like they'd been running for hours, even Mobius, who immediately began changing the license plate and the color of the Range Rover with his cog.

•

Wrung out and exhausted, they drove in silence for a while on the way to Chichen Itza, the last of the four cities. Inka fell asleep, snoring quietly, but then she abruptly sat up. "We have to contact *Maestro* Acosta to find out what is on the other tree of life stelae."

Jillian pulled out the phone. "Oh no," she said, staring at it. "It's out of battery."

"Where's the car charger?" Diego asked.

"It didn't come with one," she said. "It was barely charged when we bought it."

Mobius's frustration mounted at the primitive technology he had to deal with on this planet. If he ever saw Kaia again, he would inform her that it was nearly impossible to focus positive when it came to limited energy.

"The closest city is Valladolid. It's coming up in about thirty miles," Diego said. "We'll have to call from there. We need gas and water too."

Mobius looked behind them at the dark highway and made sure there were no headlights getting close. "We can stop briefly, but we have to get to Chichen Itza," he said, opening the map of the Mayan cities. "It's the only city with the lintel and tree of life we haven't been to."

Diego looked at his watch, something he was doing every few minutes. "We have less than seventeen hours. What if the time capsule isn't there?"

Once again, they just sat there in defeated silence.

Half an hour later, Diego pulled off the highway. He stopped at the first gas station and looked around before getting out of the car. "Good," he said, "I think we lost them."

Mobius made a face and covered his nose and mouth. "What is that smell?"

"It's air pollution," Jillian said. "From cars and factories mainly."

"It doesn't kill you?"

"No. Well, not right away, anyway."

For some reason, he was not extremely comforted by this. It felt like his lungs were being singed.

After Diego pumped the gas and paid, they headed farther into the city, passing through an impoverished neighborhood filled with dilapidated shanties. Mobius stared out the window, his mouth agape. People drained of life force, in tattered clothing, stood along the trash-laden roadside as mangy dogs wandered about searching for scraps.

At a busy intersection, a shirtless man stood between rows of traffic. He put something to his mouth, then lit a small flame in front of his face. He blew out, and a blast of fire streamed out of his mouth.

"Look at that!" Mobius yelled out. "How did he do it?"

"He put fuel in his mouth, then blew it onto the flame of the lighter," Diego replied.

"What a fantastic entelechy," Mobius exclaimed.

"A fantastic what?" Jillian asked.

"Entelechy—I think that is the word that most closely translates. His ... innate creative potential and purpose."

Diego shook his head in dismay. "That is most definitely *not* his entelechy. It's toxic and very dangerous, but he's poor. He only does it for money."

Just as the light turned green, three barefoot children, skin and bones—their hair unkempt and faces dirty—ran up to the car with their hands extended.

"What are they doing?" Mobius asked.

"Begging for money," Diego said, pulling away.

"Wait, stop! Give them some," Mobius said, but Diego was through the intersection.

Mobius put his head in his hands. "Why are there so many poor people? I don't understand."

"Neither do I," Jillian said, shaking her head.

"There are no poor people on Akara?" Inka asked.

"No," he said. "Not anymore. Not since the Rebirthing."

"Wow, that's inspiring," Jillian said, then sighed heavily. "But even if by some miracle we get through tomorrow, I just don't see how we'll ever make it to our own Rebirthing. At least not without having to go through a Ravaging, like you did. It's pretty depressing."

Inka put a hand on Jillian's shoulder. "But remember the

prophecy of light. Mobius, when I met you yesterday, you said that maybe it could be different for Earth. That it is possible for us to change without the level of suffering your planet went through."

Mobius turned in his seat to look at her. "Yes, it might be. On Akara, the Ravaging ended when people finally surrendered, not because they lost, but because they chose to stop fighting. They chose love over fear. Their desire to live in a more evolved way became more important than their survival instinct. That is how we woke up. Maybe you don't have to wait until things get as bad as they did for us. But from what I've seen, unfortunately, it seems like it's going to take things getting even worse than they are now for humans to wake up from the belief in separation that causes all the greed, conflict, and destruction."

"What exactly do you mean by the belief in separation?" Diego asked.

"The belief that you are separate beings ... separate from each other, from all of life."

Diego raised his eyebrows. "You're telling me I'm not separate from you?"

"You may be individual, but you're not separate, Diego. Like the waves on a sea. It's all one. The more access you have to the Wisdom, the more you experience the oneness." As Mobius explained all this, he realized that even though he wasn't fully awake himself, he still knew at a very deep level that what he was saying was the truth, and that alone made a difference.

Diego chuckled. "Sorry to be cynical, but what are the chances of us all waking up with seven billion people on the planet?"

"Actually," Mobius said, "it may take a lot fewer people than you think. On Akara, only a small number of people, called the Wise Ones, had a shift in consciousness, and when they did, it sparked a planet-wide awakening."

Jillian leaned forward in her seat. "Oh my God, *how?*"

Mobius paused to think, then pulled out his cog and began reading. "Quantum scientists found that individual consciousness affects the collective. Once a sufficient number of the Wise Ones realized their oneness, a critical mass was reached, which created a coherence effect on the field of consciousness across the planet."

"*Dios mío,*" Inka whispered.

"That's ... amazing," Jillian said. "So, you're saying we just need to get to a tipping point. But how many people would it take?"

"The threshold for the evolutionary leap in consciousness on Akara was found to be one percent of the population."

"Huh, interesting," Diego said. "That reminds me of something I learned in human physiology. Only one percent of the cells in our hearts regulate our heartbeat. When these pacemaker cells fire, all the other cells sync with them, and the whole heart beats together. So I guess you could say they create a coherence effect like you're talking about, Mobius. That's pretty cool."

Mobius blinked twice. "Yes, scientists on Akara have found that there are many things in nature that operate according to this kind of threshold coherence effect."

"That's amazing!" Jillian said. "So only one percent of people would have to wake up for it to impact all of humanity." She turned to Inka. "If that's it, that's doable! I mean, right?"

The shaman's eyes welled up with tears. "I think so, *mija*. It sounds like a prophecy of light to me. What a beautiful vision ... the heart of humanity beating as one."

Jillian, Inka, and Mobius launched into a several minute discussion about how to get to the 1% tipping point until Diego couldn't stand it any longer. He slapped his hand on the steering wheel and said, "Great plan, everyone. You should definitely make that happen. But first, can we get back to saving the planet from the time capsule and *then* you can go ahead and wake everyone up and save us from the Ravaging?"

Jillian rolled her eyes and Inka shook her head as Diego drove into downtown Valladolid.

"This looks like a good place to stop," he said glancing around, checking out the brightly lit, clean street, lined with colorful buildings and lots of people on the sidewalks.

The scene fascinated Mobius. It looked inviting, with humans sitting at outdoor tables, no doubt drinking *cerveza* and coffee. He was glad to see they were not poor, like the others.

"We'll have to find a café where we can charge the phone and call Acosta. I'm starving anyway," Diego said, pulling into an open parking space in front of a majestic, old building with twin spires.

"Ah, I have heard of this church," Inka said reverently, gazing up at it when they got out of the car. "The Valladolid Cathedral, *Catedral de Nuestra Señora de la Asunción. Es preciosa.*"

Mobius agreed with her; it was beautiful. As they walked down the sidewalk, he gawked at everything around him. They went into the café next to the cathedral, and while Diego ordered food at the counter, Inka and Jillian found an electrical outlet next to a table in the back, away from the other customers, who were seated up front near the windows.

"Gross. I feel disgusting," Jillian said, taking a seat. "I need a shower in the worst way."

"We all do," Diego said, bringing coffee and quesadillas for them and water and two bananas for Mobius.

"Let's call Acosta," Mobius said.

Jillian pressed redial, then set the phone in the center of the table. After several rings, Acosta's resonant voice came through the speaker. "Ah, there is the mysterious four," he said. "Did you find what you were looking for at Coba?"

"No, but we found an important clue in our search," Inka said, then explained what they saw on the tree of life etching. *"Maestro,* is it possible for you to look up pictures of the tree of life images from Tikal, Calakmul, and Chichen Itza? We need to see the detail of what's on them. It might help us find what we are looking for."

"And what exactly is it we are looking for again?" Acosta asked, a bit gruffly. "It is almost dinner time, and I have an engagement."

Inka looked at them, unsure what to say. Diego picked up the phone. "Hold on for just a moment," he said, then pressed the mute button. "Maybe we should tell him."

Jillian leaned forward, looking at Inka. "What are the chances he will hang up and call the police as soon as we mention a weapon of mass destruction?"

"He is a good man, but very conservative," she said. "It is a halfway chance he will do what you say."

"That's too high of a risk," Mobius said. "Tell him you can't say. Beg him to help us."

"What if we went to a library and tried to find the tree of life pictures online?" Jillian asked.

"Oh no," Inka said. "This is not information found on the Internet. The university has a database of Mayan images better than anywhere else in the world."

"Okay, I guess begging it is," Jillian said, unmuted the phone, and pointed at Inka.

Inka sounded like a little girl. She was obviously intimidated by this man. "*Maestro*, I am so sorry but—" she started to say, but he interrupted her.

"I know, I know," he said impatiently. "It is all very secret. If I find out you are looking for gold treasure or the fountain of youth or some such nonsense, I will lay waste to your reputation, *Senõra* Mazte."

Inka blurted out a string of Spanish so fast that Mobius had no idea what she was saying; since they'd been speaking only English for Jillian, his Spanish was slipping away. It was obvious, however, that Inka was reassuring the professor that they were not looking for nonsense.

"Fine, fine," Acosta said. "Just know I will require that you tell me everything once you have found whatever it is that you're after." He took a breath and exhaled his annoyance. "So while you were having your little meeting, I found your trees of life from the cities in question. Tell me what I'm looking for."

"At the center of the tree trunk, do you see the glyph from the lintels that has the triangle on the bottom and circle on top? On the tree, it might actually be upside down," Mobius said.

After a few moments, Acosta answered. "Yes, yes, on three of them I see that glyph. You're right, it's upside down compared to the ones on the lintels. When I zoom in, I can see it. How fascinating. I'm not sure if there is one at Chichen Itza. The glyph is barely visible."

"Can you look again, Professor?" Inka asked. "It is very important."

"I am looking," Acosta said. "The glyph may well be there— faint markings suggest it's possible. But this stela is extremely worn."

"Oh no," Mobius said. He nearly fell out of his chair in

AWAKE: THE LEGACY OF AKARA

frustration, almost certain they weren't going to solve the puzzle of the time capsule's location.

"You know, there is a good chance you could see it in person," Acosta said. "I have seen details in person that didn't show up in pictures a number of times. If you are in Valladolid, just go to Chichen Itza in the morning. It's December 21st, the winter solstice. If you are there in the morning, you will see the descent of the shadow snake down the side of *El Castillo* temple. It only happens twice a year, when the angle of the sun makes it look like the shadow is a snake crawling down the pyramid steps. And you will be there for the end of the calendar. It should be an incredible scene—" He stopped abruptly and paused for a moment. "Wait a minute. Does any of this have to do with the end of the calendar?"

Inka looked like she was going to have a seizure, so Mobius responded. "We promise we'll tell you everything very soon."

Jillian and Diego looked at him, and he shrugged. What choice did he have?

"Professor, will you please email us the pictures of the tree of life images from all four cities?" Diego asked.

Acosta grumbled loudly, but he took down Diego's email address. "Okay, there you go," he said. "They're sent."

"Professor, I hate to ask you for anything more," Inka said. "But could you please keep your phone nearby in case we need you?"

"Of course! I have nothing better to do," he said irritably. "I have a dinner tonight with colleagues I haven't seen in years, and tomorrow we are having a fiesta here at the university to celebrate the end of the calendar, but I will keep my phone on me. Don't call unless you have to."

"We won't," Inka said. "Of course not. Thank you again."

Jillian disconnected the call. "Okay, what now?"

"We've got to get to Chichen Itza," Mobius said. "The time capsule has to be there. It's the last of the four cities with the tree of life stela."

"Even if it's there, it's not going to be easy to find," Diego said. "It is the most popular of all the Mayan ruins. I'm sure they have the tightest security—barbed wire fences, lots of guards. *Todito.* The works."

"No need to worry about that now," Inka said. "Before we go to Chichen Itza, we should get the pictures from Acosta printed out so we can look at them. There may be more clues, some kind of a shamanic code left behind to help Kukulcan find the time capsule."

"She's right," Jillian said. "We've been running around like chickens with our heads cut off. Let's use any help we can get."

"I'm actually with them on this," Diego said.

"Fine," Mobius said. "*Ándale* then. *Ándale.*"

Jillian stood up. "Okay, okay, we're '*ándale*-ing.'" As they walked out of the café, she turned to Mobius. "Even if you find the capsule in time, you have to disarm the damn thing. Do you have any ideas about how you're going to pull that off?"

"I don't know. I'm going to have to make the leap, I guess."

Diego shook his head in dismay. "I still don't even know what that means. But I do know this—it's going to have to be one big damn leap."

CHAPTER FORTY

CROSSHAIRS

M inutes later, they stood outside a storefront only a few blocks away. Over the door hung a hand-painted sign that said *Copias Valladolid.*

"Wow," Jillian said. "Staples it's not. Do you think it's even open this late?"

Diego sighed. "I hope so. And that it's better inside than it looks from out here because we need Internet access too."

The door to the copy shop was locked, but the light was on inside, so Diego knocked on the glass. They were relieved when a young man came from the back and opened the door for them.

"We are closed," the clerk said in Spanish. He looked to be seventeen or eighteen, and his face was cherubic even with a scruff of hair on his chin. "I was just here playing video games after work."

"So you have an Internet connection then?" Diego asked, and the young man nodded.

"*Gracias a Dios,*" Inka said.

"We need your help badly," Diego said. "We will pay you well."

The clerk let them inside the shop filled with clutter, stacks of paper, and a single, very old copy machine.

"*Gracias, senõr,*" Diego said. "Do you speak English? The lady here doesn't speak Spanish and likes to know what is going on."

"*Sí, claro.* I mean yes, *senõrita,* for you I will speak English with gladness," he said to Jillian, smiling and blushing. "I am Francisco." He laughed nervously, and Diego saw himself in the young man, so awkward around girls when he was that age.

"We need to print out some images," Diego said.

Because of Francisco's instant crush on Jillian—and her egging it on by telling him how sweet and adorable he was—he worked feverishly for them.

As soon as the tree of life images from each city were downloaded from the email Acosta had sent, they printed them out, and Diego spread them across the counter. The trees were all very similar except for some slight variations. Like the one at Coba, each tree bore an emblem of its respective city glyph above it and had the inverted spaceship glyph at the center of its trunk (except for the one at Chichen Itza, where the center glyph was indecipherable). However, each tree featured a different enlarged glyph—similar to the Itzamna glyph at Coba—somewhere amidst its branches or roots. On the Tikal tree, a Pleiades glyph sat among the upper right branches; on Calakmul's, the serpent forming the Akaran star constellation sat in the lower right branches. Because the glyphs on the tree at Chichen Itza were barely visible, they couldn't tell if one of them was larger than the others.

"Three out of the four cities have one of the glyphs from the lintels," Mobius said. "What does this mean?"

Inka leaned in and examined the trees more closely. "Maybe the message will become clear if we create one tree with all the glyphs on it and can look at it all at once."

Jillian asked Francisco for a piece of onionskin paper, then traced the tree of life and placed all of the glyphs onto a single tree in their exact locations. Everyone hovered around and looked down on the image.

"This makes no sense," Jillian said. "It looks to me like Itzamna created all this to lead us on a wild goose chase."

"I don't think so," Inka said. "I can feel the purity of the intention behind this."

"*Perdóname,*" Francisco interrupted. "I must close the shop now."

"Of course, of course. We're sorry to have kept you," Jillian said.

"*Está bien,*" Diego looked at his watch, shocked to see how much time had passed. "It's after ten o'clock. We need to get to Chichen Itza. It's our only hope."

Inka folded the onionskin paper drawing and put it in her bag as Diego gave Francisco a hundred-dollar bill.

"*¡Muchas gracias!*" Francisco said, staring at the money, turning it over and over in disbelief. "This is too much, *señor*. But I will take it with gladness anyway." He walked them to the door, and when he noticed that Jillian was right behind him, he pushed it open and stepped outside to hold it for her. "Thank you for the coming," he said smiling. "This was most interesting—" Francisco's words were cut off abruptly by gunfire blasting through the night air and hitting him in his chest.

Jillian screamed, and Diego yanked her back into the store. They all dove for the ground just as a barrage of bullets blew out the storefront glass, shattering it all over them. Suddenly, the cacophony stopped, and the momentary silence was filled with death and fear. Francisco's body lay propping the door open where he fell.

"Jillian Savoy," a familiar voice called from outside. "Come out, and your friends will not get hurt."

Jillian began to sob.

Diego held her tighter. "It's Menendez."

"The man with the mask?" Mobius asked. "The one who shot Kaia?"

"Yes."

"Tell me you do not mean *Manuel* Menendez," Inka said to Diego as she lay next to Mobius, her hair sprinkled with shards of glass.

"Yes," Diego said. "He is after Jillian for ransom money. And to restore his pride too, I'm sure."

Huge tears dropped from Inka's eyes. "His *pistoleros* killed my cousin. He makes life in my village hell. He will kill us all."

"Come on," Diego said, fueled by adrenaline. "Maybe there's a back door. Stay low."

"Jillian! We have business to finish. I will give you thirty seconds to come out," Menendez shouted.

They crawled into the small back room and found a wooden door behind a stack of boxes. "The only reason they're not forcing their way in here right now is because they must be afraid of Mobius," Diego said. "But that could change any second." He told the others to stay down, then he stood up and moved the boxes out of the way.

"How long do you think before the police get here?" Jillian asked.

"Long after we need them," Diego said.

"What?" Mobius said. "What good are they if they don't come at a time like this?"

"I'm sure Menendez's gang pays off the cops. The *narcos* have the local police in their back pockets more often than not," Diego said, trying to ignore the fact that he was part of that equation, and that's how he knew the practice so well. "Okay, come on."

They got to their feet, and he carefully opened the door and looked outside into the poorly lit alley. Instantly, someone had a grip on his hair and was pulling him out the door. "Go back!" he screamed to the others. "Go back!"

Mobius pulled the door shut and locked it, leaving Diego on his own with the three thugs they'd seen at Coba. The largest one had his arm around Diego's throat and a gun to his head, while another called Menendez on his phone. A minute later, a Mercedes pulled into the alley, and Menendez got out of the car with one of his huge deputies. His eye and lip were bruised from the beatings Mobius and Diego had given him, but an incongruous bright white smile spread across his battered face, which Diego saw in full for the first time.

Menendez walked to Diego, his snakeskin cowboy boots gleaming even in the dim light. Without taking a breath, the drug lord slammed his fist into Diego's belly, and it felt like his lungs and guts caved in together; he stood gasping for air, held up only by the ham hock around his throat. "You should never have defied me," he said, then nodded to the big deputy he came with. "Toro, get their attention."

The man banged on the back door of the shop with the butt of his automatic rifle. "Jillian," Menendez said loudly. "I have Diego, and I am going to put a bullet in his head if you don't come out here now."

"No! Don't come out!" Diego screamed, and Menendez punched him again, cutting the sound off in his throat.

"And no tricks by the *extraterrestre*," Menendez said. "If I see anything, I will start shooting, and I will kill him right after I take care of Diego."

The door opened, and Diego struggled to get free, but the thug tightened his massive arm around Diego's neck, leaving Diego helpless. Jillian walked out with her hands up as Mobius and Inka yelled from inside for her to come back, but she ignored them and pushed the door shut behind her.

"Here I am," she said, and the man at the door grabbed her arm and put his gun on her. "Don't hurt him, please."

Menendez chuckled. "You never told her, did you?" he asked Diego, then looked back at her. "Your boyfriend here was working for me, *señorita*. That is why my men stopped him—because he owed me some information. He took a large amount of money from me, and it was time to do his job. Don't you see? If it weren't for this loser, I would have never found you."

Jillian stared at Diego with a look of such horror that he wished Menendez would go ahead and kill him on the spot. "I'm sorry," he said to Jillian. "I'm so, so sorry."

Menendez looked around at his men. "Kill Diego and anyone else in there, but not the *extraterrestre*. Bring that *monstruo* with us."

Before they had time to move, several gunshots blasted through the air, and Diego heard a bullet whiz past his ear. The man holding him crashed to the ground like dead weight. Jillian screamed, and the thug holding her dropped his gun. As it clattered to the concrete, he swayed for a moment, then fell face-first to the ground. Diego lunged for Jillian, but Menendez got to her first and jerked her away. The Mercedes pulled up, blocking Diego's path, and Menendez shoved her into the car. "Toro, get in!" he yelled, and the giant deputy dove in on the other side, then the car screamed down the alley.

Diego ran yelling after the Mercedes until he heard car tires screeching behind him. He turned back toward the copy shop to see a dark-colored Jeep Grand Cherokee racing toward him. He figured it was part of Menendez's entourage, but he couldn't make himself move again. He just didn't care anymore, and he stood there frozen. He had no doubt he would be either run down or shot, but the SUV screeched to a stop, and a white man leaned out the driver's side window, yelling, "Get in! *¡Entra ahora!*"

The man said it with such force that Diego was jolted into action again. He ran to the passenger side door and jumped in. Just as the Jeep pulled away, Diego turned back and saw Mobius open the door of the copy shop and watch them go, his sunglasses off, so Diego could see the look of panic and bewilderment in his enormous eyes.

"Who are you?" Diego turned and asked the driver of the Jeep. The man tore around a corner and followed the Mercedes as it raced through the city streets, running stoplights and wreaking havoc as it went.

"Scott Westbrook," he said. "Retired Navy SEAL. The Savoy family hired me to find Jillian ... and you."

Maybe 40 years old, Scott was tall, damn near movie-star good-looking, and Diego could tell he was clearly cut under his bulletproof vest, biceps flexing with each turn of the steering wheel. Diego wasn't sure if he should trust him, but he couldn't figure out why he would be lying.

"Damnit! I was two fucking minutes too late," Scott said as he slammed the steering wheel with the heel of his hand.

Up ahead, the Mercedes ran a stoplight, causing a car to plow into a corner market and other cars to crash into each other. Scott deftly swerved around the pile-up and flew down a hill after Menendez.

"You weren't too late to save my life," Diego said, buckling his seat belt.

"That's true, and I'm glad, Diego," he said. "But I was hired to save Jillian."

"Good," he said. "We have to get her back. Wait ... How do you know my name?"

As he continued the chase, Scott barraged Diego with questions. "You were spotted with a tall young man and a Latina woman. Who are those people? And what are you doing in Mexico if you escaped from Menendez in Guatemala, and why haven't you contacted Jillian's family, or yours for that matter? And what the hell were you doing making photocopies?"

Diego sat there in silence trying to figure out what to tell Scott, who was clearly suspicious of him, but the look on Jillian's face when Menendez told her about him kept playing over and over in his mind. It felt like a razor slashing at his flesh, taking pieces of him each time he relived it. He was also paralyzed by the thought that the time capsule was still ticking down to devastation. But there was nothing he could do about that now. Mobius and Inka were on their own.

Scott was too preoccupied with catching Menendez to force any answers from Diego, especially when the Mercedes screeched down a highway on-ramp and sailed out onto the open road.

"You know how to use a firearm, right?" Scott said to Diego.

"Of course. I'm a park ranger," Diego shot back.

"Okay, *park ranger*," Scott said with a laugh. "Take my gun."

Cocky, Captain America pendejo, Diego thought as Scott retrieved a Glock-19 from a holster attached to the steering wheel column. "I'm paramilitary, you know," Diego said, taking the gun. "Guatemalan rangers are not like your *gringo* park rangers. We have real power." He wished he still had on his fatigues instead of the ridiculous tourist garb he had changed into.

"Got it," Scott said, and mockingly saluted him. "Shoot out the tires. You should be able to get a bead on them now that we're on the highway."

Diego clicked off the safety and leaned out the window. The Jeep was going so fast that the air blasted him hard and buffeted the gun around even though he held it with both hands. The wind made his eyes water, reducing the Mercedes to nothing more than moving red taillights in the dark. He started shooting, aiming at the lower part of the car and praying that Jillian was crouching down in case he missed high. The Mercedes swerved back and forth across the two-lane highway, running cars off the road.

"He's leaning out!" Scott shouted. "Shoot him!"

"What?" Just as he squinted his eyes enough to make out Menendez aiming at them, the *narco* boss fired an assault rifle and unleashed a shower of ammunition that battered the Jeep and blew out one of its tires.

"Damn it!" Scott yelled, steering the speeding SUV as well as he could, but it careened across the road and plowed through a field until it came to a shuddering stop in a cloud of dirt.

.

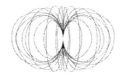

CHAPTER FORTY-ONE

PRAY

The copy shop was perfectly silent for a few moments after Mobius watched Diego and the vehicle he had jumped into disappear. It seemed impossible that such destruction could have just occurred in this quiet place. "They're gone," he said to Inka as he helped her off the floor of the storeroom.

"God help us," she said, and the pain in her eyes seemed old and practiced.

Police sirens whined in the distance. "Perfect timing to miss everything," Inka said. "Come quick, we have to leave. Let's go out the front. We can't get caught in the alley."

Mobius was still in a state of shock, and she had to pull on his arm to get him to move. When she dragged him to the front door, he stopped and looked down on Francisco's lifeless body, overwhelming grief gripping his chest. "We can't just leave him here."

"I'm sorry, but we have to." Inka pulled him away but said a prayer aloud for Francisco's soul as they ran out into the night. Mobius followed her blindly down the deserted sidewalk, and they turned a corner just as several police cars arrived at the shop behind them.

"We have to hide somewhere until they are gone," she said.

"What about in the car?"

"Diego has the keys. But we can go somewhere else. Come."

She peered around the corner at the commotion in front of the copy shop, then they ran across the street and down an alley heading back in the direction of the Range Rover. When they turned onto a main street, Inka slowed to a walk. "Put your glasses back on," she said. "And keep your hands in your pockets. You have to act like you are blind. Otherwise, at night it looks suspicious. I'm going to lead you." She held onto his arm, then turned a corner and walked them in front of the Range Rover. Without slowing down, she led him up the steps of the enormous cathedral and through a huge, intricately carved door. He was surprised the building was still open this late; humans seemed obsessed with locking things up. Inka pulled him to a pew as far away from the few other people inside as possible.

"We have to stay here for a while," she whispered. "They will be acting like they are trying to find the *criminales*, but they're just looking to arrest someone to make it all look real. I am sure they are rounding people up at this moment."

"You seem to know a lot about this insanity," Mobius said.

She sighed. "Yes, I know it too well."

"What do you think will happen to Jillian and Diego?"

"I don't know," she said. "All we can do is pray."

"We still have to get to Chichen Itza."

"I don't know how we will get there, but you are right, we have to go." She bowed her head and closed her eyes, and Mobius looked around.

"What is this place?" he asked.

"A church—a place people come to pray and worship God."

The church was magnificent, hushed, and harboring a resonant, peaceful energy. Mobius looked up at the large image in the front of the vaulted room—a nearly naked man hanging in agony, his arms stretched out from his sides. *That must be Mary's son Jesus that Diego and Inka told me about.* Looking at his tortured figure, Mobius's heart hurt. Jesus seemed to symbolize the suffering of the entire human race, but from what they said, he overcame his persecution and rose above it. Mobius's prayer as he sat there was that Earth would experience a similar transformation out of darkness and pain—that the prophecy of light Inka had spoken of would come to pass. Out of nowhere, he began to cry, his mouth opening and closing, the soft moans swallowed quickly by the lingering silence. He asked the Wisdom to help him get to the time capsule and disarm it in time so that not only his friends, but all the people on Earth, had a chance one day to experience their own Rebirthing.

"Does anyone know anything about that Range Rover parked out front?" a deep male voice said from behind them in Spanish. He turned and saw a man in a uniform standing there.

"Officer, officer," another man in a long black robe said, hurrying to him. "This is a place of worship."

"I'm sorry, Father," the policeman said, so quietly Mobius could barely hear him. "A man has been murdered down the street, and we are trying to find the killer."

"Stop looking at him," Inka whispered to Mobius. "It's a police officer. Remember you are blind. And try not to speak. Act like you are mentally slow if you have to."

"What?" He was not sure what she meant by that, but he didn't have time to find out because the uniformed officer walked to the end of their bench and stopped.

"Do you own the black Range Rover parked outside?" he asked.

"No," Inka said. "I have never owned a car in my life."

"Do you know anything about it? Did you see anyone get in or out of it?"

"No, *senōr*."

He looked her over—tiny, middle-aged, clearly a peasant—then nodded toward Mobius. "Take off your sunglasses."

"He is blind," she said. "Since birth."

The officer stood there staring at them, and Mobius's heart crashed against his rib cage. "Have you seen anyone or anything unusual since you have been here?"

"No, *senōr*," Inka said. "Nothing. We have been praying quietly for some time."

"What about you?" he asked Mobius.

Mobius almost turned to look at him but stopped himself. "I, uh, no, I did not see anything unusual ... because I do not see anything at all."

Out of the corner of his eye, Mobius could see the officer's jaw working, and he could tell his anger was fueled by embarrassment—a dangerous recipe Mobius knew all too well. If the uniformed man kept standing there, he felt as if he were going to run out of the church. The walls were closing in on him like the prison the man would put him in if he realized who or what Mobius was. All it would take was for the officer to reach out and pluck the glasses off his face.

Finally, after what seemed like forever, the officer walked away, and Inka and Mobius both breathed again. "Let's get out of here," Mobius said.

"We need to wait for a while after he leaves, and then we can go," she said. "We can't do anything suspicious right now."

Mobius fidgeted in the pew, not sure how much longer he

could sit there, wishing he could take out his cog and play with it to distract himself from everything. Instead, he ran his finger over the engraved words *Mobius* and *Make the Leap* on his flyer bracelet. Bombarded with thoughts of Kaia, Nava, Piphus, Jillian, Diego, poor Francisco, and the awful ticking time capsule, doubt began to gain traction in his mind. *We made a mistake by stealing a ship. And by landing in the middle of those men whose energy signatures were distorted. I'm never going to get to the time capsule in time. I shouldn't be the one doing this.*

Finally, he breathed deeply and resolved to let the looping thoughts of regret retreat to the background. He had been taught to do this in school and at home, but as an Anomaly, he'd never had a natural ability for it. Since he'd been on Earth, facing perils he'd never known before, he'd seen more clearly than ever that his tyrannical thoughts did not offer any answers—and worse, they weakened his life force. Using the techniques of mindfulness he'd learned only half-heartedly, he was able to keep from getting caught in a toxic spin. The thoughts didn't stop completely, but he was able to consciously step back from them and not be so affected by their fearmongering.

If I ever get out of this mess and back to Akara, he thought, *I am going to study under a master teacher and learn better how to calm my mind.* He moved into meditation as best he could, until Inka finally said it was safe to go.

Outside, they looked up and down the nearly deserted street and turned in the opposite direction from the copy shop. It was after midnight according to a clock inside a closed-up cell phone store. "Oh, please tell me you have the cell phone," Mobius said.

"No, unfortunately," Inka said. "Jillian does."

"Great. So *Maestro* Acosta can't reach us." As he had done

dozens of times, Mobius pulled out his cog for any indication that someone from Akara had been trying to reach him. "Still nothing. How can we get to Chichen Itza?" he asked, tired of not knowing how anything worked on Earth.

"I don't have enough money to pay for a taxi or a bus," she said. "And it's too late anyway. We will have to go out on the highway and hitchhike."

When she explained what hitchhiking was, and he thought about all the walking, his stomach growled. "I'm really hungry again," he said apologetically.

She smiled a little, but the laughter had gone completely out of her eyes since Menendez had showed up. "Don't worry," she said. "I can afford bananas."

She entered a twenty-four-hour market and came out with water and the life-sustaining yellow mushy fruit. She handed him a banana and took one for herself. "The man inside said the road to Chichen Itza is this way. He said there is not much traffic on that road this late at night, but what choice do we have?"

"If you don't know, I sure don't," he said. "On Akara, we would check out uni-hovers."

"Please tell me about your planet while we walk. I want to know everything."

CHAPTER FORTY-TWO

EL REY

Diego sat in the passenger seat next to Scott, trying to get his bearings. The cloud of dirt hadn't even settled back onto the field where they were stranded before Scott was on the phone. "He's on Highway 180D headed toward Cancun, and he's got Jillian," he said in Spanish that had no hint of a proper accent. "He shot out one of my tires, so I'm delayed. Get your guys on him and meet me in Cancun. I'll be there in a few hours."

"Who was that?" Diego asked when Scott hung up.

"A friend at the *Policía Federal de México*," Scott said. "I worked with him on a mission when I was a SEAL."

They got out of the car, and Diego looked around. The nearly full moon lit up the barren landscape; they were stranded in the middle of nowhere except for an occasional car passing on the highway. He looked back at Scott, who was suddenly gone. Diego ran around the car to find the American bent to the ground holding a handful of dirt.

"It's too soft to get a jack to hold," he said. "We'll have to push it out to the road."

Even though he could still feel the adrenaline pumping through him from all the chaos, Diego was tired on top of being wired, and his body slumped at the thought of pushing 2,000 kilos across a field of loose soil. He couldn't even get worked up about the time capsule anymore. All he had the energy to care about was Jillian and sleep. Scott put the car in neutral, and they took positions in front to push it backward and retrace the path to the highway.

"Okay, one-two-three," Scott said. As Diego leaned into the vehicle, he saw Jillian's face smiling at him, laughing at something he'd said. His heart was breaking, but his body grew stronger from the desire to somehow make it right with her. It made no difference—the suv only moved a few feet, then rolled back toward them.

"Come on," Scott said. "Harder!"

They heaved again, straining with all their might, but the vehicle went only a few feet more, and again rolled back to where it had stopped. It felt as if they were trying to move a tank. Diego turned and sat on the bumper, his chest rising and falling.

"The flat tire, soft ground, and incline are killing us," Scott said, bent over breathing heavily.

"Call the *Federales*," Diego said. "If you have friends, have them come help us."

"The closest *Federales* are ninety minutes away in Cancun," he replied. "There's no way they're going to use the manpower to come get us when Menendez is heading right to them."

"So what do we do?"

Their breathing was finally starting to slow down. "I'm open to ideas," Scott said.

Diego looked up at the moon. "I know what Jillian would say."

"What?" Scott stood up and looked at him. But Diego was too embarrassed to tell him about trusting the flow, especially in that moment when it seemed like the flow was circling the toilet.

"So, what would she—?" Scott was interrupted by the sound of car brakes squealing out on the highway about twenty-five yards from where they stood.

"*¡Hola!*" a man's voice called out. "*¿Necesita ayuda?*" Do you need help?

"*¡Sí!*" Scott called back. "*¡Sí! ¡Por favor!*"

Diego looked up at the fat moon again, and it was like the eye of God gazing down on him. "*Gracias,*" he said silently.

Six people headed toward them, an entire Mexican family. Diego was grateful to see three men—a father and his two sons in their late teens—as well as a mother and two younger girls. All six of them helped push the car. Even the little girls stood at the wheel wells and grunted with their efforts. Slowly, the SUV backed up toward the highway as they all yelled at the top of their lungs to push and keep going. When the father called out in Spanish, "Show how macho you are!" they all laughed together. Being around this family made Diego think of his mother and sisters, and a sudden desire to see them again blazed inside him so hot that it fueled a final push of the SUV off the dirt and onto the shoulder of the highway.

He and Scott thanked the family for their help, but they wouldn't leave until the tire was changed and Scott pulled the SUV out onto the highway.

"What now?" Diego asked, part of him wishing he were driving away in blissful ignorance with that sweet family.

"The only place Menendez can go from here to hide is Cancun," he said. "He's got people there. Ortiz, my friend at the PF, has the latest information on the Cancun *narco* cells. We worked together on a failed op to grab Menendez, the leader of the *El Rey* drug cartel. We thought we had him cornered, but when we got there he had disappeared. The PF call him *El Fantasma*."

"The ghost?" Diego said, his eyes growing wide. "Menendez is *El Fantasma*? I had no idea." Though Diego knew Menendez was a powerful *narco* with far-reaching influence, he didn't realize he was the infamous *El Fantasma*, one of the most dangerous and hunted drug lords in the world. Diego felt nauseated at the realization of exactly whom he had sold his soul to.

"How did Jillian's family hire you?" he asked Scott, changing the subject.

"They have a K and R insurance policy on their family."

Diego looked at him, confused. "K and R?"

"Kidnap and ransom. All the wealthiest families in the world have K and R policies. They're targets for this kind of thing. I'm the company's top crisis management consultant for Mexico and Central America. I recommended a rescue attempt given my assessment of the situation. If it doesn't work, the Savoys will pay the ransom and the insurance policy will reimburse them. My employer would like to avoid that, of course."

She was already at risk for this sort of thing, and I took her right into the mouth of the tiger, Diego thought.

"But when I found out it was Manuel Menendez who had kidnapped Jillian, I almost offered to come down here for nothing."

"A real American hero," Diego sneered.

"This guy has eluded capture by the best special forces in the world, and now he finally shows himself," Scott said. "Call it whatever you want, but I'm here to take his ass down."

"And get paid what? Half a million dollars? A million? Don't get me wrong. You deserve it if you get her back. I'm just curious what a billionaire's daughter is worth these days."

"What is she worth to you?" Scott glanced at Diego sideways.

"A lot more than that."

"Oh really?"

Diego looked out his window.

"You fell in love with her, didn't you? It's not uncommon in a captive situation."

Diego kept his eyes glued to the passing moonlit landscape outside. "You don't know anything about it."

"Okay fine, but in order to get your new girlfriend back, I need you to tell me everything. What in the hell are you doing in Mexico, and who are those people you were with?"

Diego turned further away from Scott's eyes boring into him. He didn't know what to say. That aliens dropped out of the sky and were trying to save Earth from a doomsday device? That he was on the take from Menendez and was responsible for Jillian's kidnapping? He couldn't figure out a decent lie and knew it wouldn't hold up anyway. This guy had interrogated people for a living. After a long silence, Diego finally spoke. "If I told you, you wouldn't believe me, so I'm begging the ninth."

"You mean pleading the fifth. I know you spent a few years in college in San Diego, but you got that one wrong."

"Fifth, ninth. Whatever the number, I'm not talking," he said, trying to hide that he was shaken by the fact that Scott knew about his past. *Could he know I was on the take from Menendez?*

"This doesn't look good for you, Diego," Scott said.

Diego peered at Scott out of the corner of his eye. He felt trapped, and now Scott was more than just a little suspicious. But the SEAL was the only chance of getting Jillian back, so he fought the urge to run as soon as the car came to a stop.

"If you're not going to tell me why you're in Mexico, can you tell me how you escaped?" he asked, but Diego stayed silent. "Why you went to Coba?" Diego said nothing. "Anything that might help get Jillian back?"

"No," Diego said adamantly. "If I knew anything that could get her back, I would tell you."

"Do I need to treat you as a hostile, Diego?"

"No you don't, Scott. I was kidnapped with Jillian and helped her escape. I tried to protect her." He put his head in his hands. "My God, what if he kills her? I don't think it's just about the money for him anymore. I kicked his ass before we got away, and he lost her in front of his men. The look in his eyes back there was crazed. He's proving his *machismo*, and he will kill her to do it if he thinks it's the only way."

Scott was quiet for a few minutes, then reached behind his seat and handed Diego a bottle of water and a protein bar. "Here, I'm sure you're hungry. So you kicked Menendez's ass?"

Diego nodded.

"I'm glad somebody has," he said.

I may have just earned myself a little respect, Diego thought. He leaned his head against the car window and took a bite of the bar, but he was so tired that he passed out while he was still chewing.

•

Diego awoke to Scott talking on the phone again. The digital clock on the dash said 3:34 a.m., and they were sitting on the side of a city street, obviously somewhere in Cancun. Less than eight hours until the time capsule swallowed the planet. Fear surged through Diego like it had at Tikal when he'd realized for the first time that the end of the calendar really did mean the end of the world.

As soon as Scott hung up, Diego said, "We have to find her *now*. What's going on? Why are we sitting here?" Now that he'd had some sleep, he had the energy to think that maybe somehow he could still get to Mobius once they got Jillian back. He growled like a rabid animal and yanked on his hair. "Where the hell is she?"

"You need to calm down, park ranger," Scott said, then waited until Diego began breathing normally again. "I can't work with you if you're going to lose it, okay?"

Diego nodded. "Okay, okay."

"Menendez's Mercedes was spotted on a few security cameras about an hour ago, but nothing since," Scott said. "Ortiz has had the known *El Rey* locations under surveillance since I called him, but there hasn't been any activity."

"What does that mean?" Diego asked.

"Unfortunately, it means we have no idea where they are."

CHAPTER FORTY-THREE

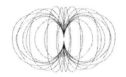

CHICHEN ITZA

Mobius and Inka walked for hours along the fifty-two mile stretch of highway between Valladolid and Chichen Itza, trying and failing to get a ride from the rare passing car. They pushed themselves until Inka couldn't walk another step, and Mobius made her get onto his back. He felt like he had failed in his mission already, but he just kept putting one foot in front of the other, because to stop would be intolerable. If he were about to die along with billions of life forms on Earth, it would not be because he quit.

After about an hour, Inka couldn't stay on his back any longer—her arms and hips hurt too much—and she begged him to let her sit down for just a few minutes. They leaned against a tree, and despite trying hard to stay awake, fatigue and lack of sleep overtook Mobius, and he was out within seconds.

The sound of cars rushing past one after the other on the highway woke him with a start. "What's going on?" he asked Inka, who was just waking up too. The sun had already risen, and he was flooded with panic, afraid that it was getting close to 11:11.

Inka groaned as she pushed herself to her feet. "It's morning. We must go."

"What time is it?" he asked.

She looked at her watch. "Eight-twenty," she said, and sounded as sad as he felt. "Less than three hours left."

They walked out to the highway, and within minutes got a ride from a group of people Inka described to Mobius as "hippies," who were driving an odd-looking rectangular vehicle called a vw Combi. He liked them all immediately, especially because they had the best collection of hair he'd seen on Earth so far. But they seemed so happy and excited about going to Chichen Itza, it was almost too much to bear. He saw tears in Inka's eyes as she stared out the window, and he knew she was thinking about her family. The guilt he felt couldn't be much more than if he had planted the time capsule himself.

•

When they finally arrived at Chichen Itza, the parking lot was already full, and people were flowing in through the gates. Inka said she didn't have close to enough money to pay the two-hun-dred-peso entrance fee each, so they blended into a group going through the entrance, and were able to sneak in.

Inside the majestic, ancient city of stepped pyramids with its own rarefied beauty, throngs of people gathered in front of *El Castillo*, The Castle. This grand Temple of Kukulcan soared above the central plaza. The crowd, quiet and speaking in hushed tones, knew something special was about to happen.

"Look," Inka said, pointing. "The descent of Kukulcan has begun," she whispered as she pulled Mobius to the front of the crowd. "Can you see the shadow snake start to make its way down the pyramid?"

The pyramid was by far the best preserved of any Mobius had seen. On the front of the structure, a staircase with walls on each side ran up the center of the stepped pyramid. At the bottom of each wall, a large carved serpent head sat on the ground with its mouth open. Mobius studied the pyramid to try to see what she was talking about. "All I see is a small sliver of shadow at the top."

"The whole process takes a while," Inka explained. "The angle of the sun casts shadows from the stepped pyramid onto the staircase wall, making it look like a snake is descending the pyramid. At the bottom, the body of the snake connects to the serpent head on the ground."

"This is incredible," Mobius said. "What a feat of engineering and astronomy, and it only happens twice a year?"

"Yes, on the winter and summer solstices," Inka said. "It is incredible. I've always wanted to see it."

"Do you think this has anything to do with the time capsule and Itzamna?"

"I don't know," she said, looking up at him. "But unless you can make yourself invisible, there is no way for you to get to the top of the pyramid to check for a hidden passageway."

"It's okay," Mobius said. "It's not here."

"How do you know?"

"I can feel it. I have known the time capsule wasn't at any of the three other cities either, but I didn't trust my intuition."

"Does your intuition tell you where it is, then?" Inka asked.

"No, I have only known when we've gotten to each city that it wasn't there."

"If it's not here, what do we do now?"

He put a hand on her shoulder. "The only thing left is to find the tree of life stela to see if there is an enlarged glyph. Maybe it will tell us something."

She nodded and looked up at him. "Can you see the stela from here?"

Mobius scanned the area, his head above the surrounding people, and located a prominent stone slab nearby. "Yes, come on," he said, but when he tried to push through the crowd, people looked at him angrily and didn't move.

"Let me try," Inka said. "Sometimes it actually helps to be small and female." She took the lead, and slowly the crowd opened around her.

Even from a distance, Mobius could tell that the stela was worn and crumbling and not in good condition. They finally made their way through the mass of spectators to the tree of life etched on the stone. Above the tree, the stela bore the city glyph for Chichen Itza, like the others did for their respective cities. Mobius glanced around for a moment, then lowered his glasses on his nose to examine it more carefully, quickly placing his hand back in his pocket. "Look, they're hard to make out, but there's the spaceship glyph at the center and an enlarged glyph like there were on the other trees. It's in the lower roots on the left," he said, starting to point, but Inka quickly grabbed his arm and shoved his hand back in his pocket again.

"You can see that?" Inka asked. "I can barely make it out."

He leaned closer. "Yes, look, it's the feathered serpent, the glyph of Kukulcan."

"Of course," Inka sighed. "It's the last of the five glyphs from the lintels. And this is obviously the city of Kukulcan."

"Yes, but what does it mean?" Mobius asked.

Inka pulled out the onionskin paper and a pencil and drew the remaining glyph on the composite tree of life. "I wish I knew."

Mobius threw his head back, deflated. "We are getting nowhere once again. Is there any significance to the placement of the glyphs? There are two in the branches and two in the roots."

"Perhaps," she said. "I need to sit and enter the shamanic realm."

"There's no time for that!" Mobius groaned. "The time capsule isn't here. It's over. We're all going to die." This time, instead of disappointment or sadness, rage at Itzamna and the ignorance that could create something so evil rose up inside of him, and he felt as if he were going to explode from it. "I wish I could put my hands around his throat," he said through gritted teeth.

Inka gazed up at him, her keen little eyes wiser and older than the stela they stood next to. "Mobius, if you let anger overtake you, Itzamna has won. One of my teachers used to say, 'You cannot beat at the darkness with a stick. You must shine a light.'"

Mobius stopped. "Oh, how I love you, Inka," he said in his own language, the first time he'd used it since he'd been on Earth.

She looked up at him, waiting.

"I said I love you. I love you all—I wish you could see what amazing beings you are and that your planet is a precious jewel. I want to save you, but I can't, and I am so sorry." He looked up at the temple. "I want to go up there and tell everyone how sorry I am. It is nothing, but it is all I have to offer."

Standing there pondering how he was going to get to the top, he noticed that the shadow snake was now complete, having undulated all the way down the pyramid, ending at the serpent head at the bottom. "Where in the world is he going?" he wondered aloud. After a few seconds, the answer came to him. He looked down at Inka and shouted, "The time capsule! He's going in the direction of the time capsule."

Inka grabbed his forearms. "Yes! Of course! Kukulcan is going to devour it. It's another clue."

"What time is it?" he asked.

She checked her watch. "9:15."

"We only have two hours!" he said, starting to push through the crowd. "We have to go! We'll just head in the direction the shadow snake is going. It will lead us to the capsule."

"Wait," she cried, holding on to the back of his T-shirt to stay with him. "We don't know which city it is pointing to. And we can't get there on foot."

Mobius didn't stop, continuing to barrel his way through people, who cursed him as he went, but he didn't have time to be polite. He and Inka were almost through the enormous horde, but out of nowhere a little girl moved in front of him, and he ran into her, knocking her forcefully to the ground. She began to wail, and when he bent over to help her up, she saw his four-fingered hands and scrambled backward screaming, "*¡Papa! ¡Papa!*" Her father, a large man with a barrel chest, yelled, "*¡Toma esto, pendejo!*" and punched Mobius in the face. Dozens of people turned to look as Mobius's sunglasses and hat went flying. He stumbled sideways and, without thinking, put his hands in front of his face to protect himself. Suddenly, people were shrieking and yelling, and everyone took a step back from him as if he were a venomous snake.

"He was born with disabilities," Inka yelled in a quivering voice, repeating it in both English and Spanish, yet people still stared at him in horror. "He is not dangerous. It was an accident."

There was a moment when they began to look at him a little differently, as if they were questioning themselves. But then their faces changed again, and their expressions were more horrified than before. "His nose is—" a woman began, but her words were drowned out because suddenly, they were all pointing and screaming.

"His blood is purple!"

"*¡Su sangre es violeta!*"

"Look at his eyes! He's not human!"

Mobius wiped at his nose with the back of his hand, and egg-plant-colored blood smeared across it.

Several people had pulled out their phones and were capturing the scene on video.

"We need to go!" Inka said, and pushed him hard.

With the force of the hunted, he leapt away, running at full speed in an instant, but through the chaos, he heard Inka's voice—"Mobius!" He turned to see that she was running as hard as she could go, but he had left her far behind. In a few strides, he was back at her side, and when he picked her up, the crowd surged toward him. His heart felt as if it were going up in a mushroom cloud of fear. Again, he turned and ran, covering huge amounts of space with each stride even as he held Inka like a baby in his arms.

"Mobius!" Inka yelled as he raced through the huge parking lot. "Where are you going?"

"I don't know!" he screamed. "Away!"

"This is not the direction of the shadow snake. What about the time capsule?"

He looked around at the wild landscape stretching out forever in every direction and realized how stupid he was for thinking ... What was he thinking? That he could run all the way to the time capsule—wherever it might be—and disarm it in less than two hours? He stopped running and put Inka down. *Let them do what they want to me. There is no way to get to the capsule in time. We're all dead anyway.*

CHAPTER FORTY-FOUR

EL FANTASMA

Scott and Diego still hadn't found Jillian and her captors and had no clue as to where they might be. They'd driven to all of the *El Rey* cartel's known hideouts and had talked to the cops who were staking them out. No one had seen or heard anything. Finding Menendez was starting to seem impossible to Diego; he could see why the *narco*'s nickname was *El Fantasma*. "So where to now?" he asked as Scott drove.

"Cheap hotels," Scott replied and turned west, heading inland.

"How many of those are in Cancun?" Diego said, annoyed. "Three hundred or so?"

"We can eliminate the ones in the tourist zone near the beaches, so that takes it down by ninety percent," he said. "Menendez wouldn't want to be hemmed in by the water, and he knows we're watching the coastline in case he tries to get away by boat."

"I guess that makes sense."

Scott glanced at him. "Thanks for your overwhelming confidence, *amigo*. The truth is, he'd find the most support and protection in the worst part of town. A lot of poor, young people look at these guys like modern day Robin Hoods. Being called a *narco* is a badge of honor."

"It's the same in Guatemala. Crime is the only access poor people have to money or any sense of power."

Scott nodded. "Desperate people, desperate behavior. But for guys like Menendez, it's not even about the money anymore."

"No," Diego said. "It's not."

As they headed away from the tourist zone, the neighborhoods got worse and worse. Diego felt sick at the thought that he'd bought into the rebel glamour of gang culture. The *narco* gang promised him entry into wealth and power, but the price had been higher than he could have ever imagined; he had paid with the currency of his very being—his integrity, his self-respect, his honor.

On the outskirts of town, shantytowns began to pop up on the hillsides—dwellings made from other people's junk that sat amidst squalor and sewage. *There's poor, and then there's shantytown poor*, Diego thought. "If Menendez is hiding Jillian in one of those, we'll never find them."

"Knowing what I know about him, he wouldn't go that low," Scott said. "He has very rich taste."

"I know. I drove his Range Rover."

Scott put a hand on Diego's shoulder. "*Hombre*, why don't you just tell me what happened?"

Diego looked at Scott. "Fine, I'll tell you. I don't have anything to lose anymore," he said. "An alien ship landed in the jungle where we were being held captive by Menendez, and four aliens from a planet called Akara set us free."

Scott chuckled. "Okay, maybe not now, but it has to come out some time."

Diego figured if he didn't mention the apocalypse aspect of the story, Scott wouldn't have him arrested. And the truth was, he really *didn't* have anything to lose. How much faith could he have that a young, naïve alien on a planet he knew nothing about, and a middle-aged peasant woman from the Guatemalan jungle with no money, no wheels, and no phone, could find the time capsule and shut it down in time? He started wondering when he should call his mother and sisters to tell them he loved them one last time.

Scott drove to three run-down motels, but there were no signs of Menendez. At the fourth one, Diego saw a man wearing cowboy boots who looked vaguely familiar. The man leaned down into a Cadillac and grabbed something. When he stood up again, Diego recognized his ghoulish face and ducked down quickly.

"What is it?" Scott asked.

"That guy's name is Pedro," Diego said. "He's one of Menendez's lieutenants. He's the one who kidnapped us."

From across the street, they watched Pedro enter one of the rooms. "Okay, Scott. It's time to call the damn *Federales*," Diego insisted.

Scott shook his head. "If I do that and Jillian and Menendez aren't in there, Pedro will see a SWAT team in time to warn Menendez, and Menendez will move her again. We have to sneak up on him."

"So we go in with no backup?"

"What happened, park ranger? You were so macho earlier."

"I know that guy, and he'd be happy to cut me in half."

"You don't have to come if you don't want to."

"Your American hero act is really starting to get annoying."

"Well, you seem scared."

"I'm not scared," Diego stated emphatically. The fact was, he *was* scared, but he wasn't about to admit it to Scott.

"Just drive me up to the door and stay in the car with the engine running."

"No, I'm coming," Diego protested weakly, trying to reclaim his manhood.

"Really, Diego. I need you to drive the car."

"Fine," Diego said, relieved as they switched places. He drove Scott to the parking lot right outside the room Pedro had entered, and Scott slipped out of the car and ran, crouched down, to the door. He knocked. As soon as the door opened a crack, Scott kicked it in and started shooting. Through the open door, Diego could see a second guy sprawled across the bed, unmoving and bleeding. Scott was lying on the floor with his hands on his head, taking cover behind the bed as Pedro sprayed bullets from the bathroom, chewing up not only the bed, but also the body of the dead man on top of it.

Pedro stopped shooting for a moment, and Diego yelled out to Scott to get in the car, but Scott fired toward the bathroom, then dove under the bed and disappeared as Pedro shot back. A bullet blasted Pedro in the shoulder, knocking his body back and the weapon out of his hands as Scott suddenly popped up on the other side of the bed. By the time Scott got to his feet, Pedro had retreated into the bathroom.

"Come on out," Scott yelled in Spanish, ready to fire, his weapon pointed at the bathroom door. "Hands on top of your head."

Suddenly, Pedro's hand appeared. He grabbed for the AK-47 just outside the door, but Scott fired. The bullet ricocheted off the gun, and Pedro yanked his hand back.

To Diego's amazement, Scott holstered his weapon and rushed the bathroom door. Half a minute later, he pulled Pedro out of the bathroom, his arm around the *narco*'s throat. As Scott held the *pendejo*, Pedro elbowed him in the gut, and the war was on.

They fought for several minutes as Diego watched, impressed as hell with Scott's skills and Pedro's toughness and animal instincts.

"You want me to come in there?" Diego yelled from the car.

"Nope," he yelled back. "Almost got it."

Diego watched until Scott finally felled Pedro with a blow to his mid-section and a knee to his face. Scott handcuffed Pedro, dragged him out of the hotel room, and pushed him into the back seat of the Jeep, getting in beside the *narco* as sirens sounded in the distance.

"Not bad," Diego said, looking back at Scott.

"That means the world coming from you," Scott quipped. "Now can you get us the hell out of here?"

•

As Diego drove, Scott tried to extract Menendez's location out of Pedro by threatening to kill him in ways that even Diego believed he would carry out. Diego joined in, taunting the drug lord's henchman. "Come on, Pedro, I saw how Menendez treats you—like his little bitch, and in front of all the guys too. Are you really going to die for him?"

"If I tell you where he is, do you promise to let me live?" Pedro pleaded. "I have a family."

"Well, it's your only chance," Scott said. "So I recommend you start talking."

"Okay, okay, but you can't take me with you," Pedro whined. "He will kill me the second he sees me."

"Then you need to stay out of sight," Scott said. "Because I'm not letting you go until we know Menendez is there."

Pedro directed them to the outskirts of the city and onto a desolate, menacing dirt road. A few dilapidated dwellings lined the street here and there, but most of them appeared to be abandoned.

Diego's scalp tingled. "She's here," he said. "I can feel it."

Pedro pointed to the largest house on the road and told them Menendez was hiding Jillian inside. Scott drove behind an empty shack next door to the hideout. "We'll approach from here."

Even though the shack hid them from the *narcos'* line of sight and the house was at least fifty yards away, the noise of the Jeep's engine seemed so loud to Diego that he was afraid it would give them away, and he was relieved when Scott turned off the ignition.

With Pedro cuffed hand and foot, Scott jumped out of the car. "Wait here and keep that gun on him," he said to Diego and ran to the back of the shack to scope out the hideout.

"There are a few cars behind the house, but one is under a cover," Scott called to Diego. "I think it's the Mercedes, but I need to know for sure. Don't move."

Scott disappeared behind the shack, and Diego's heart started thumping. *Does he not understand what he's walking into?* Thankfully, five minutes later, Scott was back, and Diego took a breath for the first time since he'd left.

Scott made a short phone call before getting back into the car. "It's the Mercedes, and there are two more cars besides." He turned around and asked Pedro in Spanish, "How many guys are in there with him?"

"You promised you'd let me go if this was the house. Please," Pedro pleaded, squirming in the back seat.

"You're a free man as soon as you tell me how many," Scott said.

"Eight or ten, I don't know exactly."

"Please tell me we're not going in there alone," Diego said as Pedro continued to make a racket.

"We're not going in there alone. *Now* I call for back up."

Diego sighed with relief. *"Gracias a Dios."*

Scott called Ortiz at the *Policía Federal* and told him to bring in the troops as Pedro yelled in the background, "Let me out of here! You promised, you American *hijo de puta*! They're going to kill me!" Scott finally pointed the gun at Pedro's head, and the *narco* whimpered as he fell silent.

Scott hung up with Ortiz and told Diego, "He's coming with eight officers in a helicopter. You stay here and keep an eye on Pedro."

Pedro started bucking and kicking in the back seat. "Hey *gringo*! You got to let me go!"

"I'm not staying here," Diego shouted over him. "I want to help."

Scott checked the magazine on his pistol and ignored Diego until they heard a helicopter approaching a few minutes later. "Just stay out of the damn way and don't get shot," he said. "We've got this now."

As Scott got out of the SUV, Diego looked toward the approaching Black Hawk with *Policía Federal* written in white on the side. A massive machine gun that looked more like a rocket launcher protruded out an open helicopter door from just behind the cockpit.

The chopper landed in the middle of the road next to the shack, and a distinguished-looking Mexican PF captain with a full beard and mustache jumped out, followed by eight SWAT team commandos, armed to the teeth.

Scott shouted to the captain in Spanish, "They're in the house just east of here. Use this building for cover! Do not fire anywhere near the woman! If we can't rescue her right now, I just got the order to negotiate paying the ransom."

"You know that will not guarantee her safety," the captain said, scowling.

"I know, but it's what her family wants." He ran around the side of the shack, followed by Ortiz and his men.

Against orders, Diego got out of the car and brought up the rear, leaving Pedro flailing in the backseat. As he came around the corner, the *criminales*, who had obviously heard the helicopter, were running for their vehicles. For a split second, he saw Menendez looking out the back door of the hideout, but when the SWAT guys started firing their M-16s from positions in and around the shack, the drug lord ducked back inside.

Diego entered the shack, crouching down as low as he could with his hands on top of his head to protect himself from flying glass. All the windows were taken by the PF, so he ducked into the bathroom, climbed onto the broken toilet, and looked out of a high bathroom window to see the gangbangers firing from behind their cars, now rendered useless by bullet holes. As the full-tilt machine gun battle raged on, a dozen or more dogs raced here and there seeking cover, and people in the neighboring houses shut their curtains and doors.

The PF took out the *criminales* one by one. Diego scanned the chaos for Jillian and Menendez, but they were nowhere in sight. Finally, the battle died down, and eight bodies in cowboy boots lay on the ground surrounded by blood.

Into the disturbed quiet, Menendez yelled out from the house, "I still have the girl! If you want to talk, give me a phone number to call!"

Ortiz looked at Scott and nodded, and Scott called out his cell number. Diego went and stood next to him. He wanted to hear every word.

"This is Diego Villela," Scott said to Ortiz. "He escaped with the hostage."

Ortiz shook Diego's hand so hard it hurt, then introduced his second in command, Lieutenant García, to both Scott and Diego.

Scott's phone rang, and they looked at the caller ID; Diego was surprised to recognize the number. "He got the phone off of Jillian. It's the one we bought after we escaped," he said. "Remember, only speak English with him so Jillian can understand what you're saying."

Scott pressed the speakerphone button. "*Señor* Menendez, my name is Scott Stern," he said, giving a fake last name. "I was hired by the Savoy family. I need to speak to Jillian before we go on."

There was a muffled struggle then, "This is Jillian Savoy ..."

Diego was relieved at hearing Jillian's voice, but furious knowing that, once again, he was powerless to help her.

"Don't try to save me. You have to stop the time capsule—"

Her distressed words were suddenly cut off by Menendez. "I am going to tell you this once, then give you two minutes to decide what you are going to do, so listen carefully. You can ask your park ranger friend Diego Villela if what I am about to say is the truth or not. He knows me well because he was on my payroll. I would not have had the good fortune of finding Miss Savoy if it were not for him."

Scott and Ortiz turned to Diego in shock. Diego's stomach melted into liquid, but without missing a beat, Scott replied to Menendez, "The park ranger is dead. You shot him on the freeway."

"Ah, that is welcome news. Diego is dead, Jillian," Menendez said, but there was silence in response, and Diego was sure it was because she didn't care anymore whether he was alive or not. Menendez continued, "*Señorita* Savoy has convinced me that the reason the *extraterrestres* came is because a deadly explosion is going to happen in a few hours."

"Extra what?" Scott said.

"Because I believe her," Menendez continued, "I *will absolutely* kill her unless you bring the helicopter with a single pilot to me. Be very clear," he said. "I believe that I am going to die soon if I don't get out of here, so I have no problem killing her. None at all. Do you understand?"

Scott and Ortiz looked at Diego with faces so screwed up into question marks, he almost laughed. "Do you understand?" Menendez screamed like he had gone mad.

"Give us five minutes and call back," Ortiz said.

"You have two." The phone went dead.

Scott and Ortiz glared at Diego. "Did he say *extraterrestrials?*" Scott asked.

"What the hell is he talking about?" Ortiz added.

"I tried to tell you in the car, but you didn't believe me," Diego said to Scott.

"No, I didn't. But tell us now."

Diego recounted the entire story to Scott, Ortiz, and García as quickly as he could.

"Unbelievable," Scott said when he was finished. He scrubbed his hand down his face then looked at Ortiz. "What do you think?"

"I think they were all on *ayahuasca.*"

"We were not on drugs!"

"Captain Ortiz, maybe their story is not so unbelievable," Lieutenant García interjected. "There have been many UFO sightings in Mexico. In fact, our government is one of only a few in the world to have officially recognized UFOs."

"*¡Exactamente!*" Diego said, pointing at him. "You should listen to him."

Ortiz clenched his teeth, clearly annoyed. "Menendez said that aliens landed on the ground. That is very different from a moving light in the sky."

"The most important question at the moment is not if it's true, but if Menendez believes it," Scott said.

"He saw the aliens and the ship with his own eyes," Diego argued. "He shot one of them himself. I promise he believes it." But he wondered what the hell Menendez was thinking—trying to run from a black hole was absurd.

"Sir, if this is true, shouldn't we try to find the bomb?" García asked.

Ortiz glared at him. "We are not doing anything right now but taking down *El Fantasma* and rescuing *Señorita* Savoy."

Diego was on Lieutenant García's side—they should be doing everything possible to stop the time capsule in addition to rescuing Jillian. But Ortiz had all the power here, and it was clear he would not be convinced. His goal now was to rescue Jillian so at least they could be together when the time capsule imploded.

The phone rang again, and Scott answered. "We'll take you where you want to go and drop you off," he said to Menendez. "But Jillian stays in the helicopter. Our pilot was shot by your men, so I'll be flying. I'm the only other pilot."

Menendez paused for about thirty seconds before responding. "Fly to the far side of the house we are in and land. If anyone else is with you, Jillian dies."

"I understand," he said and hung up.

"So, what's the real plan?" Diego asked. "Menendez will just shoot you as soon you take him where he demands."

Ortiz rubbed his beard and looked at his men, then at Scott. "I will hide behind one of the body shields on board, and when I see an opportunity, I will take him out. I think only one of us in the helicopter is the best way. I can hide pretty easily."

"Sounds good," Scott said.

Ortiz turned to his lieutenant. "García, take the *narco* in Scott's vehicle to the station and get the coroner's office out here to take care of the bodies. The rest of you search the house and arrest any *narcos* who might still be alive. We'll return to pick you up when we've secured the Black Hawk."

Diego looked back and forth between Scott and Ortiz. "What about me?" he asked. "I have to do *something*."

"Just stay here and we'll come get you when we've got her," Scott said. "You have some explaining to do."

Inside the helicopter, the cabin was empty except for two seats, which faced away from the cockpit and were situated next to the open side doors. Additional passengers would have to sit on the cabin floor or stand holding on to handholds dangling from the ceiling. Ortiz jumped in and took a police shield off the wall where it hung along with other equipment. The shield, used for crowd control, was black with a clear square near the top for the carrier to see through, and was big enough to span the head to the knees. Ortiz un-holstered his pistol and backed into a rear corner of the cabin, then squatted down to hide behind the shield.

"How does it look?" he asked.

"It'll take him some focus to realize someone could be behind it," Scott said, and the other guys agreed. "We'll have a minute or two before he gets suspicious, maybe less."

"Don't let him see the top of your head through the little window," Diego said.

They all stared at him. "Who is this guy again?" Ortiz asked, looking around the shield.

Scott got into the cockpit and fired up the chopper.

"Are you sure you can fly this thing?" Diego yelled.

"What part of 'I'm an ex-Navy SEAL' wasn't clear to you?" he yelled back.

"Please bring her back safe!" he shouted.

Scott nodded in an infuriatingly cocky way, and Diego ran away from the helicopter as the rotors started spinning faster. When the Black Hawk was in the air, Diego ran to the side of the shack and watched it fly the short distance toward the house, then descend on its far side. Without thinking, he was suddenly sprinting across the distance toward the house. The PF guys behind him screamed at him to come back, and he expected to be hit with a barrage of machine gun fire erupting from the hideout, but no one shot at him.

By the time he made it across the expanse, his lungs were ready to burst—*they must be starting to load into the helicopter already.* He ran to the side of the house and peered around the corner in the hope of getting a glimpse of Jillian. Toro, the muscle-bound *El Rey* gang deputy, stepped into the Black Hawk with his AK at the ready. *Ortiz thinks Menendez is alone,* Diego thought. *It will be a different story trying to take them both down.*

His breath caught in his throat as Menendez came out holding Jillian in an arm lock in front of him. He pushed her into the helicopter, then stepped inside himself. Just as it started lifting off the ground, once again without thinking, Diego raced toward it. A strap hung from the side of the chopper, and he sprinted and grabbed the bottom of it with both hands. As his feet were raised off the ground, he realized that the strap was used to keep the sliding side door from closing, and he hoped like hell it would hold. The Black Hawk gained altitude, and he dangled below it, swinging and swaying with an ever-increasing amount of space between him and the ground below.

Inside the cabin, he heard gunshots and the sounds of fighting. The fear that Jillian could get shot propelled him, hand over hand, up the strap. He pulled himself over the edge of the open side door, but when he did, the gun came out of his pants, falling to the ground below. *"Mierda,"* he said as he grabbed onto a steel ring tie-down on the cabin floor, his legs still hanging out of the helicopter. He looked up to see that Jillian was loose from Menendez, who was lying on the cabin floor, bleeding from his leg and yelling in pain, while Toro and Ortiz were in a fight to the death. Three or four guns lay around, but none were in reach.

Toro got the captain in a death grip around his throat and dragged him toward the side door, heading directly toward Diego. As soon as Toro was close enough, Diego grabbed his leg with one hand and yanked on it with all his strength. Toro fell to the floor hard and was stunned for a moment but then pushed himself to his feet, trying to stand up in the moving helicopter. Ortiz rushed at him to shove him out the door, but at the last second, the criminal ducked and Ortiz went flying out himself, screaming as he plummeted to his death.

With a smile on his face, Toro watched Ortiz sail through the air over the tourist zone of Cancun as the chopper headed toward the open ocean. Toro looked down at Diego, and his smile turned to rage. He lifted his foot to stomp on Diego's hands as they clung to the ring, then suddenly, he stumbled forward and went hurling out the cabin door.

Diego looked up to see Jillian standing above him, a look of triumph on her face. Behind her, Menendez, *El Fantasma*, picked up his automatic weapon and stood up on one leg, holding on to the back of the seat for support, the blue sky rushing by behind him out the opposite side door.

"Jillian!" Diego screamed.

She turned, and it seemed to Diego that everything went into slow motion.

"Hold on!" Scott yelled.

Diego reached out and grabbed Jillian's ankle. Suddenly, the helicopter tilted violently up on its side, and Diego was catapulted into the cabin. Jillian fell headfirst toward Menendez, but Diego grasped the ring with one hand as he held onto her leg with the other and stopped her momentum. For a moment, Menendez stood there, his arms flailing wildly as he tried to steady himself. The background behind him had turned from sky to ocean as the gaping door now faced directly toward the ground. Then, with a whoosh, Menendez was ejected out the door and plummeted, his arms flailing, into the blue expanse.

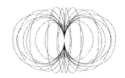

CHAPTER FORTY-FIVE

UNDISCOVERED

Inka and Mobius stood in the Chichen Itza parking lot, the angry, fearful, and curious crowd of people still coming after them. "It's over," Mobius said to her, then turned away from them and put his hands on his head, breathing hard from running. "I am not Kukulcan. I am not the feathered serpent. I don't have wings."

At that moment, he saw and heard something approaching over the jungle canopy in the distance. "What is that?"

Inka put her hand over her eyes to shade them from the sun and stared at the moving object for a few seconds. "It's a helicopter."

"A what?" he asked.

"A flying machine. And it looks like it's heading here."

Mobius looked up again, and the machine was now close enough for him to see its whirling blades and hear the fullness of its roar.

Inka shaded her eyes with her hand. "It must be some government officials for the end-of-calendar ceremony."

Behind them, the crowd was on them now. "Let her go!" they screamed, as if he held Inka against her will. He picked Inka up again and started running toward the helicopter, creating even more hysteria behind him. As he ran, he tried to think. Somehow, they had to convince the government officials to take them to the time capsule. They would fly in the direction the shadow snake pointed.

"Where are you going?" Inka cried, jangling along in his arms.

"Helicopter!" he shouted.

Inka craned her head around to look at the people surging toward them. "Mobius, they're taking pictures and video of you. This is not good."

A moment later, the helicopter descended, landing a hundred yards away from them in the middle of the two-lane highway at the turn-off to the ruins. Cars screeched to a stop on both sides of the road, and traffic began to back up as people got out of their cars to look. Increasing his speed, Mobius realized he might have to overpower whomever was in the helicopter to make them take him to the time capsule, but to his shock, Diego leaned out of the craft.

"DIEGO!!!" Mobius screamed with such ferocity that he stumbled over his own feet and went crashing to the ground at the edge of the dirt parking lot. Just before he hit, he tucked his shoulder and rolled onto his back, protecting Inka from being smashed underneath him. But now she was on top of him, and he couldn't get her off.

"Get up!" he yelled.

"I'm trying!" she yelled back, but she seemed to have no strength left in her little body, and he didn't have enough left to get her off of him. They were like an eight-legged, helpless hybrid species caught on its back.

Mobius looked at the mob. "They're almost on us," he yelled. Then suddenly, the people in front stopped so fast that they were nearly trampled by the ones bringing up the rear.

Even over the noise of the helicopter, he heard a man screaming, "Back off! *¡Atrás!* Get back!"

Mobius looked toward the helicopter and saw a man behind a huge gun, swinging it from side to side. At the same time, Diego and Jillian raced toward Inka and Mobius. "JILLIAN!!!" he screamed.

A few seconds later, Diego pulled Inka up. As Jillian helped Mobius to his feet, he hugged her hard. "I'm so glad you're okay."

"Thank you," she said with tears in her eyes. "You too. I thought I might never see you again."

"We don't have time for a reunion. Come on! Come on!" Diego shouted, and the four of them ran toward the helicopter.

"Who's that man with the giant gun?" Mobius yelled to Diego as they ran.

"That's Scott. He helped save Jillian."

"He isn't going to kill everyone, is he?"

"I hope not," Diego said as they hurled themselves into the cabin of the Black Hawk.

To Mobius's relief, Scott stopped waving the weapon and jumped into the cockpit. As the helicopter lifted off the ground, Mobius pulled his cog from his pocket and extended it toward the rabid crowd, releasing a directed electromagnetic pulse that wiped their phones clean and rendered them useless.

"Headphones," Scott hollered back at them, gesturing to the ones on his own head.

They each grabbed a set of wireless headphones hanging from the cabin wall and put them on. Mobius was relieved that the headphones muted the deafening roar of the blades. As they ascended into the sky, Scott looked back at Mobius, and a mixture of fear and fascination spun across his face as he scanned Mobius's hairless body, bronze skin, four-fingered hands, and two-toned eyes. Scott's mouth gaped open, but he forced himself to look out the cockpit window. "Diego, aren't you going to introduce me to the alien?" Scott asked, his voice coming through all their headsets.

Diego closed the sliding side doors, further cutting down the noise. "Scott, this is Mobius from Akara, just like we told you," he said wearily, and Mobius could tell he and Jillian had had to fight to get the pilot to bring them to Chichen Itza. "Mobius, this is Scott, an obnoxious American hero."

Mobius nodded at Scott, then looked at the control panel. When he saw that it was 9:55, panic rose in his throat. "We have to go in the direction of the shadow snake!"

"What the hell is the shadow snake?" Scott asked.

"Fly over the tallest pyramid," Mobius said, "I'll show you."

Scott banked toward *El Castillo* and flew low over the temple. Everyone below looked in the direction of the helicopter and pointed up at it. Mobius showed Scott the descending Kukulcan, then pointed a finger in the direction it was going. "That way!" he said. "We're looking for Mayan ruins."

Scott turned the helicopter and pushed it ahead at full speed.

"What did you find down there?" Jillian asked Mobius and Inka. "Where are we going?"

Inka pulled out the tree of life drawing and placed it on the cabin floor, then they all sat down around it. "We found the final glyph on a stela and placed it on the tree of life, here," she said, pointing. "It is the symbol for Kukulcan. We still don't know what the tree of life means, but we believe the descent of Kukulcan, the shadow snake, is a clue pointing us in the direction of the time capsule."

"So we still don't have a specific location?" Jillian said. "We're just flying in this direction, but we have no idea how far or where to?"

Mobius pulled the ruins map from his pocket and laid it on the floor next to the tree of life drawing.

Diego looked down on the map and the tree of life. "Hang on," he said. "I'm looking at this upside down." He started to move positions to sit next to the others opposite him, but then froze, looking back and forth between the drawing and the ruins map. "¡Dios mio!"

"What is it?" Mobius asked.

"The glyphs correspond geographically to the four cities we've been to!" he shouted, pointing to each glyph on the tree of life consecutively. "The Pleiades represents Tikal. The Serpent is Calakmul—the Kingdom of the Snake. Itzamna is Coba—remember the two huge stelae of him there? And Kukulcan, the shadow snake, is Chichen Itza. The tree of life is a coded map! The key to unlocking it is turning it upside down." He rotated the image one hundred eighty degrees so they too could see it. "That's why the spaceship glyph is inverted—it's a clue to turn the tree upside down."

Mobius looked back and forth between the two images and saw that on the upturned tree of life, the spaceship glyph now sat right side up, and the four glyphs perfectly corresponded to the locations of the four cities on the ruins map. "Inka was right—the spaceship glyph has to represent the time capsule. The tree of life is a map pointing to its location."

"Inka, the pencil," Jillian said.

Inka rifled through her bag. "I can't find it!"

"Seriously?" Diego asked. "What next? Scott, do you have

something to write with up there?"

Scott reached back and handed them a pen. With it, Jillian drew a line on the tree of life from the glyph representing Chichen Itza in the branches to the one representing Tikal in the roots and another from the glyph representing Coba in the branches to the one representing Calakmul in the roots. The lines formed an "X" and intersected directly on top of the spaceship glyph. "The time capsule is located at the center of the four cities!"

She then took the ruins map and did the same.

Mobius put his finger on the center of the X. "We need to go to this location!"

"Scott, we're heading south-southwest, right?" Jillian yelled.

Diego gave her a look as if to say, *How do you know that?*

"I grew up sailing," she said. "Had to learn to navigate."

"Yes, exactly forty-five degrees south-southwest," Scott yelled back.

"Then we're going in the right direction," Jillian said.

"But *mija*," Inka said. "There are no ruins at that location."

"She's right," Diego said. "There's nothing on this map because there are no ruins there. This direction just takes us deeper into the jungle in the middle of Quintana Roo."

"That's not possible," Mobius said.

Jillian's shoulders slumped. "My God, maybe Itzamna did lead us on a wild goose chase."

Even though the helicopter was making the loudest noise Mobius had ever experienced, the silence between the four of them was even more deafening.

Suddenly, Scott started talking into his headset in Spanish. "I cannot land the aircraft— I'm sorry, I can't explain right now. But Miss Savoy is aboard, so do not fire. I repeat *do not fire*. And do not pursue or she will die."

It was hard for any of the others to concentrate—at least the ones who spoke Spanish—knowing that, from the sound of it, they could be shot out of the air at any moment.

Scott turned to them with an intense look on his face. "Where exactly are we headed? We're running out of time with the Mexican government. They know we took out Menendez—there is video all over the Internet of a body falling over a busy tourist area and another one just off the beach—so they don't understand why we're still in the air. I just tried to bribe Miguel Vargas, the fucking chief of the federal police, with some of Jillian's daddy's money, and that could get me some prison time, so please tell me you know where we're going!"

Mobius brought the ruins map up to Scott. "Here, we're going here and unless we get there soon, you won't have to worry about prison time."

"There's nothing there," Scott said. "That whole area is hard-core jungle."

"Maybe we'll see something from the sky," Mobius argued.

"I can tell you what we'll see—trees. That's it. Not only that, but I barely have enough fuel to get us there, and based on what I'm looking at, that's got to be at least forty minutes from here."

"It's already 10:15," Diego said.

Scott rifled around in the console next to him. "Shit!"

"What?" Diego asked.

"There are no navigation maps on the aircraft. Even if I have enough fuel, I need a precise location."

Jillian put her head in her hands and stayed that way for a long time. But when Inka put her hand on her back, Jillian looked up. "Dr. Acosta," she said.

"What about him?" Inka asked.

"Maybe he knows something. He called the cell phone. That's how Menendez found it on me. It started ringing, and he took it away and turned it off. But when he turned it back on to call Scott with his demands, there was a voicemail beep. Acosta was the only one who had the number, so it had to be him."

"We need to call him," Mobius shouted. "Now!"

"Scott," Diego said. "We need to speak to a Mayan studies professor at Mesoamerican University. Can you have someone call him?"

Scott sighed. "I'm sure they'll be happy to do that after I just stole their multi-million-dollar aircraft. I was about to try to get ahold of García and ask him to map the coordinates for the intersection of the four cities. If I reach him, I'll ask him to contact the professor as well."

"It may be hard to reach Dr. Acosta. The university is having a fiesta for the end of the calendar," Inka explained. "I'm sure it is very loud there. He may not hear the phone."

"Copy that." When Scott got Lieutenant García on the radio, he said, "Remember what Menendez told us? The thing you didn't think was as crazy as Ortiz and I did?"

"I'm alone, Scott," García said. "I just switched off the recording. I'm supposed to call the chief if you contact me. Yes, I remember."

"Well, it's true about the alien," Scott said, but García did not respond. "Hello, García, you there?"

Jillian turned to Diego, covered her microphone, and pulled back one of Diego's earphones. "What the hell?" she yelled into his ear. "He wasn't supposed to tell anyone about Mobius."

"At this point, whatever it takes, don't you think?" Diego yelled back.

Mobius felt a distance between Diego and Jillian that wasn't there before. He could tell that her heart was closed to him, but he couldn't fathom the reason.

"Are you still with me?" Scott asked again.

"*Sí,*" García finally responded. "Is the rest of it true too? The weapon of mass destruction?"

"Affirmative."

García inhaled sharply. "When?"

"Within the hour," Scott said.

"*Dios mío,* what can I do?"

"We're trying to find the location of the weapon. Listen carefully, I need you to get a map and draw a line from Tikal to Chichen Itza and one from Calakmul to Coba. Then get me the latitude and longitude of the location where the lines intersect. You got that?"

"Affirmative," García said.

"Also, we need to talk to a professor named Dr. Acosta from the Mayan studies department at Mesoamerican University in Guatemala City. I have a number for you to call. But if you don't reach him, do whatever it takes to find him."

"I will," García said.

"Thank you," Scott said. "And it's best not to tell anyone else about this. We're doing everything that can be done, and it will only create a panic."

"I understand. I'm just not sure what to tell my superiors to keep them off your back. They're very angry—I already heard about your little attempt at a bribe."

"This is a total clusterfuck!" Scott yelled. "Give me a second to think—tell them—tell them that you think one of Menendez's men is still onboard and has a gun to my head and made me say all that stuff to the chief."

"Okay, that should work. Do you have the alien on board with you now?" García asked.

Scott didn't respond.

"*Jesucristo*, you're flying with the extraterrestrial," he said breathlessly.

"I'll answer all your questions later if we make it through this," Scott said. "But for now you've got to keep this under wraps."

"I will," García said. "But if we *do* make it through this, I want to meet the alien."

"Whatever you want!" Scott yelled. "Just get me those coordinates and call Acosta. Now!"

"*Sí, sí*, I'm on it."

When Scott finished with García, Inka said, "It sounds like if we live, you're going to be in big trouble, yes?"

Scott turned around and looked at the tiny woman in her ceremonial Mayan garb. "And ... *who* are you again?"

"Inka Mazte, a Mayan shaman," Jillian said. "And we wouldn't be here without her."

"Nice to meet—" Inka began, but stopped when she saw Mobius frantically patting himself down, turning his pockets inside out, looking all over the cabin floor.

"What is it?" Diego asked.

"My cognizer! I was going to check if there was any word from Akara. It's gone! I thought I put it back in my pocket when we were taking off at Chichen Itza. It must have fallen out of the helicopter."

"*¡Mierda!*" Diego shouted. "Mobius, you've got to be kidding. How could you let that happen?"

"Don't talk to him like that, Diego," Jillian said, bristling. "You have no right."

Diego closed his eyes for a moment, pulling himself together. "You're right. I'm sorry, Mobius." Then he turned to Jillian. "I'm so sorry. I made a terrible mistake with Menendez. Can you please forgive me?" He also silently asked for forgiveness for wanting to steal Mobius's technology.

She sighed and turned away from him.

"Jillian, please—I know you're hurt and angry, but I can't die with this between us," Diego pleaded.

She shook her head. "I don't want to be angry with you any-more, but what you did was completely fucked up. I don't know how to trust you again. I need some time."

"That's just it. We don't have time. You have to know ... I feel so much regret for what I did. You can't possibly imagine what it was like for me growing up. I was trying to make things better for my family—"

"And *yourself*," Jillian said.

"You're right. I was. But haven't I redeemed myself? Even a little?"

She softened a bit and her eyes filled with tears. "I guess a little."

"And think about it. Mobius would never have found us if we weren't in the jungle. You always talk about how things are meant to be."

"Don't push it," she said.

Mobius put a hand on both their shoulders. "I don't know exactly what is going on between you, but I do know that one of the things that saved my people was that they chose to forgive—to let go of their resentments and judgments. And you should know that the vibration of love between you was the reason we chose you as our guides."

Diego looked at Jillian hopefully, then held out his arms, and in spite of herself, she wrapped her arms around his waist and looked into his eyes. "I hope I get a chance to earn back your respect," he said. "And your trust. I love you, Jillian."

"Hey lovebirds," Scott interrupted, "I'm sorry to break this up, but García's back."

They all gathered up front again as the lieutenant's voice came over the radio. "I have Dr. Acosta for you—the university tracked him down—but unfortunately, I don't have the coordinates yet. I'm trying to get my hands on a paper map—they don't seem to exist anymore. I'm patching the professor through."

"This is Alonzo Acosta," the familiar voice crackled across the radio.

"*Maestro*, it is Inka Mazte! Do you have information for us?"

"I told you on your voicemail," he said.

"The phone was lost," she said. "Please tell us!"

There was a moment of irritated hesitation before he said, "My colleague Alejandro Diaz called me back and was surprised that I was asking about the circle and triangle glyph that you showed me."

"Why?" Inka asked.

"Because just last week, he and his colleagues discovered a lost Mayan city they are calling Awas'itza. They have seen this symbol of yours there many times. They think it may be Awas'itza's city glyph. They haven't announced their discovery yet, even to Mayan scholars. The city is still buried under the jungle, and they are trying to prevent looting and destruction of the site during the Christmas holiday."

"Dr. Acosta, where is this lost city?" Mobius asked.

"In Quintana Roo, near the Campeche border."

Mobius started blowing in and out excitedly.

"Professor, do you by chance have the GPS coordinates?" Jillian asked.

"Of course not," he said, clearly annoyed. "I'll see what I can do, but the end of the calendar is a seminal moment for every Mayan scholar in the world—they're all celebrating and being interviewed by the media."

"Dr. Acosta," Jillian yelled. "We're running out of time!"

"If the world ends at 11:11, I will know you didn't find whatever you are looking for," Acosta said. "Is that about right?"

"Yes, that's right," Inka said gravely. "Please, do whatever you can."

Scott looked at his watch. "You all should start looking now. We must be getting close."

"What exactly are we looking for again?" Jillian asked, rubbing her eyes.

"Something that looks like a Mayan temple," Mobius said.

Diego opened the side doors, and they each took hold of a hand strap and began scanning the landscape below. Mobius looked ahead, hoping that with his superior vision he might spot something the others couldn't, but the jungle seemed to be a single, flat layer of uninterrupted green as far as the eye could see. He couldn't even distinguish different trees or shades of green anymore. As Scott headed farther in the direction in which the shadow snake pointed, each passing moment felt like an hour.

Diego rubbed the back of his neck anxiously and turned to Mobius. "Even if we find it and have enough fuel, we don't know for certain that the time capsule's still there. What if it's been moved?"

"It's there," Mobius said. "I know it is."

"I hope you're right," Diego said, putting a hand on his shoulder, "because I believe you, and I have a date to share some coffee and *cerveza*."

"*And* for you to show me your hairy penis," Mobius said.

They smiled at each other, and Mobius was aware it might be the last time he ever got to joke with his friend.

García's voice came over the radio again. "Scott, I have the coordinates for you." He read off the numbers, and Scott punched them into the nav system.

"We just passed it!" Scott yelled as the location came through. "I thought I saw a road back there. Hold on." He turned the chopper hard to the right and brought them about.

"Look," Mobius said, pointing. "There's a rise in the jungle." As they passed over it, they saw a barely visible peak of stone breaking through the green.

"That has to be the top of Itzamna's temple. Let me out!" Mobius screamed.

"I have to find a place to land, and I'm almost out of fuel," Scott said as he switched off the flashing low-fuel warning light.

"There's no time. I need to get out of here now," Mobius said, looking down at the fifty-foot drop to the jungle below. "But if I jump, I don't know that I'll survive."

"No! You'll never survive," Scott yelled. "Diego, there should be a suspension rope in the back. But if I hover much longer, I'm going to run out of fuel in the air."

"Forget about us!" Jillian shouted. "We're all dead anyway if Mobius doesn't get to the time capsule."

Scott told Diego how to connect the rope, then instructed everyone to move away from the center of the cabin. He pressed a button, and a hatch in the floor opened up.

"Diego, give me your watch," Mobius said, then strapped on the timepiece—it was 10:52 a.m., nineteen minutes to go. He grabbed hold of the rope and turned toward his companions. "If I don't find it—"

Diego put his hands on his shoulders. "You can do this. I know you can."

"Mobius," Inka said. "You are Kukulcan. You came here to defeat the prophecy of darkness and help us fulfill the prophecy of light."

Jillian smiled at him. "Make the leap."

With that, Mobius stepped backward out of the open hatch and began a rapid hand over hand descent down the rope, swinging and twisting in the air. Before he reached the ground, the helicopter began to sputter and stall, teetering wildly back and forth. While he was still suspended well above the tree line, the chopper suddenly pitched hard sideways and veered away from the summit of the buried temple. Mobius let go of the rope, plummeting through the air before slamming into the top of a dense tree below. He dropped through leaves and branches, which tore at his clothes and skin, but the tree slowed his descent enough that he was finally able to grab onto a branch and stop his fall. Grunting with effort and the pain of the impact, he stabilized himself on a tree limb, then pushed himself up to standing so he could see which way he needed to go. As he did, through his wireless headphones, he heard Scott yell, "Inka, you'd better pray, we're going down!"

"No!" Mobius screamed. He ripped the headphones off his head and watched without breathing as the huge black flying machine belched a few times, then went quiet before free-falling out of the sky.

CHAPTER FORTY-SIX

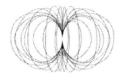

11:11

Mobius stood frozen in the top of the tree for a moment but then felt an influx of energy move through his exhausted body that propelled him into action. He scrambled down the tree onto the jungle floor and raced toward the temple. His vision came into greater focus, allowing him to dodge the trees and branches and roots that blocked his path while his long legs pumped at nearly full speed. The jungle rushed by so fast that he almost missed the signs of the lost city, but then he saw them— fallen stelae and crumbling stone structures covered by a millennium of vegetation.

Suddenly, the jungle floor began to rise, and he knew that he was climbing the temple. The ground was so steep and loose that he had to crawl upward on hands and feet. Branches hit him in the face and arms, and purple blood trickled down from the gashes in his skin, but he continued on undeterred. Grabbing onto a loose tree root, he tried to pull himself up, but it lifted out of the ground in his hand, and he pitched backward. Just before falling back down the slope, he reached up and grasped onto a low-hanging tree limb. For a moment, his feet were off the Earth and he swung backward; thankfully, the limb held, and when he swung forward again, he let go and dropped back to the ground. Regaining his footing, he scrambled upward again, finally reaching the summit of the mountain of stone a few minutes later.

For the first time since he'd arrived on Earth, Mobius was completely out of breath, and he had to bend over for a few seconds. From the helicopter, this had looked simply like the summit of a hill with rock peeking through, but now he could see a doorway covered by crumbling stone and dirt. *This must be the roof comb,* he thought. Boot tracks surrounded the entry, and Mobius could tell some of the debris in front of the doorway had been removed. One relic that did remain, however, was the huge round stone carving that King K'awiil had presented to Itzamna on the day of the temple's dedication. It lay on the ground, broken, covered in a layer of lichen.

As he began throwing rocks and debris out of the way, dozens of black flying creatures swarmed out of the doorway, making a terrifying screeching noise. He stumbled backward, a primal scream erupting from deep inside his belly. Before he could lose his nerve, he dove head-first into the opening, tumbling into a dark inner chamber and landing with a sickening thud that knocked the breath out of him.

He stood up but remained frozen in place, clueless of his surroundings, and terrified of the dark and what other eerie things might be down there. Even though his eyes had transitioned entirely to orange to take in as much light as possible, he couldn't see a thing after having been in the bright sunshine. The energy of this place felt heavy and bleak, and it made him want to get as far away as he could. Instinctively, he reached for his cog to use as a light but remembered that it was gone.

The watch on his wrist ticked away the seconds, and he became frantic, desperately reaching around in the dark for the time capsule, as if it might just be lying around. "I'm not going to find it. They're all going to die!" he yelled aloud in his own tongue, as his arms flailed wildly. The depth of his rage jolted him out of his panic, and suddenly he became still. He knew he had to get centered, or the Earth would be lost. Consciously slowing his breath, Mobius inhaled and exhaled the primeval air of the chamber. He set a clear intention to access the Wisdom, then asked it to show him the way.

He felt his fear and anger recede and a still, aware, timeless presence rise to the forefront of his consciousness. Suddenly, the dark chamber began to glow. Mobius looked down to see that he was the source of the light; his energy body had lit up for the first time ever. He stood breathless.

Out of the fullness of this silence, he heard a voice say, "Mobius, can you hear me?" But it was not in English or Spanish. It was in Akaran, and his energy soared when he recognized the voice as Nava's. It took him a moment to realize that she must be communicating with him telepathically since his neurolink was out. *I can hear her!*

"Nava," he said inwardly. "Where are you?"

"We're at the edge of Earth's atmosphere above Tikal," she said. "I've been trying to contact you since we couldn't reach you through your neurolink or cog, but you weren't open enough until now. Have you found the time capsule?"

"I'm in Itzamna's temple. I just have to locate it," he said. "How fast can you get here? I need your help. We're running out of time. It's going to detonate at 11:11."

"We're on our way, but I don't think we'll make it in time to help you find it."

He didn't respond.

"Mobius, you can do this. Access the Wisdom, you can trust it."

He turned his attention away from Nava and began moving around the chamber, lighting it up as he went. Surprisingly, the walls were uniform and smooth, unlike any of the other temples he'd been to. He didn't notice anything that might lead to another chamber, so he ran his hands along the walls, hoping to feel something that he couldn't see. When he found nothing, his chin dropped to his chest. As the seconds passed, the light from his energy field began to fade and was just about to go dark when he noticed something that made it glow even brighter than before. Beneath his feet, under a layer of silt and grime, lay a giant Mayan calendar covering the entire floor.

Examining it closely, he realized that it was oriented toward the temple's entryway, and he moved to inspect it from there. The calendar was comprised of the familiar set of concentric circles with Itzamna's face in the center. But something about it was off—the serpent headpiece was missing. *Why isn't it there?* Then he saw it—the circle surrounding the central mask was offset. The serpent sat coiled amidst many other glyphs, diagonal to Itzamna's head rather than directly on top of it.

Instinctively, Mobius dropped to the ground and pushed on the second circle with all his might. As he strained beyond the strength he had left in his body, the circle finally budged, and he cried out when it turned and clicked into place. As it did, two handholds emerged out of the floor on either side of the central etching. He grabbed them and pulled upward, grunting as his muscles screamed in pain. The hefty disc of stone finally came loose, and he shoved it aside. His heart leapt when he saw a dark passageway underneath.

The opening was just wide enough for Mobius to squeeze through and begin his descent into the bowels of darkness, lighting it up with his energy body as he went. He rushed down a steep, narrow spiral staircase, at times brushing against the walls with his shoulders, the space was so tight. He descended so far that he knew he must have gone well underneath the temple's foundation.

The stairs ended abruptly at a wall, which almost made him begin fish blowing as he faced yet another obstacle. In front of him stood a doorway-sized etching of the 13th baktun—the symbol for the end of the world—with its two columns of stacked glyphs and winged crown, just like the one Inka had shown the crowd at Tikal and the one on the T-shirt he wore. Above the door hung a rectangular wood lintel with five glyphs, matching those at the other four cities.

He pushed on the door with all his strength, desperately scanning for anything that would move the massive sealed stone barrier. It didn't budge. Stepping back, chest heaving, he gazed up at the lintel again and noticed that the Itzamna glyph was on the far right and Kukulcan on the left. *That's backward*, he thought. *Itzamna is always the first and Kukulcan the last glyph in the series.* "Why is this reversed? What does it mean?" he asked aloud. That's when he noticed that instead of a continuous woodcarving, the lintel had nearly imperceptible seams between each glyph. He stood on his tiptoes and pushed upward on the Kukulcan glyph, and with some effort, slid it out and held it in his trembling hand. Next, he removed the Itzamna glyph, then replaced both of them, but this time in their correct locations so that the lintel was in the proper sequence—Itzamna, Pleiades, Spaceship, Serpent constellation, Kukulcan. Nothing happened. He pushed on the door again, but it didn't move.

On top of his ragged breath and thumping heart, he heard an inner voice, one he'd come to recognize as the Wisdom. "The spaceship," it said, and immediately he understood. He removed the central glyph from the lintel, turned it upside down, then forcefully slid it back into place.

This time the door cracked open with a loud whooshing sound as air rushed past Mobius; the smell was ancient. He leaned into the door, pushing it inward just enough to squeeze through the narrow opening. Stepping inside, he saw that the door had been coated with an amber material, rubbery to the touch. He looked down to find himself standing amidst the skeletal remains of the people who had sealed the chamber door from the inside. The rubber sealant must have been used to create a low oxygen and moisture-free environment to preserve the contents of the tomb. The place was so spooky, Mobius's knees felt like they had turned to myomeal, and his breath came in shallow sips. "For the way of peace," he stammered aloud and heard the terror in his own voice.

Two stone sarcophagi etched with elaborate hieroglyphs sat in the middle of the chamber. Mobius knew from the mission log that one of them had to contain King K'awiil. He made his way first to the sarcophagus on the left, the bones crunching underfoot, and looked down on it. The all-too-familiar image of Itzamna stared back at him. He shuddered all over. The body of the deranged tyrant must lay inside.

Looking over at the second sarcophagus, which had to be King K'awiil's, he couldn't believe what he saw—an etching of the tree of life, right side up, with all four glyphs amidst its branches and roots, and the spaceship glyph at the center of the trunk. Seeing the full map on his tomb, Mobius suddenly recalled the look of horror on the king's face when Itzamna told him about the time capsule, and it all made sense. *It was K'awiil who left the clues! He must have died after Itzamna and worked with a secret society like Jillian said. They used symbols to create a map that would only be understood by someone from Akara. How ingenious! And courageous. But how did he learn the symbols?* His eyes fell on the glyph of the feathered snake. *Of course! Itzamna's rebel crewmember from Enshala—the feathered snake is from her region.*

Mobius refocused, looking back at Itzamna's sarcophagus. *The time capsule must be buried with him.* He pushed as hard as he could on the massive lid, sucking down the small amount of air coming in from the stairway. Finally, the huge slab began to move. Inside, Itzamna's enormous skeleton, a creepy collection of bones topped by a skull that seemed to be frozen in an eternal scream, was crowned with a withered headdress and adorned with the huge jade pendant K'awiil had given him, as well as jade bracelets and belt.

Mobius reached into the coffin, the jade and bones clanking together as he tried to feel around underneath the skeleton for something—anything—that could be the time capsule. He didn't know exactly what he was looking for, but Piphus had said it would be small. Unable to see what he was doing, Mobius struggled to shove the lid off completely, and it fell with a gut-wrenching clamor onto the bones below. He climbed into the sarcophagus with Itzamna, dropped down on his knees and felt around, his face inches away from Itzamna's skull. His empty stomach threatened to come up at any moment. An irrational fear swept through him that Itzamna was going to sit up, clench one hand around his throat, and yank out his undefended heart with the other. Suddenly, it dawned on him. *What am I doing? It can't be buried with him! Itzamna hid the time capsule himself.*

367

Quickly, he glanced at the watch and saw that it was 11:05. *"Where is it?"* he yelled at King K'awiil's sarcophagus, and his eyes landed on the tree of life etching again. This time he noticed that the spaceship glyph was neither upside down nor right side up but rotated ninety degrees to the right. *Why is it sideways?* he wondered and realized it must be another clue.

His eyes followed the direction in which the spaceship was turned. It seemed to point toward the wall on the right side of the chamber, and he scanned the wall frantically. Many etchings were incised all over the wall, most of which he recognized from other sites, but then he saw one unlike any of the others, and he gasped. He jumped out of the sarcophagus and rushed to the wall, where he could now hear a low, ominous rumbling sound coming from behind it.

In the wall, at shoulder height, was a golden metallic imprint of a right hand. But it was not of an earthly source; the long lean hand had only four fingers. The weapons security exhibit in the Discovery Corps atrium flashed through Mobius's mind. *Only Itzamna's biometrics can open this!* And yet, something impelled him to reach up and place his own hand on the imprint. It was a perfect match. A wave of energy pulsed through his body. *My hand may be a fit, but my* DNA *can't be,* he thought and was about to pull his hand away when the crypt began to tremble. Pieces of the stone wall surrounding the square etching to the left of the handprint—a terrifying rendering of Itzamna, mouth open and tongue extended—began to crumble and fall to the floor, leaving a gap around the image. *How is this possible?*

Mobius then heard the whooshing sound of a pneumatic seal releasing, followed by a mechanized whirring as the square etching pushed out from the wall. Inside the small alcove, a smooth, transparent pyramid, just bigger than his hand, vibrated, roared, and glowed from the fluorescent green and orange chemical maelstrom roiling inside. The time capsule! He snatched it from its perch and ran.

As he held the hot, almost weightless object filled with protoxan, he could not imagine how so much destruction could be contained in such a small space. He envisioned it opening—its four sides folding back, like noxious flower petals—exposing the super-condensed gas to catalyzing oxygen. He felt like he was holding a star in his hands just before it exploded into a supernova. Climbing the stairway as fast as he could, he called out to Nava telepathically, "I have it! It's about to open. I need to know how to stop it."

"Bring it to the surface, Mobius. We are right above you."

"Just tell me—" he began to protest. "I'll do it!"

"Mobius, you can't," she said. "Bring it now."

He continued up the stairs, taking them three at a time. By the time he reached the upper chamber, his legs and lungs felt like they were going to go up in flames. Looking up, he saw a shaft of light coming through the opening several feet above his head.

He yanked off his shirt and laid it on the ground, then placed the pyramid on top. He wrapped the fabric around the time capsule, knotted it, and placed the tie holds between his teeth. Carrying the makeshift pack in his mouth, he climbed, using small crevices in the wall as hand and foot holds. When he reached the top of the chamber, he grabbed at the ground, finding tree roots for leverage, and hoisted himself out of the temple. As he raced toward the peak of the buried pyramid, he unwrapped the instrument of death and cradled it in his arms. A searing heat that seemed to increase by the second radiated into his chest and face, and he had to fight the urge to throw the device to the ground.

At the apex of the hill, he looked up to see a blue and silver spaceship much larger than the *Concordance* approach him noiselessly. The underside of the ship opened, and a platform carrying Nava descended toward him. Seconds later, she hovered just above him with an outstretched hand. "Give it to me." He passed her the pyramid, then climbed aboard the platform.

"You know how to disarm it?" he asked, gasping for air, light-headed from exertion and from being so close to her.

"No," she said. "We were planning to take it into remote space and eject it, but now we don't have time." She placed the time capsule into a clear quarantine chamber and injected retainite into it.

Mobius watched as the liquid shaped itself around the pyramid and solidified. "So the retainite will stop it from imploding?" he asked, his voice filled with hope.

She shook her head. "No, but we think it may contain the reaction long enough for us to make the leap."

Mobius looked at his watch and yelled out, "It's 11:10. We have to go!"

"Piphus, bring me up," she said into her comm. As the platform started to move, Nava pushed Mobius backward with both hands.

He fell off the platform, arms and legs flailing. "What are you doing?" he screamed before landing hard on the ground.

"I can't let you come," she said.

Mobius lay on his back, helpless, as the platform retracted, and Nava ascended into the ship. Just before she disappeared from view, she called out, "Mobius, I love you!"

The ship lifted off so fast it caused the surrounding jungle to ripple outward in waves. Mobius watched it arc through the sky like an upward shooting star and recede into a pinprick before it disappeared. He shouted triumphantly and thrust a fist into the air, thinking it had safely made the leap. But suddenly, a brilliant flash of light burst across the sky, then collapsed in on itself, beginning to create a black hole. Just as suddenly, the blast vanished into the quantum field.

Mobius stared up into the sky, stunned. The ship had imploded out of existence, and his heart imploded with it.

CHAPTER FORTY-SEVEN

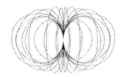

PROPHECY OF LIGHT

For the longest time, Mobius didn't move. He lay on the ground with his eyes shut and mouth opening and closing, low moans emanating from deep inside his aching chest. Nava's last words played over and over in his mind as strands of disjointed thought floated in and around them. *I saved Earth, but Nava's dead. So are Diego and the others. I'm stranded here alone.* Closing his eyes tighter, he tried to squeeze out the barrage of inner noise and the pain of unbearable loss. He wanted to melt out of existence and be finished with it all, and he wished desperately that he had been aboard the ship with Nava.

Faintly at first, but then louder and louder, he heard a rustling sound down the hill. He turned his head and, through glazed eyes, saw four blurry figures moving toward him from below. Impossibly, it looked like his Earth friends were making their way toward him. *I must be hallucinating.* The figures began calling his name and started to run toward him, and when he was certain he was lucid and that they were really alive, he put his hands over his face and wailed in gratitude and relief.

"Mobius!" he heard again, this time directly over him. He took his hands from his face to see Jillian fall to her knees next to him.

"You're alive! We thought you were on the ship."

Diego and Inka dropped to the ground next to her.

"You did it!" Diego shouted.

"You saved us," Inka said, tears in her eyes.

Mobius shook his head. "But everyone on the ship died."

"What happened?" Diego asked. "We saw an explosion in the sky and thought it was creating a black hole."

Mobius was silent for a moment before he could form the words. "It was starting to. They must have been making the leap when the time capsule opened, or it would have created a black hole. But the reaction got pulled into the quantum field."

"So maybe they're still alive," Diego said. "You told us you jump out of space-time and then back in."

Mobius shook his head. "No. I saw the explosion destroy the ship as it was making the leap."

They were all silent for a moment in the face of the sacrifice he and his fellow Akarans had made to save Earth. "I'm so sorry," Jillian said softly.

Mobius sat up and looked at each of them. "How are you alive? I watched you crash."

"I had everyone strap into the seats, and the jungle caught our fall," Scott said, standing over them.

"It was a miracle," Inka said.

"I don't know if it was a miracle, but it was incredible that no one was injured," Scott said. "It *is* going to take a miracle to evade the *Federales*. They'll be coming for us. We've got to get out of here."

Mobius collapsed back onto the ground and closed his eyes. "I don't care."

"Please, we have to get you hidden," Jillian pleaded.

Inka took his hand. "*Mijo*, I know you are hurting. But you saved our people. You saved our planet. One day the story of why the world did not end will have to be told, but for now you must save yourself."

Mobius didn't move.

Scott wiped the sweat off his forehead with his sleeve and turned to the others. "If the government—any government—finds out about him, he will be in serious danger, especially after the explosion. The optics on that are *not* good," he said, gesturing toward the sky. "They will definitely treat him as a hostile."

Inka shook her head. "They already know about him. Many people saw him at Chichen Itza."

"Oh God, that's right," Jillian said.

"Mobius, you've got to get up," Diego said, extending his hand to help Mobius, who remained motionless. "Come on, *amigo*. You're not thinking straight. Besides, we have some *cerveza* and coffee to share."

Mobius finally opened his eyes, smiled slightly at Diego, then reached up and took his hand. As Diego pulled him to his feet, Mobius winced. He looked down at his palms—they were raw and bloody.

"What happened?" Diego asked.

"I don't know," Mobius said vacantly. "It must have been when I uncovered the entry to the stairs ... or when I pushed the lid off Itzamna."

They looked at him wide-eyed. "Itzamna?" Inka exclaimed.

"He's buried down there with K'awiil. The king is the one who left the clues."

"What?" Inka asked, interrupting him. "You have to get me down there. I need to do a ceremony to clear Itzamna's energy from the Earth." She started digging furiously in her cloth bag.

Scott ran his hands through his hair. "I have to tell you, *nothing* in my SEAL training prepared me for this. You have to *exorcise* alien bones? I'm sure it's important in some way I'll never understand, but you'll have to find another time to do it. Because right now we have to go."

"He's right," Mobius said, his eyes on the horizon. "Helicopters are heading this way."

Scott whipped around and scanned the skyline in the direction Mobius was facing. "I don't see anything."

"I can see much farther than you can," Mobius said.

"Then move, move, move!" Scott yelled, and the five of them slipped and slid down the temple mountain.

•

Shadows and light danced on the wall of the cave as a fire flickered in front of Mobius, Diego, and Inka. For the last few hours, they had been in hiding after fleeing to a tiny village near the lost Mayan city. The local shaman had brought them here; Inka had convinced him that Mobius was Kukulcan and that he had averted the prophecy of darkness and saved the world.

Jillian and Scott had stayed behind to turn themselves over to the *Federales*. The plan was to deny any knowledge of the alleged alien and tell them that Diego died falling from the helicopter. They'd all decided that Diego staying with Mobius was their best chance to protect the alien, and they knew that if Diego showed himself, he'd be apprehended. Menendez had already outed Diego to Captain Ortiz. Plus, the authorities had Pedro in custody, and the *narco* surely would be revealing all the details of the jungle ranger's involvement with the drug gang.

The shaman, a wiry old man with dark skin and bright eyes,

entered the cave with water and food. He set the bowls down in front of them, then bowed to Mobius, gazing at him awestruck, before exiting the cave.

"Why does he keep doing that?" Mobius asked Inka.

"Because you are Kukulcan," she answered.

"No, I am not," he insisted. "This is how they treated Itzamna and look what happened."

"I will tell him not to worship you, but you are Kukulcan. You are the feathered serpent, a being that exists only on Akara. Your hand opened the chamber where the time capsule was hidden. You defeated the prophecy of darkness, and you are still here in order to help humanity fulfill the prophecy of light—to bring about a Rebirthing on Earth. It is your destiny, *mijo*."

Diego looked at Mobius. "How are you going to fulfill it?"

"I don't know. All I can do is access the Wisdom and see where it leads."

"Yes, let us enter the timeless realm," Inka said.

Mobius and Inka closed their eyes, and for the first time, Diego joined them.

The fire warmed their faces as they meditated, merging with the stillness. After several minutes of silence, Mobius's eyes suddenly flew open. "She's alive!" he yelled out. "For the way of peace, she's alive!"

EPILOGUE

The young woman woke up shivering, cold seeping into her bones. Her body ached all over as she sat up. Blinding light glinted off brilliant white snow that covered the stark, foreign landscape, and she squinted against it. As she tried to stand, a searing hot pain shot up her leg and sent her back to the frozen ground. She put her hand up to shade her eyes from the intense singular sun and noticed a bracelet that changed colors on her wrist. Something was written there, and when she read it, she realized that it was her name—Nava.

A small escape pod lay nearby, smoking and damaged, and when she saw it, she realized she wasn't home. In the distance, dark silhouettes moved toward her—four-legged creatures with riders atop them, galloping at an alarming rate. *Where am I?* she wondered.

And then, she remembered. *Earth.*

END OF BOOK ONE

The Story behind the Story

To find out about the incredible true story that inspired *Awake*,

go to: www.awakethenovel.com/truestory

ACKNOWLEDGMENTS

To begin, we must give gratitude to the Wisdom—the invisible quantum field of infinite love, intelligence, and creativity— the Source from which this novel was born, and which synchronistically brought about our collaboration.

This book took seven years to complete, and in that time, so many people gave their time, energy, expertise, and support.

First and foremost, we want to thank Pamela Koenig, our "executive angel." She not only financed the publication of this novel but also worked on everything from being our primary reader (she probably read this book ten times) to assisting with the nuts and bolts of every step it took to produce and get out into the world. Before even reading a draft of the novel, Pam felt a calling to support it. Her doing so lifted it from a manuscript on our computers to an actual published book. We are forever grateful.

We wanted to be certain to honor the Guatemalan and Mayan cultures and people, and we could not have done this without Edwin Villela and Dr. Brent Woodfill. A very special thank you to them both:

Edwin Villela, President of the Guatemalan Association of San Diego, read the novel and reviewed it for authenticity and accuracy regarding the Guatemalan people, places, and language. He was so kind, giving his time, knowledge, and undying support throughout the process, that we had to name Diego after him. So many times, we reached out and asked questions about everything from usage of a word to accuracy of a description, and in no time, he would respond in the most gracious possible way.

Dr. Brent Woodfill, a Mayan scholar at Winthrop University, checked all of the Mayan aspects of the novel for authenticity and accuracy. Blessedly, he also just happens to have a degree in English. So, while he corrected and added a number of factual elements, he also understood that we needed a bit of creative leeway for the demands of the story. His combination of scholarly rigor and literary license was a dream come true. Rest assured, any inaccuracies are on us, not him. We are also grateful to Tom Olson of the Maya Society of Minnesota for connecting us to Dr. Woodfill.

We received incredible assistance and encouragement from our Aerospace Engineer and Remote Sensing Calibration, Characterization, and Validation Specialist known as "Hellwinger," out of Pasadena, California. A huge sci-fi fan, he emailed us after reading an early draft: "Wow. End of Book One! Very entertaining read with gritty descriptions. A real roller coaster—and it's not over! Where's book two!?!" His words were like manna from heaven. He vetted all the visionary science in the novel for its theoretical plausibility. In a number of places, he corrected or enhanced details and gave us accurate scientific and mathematical phrasing. But he didn't stop there; he gave us feedback on the story as well, and we implemented many of his comments, which made the book better. Hellwinger was a constant and reliable consultant and supporter throughout this entire process, and we are so, so grateful. And thank you so much to Sarah Lundeen for referring him.

Mike Taron read the novel very early on and helped figure out the science behind Protoxan. His suggestions were invaluable in coming up with a unique way to stabilize wormholes and travel through space as well as how the time capsule itself functions. Also, many thanks to Jennifer Taron for her feedback, and to both of them for their amazing enthusiasm for the book even when it was just a glimmer of what it turned out to be.

A big shout out to our copy editor and proofreader, Genet Jones, The Thoughtful Wordsmith, for her OCD level attention to detail and her geekdom about grammar, her patience with all our revisions after our so-called "final draft," and her generosity with her time.

A huge thank you to Bill Young of the Oklahoma Department of Libraries who has been a big supporter and valuable source of information. Bill referred us to Adrienne Butler, public library consultant at the Oklahoma Department of Libraries. We are grateful to her for reviewing the manuscript and for her incredible graciousness with her time and vast knowledge.

As we worked on the manuscript over the years, so many people read different drafts and gave us invaluable feedback. Not only that but also their enthusiasm for the material provided the energy that kept moving it toward completion.

To all those who endorsed our book, we thank you for your belief in the novel. Two people in particular went above and beyond—Rick Archer and Daniel Schmidt. They not only gave us beautiful quotes but supported *Awake* getting out into the world, and they served as connectors to others who have helped us as well.

Warmest thanks go to our beloved readers: Brenda Adelman, Teri Breier, Dana Carpenter, Robin Colucci, John Hruby, Pamela

Lane, Lyssa Reese, Evie Stern, Leo Stern, Emily Stuart, Madi Stuart, and Sydney Tucker.

Also, we are grateful for those who gave us feedback on plot, pacing, world building and character development of the opening chapters: Bill Cooper, Dustin Dunbar, Stephen Klein, Jami Lula, Will Lula, Alixson Soukup, Julie Sponsler, Barb Wade, Tim Wade, Quinn Wade, and the awesome teens of Boy Scout Troop 67 of Santa Monica, California.

Thank you to Maya Felsenstein, Alon Gilboa, Caren Padawer, and Julie Sponsler for your input on our cover design.

Our deepest, heartfelt gratitude goes to Mark Lersch, who held the highest vision for us and gave us a spiritual anchor in the midst of all the ups and downs. His love, counsel, kindness, and wisdom were invaluable. And if there are awake aliens on Earth, he is surely one of them.

So much gratitude goes to the many teachers who've inspired us. We wish to thank:

Drs. Ron and Mary Hulnick, co-directors of the University of Santa Monica, from which we both received master's degrees in spiritual psychology. This book simply would not exist without them. Not only is USM where we met, but also, we could not have written the novel without doing the work in consciousness that we learned in the program. In addition, USM is where Dayna wrote her first novel, which began her writing career. The influence and support of Ron and Mary have been utterly profound to us both.

Adyashanti for being a true embodiment of the Wisdom.

Maharishi Mahesh Yogi for inspiring the idea that a critical mass of beings waking up can create a coherence effect on collective consciousness.

Paramahamsa Yogananda, who said, "A room may be in

darkness for thousands of years, but if a light is brought into it, in that very instant the darkness vanishes.... You cannot ... beat darkness out of a room with a stick." We paraphrased this beautiful teaching and used it in the novel.

We are thankful to T.S. Eliot for originating the idea of what is today known as the "DIKW principle" or "wisdom hierarchy." This inspired our Discovery Corps motto, "From data to information to knowledge to Wisdom ... Make the Leap."

We have to express huge appreciation to the amazing people at Wikipedia, who provide the world reliable information at our fingertips. Without it this novel could not have been written. We make a monthly donation to them and encourage everyone who uses Wikipedia to do so. This not-for-profit service that we all take for granted would thrive indefinitely if its users were to give just $2.75 per month.

Finally, a tremendous thank you to the celestial being who, in 1993, first ignited a spark of inspiration to write a novel about an awakened alien civilization. And to Chris White, who was part of the mystery and wonder that night. Also, to John Ashcraft, who kindled that spark into a flame in 2013, when at a Mayan museum exhibition, he made the offhand remark, "You know they had help from aliens."

If there is anyone we have left out, we are deeply sorry. If Jillian could forgive Diego and Chad Lowe could forgive Hillary Swank, we hope you can forgive us.

About the Authors

DAYNA DUNBAR is an award-winning novelist published by Ballantine Books. Both her novels—*The Saints and Sinners of Okay County* and *The Wings that Fly Us Home*—were selected for the exclusive Ballantine Reader's Circle. Fannie Flagg, #1 *New York Times* bestselling author of *Fried Green Tomatoes at the Whistle Stop Café*, described her first book as: "Beautifully written .... A funny and poignant story."

JULIA NADINE PADAWER is a former award-winning Madison Avenue advertising executive. She is currently a spiritual and life purpose coach as well as a writer. Both women hold master's degrees in spiritual psychology from the University of Santa Monica, where they met and began their creative collaboration.

awakethenovel.com

Made in the USA
Middletown, DE
06 October 2021